My BROTHER'S KEEPER

Randy A Green

Acknowledgment

This incredibly beautiful cover is the work of my cousin Diane Johnson. Once again, despite health issues, she gallantly produced this incredible work of art.

Her talent for listening intently while grasping every detail of what I hoped to convey with this story via the book cover never ceases to amaze me.

After a one-hour conversation she uses her God given talents to magically bring my imagination to life. I am eternally grateful for her as my book cover artist and even more grateful that she is my cousin and friend. Thank you Diane, I love you dearly.

PART I

Chapter 1

There were little to no upsides working with Jimmy, I didn't care much for working with anyone, but especially Jimmy Romano. Jimmy was loud and constantly yapping about how he was going to run the outfit someday and it was only a matter of time before he would become a boss. Not only was he a loudmouth, he enjoyed talking openly about who he would "take care of" once he was in charge and that he wouldn't take any crap from anyone like his old man did. He couldn't string together a cogent sentence without the use of foul language, he had no filter, regardless of who might be in the room, he loved cursing. I'm sure it made him feel tough, but he was far from that. He was annoying as hell, but there wasn't much anyone could do or say about it because he was also the boss's son.

The boss was Big Paul Romano, and he was, for the most part, a decent guy, if there was such a thing for guys in this line of work. He wasn't quick to pull the trigger on anyone, but he wasn't scared to either. He worked his way up the ranks like all good, wise guys do. He had been a good soldier, enforcer, collector, peacemaker, innovator, and negotiator and now he was the boss of his own crew. There were a lot of occupations in between captain and soldiers, and he had been good at all of them. He was a creative boss who thought of new ways to enhance his pockets. His son was nowhere close to being cut from the same material as his dad, and never would be.

Everyone thought that Big Paul was named "Big Paul" because of his physical size, he was a pretty big guy at 6 feet tall and nearly 300lbs but it wasn't. He received the nickname from a kid he used to run with when they were teenagers, John Calabrese. John and Paul were inseparable growing up, they did everything together, played ball, threw dice, stole merchandise, and even went on dates with their girlfriends together. John isn't around to tell the story any longer, he disappeared not long after he was married, but everyone repeats the story with laughter like they were actually there. It seems that the story goes like this, John and Paul were on a double date where they took two girls to a drive-in movie. Apparently, Paul and his date were in the back seat, and John and his date were in the front seat. As the evening progressed, the boys and the girls were doing what boys and girls do at the drive-in when the girl that Paul was with yelled "It's too Big!" If anyone had been there for real, they would have known that the girl was referring to the size of the drink cup and it wouldn't fit in the back-seat cup holder. The two would crack jokes about it, and as time went by, the cup was left out of the story and through many embellished versions and several years it just became the fact that big Paul was big Paul because he was a well-endowed male. Big Paul never tried to correct the story, really, what guy would?

Big Paul was already 50 years old when Jimmy came along as the 1st son of Paul and Annamarie Romano. Annamarie was Paul's second wife, his first wife passed away due to a brain aneurism. She went to bed one night and just never woke up. The funeral was massive, long lines of cars and thousands of flowers. It was hard to tell when a boss's wife dies if she gets all those flowers because she was loved so much, or people were just trying to curry favor. One thing was for certain, no one ever wanted to be on the list of people that didn't show respect, it was not a healthy list.

Big Paul waited almost two years before he would even be seen in public with her, but everyone knew she was taking care of him less than a week after his wife's funeral. She took care of everything, and big Paul was happy with the arrangement. The two would meet at his lake house, his apartment, or her apartment but never at his house. He was firm about the unwritten, Italian acceptable grieving period of two years for a widower, but everyone was certain that she would be the only person alive today that could actually verify if the stories about Big Paul were true.

Nobody cared really, they knew he was faithful to his wife while she was alive, but he had always had a thing for Annamarie. She ran the corner market that was left to her by her father. Big Paul liked to stop there and pick up some bread for dinner or some fruit for the office, but most of his henchman knew he just loved to see her, look at her and hopefully talk to her for a while. She pretended to blow him off most of the time, in a nice way, of course, but she always tried to keep her distance in public. She knew he liked her; she knew he was married, and she knew he was dangerous and that is what drew her to him. She was also 20 years younger than him, and she wanted lots of kids. Everyone that really knew her said she was a good woman; she just wouldn't let Big Paul discipline her baby boy under any circumstances and his behavior as an adult proved why that was a mistake. Jimmy needed a good parental ass kicking, but he never got one.

Where the hell are you going? I asked the question, but I already knew the answer, "you know damn well where we are going!" Jimmy shouted back at me like I was a nobody, but I had been doing this for nearly 20 years. I had seen all there was to see about this business, and I knew that sometimes things just didn't go your way, but you had to be able to roll with whatever came up. Jimmy was a loose cannon and he outranked me, not in rank really, but in family ties. I could have cracked him in the mouth, drug him out of the car and beat the hell out of him if it were a rank thing, but it wasn't. His dad would have filled my boots with cement and dropped me in his family pool just so he could watch me struggle and drown. That was perhaps one of the consequences of smacking Little Jimmy in the mouth.

He pulled the car into the back of the pharmacy and put the car in park. "I'll be back in a minute," I knew what he was doing, he was collecting a gambling debt from Bobby Weinstein. You see Bobby Weinstein was the local pharmacist and for all practical purposes he had a gambling problem. Despite his gambling problem, he managed to run a successful pharmacy, be a great dad, granddad, and an upstanding member of the community. He was president of the local Lyon's club; he sponsored a Pop Warner football team every year and he was in the synagogue as much as he was in the pharmacy. If it weren't for his passion for sports and betting, he would have been damn near flawless and probably happier. He created his own stress.

I thought he was actually a pretty good gambler, seemed to me like he won more than he lost but when he lost, he always lost big. He managed to stay out of Big Paul's cross hairs for many years, but he was on a rough streak here lately. He owed Big Paul 5 large plus 2 points that he hadn't paid yet. Little Jimmy hated Bobby and it would please him so much if he would have been given the green light to eliminate the problem but deep down, I think Big Paul always knew that Bobby was good for whatever he owed. Bobby never tried to hide, and he always paid his debts. To me he was a good associate; he was constantly creating cash flow. To Jimmy he was an ungrateful piece of garbage who took advantage of his status with Big Paul.

"Wait in the car my ass." He tried his best to boss me around, but I wouldn't have any of it. It would make him so mad, he would slam doors, break things, he even smashed his cell phone on the hood of the car, making a dent in the hood of his own Mercedes and breaking his phone. I got out and walked into the pharmacy after Jimmy threw his fit and gave me an incredible profanity laced lecture about him being the boss and I was just a peon. When I walked up to him in the back of that pharmacy, standing there, nose to nose with this idiot, the thoughts of ending his pathetic life first entered my mind. I knew the consequence of that action, so I merely pushed him out of my way and entered the pharmacy first. Jimmy didn't like that one bit and was still yelling at me from behind when we entered the back hallway of the pharmacy. I was ok with that until he brought my brother into it.

"You screw with me like that again and I will make sure that moron brother of yours never so much as hugs his Teddy Bear again!" I heard that, and I spun around and placed one hand on his neck and slammed him against the wall. I got so close to his face that he could smell the garlic I had on my eggs a few hours ago, "I don't give a shit who your daddy is you worthless piece of human debris, you threaten my brother again and no one will ever find your mutilated corpse except coyotes, you got that you drooling little oxygen thief?" I could only hear him gag and I really didn't expect to hear an answer because I have always had a vice like grip when I was mad. Jimmy crossed the line and the spoiled little brat needed to know it. His eyes became as wide as silver dollars and he tried to blink but he couldn't even do that, he tried to nod but that wasn't very emphatic, so I let him go. He started to speak, and I grabbed his throat again and slammed him back up against the wall. You see, I know these types, they are legacy bullies, and they grow up thinking they are bad asses because nobody ever fights back because they are afraid of ending up at the bottom of the lake. But for today, I needed to establish what the rules of working with me were, not the other way around and he needed to know my little brother was off limits. "Don't come back with something cute you little shit! I can hear the coyotes chomping on your bones right now!" I let go and turned towards the pharmacy. You kind of need to know a little about my brother, he has Down Syndrome, he's 15 and I am 39. Our parents were killed in a plane crash a few years back. Our dad had his own accounting firm and honestly did quite well, but I hated accounting, so I never wanted to follow in his footsteps. He sold the firm to a bigger company for a bundle of money, which is why he could afford to buy a plane. I remember he caught the flying bug right after I graduated from college. My Dad loved to fly so much that he bought a single engine Piper Malibu that could flat out haul ass. He and mom would take trips all over the United States in that thing and loved every second of it, right up until that plane crashed into the side of a mountain. It was a trip to Colorado that ended up being their last. Luckily, Teddy was not with them at the time the plane went down, or I would have had no family left except for an uncle that lived in Brooklyn, and we weren't even remotely close. He was my dad's brother, and they didn't speak much. Something had happened between the two of them many years ago that left their relationship fractured. I don't think they hated each other but they didn't go out of their way to see or speak to each other either.

Yeah, you heard it right, I actually have a college degree, a major in Finance and a minor in Economics. I hate wearing a tie, but I like playing the market. This job I have, where I collect debts for the boss, just seemed better suited for me, plus the cash was quick and easy if you could stomach it. I had no problems handling any task I was assigned. Teddy and me got some money passed on to us when my parents were killed, I am certainly not complaining about that part, but I never wanted the money that was left to us to define me. I wanted to make my own way and when the time came, I could make sure Teddy had everything he needed to make it in life should something happen to me.

My little brother was definitely an accident, I had no idea that my parents still had sex at that age, but as my parents liked to say, he was the best and most fun accident they ever had. Obviously, my mother got pregnant with him very late in life, a time when she should have been begging me to get started on grandkids. If she were alive today, she would still be waiting on grandkids from me. Based off my profession, I figured no woman would ever have anything to do with me, at least that is what I told myself. I told myself that ladies wouldn't like me because of what I did, and it never even crossed my mind that it might be because I wasn't good looking or desirable. Nope that couldn't be it, but I knew it was.

The doctors could tell he was gonna be a down kid in the womb and because of my mother's age at the time, they all urged her to have an abortion. They said he might kill her during birth and even if she survived the birth, at her age, he would be just too much to for her to handle.

Now my mom was a devout catholic and she wouldn't hear of such talk. She was bound and determined to have Theodore and she did. Teddy turned out to be the best thing that ever happened to my parents and if I am totally honest, he's the best thing that ever happened to me. He tries harder than any person I know just to learn the simple things like tie his shoes or play a game but once he learns it, he never looks back. It wasn't easy when I first became Teddy's guardian, there were times I cursed my parents for dying and leaving me with such a heavy responsibility.

There are a ton of things that I have done that I'm not real proud of but there was no way that I could have looked after Teddy after my mom and dad were killed if I had a regular job. Teddy was 5 when their plane went down, and Teddy has been with me ever since. He is really the only good thing in my life. I tell myself that he is the good balance to all my bad. This job and the money I make pay for some really cool schools and other stuff for Theodore. Schools I wouldn't be able to afford if I were still trying to make it in corporate America.

Anyway, my little brother Theodore or Teddy as I call him, has a heart of a lion and more character than I will ever have. He sees love everywhere he goes, and he wants to show affection. He will hug strangers and it's an amazing thing to watch. He could pick the toughest, most mean looking man or woman, run up to them and hug them and they all turn into little globs of blubbering teddy bears. He has a way of breaking the ice with people and he always seems to find the good in people no matter how bad they are. He even hugged Jimmy the first time they met. It was comical to watch when it happened, Jimmy never turns off his tough guy persona and he acted like he had just been mugged. Now you know about Teddy, so we better get back to reality and the hallway we were standing in.

Bobby Weinstein heard the commotion, and he was already standing in the hallway with his hand on his forehead. I could see that Bobby wasn't happy to see us because it easily showed on his face. He tended to pat the sweat on his forehead with a handkerchief when he was nervous. This wasn't Bobby's first visit from us, in fact, it was more like my 5th visit to Bobby for sure. There may have been other guys that visited besides me, but I only count the ones I know of. Bobby loved to gamble and like I said, he was pretty good at it but sometimes he would pull a bonehead move and trust some of those sports guys on TV instead of sticking to what he knew. When he trusted the sports morons, he would lay down too much and get overextended with the bookies and that's where big Paul would come in and rescue him, but even as good natured as big Paul was, he had a limit. Bobby had exceeded his limit and made the mistake of hanging up on Big Paul when he called to talk about it, with the excuse of "I've got a customer."

Now it's common knowledge that Bobby was a good pharmacist, and it was probably true that he had a customer, but you just don't hang up on big Paul, that's just bad etiquette. The whole neighborhood knew that sometimes Bobby would let a customer slide on a payment when they were having a tough time or he would slip them sample drugs until they could get on their feet but again, you don't hang up the phone when Paul ain't ready to quit talking. It really makes the situation worse.

Like I said, I have visited Bobby a few times already, I broke his nose once by accident really, but it sent the right message. A broken nose bleeds like there is no tomorrow and he sure bled that day. Now I do have to admit that I did break his pinky finger and it was tough watching him cry but I tell myself that it wasn't me that made the bets and if he would just get his act together and quit gambling, he would be a stand-up guy. Out of all the pressure tactics I've used on Bobby, I can safely say that I have never done it in front of any of his family or customers. Regardless of how I make a living or what you might think of me, I'm not a thug and that is what I consider "thug" behavior. Today, turned out to be one big shit show for sure.

Chapter 2

Go Back to Jersey!

Bobby must have seen me throttle Jimmy in the back hallway and knew that I was in no mood for small talk. Bobby knew the hierarchy too; he knew that Jimmy was big Paul's son, and he also knew that Jimmy was a loose cannon and unpredictable. I'm not an oversized guy but I'm thick, big boned as my mother used to say, you know, big ass, big forearms, and EE shoes. My dad loved to watch me play football because he said I was a murderer on the gridiron, I was pushing kids all over the place, he said I had a "low center of gravity." Now, you gotta know there are lots of knuckle draggers like me in the organization but most of them are shorter than me. I made it all the way to 6 feet. That's about four inches taller than my dad and a foot taller than my mom. My dad never approved of my work though. My mom loved me anyway.

"This isn't a good time guys, seriously, I have lots of customers and I have family in the store." Bobby grimaced like he wished they weren't there and pointed over his shoulder to illustrate where the customers and family were. "I promise, tell Mr. Romano I am good for it." Bobby clasped his hands together like he was praying, "YOU of all people should know I am good for it!" He looked over his shoulder and I could tell that he didn't want anyone, customers, or family to know what was going on in the back hallway and he looked at me with the utmost scared eyes that I have ever seen. This wasn't normal for Bobby, he was never scared of getting kicked around, this was something else. "Come with me Bobby," I motioned for him to come towards me, but he kept looking over his shoulder like he didn't want us to see who was in the store but then he looked over my shoulder and his eyes got even wider.

I turned to see Jimmy walking slowly towards us, he had his gun out but he wasn't pointing it at anyone, he just let it hang by his side as he walked. I turned my wide frame in the hallway leaving no room for him to get by, "Put that away Jimmy, it ain't necessary." Jimmy glanced at me and tried to get by but as he did, he raised the gun, I thought he was going to shoot me so I reacted, what else could I do? I pinned the arm holding the gun against the wall and gave him a soft shot with my elbow to the chest. I swear it wasn't a very hard shot, but it sent him to the floor. I caught the gun out of midair before it fell to the ground. I was afraid as crazy as Jimmy was, he may have already taken it off safety and I didn't want it hitting the floor and accidently shooting someone, including me. I never really carried a gun; I didn't like them much which I guess makes me a bad wise guy, but I felt like I could get by without one. The only time I carried a gun was if the assignment was a tough collection. Like I said, Big Paul rarely sent me on a tough one, but he wasn't scared too either.

Needless to say, Jimmy was furious, he bounced back up from the floor and unleashed another profanity laced tirade on me and Bobby. He was unleashing language that would make a sailor blush and he was screaming at the top of his lungs. That's when I saw the other guy's step into the hallway behind Bobby, leaving Bobby stuck in the middle and I knew "THEM" the minute I saw them, it was the Jersey crew.

The Jersey crew was a part of a different family and I bet you can guess, our family and theirs didn't get along very well. The leader of the two smiled and said, "Hey why don't you two Moron's go back to catholic school and suck some priest peckers." These guys always had something cute to say. I knew one of them, but I was not familiar with the other, they were both leg breakers for sure, but I had to admit, at least one of them knew how to handle themselves in a fight. They were both as wide as me and if I were with anyone else but Jimmy, I would feel better about the odds of kicking the hell out of these guys, but at the moment I figured I had a 60-40 chance if things got rough, and that was 40 for me and 60 for them. "Why would we do that when they got you two cock holsters to blow them?" They stopped laughing and looked like they were about to do something that I wished they wouldn't. We were both there to collect and this could easily be worked out, but Jimmy was a loose cannon, and I had no idea what he would do. I also knew the minute I saw them that Bobby was trying to rob Peter to pay Paul, no pun intended and now he was getting yanked from both Jersey and New York. It was a bad move because it shows no faith in your friends or worse, you think your friends are morons and won't find out. I considered Bobby a friend and so did Big Paul, but now he had really messed things up. If Jimmy and me had to duke it out with these goons, big Paul would be pissed off for sure. He may not let Bobby off easy this time around.

The one guy I knew was Carmine, he was sort of the leader of the Jersey crew, took a step around Bobby and was standing in front of me now. He had this strange cologne on that smelled like nothing I could really describe except that it was strong, and it pissed me off. No way any decent man was gonna pick up any girls smelling like that. I actually found it revolting, so much that I wanted to kick his ass for having the audacity to wear that crap. I gave a disgusted but sort of confused look to Bobby, "Bobby, why you treat us like that huh?" Bobby could see that I was serious, and his face went red, "I'm sorry X, I had a sure thing." You see what I mean; I've known Bobby a long time, long enough for him to call me X. Only my closest friends called me X, everyone else were required to call me Xavier. Carmine pushed passed Bobby and was now in front of me. He took one of his short fat greasy fingers and poked me in the chest but as he poked me, he said, "Fuck off X, we got dibs."

Seeing how I wasn't really in a good mood anyway; I knocked his fat finger away with my left hand and gave him a serious upper cut with my right hand that landed flush against the bottom of his chin. Carmine went down easier than I expected. I saw the other guy behind Bobby reach under his coat and I thought he was gonna try something stupid, so I grabbed Bobby by the shirt collar and yanked him towards me and then behind me. He tumbled and fell which left me standing directly in front of the other guy. It all happened so quick that he didn't have a lot of time to react effectively, but he still managed to yank his gun out of his holster and get off a shot, I didn't feel anything, so I took another quick step and cracked him right on the nose. He went down quicker than I expected too, so I guess I miscalculated the odds.

Now there is a small hallway full of wise guys and one pharmacist that liked to gamble. I looked down at the guy with the now broken nose that was bleeding profusely and realized I hadn't knocked him out. I felt bad for him because he was bleeding so badly and he was now looking up at me with wide, frightened eyes so the only decent thing I could do was to finish the job, I brought the heel of my boot down on his forehead and it was nap time for Mr. Flat nose. I have to admit, I expected more of a rumble than these two brought to the game. I turned to see if Bobby was ok, I slung him pretty hard. As I turned to look, I realized I was the only man standing in the hallway.

I turned back to look at Mr. Flat Nose just to make sure he didn't wake up and try to shoot me again. I took a step back, looked around and found his gun. I picked it up and put it in my pocket. I already had Jimmy's gun that I stuck in the back of my pants, now I checked for Carmines, and I was surprised to see he didn't carry one either. "Jesus H Jimmy- you're bleeding." I looked at Jimmy and he was leaking blood out of the side of his pants. "Let me see!" Bobby was now trying to scramble to his feet as I was trying to get Jimmy's pants down so I could see where he was bleeding, "Are you hit Bobby?" Bobby looked all over himself and decided he had not been hit and shook his head, "Then give me your belt!" Bobby stood there for a second too long and this time I yelled even louder, "Give me your damn belt!" By that time, I found where Jimmy was leaking, it was his left thigh and geez it was a gusher. "If I don't get a tourniquet around this leg, he is gonna bleed to death!" Bobby handed me his belt and as soon as I got the belt snug around his upper thigh, the bleeding slowed down considerably. "Help me get him up."

Bobby did as he was told and we both carried him back to Jimmy's car where I was trying to put him in the back seat when I heard Bobby say, "what do I do about those men in my hallway?" I was trying to get Bobby's legs inside the car and when I finally did, I slammed the door shut and turned to Bobby, "not my problem, it's yours, you created it, so you figure it out but let me tell you this," I opened the driver side door, "you better pray that young Jimmy here doesn't die because if he does, big Paul is gonna blame you."

Chapter 3

Ice Cream You Scream

I don't like to carry a cell phone; they are just too damn busy. Every time I tried to carry one, I would catch myself checking stocks too much throughout the day. I needed one for the school to call me if something happened to Teddy and of course I had to have one for Big Paul to reach me, but I really don't like the damn things. I see grown men with their heads down looking at their stupid phones running into shit as they walk around. Today of all days I intentionally left the phone at home so considering the current circumstances I was kinda wishing I had it now though. If I did, I would call big Paul and ask him what he wanted me to do but instead I had to try and get back to the ice cream shop where Big Paul hung out. There was no way I could take him with a gunshot wound to a real hospital.

The shop was a legitimate corner ice cream store ran by a cute lady that had no ties to us at all, but she kept an office and a pretty good size back-room area for big Paul and his crew. It was strange but because of the entrance that Big Paul and the crew used, nobody ever knew there was anything going on. There would be high stakes poker almost every night where thousands of dollars would be won or lost. Big Paul paid her a grand a week for the space and they both stayed out of each other's business.

Now I was gonna have to crash the ice cream store and dump his half dead son in his lap. He wasn't gonna be happy but at least I was delivering him alive, plus I was gonna have to tell him that me and the Jersey crew cracked heads in Bobby's store, and I wasn't sure if Bobby would call the cops are not. If he were smart, he wouldn't but who knows. Bobby was panicked now.

I came through the back door carrying Jimmy fireman style because even though he was small, he was dead weight, and he was hard to carry. "Long story but the quick of it is, he needs a doctor in a bad way boss." Big Paul jumped up from the couch he appeared to be napping on, the paper that was laying on his chest fell to the floor. "Good Christ what happened?" I set Jimmy down on the now vacant couch and helped him lay back. Once I had his feet elevated, I responded, "Jersey crew got in the way, it was a harmless encounter at first, but I think they had a new guy that panicked and fired off a couple shots, missed me and Bobby but Jimmy took one in the leg. I think it hit an artery."

Big Paul, ran to his desk and called a number, all I heard was "Now." I was impressed that in less than ten minutes there was practically a mini surgery area set up right there in big Paul's office, equipped with nurses, a doctor and equipment. I sat in the back of the office on one of the high back chairs with big Paul watching with me. He asked a few questions, and I gave him the honest answers. It surprised me when he said, "I put him with you because I knew you'd look out for him." The only thing I could think to say was the truth, "He'd already be dead if I hadn't been there."

It was two hours later when the doctor looked up and said, "I think we got it." Everyone was working around the table where Jimmy was laying with a tube stuck down his throat. "The bullet tore the hell out of his femoral artery, whoever tied that tourniquet did it at just the right spot that we might be able to save the leg." I never blinked or looked at big Paul, there wasn't any point in hammering my point any more than I already had. I was feeling pretty good about the situation and big Paul as he had a way of doing brought a little internal panic back into the situation. "What do you mean you THINK you can save the leg?" The doctor peeled off his gloves and threw them in the trash can next to big Paul's desk. "Have to see blood flow established again, I basically had to scrounge around his body to find a suitable part for vein repair." Big Paul got up from his chair and walked directly to the doctor. "He better not lose that leg! I pay you a frickin fortune for this shit!" To the doctor's credit he didn't flinch, "You pay me to plug bullet holes, and that I have done, you don't pay me to be a miracle worker but what I did just now is pretty damn close, of course you can always get a second opinion." I didn't smile out loud, but I always enjoyed it when common folk popped off to Big Paul and the Doc had just put him in his place. The Doc was right, it was damn hard to find a Doc who would do what this one had just done on such short notice and from what I understand, this Doc didn't even have a gambling problem or wasn't in debt. Most of the time a doctor would only help like this if he was being pinched due to some gambling debts. In this case, I think the Doc just liked the tax-free money.

"Keep him stable for the next three days, nothing solid to eat, liquid diet." He pulled a pad from his coat pocket, "I am writing you a prescription for Percocet to help with the pain and a blood thinner to ensure there is no clotting that might cause issues later." He ripped the sheet off the pad and handed it to Big Paul. Paul stuck it in his shirt pocket. "Can I get him home?" The doctor shot big Paul a look like he had two heads. "If you do, you risk blowing out his stitches by moving him and he will bleed to death in minutes." I could see that big Paul was upset and at this point I wasn't sure if he was upset that his son had to stay in his office, or if he was upset with me for not being the one that got shot. Either way I was ready to get out of this situation. "Fine Doc! He will stay right here." When the doctor rolled the last piece of equipment out and closed the door behind him, the room became quiet and uncomfortable.

I listened to Big Paul breathe through his nose for a while, longer than I should have. He had an annoying way of breathing through his nose, and it would not only cause his mustache hairs to flutter but it would make a high-pitched whistling sound. If it would have been anyone else but Big Paul, I would have asked him to breathe a few bars of "Dixie" or some other catchy tune, at least that way it would be less annoying. Finally, Big Paul broke the silence, "You need to start making some plans to cross the Hudson, soon." I started to say something, but he continued, "Once you find our friends, you'll need to show them a good time," I was nodding my head like I agreed with him, but I couldn't disagree more. He was talking about retaliation against the Jersey crew and a different family. That kind of action is really bad business, and a lot of people could get caught up in it and it never ends well. "And once you show our friends a good time, make sure you pick up the last prescription from Bobby, we will be changing pharmacies, I heard there are cheaper places to do business."

Big Paul believed that he was always being surveilled which may be true but if he were, the feds sure let him get away with all kinds of stuff in the back of that ice cream shop because in the 5 years he'd been there, we never even so much as got a post card from them and that's why he always spoke in code when something had to do with the bad side of this business. He had just asked me to go get Carmine and the other doofus that shot Jimmy and once I had that done, I was supposed to close the account at Bobby's pharmacy which meant that Bobby had probably placed his last bet. My stomach was churning, this was just a bad idea for a lot of reasons, but the main reason was that I hated making a final collection. "Uh Boss, you know that showing guys a good time aint my specialty, what about Leo and one of his boys?" For the sake of being surveilled I continued to speak in code, "Leo loves showing guys a good time." Big Paul got up from the chair and walked over to where Jimmy was now laying on the roll-away hospital bed that had been brought in and then he placed his hand on Jimmy's forehead. "Leo don't know the guys as well as you, we want to make sure the right guys have more fun than they can stand," he rubbed Jimmy's forehead with the care and concern you would expect from a father, "you can go now." When big Paul told you that you can go, that meant leave, so I said "yes sir" as I closed the door behind me.

Chapter 4

Ship in a bottle

I left the ice cream shop confused as ever. I saved Jimmy from certain death, yet I felt like Big Paul was blaming me for it, which was never a good situation to be in. I've certainly pissed off big Paul before, but this just seemed different. I couldn't worry about it right now though because I needed to pick Teddy up from Madison's place. Madison Reynolds was a Special-Ed teacher at an elementary school but had signed on to help teach Teddy on her personal time. It cost me 60 grand a year to have her work with him, but it was well worth it.

At first, she worked under an hourly rate and would schedule times to come to our place and work with him after school but after a while, her and Teddy hit it off so well that she started taking Teddy back to her house after school or I would drop him off. If I had to make some collections that required overnight work, she would let Teddy stay with her. She was so good at helping Teddy that one day I handed her an envelope with 30 grand in it and told her that I would give her another 30 at the end of the year if she would help me when I needed it. It was safe to say that I liked her because of the way she treated Teddy. She never asked me about my work other than an occasional question about the market. I told her that I was a foreign market trader and I had to work some weird hours to keep up with the trends worldwide. That really wasn't a lie; I played the market but rarely was it foreign.

Madison was an attractive woman, but I had no interest in her, really anyone, but especially someone that was 15 years younger than me. She and Teddy were just about the same height and when they were together, I swear he was smarter, more engaging, and happier.

We found Madison when we placed an ad in one of those hiring sites where people can apply for the job online and we got to pick the ones we liked. Teddy and me set up all the interviews. Teddy had a blast with the process; he was so excited that I let him help me decide who we would pick. I told him what I was looking for and asked him what he liked in people. We wrote down all these things and as we interviewed each one, we would try and check them off the list. One of Teddy's first qualifications was that they had to like the zoo because Teddy loved the zoo and his second one was that they had to be really nice.

Teddy was very serious about the process and made me take him to a tailor so he could have a suit made. He picked out a dark navy material and asked for a vest to go with it. He wanted the vest to be brown though. Personally, I didn't care much for the combination, but I loved to see that kid smile and when we went back to try on the finished product, you should have seen that smile. He was as happy as I have ever seen him, including the Christmas when he got his first iPad and I had to admit, the color combination looked pretty good on him. Despite my objections, Teddy slept in that suit the first night we brought it home.

Madison was our 5th interview that day and looking back on it, I wish she had been our first. If she had, then it would have saved a lot of time. Teddy asked them questions he had written down, questions like; what their favorite animal at the zoo was and if they didn't have a favorite animal what their favorite football team was. Teddy loved the Jets; he would give them a star on his interview sheet if they mentioned the jets or zoo animals. The first four were nice except one. I did like this one guy alot, but Teddy didn't because he really got into the details of Down syndrome and was adamant that Down kids are to be pushed as hard as possible and not to be treated softly or separated from the rest of the class. I wanted that for Teddy too and we were hitting it off pretty well, but Teddy just didn't light up around him and that was unusual for Teddy. Just meeting a new person was a special thing for Teddy, he loved that interaction with people, he craved it like candy. Now, the other three interviews before Madison didn't have a shot at all, they were lousy interviews. One lady began to tell me that I needed to "understand" the dynamics of Down kids and stop trying to repair Teddy and just accept him as he is. I told her that I wished someone had tried to repair her instead of accepting her the way she was and showed her sorry ass to the door and as I was ushering her out, Madison was standing in the doorway. We saw each other and she smiled but she did something different than all the other interviews, she stuck out her hand to Teddy, not me, and said, "I'm Madison, I am here to interview for the job you posted." You get that? She introduced herself to Teddy, not me! She put him in control right away and he ate it up.

That was it, we didn't need to interview anyone else, Teddy took over the interview and he held court for almost two hours. She never faltered and I will be damned if she wasn't a Jets fan, and she wasn't faking it either! Teddy drilled her about the 1969 super bowl winning team, and she knew everything about that team, almost as much as Teddy. He was definitely hooked. I hardly spoke during the entire interview; I just sat back and watched her react to my baby brother like he was her own brother and man did Teddy respond to her. He was having so much fun that he forgot I was even in the room and I had to interrupt him at the end of the second hour to ask if it would be ok if I asked some questions of my own, he reluctantly let me but instead of sitting across the kitchen table like he had done with the other interviews, he changed seats and sat by her while I sat alone across the table now interviewing her and Teddy. Teddy would frown at me if he thought I was being too mean in my interview questions. It is safe to say that Madison was one of those rare finds that filled the gap in our life perfectly. So perfectly that before she got up to leave, Teddy hugged her and asked he if she wanted to spend the night.

"Uh Teddy, that's a highly improper interview question that could get us both in legal trouble so let's just tell Ms. Madison that we appreciate her time, and we will let her know the outcome of our decision by the end of the week." Teddy was not happy with that response but Madison laughed at my response and turned to look at Teddy, he was almost as tall as her but not quite, She put both of her hands on each side of the huge grin that was on his face and said, "Teddy, that's very nice of you to ask but I already have plans and even if I don't get the job, I know I've got a new friend and that's more important." Teddy grabbed her and hugged her in the only way Teddy could hug someone and that was with full strength. Sometimes it could be crushing but again, it appeared that Madison got as much out of the hug as Teddy did. All I could think of at that moment was, "Damn, she is perfect." As it turns out, she was.

Not long after Madison took over as Teddy's tutor and caregiver, I rang the doorbell to Madison's place, and she answered the door. She smiled as she saw me, she quickly put her index finger up to her lips to indicate that I shouldn't talk, "Hi Xavier!" I was a little confused, but she winked and glanced over her shoulder, and I knew what that meant, Teddy had a surprise for me, or he was hiding from me and intended to scare me. He hatched these plans quite often and he would work on them all day. "Uh Madison, say, if you have seen Teddy tell him I'd like to talk to him about some very important matters." She smiled, if he was hiding, she would say something like she hadn't seen him, and that I was more than welcome to come in and look around at which time Teddy would spring out of some closet or box or behind the couch and it was my job to pretend like I was scared out of my wits. If he had a surprise, she would say something like, Teddy is waiting to see you in the office or something like that. You get the idea . . . Today she bowed gracefully and in her best British accent she said, "Master Theodore awaits you in the parlor." When she was finished with the graceful bow, she winked and smiled at me, "Right this way sir."

I walked down the hallway that led to the living room and when I saw Teddy, he was smiling from ear to ear. He was holding one of those bottles that had a ship in it. It was a big bottle that he had to hold with two hands in order for me to see the whole thing. "Happy Birthday!" he yelled as he held the bottle high so I could see it better. I had completely forgot that it was my birthday and somehow, he remembered or maybe he had some help from Madison but either way this was his gift for me. Knowing Teddy like I know Teddy, he had gone to great lengths to find the present that meant the most to him. I didn't know what the ship in bottle meant but it wouldn't matter, you knew when Teddy gave you a gift it was a gift directly from his heart. He took Christmas and birthdays very seriously.

"Holy smokes would you look at that!" I grinned and put my hand on my heart and then my forehead to give it more drama. If Teddy thought for one second that he had not picked out the best gift ever, he would be crushed and would carry that hurt around until he was given a chance to repair whatever damage he thought he had done. "I have always wanted a ship in the bottle!" His smile got bigger as I had just confirmed for him that he had done a great job. I walked over to him and put my hands on the bottle as if I was going to take it from him, but he said, "Not yet!," he looked around me towards

Madison's kitchen where she had snuck behind me and lit a cake that obviously had all 40 candles on it and somehow Madison had managed to light them all. It looked like an inferno, and I seriously thought I would need a fire extinguisher to put them out. "You have to blow out the candles and make a wish!" I pretended to be shocked at the cake and all the fuss, which added to Teddy's excitement. "Oh my God! Look at all those candles Teddy! You gotta help me blow them out!"

So, you can see that I am not as bad of a guy as most folks think I am. I do some things that I can't explain other than the money is good, and it helps me give Teddy the best possible care I can give him. I tell myself that some of the people that I have had to make a final collection on, put themselves in that position and if they just stayed away from the drugs and the gambling, they would still be around.

I smiled at Madison and mouthed the words "thank you" to her because there was no way that Teddy could do any of this without her. She was becoming a very big part of Teddy's life and mine and I hated it. In my line of work, you really can't have close friends and you can't have feelings for people. It was dangerous enough to have Teddy in my life because my feelings for him made me weak. And now my feelings for Madison would make me even weaker and that was even more dangerous. I am very careful about loose ends; I have never even been talked to by the cops much less arrested. I am smart, I do things the right way and I don't leave any evidence. That's why I make the money I make.

"You said you wanted to go sailing one day so this is the next best thing!" I put my arms around Teddy and hugged him; he was as comforting as a warm blanket. Like I said, Teddy never gave a hug he didn't mean. "You can put it on your desk at work!" I'm sure that somewhere along the line I told Teddy that I had an office and there was no reason for him to believe any different. He went to a fine school, and he was getting premium, top-notch tutoring from Madison, why spoil happy by telling him the truth? "You bet buddy! I will put it on my desk at work."

After we had all those candles removed from the cake, me, Teddy, and Madison sat and talked and laughed at all the things that Teddy said. He started telling me all the places I could go sailing and I was pretty impressed with his knowledge of geography. He mentally sailed us around the Gulf of Mexico and all the way down the coast of Florida and then on to the Bahamas.' "Teddy has been studying geography plus he is fixated on pirates right now." Madison smiled at me, a smile I hadn't seen before. From where she was sitting at the table, right next to me with Teddy sitting at the head of the table, she placed her hand on my leg under the table. Did I tell you I had no interest in Madison? Teddy made an "arhhh" sound trying to mimic a pirate as Madison moved a little higher on my leg. "Hey Xavier, what is a Pirate's favorite letter?" I almost didn't hear him as I was channeling every ounce of spiritual karma I had in me to get Madison to remove her hand from my leg. I knew to play along, "Uh, that's a tough one, I bet its G for Gold?" Teddy shook his head no, "Ok it's probably a T for Treasure then?" Teddy was smiling and shaking is his no, "I give up then, what is a pirate's favorite letter?" Teddy laughed and said "RRRR" as he drew the R out as long as he could before he started laughing.

I stood up; it was the only thing I could think to do. Her hand on my leg surprised me more than I can even describe. She never once flirted with me or acted like she had any interest at all, and this really caught me off guard. I didn't need this kind of attention, nor did I want it. I also didn't want to upset her because she was far more important to Teddy than she was to me. I didn't need to risk upsetting her and maybe ending what I considered to be a very good thing. "Hey Teddy, I think it's time we head home," Teddy wasn't very receptive to this and showed his displeasure with a frown, "now, come on man we gotta go, I have to get up early tomorrow." Teddy always understood how to accept things he didn't agree with and move on. He definitely wanted to stay with Madison, but he also knew he needed to do what I said.

By now, I started to move away from the table and as I stood up, her hand fell off my leg, I never made eye contact with her because I was scared of what I might see. I didn't want to see her look of either disappointment or the look of playfulness. Lord knows since I took over as Teddy's guardian, I haven't played at all, and I could probably use a little mature fun with someone willing, but it wasn't going to be Madison. No matter how beautiful she was or how much I would enjoy her touch, it just couldn't be Madison. That much I knew.

"Tell Madison thank you for the birthday party help." Teddy glowed as he thanked Madison for helping him pick out the ship in the bottle that he insisted on carrying for me as we left. I finally made eye contact with Madison, and I did the best I could to relay how I was feeling at the moment with my eyes, but you really can't tell someone they are highly attractive, and you are grateful for their efforts, but you just can't go in that direction with them, with nothing more than your eyes. "Thank you, Madison, really. It was quite a surprise."

Teddy and I took the elevator down to the lobby of Madison's apartment building, he talked the whole way down the elevator, mainly about how he was going to learn to build a ship in the bottle, but he wanted to build a car in the bottle. He was convinced that no one else had that idea and he could make lots of money if he put a Ferrari in a bottle. Teddy loved Ferrari's; he was hooked on an old TV show where the lead character drove a Ferrari everywhere he went.

As we stepped out of the elevator and into the Lobby, the attendant smiled and greeted us, he was a nice man, he knew me because I was there damn near every day. "Hey Mr. Thomas!" I nodded and waved at him and felt a little embarrassed that as many times as I have seen him, I didn't know his name, "say Mr. Thomas, there were two guys outside earlier that wanted me to give them an elevator card to come see you, but I wouldn't do it. They said they were friends of yours and I told them that I would ring the apartment first," He acted a little nervous, "but when I picked up the phone, they told me not to bother and they would catch up with you later." He gave me a nervous smile, "I hope I did the right thing for you sir." I couldn't help but like this guy, he was nice, and he was doing his job. "No problem at all." I looked at Teddy and then back towards the doorman, "Oh hell, I forgot my keys, come on Teddy lets go back up." I started to turn towards the elevator and stopped, I walked over to where he was standing, "say I feel bad, I never caught your name," He gave me a crooked nervous smile again and said, "Delbert, just like the comic strip without the I." I laughed, that makes it easy to remember, forgive me in advance if I call you Dilbert." He had probably heard that a thousand times, I fished around in my pocket and pulled out my money clip, I thumbed three 100-dollar bills out, then looked down at Teddy and then glanced up like I was looking at Madison's apartment and thumbed 2 more 100-dollar bills out. I handed Delbert 500 bucks, and his face went white. "I can't take this Mr. Thomas; this is way too much but thank you." I put my hand up to stop him, "listen Delbert, Teddy and Madison are the only two people I have in my life that I give a shit about," I pushed his hand that still held the money back towards him, "you just keep doing a good job." I turned, "come on Teddy, let's go get my keys."

Chapter 5

Delbert the Doorman

Nobody knows where Teddy hangs out after school, which means that nobody knows about Madison, and I would just as soon keep it that way. It bothers me a lot that two guys show up at Madison's apartment building looking for me. It should have occurred to me before, but I need to get some things cleared up with Madison. It isn't fair for her to help me the way she does and not know that there could be a chance that someone might use her to get to me. The doorman had done a pretty cool thing for me, and he didn't even know it. Those guys were not my friends, and they were not there to wish me a happy birthday. I didn't know who they were, but I needed to find out. They would be waiting on me when I left the building and having Teddy with me would drastically decrease my odds. You remember I don't carry a gun, not because I don't like them, but because I don't want Teddy anywhere near a gun. His curiosity is incredible, and he would want to know everything about it, and he would sneak around and try and find where I hide it. I keep what I need in a small storage unit. Madison opened the door and was surprised to see us, "What did you forget guys?" She opened the door wide and allowed me and Teddy to step into the living room area, "I think I left my keys somewhere around here," as I said it, I raised my eyebrows and looked at Teddy, "Say Teddy can you give me and Madison a minute, maybe play a video game while we talk?" he smiled; gave Madison another hug then took off to the little game room just down the hall from the main room. Madison was smiling at me, and I had an idea as to why, but I would clear that up later, "I think there are some guys waiting for me downstairs that …", I was still tap dancing around the subject as best as I could, "they might have some bad intentions." Madison's smile changed very quickly to a concerned look, "are you in trouble?" I shook my head and decided to make up a story. "Listen, Madison, I uhh," this was much harder than I expected, "I uhh, I really am a stockbroker," I looked down the hall to make sure Teddy hadn't snuck out to eaves drop, which he loved to do. I lowered my voice just in case he might be listening, "uhh, my method of making a living gets a little rough sometimes, people don't always make a fortune in the stock market and sometimes they lose money." Madison cocked her head to one side and folded her arms in a playful yet serious way of enticing me to continue, "I try to keep my clients between the ditches so to speak but they don't always listen to my advice."

Madison cocked her head to the other side, which clearly meant that she wanted more information. Now I think it would have been easier for her to just ask questions and let me fill in the blanks as much as I could, but women confuse the hell out of me sometimes. One minute she has her hand on my thigh under the table and the next minute she is giving me the scorned wife look. Honestly, I didn't care much for that either. "Go on," was all she said.

I told her about a client that had lost a lot of money and was now blaming me, I threw in a bunch of stuff about stock futures along with a quick lesson about margin calls, but it was only to add color to a made-up story. "I have this one client that I didn't realize made money in unconventional ways and thought he would take a stab at the market and lost a bundle." I paused then continued, "He thinks I should have told him not to make some of the trades he wanted me to make only he forgot that I did that very thing." I tried to read her body language to see if the story was working, "He wants to rough me up and make me pay back his losses but that ain't how it works. I just need to go visit with these guys without Teddy, because I don't want to scare him and then I will be right back."

I thought she was getting upset but then she smiled, she took a few steps closer to me, put her hands on both sides of my face and planted a kiss right smack on my lips. When she pulled away, she laughed "I want you to be careful, this guy sounds bad." I was taken back by the kiss but now was not the time to dwell on it. "So, listen, I need Teddy to stay with you for just a little bit but . . . if I don't come back, here is a number I want you to call," I reached in my coat pocket and grabbed my pen, I wrote the number down on a scratch pad I kept on me and gave it to her. "She will take care of everything."

She took the paper and looked at it, "there is no name, just a number?" I looked at the paper in her hand, "It's better that way, just call it." I started to turn around but then turned back to look at her. "At the table tonight," she smiled, "what was that for?." She smiled even bigger, "You look lonely Xavier, you look like you need company, the company of a woman," she paused and looked down at the paper in her hand, "now I know why." Madison looked at me with the saddest eyes I have ever seen, and I didn't know what to say, I was already too close to her and if one of my colleagues or past business associates found out that she was important to me, they would eventually get around to using her against me. "Listen, you are drop dead gorgeous, and some guy some day is gonna be very happy to have you by his side, but it can't be me." I turned towards the door and without looking back, "I will be back in a few minutes but if I ain't, you know what to do."

I turned the knob on the door handle, "Don't open the door for anyone you don't know." I got back on the elevator and rode it down to the 2nd floor, I wanted to take the stairwell to the lobby from there. If they could somehow see the elevator though the windows outside, then that would let them know where I was. I needed to exit the building and into the parking garage without being seen. Once I got to the first floor, I took the stairs closest to the front of the building. I peeked outside the door into the lobby and could see the doorman standing next to the counter looking at his phone. I slowly made my way towards the desk without ever stepping in front of the lobby door windows. Once I was close enough to the desk for Delbert to hear me, "Hey Delbert, keep looking at your phone," surprisingly he did as he was told, "What's up Mr. Thomas" I smiled, damn this guy was good, he knew my voice too." Is there an employee entrance or some way to get to the parking garage without being seen?" Delbert continued to look down at his phone, "Yes sir, stay right where you are, and I will come let you in the back office and then into the garage."

Delbert continued to look at his phone for a few more seconds then shoved it in his pants pocket and moved behind the counter, grabbed something from under the counter and then turned down the hallway I was standing in, "I really appreciate this my friend." He opened a door that I always thought was a janitor closet and it opened up into a pretty nice size office that was beautifully furnished and well decorated. It took me by surprise, and it must have shown on my face "They give us a nice place to work and get away during the slow times, plus the super has some exquisite taste." He laughed as he walked me though the office to another door that looked like a closet and when he opened it, I was once again surprised. It opened into a dark stairwell that led down to the parking garage level. He opened that door, and we were staring directly at a brick wall with just a few feet of space to step out, it was so small that I had to turn sideways to follow him. After a few shuffled steps he stopped, "Now, when you take another step, you will be in the parking garage." He patted me on the shoulder, "no one knows this is here but me and the Super, and now you. Unfortunately, you can't come back in this way unless I let you in." I smiled as he squeezed himself between the wall and me and I started to say something, but I froze as I could clearly feel his hand on me in a place that it shouldn't have been. He only brushed it as he passed but it was clearly intentional. "Uh, thanks Dilbert, uh Delbert." He laughed and went back through the door we had just exited. I watched him swipe his employee card or badge and disappear. Man, oh man, I have never in my life had a guy grab my stuff before! I didn't know what to think. At least it confirmed that I wasn't gay, not that there would be anything wrong with that, I am in no position to judge.

I slowly stepped out into the parking garage and gave it a good once over. There was a good chance they knew what I drove and by now they were either close by my car which was a 1976 Chevy Monte Carlo or in my car. I bought it used but it had low miles, and it was super clean. It looked brand new, but I didn't like the interior, so I had it reupholstered in a cream-colored leather, none of that roll and tuck shit just the nice, classy, soft kind. The outside was gray or silver, it depended on my mood that day. The car did not stand out and that is what I liked about it. I certainly had the money to buy something nicer, but I had no reason to, I preferred to stay anonymous if I could.

A cloud of smoke caught my eye as I continued to survey the parking garage, it wasn't unusual for people to come down to the parking garage to have a quick smoke and then head back up to their apartment, but those folks usually hung out by the elevator and not in their cars. This smoke cloud was coming from one of the cars that was parked semi-close to my Monte Carlo. I crouched down and slowly made my way to where the smoke was coming from. I was behind them so I could see the plates were Jersey. There were two guys in the car, and both were smoking a cigarette. Now was the time to act if I was going to. I could have easily gone back upstairs, called an Uber, then me and Teddy could have gone home with no trouble, but I really needed to end this little squabble now. These guys got embarrassed by what had happened earlier today, and they wanted some payback. I wasn't sure if they just wanted to rough me up and break a few bones or if they wanted to cast me for cement shoes. I didn't want to hurt them I just needed them to know that this was over, and we all had better things to do. I eased up to the back of their car so a rearview or side mirror couldn't spot me. The fact that they were smoking was to my advantage because they didn't have both hands free. I went for the guy in the passenger seat first because he didn't have a steering wheel in front of him, which would limit the driver's ability to move quickly. The passenger window was down so I quickly reached for the cigarette hand that was hanging out the window, gabbed the cigarette and tossed it into the guy's lap. As he was trying to get the hot burning cigarette out of his crotch I reached inside his jacket and felt for the gun that he would have concealed there and yanked it from its holster. I was right, the driver was Carmine, and he couldn't get to his gun because his hand got caught in the steering wheel. If he would have just tossed out the cigarette he was smoking and used that hand, he might have got the jump on me but for some stupid reason he continued to hang on to the cigarette. I had the passenger side guys gun pointed at them before they could do anything. The passenger guy was still squirming trying to get out of the way of the hot cigarette. It was actually kind of comical to watch but now was not the time to laugh.

"Put your weapon on the dash and get out of the car." I didn't yell, I mainly didn't want to attract attention, but I also didn't want these guys to get jumpy and try to do something stupid. I watched him pull his gun out and place it on the dash then step out of the car. Once the driver was out of the car, I backed away from the passenger door and motioned for the other guy to step out. Once the passenger was out of the car, I almost laughed because he had a big bandage on his forehead. It looked like he was wearing a Kotex on his head.

Both men looked sheepish now, they looked like a couple of kids that didn't get the Christmas present they wanted. I kept the gun pointed at them both, but I kept it low with my elbow bent. "Fella's, you gotta learn how to let things go" I looked at Carmine, "your pal here started shooting when there was no need and now the boss's son might lose a leg or even die because of it." I took the gun and put it in the back of my pants under my shirt. I reached inside their car and took the gun that was on the dash, dropped the clip on the concrete floor of the parking garage and then kicked it so that it would slide under a car further away from where we were. I racked the shell in the chamber so it would pop out and I caught it in midair. I then threw it as far as I could. Neither man said a word, they just stood there, embarrassed for sure.

"You know my boss is pissed, he already told me to book passage to Jersey and find you two dipshits and now you've made it easy." I smiled, "But tonight is your lucky night, I don't have time to handle you two pricks, so I am sending you back to Jersey." I threw the now empty gun at Carmine and he impressed me when he caught it with one hand, "why don't you guys pretend like the doctor has just told you that you have two months to live," I took the gun out of the back of my pants, it was cylindered so I kicked the cylinder out and dropped the shells in my hand and then I stuck them in my pants pocket. I threw that empty gun at Mr. Kotex, and it was no surprise to me that he dropped it. "Live it up gentleman, you got two months, bet big, hug your kids, visit your estate lawyers and hump your gals or pets, whichever it is, but two months is all you got." I looked around the parking garage, "The exit is that way and I don't validate. Get your asses out of here, now." I opened the driver door to their car and pointed at Carmine who took the hint and climbed in. I closed his door and looked at Mr. Kotex as if he were stupid for not taking the hint. When he finally did, he climbed in the passenger seat. I watched the car pull out of the garage.

Chapter 6

The Gambler's Debt

After Madison made me tell her who I was and hold my driver's license up to the peephole, she opened the door. I was happy that she took our conversation serious, and I even told her that. I could see the look on her face after she opened the door and I felt bad for her, she was now scared to open her own door. "I'm sorry kid, I don't know what to say." She looked down at the floor and then backed up to me, "come in and let's have a drink, we should talk some more." I could hear that Teddy was still playing video games because he liked it loud for the explosions and everything else that was in those games. I never liked the games though, I thought they were simply too violent, but Teddy loved them, so I let it go.

She went to the kitchen where she fumbled around in the cabinets looking for glasses first and then the bottle. "I don't normally use these glasses," they clanked as she carried the two glasses with one hand, "they are actual crystal, my dad used them when he was having his wind down drink as he liked to call it." I was starting to feel even worse because out of all the time we spent with Madison, I never really got to know her. I had a feeling that her dad was dead and that's why she had the glasses. Geez, what if her old man had died while she was working for me and helping Teddy and I didn't even know it. What a piece of shit I would be. "This is Blanton's single barrel bourbon whiskey, it was my dad's favorite drink, it is hard to get now, I think it is all marketing but hey, what do I know." She sat the glasses down on the dining room table, "come sit down."

I wasn't much of a drinker, and I had no idea if Blanton's was good or bad and I really wasn't in the mood to have drink but after what she learned about me tonight, I simply needed to comply. She poured some of the whiskey in each glass, not much though. "Poppa liked it "*neat*," he would sip on this little amount for an hour before dinner," she picked up her glass and looked at it as if it were a magical potion, "He was my protector, he was my rock." She extended her glass towards me, and I picked up my glass and clanked it against hers, "to our protectors." I took a drink and had to admit that it tasted pretty good. It didn't have that burning sensation in my throat like I expected. It smelled very good too, "wow this is pretty good stuff." She smiled and smelled the aroma then drank it all down in one swallow. She poured another small amount into her glass and as she was pouring, "is your pops still around?" I wasn't sure if I had asked the question delicately enough, but she answered anyway, "I don't know, he never came home from work one Friday. It's been four years now." She took a smaller drink from her glass, "We have no idea where he is."

Now I couldn't imagine having my old man walk out on my mom, or me, he just wasn't that type. My dad was steady as a rock. He went to church every Sunday and took me along with him until I was old enough to opt out. He never put up a fuss about me not going but I could tell he wished I would. I am not sure they liked the message they received at church as much as they liked the thought of belonging to something good. My dad used to say that there was so much bad in the world that he needed a good place to get away from it for a few hours. After looking at her stare at her glass I felt like I needed to break the silence "I am sorry to hear that, I didn't know." She looked up and gave a fake smile, "It was hard on my mom for sure." I sat and listened to her tell me her life story, it seemed as though she was hell bent on giving me every detail that she could possibly give. "My mother suffered from depression after he left, she blamed herself every day, she'd say she should have been a better wife and that she should have taken better care of him." I could see a tear running down her cheek as she stared at the glass of bourbon. "We couldn't even cash in on his insurance because he never turned up dead or alive," she looked up at me, "we lost everything, the house, the car, EVERYTHING." I tried to be sympathetic, but sympathy just wasn't my strong suit. "I'm sorry all of that happened to you, but you have come out of it just fine, you need to put it behind you and enjoy what you have, not worry about what you don't have." She gave me a look after I said that and told me if she had a gun, she would have shot me. "Do you know what it is like to not know why your dad left you? Or why he hasn't tried to contact you?" She looked like she was going to throw her glass across the kitchen, "or if it's your fault he left?" She lowered her glass back down to the table and stared at it.

So maybe it wasn't the best response I could have given her, but my intentions were good, right? I wasn't going to say anything else that could put me in deeper hot water, so I just apologized but she wasn't done. "It killed my mother, the stress of it, the bill collectors didn't give a hoot whether he was missing or not, they just wanted their money." She took a sip from the glass but then turned it completely up and finished the rest, "with the money you give me to tutor Teddy, I have been able to pay off all his debts." She put her hand on top of mine, "I am sorry I snapped at you, what you have done for me is overwhelming to say the least." Madison removed her hand from mine and took the glass that I was using and drank it too. "You pay me too much; you know that, right?" She was looking at me as if she expected me to say something, so I wasn't about to say anything else stupid, "Teddy doesn't think so, and that's all that matters." She got up from the table and went to the sink, "Yeah well Teddy is a special kid that deserves the best," I knew what to say to that, so I said it, "and you are the best."

She turned away from the sink and walked back over to me and stood over me long enough to make me feel a little uncomfortable, then she put her hand on my shoulder, "I am sorry I was so forward, I should know better, and it won't happen again." She was looking at me with the calmest expression now and I marveled at how she just went through an entire roller coaster ride of emotions with me and now she was back to the person I knew before I had to tell her what my job really was. This is the main reason I don't date girls, I can't compete with that kind of honesty and raw emotion, nor do I want to. This girl just swallowed her pride a little, fixed what she thought was a mistake and was ready to move on and my mind was still stuck on the two goof balls from Jersey that I had sent packing just a few minutes ago. I looked up at her to see her smiling at me, most normal guys would have run with her advances and would probably have her clothes off with her heels pointed toward the ceiling by now, but not me. Damn she was beautiful, smart, soft, young, and I was not even close to interested, well, maybe a little. I concluded as I was sitting at that table that night, that there was possibly something wrong with me in the love department. Don't get me wrong, I like looking at women as much as the next guy, but I don't like the dating scene, and being polite and getting to know someone that well. I am too busy for that stuff and besides, I don't want anyone that close to me. Madison tried to pour some more whiskey in my glass, but I didn't want any, so I put my hand over the top of the glass, "I am afraid I don't handle alcohol all that well and I have to drive Teddy home." She smiled and put the top back on the bottle but before she did, she poured herself another drink only this pour was quite a bit more than the previous ones she had poured. "If you want to find Teddy another tutor now, I will understand." I had no idea what the hell she was talking about, and it had to have shown on my face. "Like I said, I paid off all my father's debts and my mother's funeral with the money I got from you." She was talking to me, but she was now staring off somewhere, not anywhere in particular but it was as if she was seeing something in the room that I couldn't see. I was still trying to figure out how Madison could change moods and emotions so rapidly that it kept me confused. "I told you already, Teddy and me don't want anyone else, we want you." She didn't change expressions, but she changed the location of her stare to somewhere else, to me it looked like she was switching back and forth from looking at the refrigerator and then to the oven, but she was certainly not looking at me. "You know I used to help him in the store all the time," she took a sip from her glass, "He owned a sporting goods store, and it was the best sporting goods store in the state of New York" she smiled now, "at least that's what Dad used to say, he even had a big sign made that said that exact thing," she raised the hand that had the glass in it and to me it appeared she was now looking at the front of the store, and she was pointing with her glass in hand, "THE BEST SPORTING GOODS STORE IN THE WORLD."

I immediately took the bottle that was sitting in front of us and poured a healthy amount into my glass. She heard me pour it and snapped out of the little trance she was in, "I thought you said you didn't handle alcohol well?" I could feel the beads of sweat pop out on my forehead and the back of my neck, instead of sipping the contents of my glass, I downed it just as she had done earlier and then I softly set the glass back on the table. "You say that was the sign on the building huh?" Images of that sign were bursting in my head now and I was hoping a good shot of that bourbon would help them go away but it only made it worse. "You never told me your dad had a sporting goods store in the city," she poured some more Blanton's in my glass and this time I didn't argue. "Why would I, we don't have it anymore. Mom sold it for a fraction of what it was worth just so we could get by for a few years." She went over to a drawer in the kitchen and pulled out a big brown envelope and dumped the contents out on the table in front of us. It was pictures, a bunch of pictures of her and her dad, her mom, their house she grew up in and the sporting goods store. She sifted through the pile of pictures until she found the specific one she was looking for. It was a picture of her and her dad when she was just a little girl, and he was holding her on his hip in front of the store with the sign that said *Oh-G Sporting Goods* in big letters and right under that was the words "*The best sporting goods store in the world*!" I looked at the picture but didn't touch it, even when she tried to hand it to me, I didn't touch it. "I'm gonna check on Teddy. I uh . . . we, me, and Teddy, we gotta get going."

I touched the rim of the glass to my lips as I continued to stare down at the picture of a man holding a little girl in front of a sporting goods store. I tilted the glass, drank all the contents, and then set the glass back down on the table. She was looking directly at me as if she knew but I knew that she didn't, no one did, no one except the man who ordered it to be done, Big Paul. Her dad would never be found, and I knew it but couldn't tell her. I didn't know where he was buried or if he was buried at all, but her dad was a gambler and got sideways with big Paul. I had nothing to do with it, but I knew about it and that was bad enough. "What's the matter Xavier?" I shook my head as I stood up and shouted for Teddy to end the game and grab his stuff. "Nothing, I just realized what time it is and we gotta get going." I walked down the hallway that led to the little game room, "Come on Teddy, say bye to Madison, we gotta get going," Teddy dropped the game controller and turned the power off the TV then ran directly past me and right into the waiting arms of Madison. There was no doubt that Teddy loved her, and I couldn't blame him.

Chapter 7

What's a Dingleberry?

Teddy slid into the passenger seat and buckled up, he was a stickler for safety and wouldn't let you even think about putting the car into drive if you weren't already buckled up too. He was also in command of the radio and the temperature. Teddy tended to be hot natured so we would struggle with the temperature in the car if we drove for long stretches. I was very cold natured; I hated the cold, and I couldn't wait to eventually move to Florida or Arizona when the time came. I was the kind of guy that liked to wear shorts on Christmas day if I could. Living in New York, there was never any chance of that happening.

After I got Teddy back to the house, he was still wound up and wanted nothing to do with bedtime. No matter how much I explained how grumpy he would be in the morning when I woke him up for school, he wouldn't listen and to tell you the truth, right before bedtime was my favorite time with him. When he felt like the day was about to end, he had to empty his mind of everything he observed that day like people empty their pockets before they take their pants off. I was always surprised by how much detail he stored in his head and that he needed answers to so many questions before he closed his eyes. I did the best I could to answer them one by one, some were easy, such as, why do some men wear ties, and some men don't and others were much more difficult and required way more thought on my part such as, why are there so many different churches and does God favor one over the other? To me, the questions were fun and after each question he would lay in bed and listen to the answer, sometimes he would have follow-up questions and sometimes he wouldn't. Sometimes, his follow up questions wouldn't get asked until days later which always caught me off guard because it meant that he was still thinking about my answer and that made me question my own knowledge of his interests.

"You gotta go to sleep Teddy boy, we stayed at Madison's too long and you have school tomorrow big man," as he leaned back and put his head on the pillow, he put both of his hands behind his head and laced his fingers together to form a cradle for his head and smiled. "I think Madison should come live with us," I smiled because it wasn't the first time that he brought it up, in fact, since the very first time he had any contact with Madison, he was hooked. He made it no secret that he wanted her to live with us, I couldn't really tell if he was trying to play cupid with Madison but either way, he definitely thought that Madison hung the moon. "Is that so?" He closed his eyes as he spoke, "she would make a great mom."

I sat down on the bed next to Teddy so I could talk to him without seeming like I was looking down at him, "Listen, I think Madison is pretty damn good too, but she isn't going to be your mother." Teddy always processed all the information you could give him and more times than not, Teddy came to the right conclusion without an argument but that was only if you managed to answer all his questions. Teddy was smart and it would frustrate me at times and piss me off that people would see his outward appearance and automatically assume that he was anything but intelligent. "Why don't you like her X?" I put my hand on his leg that was under the covers now, "I do like her, very much so, I actually love the way she looks after you and cares for you, but I don't like her the way that you want me to." He unlaced his fingers that were behind his head and let his arms fall to his sides. I could see by the look on his face that he was disappointed, but you have to understand that Teddy and me have had this conversation several times already. Teddy was tenacious when he wanted something and if you stripped away all the conversations of Madison, what he really wanted was to bring his mother back. He got that motherly kind of love from Madison that I couldn't give, and I understood that. "Go to sleep now Teddy monster, the school bell will ring before you know it.

I kissed Teddy on the forehead like I always do and turned to walk out of the room and just about the time I started to turn the light off Teddy said, "what's a dingle berry?" I stopped and turned back to look at Teddy who was clearly looking at me with inquisitive eyes waiting on me to answer his question. With Teddy and me there were no off-limit boundaries installed between the two of us. I never lied to Teddy except when it came to what I did for a living, "why, what do you think it is? What's the context?" He rose up on one elbow, "a kid at school said I was the best dingle berry he had ever met, and everyone laughed when he said it, but I didn't know what it was, so I didn't say anything back." He laid back down on the pillow and looked up at the ceiling again, "I know what a strawberry is, and what a blueberry is and lots of other berries, but I don't know what a dingle berry is."

I turned and went back to his bed and sat down because this was probably going to be a long conversation now. Because Teddy was a Down syndrome kid, he was an easy target for bullies and jokes but sometimes, kids were just playing and joking with him like they would any of their other friends which is the way I wanted it for Teddy. I wanted him to be just another kid in school. It was always a tightrope for me to walk because kids picked on kids and that was just a fact of life. I wanted to make sure that Teddy was being picked on because he was a kid, not a Down kid. I knew I couldn't protect him from everything so I would have these long conversations with him to understand the context. I mean, hell, I had buddies in school that would call me names like "hey dumbass, you forgot your book" but that was always good-natured stuff that friends did to each other. Figuring out if the words thrown at Teddy were good natured or just mean was always my mission during these conversations.

"Who is the kid that called you a dingle berry? Do you like him? Is he a friend?" I let those questions hang in the air for a minute so Teddy would have time to think it through. "Well, I think of him as a friend, he is nice to me and the girls like him a lot." I knew he had more to say so I held back my initial line of questioning because as far as Teddy was concerned, everyone was a friend, even when I knew they weren't. "He has sex with a lot of girls." Well, I didn't see that one coming and I sure as hell wasn't prepared to have the birds and bee's conversation tonight but with Teddy, it was best to squeeze out the sponge he stored his thousands of observations in as often as possible or he would get mentally bogged down.

"Ok, wow, do you know what sex is?" I asked the question before I was ready and now had to course correct, "wait, lets come back to that. "Tell me about your friendship with this guy, what's him name?" Teddy sort of turned and sat up on one elbow, "His name is Daniel, Daniel Garcia but everyone calls him Danny." I thought about what to say next, but Teddy wasn't finished. "He is interesting." I shook my head; I don't think I ever recall Teddy using the term interesting like that. "Why do you say he is interesting?" Teddy smiled, "Well, like I said, girls like him a lot and when we eat in the cafeteria together, everyone treats me normal." I was beginning to feel better about this conversation than I had originally thought. In my mind I was expecting to hear that this kid just picked on

Teddy, but apparently this kid actually protects Teddy, at least that is what I thought I was hearing. "How often do you and Danny eat in the cafeteria together?" Teddy wasted no time in answering and his smile got even bigger, "Oh every day! Danny saves me a seat because it takes me a little longer to get to the cafeteria because he goes there right out of Algebra and I go there right out of U.S. History," he paused, "they are at totally opposite sides of the school."

I was relieved, I was liking this Danny kid more and more, but I was also prepared to hunt him down and break a few of his fingers while I whisper in his ear who Theodore Walter Thomas was to me. Hey, I don't care how old or young the kid is, if you pick on Teddy, I will find you and you won't pick on him anymore, it's just as simple as that. "If you and Danny hang out so much, how come you never told me about him?" Teddy put some real thought into that question because he looked down at the floor off to the side of the bed and held that stare for quite a while before he looked up at me, "I don't really know, I am not trying to hide anything X." He looked at me with eyes that were changing, and it hit me that I wasn't being as involved in Teddy's life as I needed to be. I wasn't asking all the questions that a dad should ask a son. Teddy was my little brother but there were days that he needed a father instead of a big brother. "Oh, I don't think you are trying to hide anything Teddy." I smiled at him and patted the leg that was closest to me under the covers. "Tell me more, I want to know about the girls my man." Teddy grinned with a grin that only Teddy could grin, "uh oh, hang on little brother, I am gonna go get a cup of coffee." I was thinking that this was going to be a long conversation and would need something to help boost my energy but when I came back with a cup of coffee in my hand, Teddy was already fast asleep. Teddy had always been quick to crash. His mind and body went full speed all day and when it came time to shut it down and give it a rest, he wasted no time. He was done for tonight, but I now knew that the conversation about the birds and the bees was looking more and more eminent.

I turned off all of Teddy's lights and shut the door, leaving him to sleep and maybe dream about the girls. When I made it back to the kitchen I sat down at the bar and opened my laptop, it was old and heavy, and I loved it. It had a 17-inch screen which they didn't even make any more but the guy at the mac store installed a new hard drive for me over a year ago and the thing worked beautifully for what I needed, and what I needed was to watch overseas market trading to see if I could spot a trend that would take off at the bell here in the states. It wasn't easy and there were lots of people better at it than me, but I loved to look. To me, it was like spotting a rose popping up out of a Queens's sidewalk, it didn't happen often, but it was always possible. Just a year ago I pegged a small upstart Ecuadorian pharmaceutical company that managed to patent a dietary supplement that didn't curve your appetite like all the others did but increased your appetite for a bunch of foods that were good for you. They had a whole market study that showed the people who took the pill once at night before they went to bed would wake up the next morning with veracious appetites for broccoli, carrots, and stuff they would normally avoid.

Now who knows if it actually worked but I knew they were going public and went in big on the IPO, so big that I didn't sleep for a few days because after it hit the market, nothing happened. The stock just sat there at the opening price and then the worst possible thing for a trader happened and the stock crashed. I had just about everything me and Teddy had tucked away in that stock. I watched all my savings evaporate in one day and then, something happened, word got out, who knows, but I woke up one morning about a week later and found that the stock had skyrocketed well past the IPO price I paid. Teddy and me made a bundle that day and I can promise you once I saw that rocket ship take off, I clicked the sell button, and the money was deposited in my bank. I could never do the stock trading for anyone else but me, if that would have been someone else's money that I nearly lost, I wouldn't be able to face them. As far as I know that stock was still trending up the last time I looked but I'm not greedy.

Chapter 8

The Crossing Guard

I woke up with Teddy next to me, it wasn't uncommon for Teddy to get up in the middle of the night and crawl in bed with me, it was uncommon for me to not wake up when he did it. I was usually a light sleeper, but I must have been tired. I was one of those guys that never needed an alarm. I was usually awake before 6am regardless of what time I went to bed. I used to call it a curse when I was younger but now it was a blessing. I always had a few minutes alone in the morning to think through things and plan the day.

As for Teddy, he would wake up and more than likely start thinking about our parents and would just feel lonely. He didn't get scared or anything like that, but Teddy didn't care much for feeling lonely and he would often have those lonely feelings caused by the death of a parent at his age. Don't get me wrong, he could stay in his room all day by himself and stay occupied but only if he knew someone was in the house with him.

After I got out of the shower and dressed, I woke Teddy so he could begin the process of getting showered and dressed. Teddy did not enjoy this part of the day. He would move so slowly, and he would get stuck on all kinds of things other than getting dressed. I would have to stay on him all morning in order to have him ready for school. I had the routine down very well and we were never late. This morning Teddy started looking for one of his sneakers but got distracted when he found an old coloring book under his bed that he must have used about 10 years ago. He began flipping through the pages and studying each one as if he was trying to find the hidden meaning of his artwork. If I didn't say anything or push him along, he would get stuck looking at that coloring book for the next hour. I couldn't blame him though, I struggled sometimes with my own attention span. I made a note to clean out everything that was under Teddy's bed.

I sat at the kitchen bar reading the paper while looking at the results of the overnight trading. I loved to read the newspaper. I know I could probably get more information if I used the internet better than I currently did but My God, you could get lost on the internet and you could also be manipulated much easier. The way I looked at it, if every internet site were saying the same thing, you couldn't form your own opinion. To me, reading an article in print made me think about it and it even made me more skeptical. I guess I am just old fashioned that way and will more than likely have to give up the old, printed newspaper at some point and time because there probably wouldn't be a printed version anywhere to be found. There were no big surprises in the paper and on my trade site. I was glad I hadn't pulled the trigger on an environmental stock out of India that looked promising at first. I was paying attention to it every day for the last week as it had climbed almost 30% in the last few days but overnight it crashed. The company was called Eraydrop Technologies, and were supposed to increase the cell absorption rate on solar panels allowing them to retain more sunlight which extended the use of solar power during cloudy days but apparently it was somewhat of a hyped hoax and got caught flat footed by the media and the stock tanked. I still thought it was a good stock and would more than likely consider buying it while it was down. They were definitely onto something because they also stated that their solar panels were a sixteenth the size of the current solar panels used on homes now but currently, they were promising more than they could deliver.

My cell phone was laying on the counter next to me so I could easily hear it buzz, it took me a minute to find it under some of the sections of newspaper I had already perused and discarded. I never stored names in my phone, that could be dangerous, in my business, numbers were always changing anyway so it would be difficult to keep up with, the only number I had stored in my phone was Teddy's school and Madison. I wanted to make sure that I knew when Teddy needed me.

"Hello," that was all you ever got with me and if in the first few sentences, I couldn't figure out who you were, I just hung up. The voice on the other end I knew very well because I had been his employee for nearly the last 20 years, "Forget about the trip to Jersey for now and let's get some ice cream." Big Paul was a man of few words on the phone but in person, he could talk all day about a wide variety of subjects. Big Paul was smart, and he loved to read. He read stuff that I wouldn't even think about reading and what was confusingly interesting about big Paul, he retained most of it.

Big Paul always conducted his life as if someone was watching it. He used to tell me that if I wouldn't want to read my words printed in the New York Times, and then never say anything on the phone about our business so we were always "meeting for ice cream" or "going for a drive". I was always nervous about the drives though, a "Sunday drive" usually didn't turn out well for someone so every time I was asked to go for a drive, I made sure that Teddy was at Madison's and all his paperwork was in order. I know it seems like a nerve-racking way to live but it paid the bills quite well and so far, I had managed to stay on everyone's good side. Since big Paul asked to meet for ice cream today, I was comfortable that everything was just fine.

As I was taking a sip of my coffee I hear, "Good morning, Dingleberry." It reminded me that Teddy and I had not finished the conversation from last night and I would need to at least finish this dingleberry part of the conversation before school. I could see Teddy calling one of his favorite teachers a dingleberry. Teddy sat down at the bar next to me and poured some cereal into a bowl that I had already retrieved from the cupboard for him. "Say Teddy bud, let's finish that conversation about the word dingleberry we had last night." Teddy poured his milk and started looking for his spoon, which I forgot to grab when I was preparing for his arrival, so I got up and grabbed a spoon from the drawer and handed it to him. Teddy was a little grumpy which was not out of the ordinary but he managed to smile, "it's ok, I figured it out", Teddy shoveled a mountain of fruit loops into his mouth but continued to talk, a habit of his that I was desperately trying to break but was not having much luck with, "It's just whah gise cuh e uth . . . " he was very focused on his fruit loops so I let him chew up what he had in his mouth, "don't talk with your mouth full Teddy", he nodded that he understood. Before he could shovel some more fruit loops in his mouth, I put my hand on his wrist to keep him from raising the spoon, "now, what did you just say?" He grinned, "It's just what guys that are best friends call each other." I was somewhat satisfied that Teddy understood the concept, but I followed up just to make sure, "so you understand that the word dingleberry can be considered bad and that maybe, even close friends would take offense at being called a dingleberry?" Teddy nodded in agreement, and I considered the matter closed for now. "You got your books?" Teddy was fumbling through his backpack looking for something, "I have my books, but I can't find my homework." I do my best to try and let Teddy figure things out on his own and I am quite proud of how independent he has become. I like to think that the things I am doing with his education and how I treat him are making him more independent by the day but in reality, it probably has more to do with Madison than me. She has been a miracle worker when it comes to Teddy. "Where did you last have it?" He looked around the room while he was thinking and then he must have remembered where he put it because he ran out of the living room and into his bedroom and he was back in a flash holding several sheets of paper. "I found it." I was still sitting at the bar when there was a knock on the door. I spun off the bar stool to go answer it but before I could get there, Teddy was already at the door, "uh Teddy hang on, I will open it. Teddy turned away from the door with a frustrated and disappointed look on his face. I wasn't quite ready for Teddy to open doors and allow guests in the house, not in my line of work.

I pulled Teddy's arm to slowly tug him away from the front door. I stood beside the door, not in front of it, that was a tactical mistake that I had learned a long time ago not to make. "Who is it?" A very high-pitched female voice returned an answer "DHL delivery". Her voice was crystal clear; I had never heard anyone sound like she did.

It was unusual to get packages at the door because I hardly ever bought anything over the Internet, but this was DHL, so it was more than likely documents that continued to trickle in from our parents' estate, "just leave it by the door." The female voice on the other side of the door, "Sorry, you have to sign for it. If you don't want to sign for it, I can leave the address and number to the branch office, and you can pick it up there." Her voice boomed through the doorway, it was so clear and precise that it almost came out as sounding sexy. I know that is weird but hey, maybe the door between us was like a refractive prism that turned a woman's voice sexy. After I laughed at my own stupid thoughts, I told her to leave an address and I would go pick it up later.

"Teddy, let's go, little bro, time to go." Teddy grabbed his backpack and we both headed out the door. I grabbed the sticky note that the DHL driver left on the door. "What's the note say dingleberry?" Teddy was laughing when he said it; I grabbed him and put him in a headlock. It was playful, "I will make you eat this note you little butt head." I rubbed his head, and he laughed even harder.

Once we were in the car, Teddy started to screw with the radio like he always did. "I want to hear some Christmas music." I rolled my eyes, Teddy always wanted to listen to Christmas music, hell it could be the middle of July and I would hear Christmas music coming from his room. He found the satellite channel that played nothing, but Christmas music and Perry Como started belting out that it was the most wonderful time of the year. "Buddy it's October, we haven't even gone trick or treating yet." Teddy smiled like he always did. To tell you the truth, I kinda liked Christmas music too so I really didn't mind. Teddy turned the music down so I could now hear Nat King Cole softly sing one of the best Christmas songs ever, then Teddy spoke, "am I supposed to have sex when I like a girl?" That question really caught me off guard and I had to focus on my driving in order to get through that question. I knew it would come someday; "no, not every girl" was all I could say for the moment. I was trying to gather my thoughts so that I wouldn't screw this conversation up, but I really wasn't ready for this today. "Sex is like saying you love someone", I searched for the right words because I could tell he was listening intently. "You are going to like lots of girls over time, but you don't want to have sex with every girl you like otherwise you are just a man slut." I wish I hadn't picked those words because I could see a thousand more questions bubbling up in Teddy's head. "And not only that, not every girl will want to have sex with you."

I turned into the school parking lot and entered the loop that parents use to drop their kids off at the front door. The school traffic cop was standing there smiling like she was every morning. She was an older lady, at least older than me, but she was put together very well. She always had this air about her that she was a big executive or something in another life because she was always in control of everything, her surroundings and especially her appearance. She was always dressed well, and I wouldn't have a problem being seen having dinner with her

"Maybe I should ask Ms. Hunsicker about it?" I shot Teddy a look that I hoped would indicate to him that asking Ms. Hunsicker about sex was a very bad idea, "Buddy we don't really talk about that kind of stuff with women, let's resume this conversation tonight after I pick you up from Madison's." I was about to give some more instructions, but Ms. Hunsicker opened the passenger door for Teddy, and he jumped out of the car and hugged her. He must not have asked her about it because he practically ran up the walkway and into the school before I could even say bye.

I started to put the car into gear when I heard the tap on the window, I looked over and Ms. Hunsicker was staring at me through the window, so I rolled the window down. "I just want you to know that if you ever need any help with Teddy or just help in general, I am available." She smiled at me; a smile that made her look even prettier than she already was. "I appreciate that, but I think we got everything under control but it's always good to have a backup plan if needed." I nodded to her as I was rolling up the window; small talk was not one of my strong points. I didn't quite get the window rolled up before she spoke again, "would you like to have dinner with me sometime soon?" At first, I wasn't sure I heard correctly, "I'm sorry I almost had the window up, did you ask me a question?" I was rolling the window back down so I could hear better but in truth, I was certain I heard her correctly the first time. "Yes, I wanted to know if you would like to have dinner with me?" She smiled again and this time I saw just how perfect her teeth were and just how beautiful she was. Her blonde hair and hazel green eyes were probably as clear as I had ever seen, maybe I was wrong, maybe she was younger than me. Either way, she caught me off guard.

So, based off her body language and the way she treats Teddy, I believe that Madison would like to develop a relationship with me. I could be overthinking things but not likely. Now, the crossing guard at Teddy's school wants to go out with me? I am certainly no prize, so why was this happening? I had no idea, but I was not interested in a relationship with anyone. These ladies were very attractive, and any guy would be happy to be seen with them but not me. "I uh," I searched for the right words, "I uh just don't have time for dating, really, I appreciate it, but I just don't have time." I smiled a semi-smile, and I could feel my face getting red, so I nodded again and pressed my foot on the accelerator, she said something but this time I didn't hang around to hear the response.

Chapter 9

Meet Ruby

Ipulled into the lot across from the ice cream shop and made my way to the back entrance. I didn't bother knocking because if you knew about this door and what it led to, you already were in too deep to care. "Hey how's he doing?" I could see Jimmy still laying on the hospital bed with an IV in his arm. "Doc took the breathing tube out this morning and said he is on the mend." Big Paul was standing over the bed looking down at his son. "Say's he needs to stay away from bullets and dumbasses for a while." Big Paul always had a subtle way of joking that skirted the lines of jokes and reality really well. "I guess he won't be working with me anymore then." Big Paul turned to look at me and produced a half grin. "Nah, you are the smart one in this outfit kid." He turned back to look down at Jimmy but continued to speak, "Weinstein stopped by and manned up this morning." I nodded and was tempted to look around for traces of blood on the floor, but I knew that Big Paul was too smart to use his office as a place to settle scores. I was impressed with Bobby Weinstein for having the courage to stop by here. "Yeah, he paid off his debt plus 50 points. Way more than he owed for sure."

Big Paul then turned and made his way to the little half kitchen and poured some hot water into his cup then dipped his Lipton Blackberry-Pomegranate tea bag into the cup. He quit drinking coffee to try and sleep better but the jury was still out on whether it had helped or not. I personally thought it made him grumpier. "He also told me that you tried to diffuse the situation." I wasn't sure where this was going so, I wanted to keep my answers short, "I didn't do a good enough job of it." Big Paul sipped from his teacup then made an awful face, "I hate this shit." I couldn't resist, "then don't drink it." He laughed a small burly laugh then turned to look at me, "he said you managed to keep the whole place from being shot up." I shrugged my shoulders; I was definitely not sure where this was going.

He walked over to where his son was still lying on the hospital bed, "He's a hot head, I know it, but he is my only son." He continued to stare down at Jimmy who looked to me like he has one foot in the grave already, but I would never say that out loud, "that's why I try to keep you close to him as possible." Since he had his back to me, he looked over his shoulder at me in a quick glance, "and I know you hate working with him." I couldn't figure out where he was going with this conversation, so I didn't say anything. Big Paul may have sounded like he was rambling or just thinking out loud, but he was always going somewhere with his thoughts and questions, that's why you have to be extra careful how you answered the man. He liked to trap people in their own words in order to find out who was lying to him and who was not, and he was very good at it.

He turned away from looking at Jimmy and squared his body up, so he was looking directly at me, "how long are you gonna do this job?" I couldn't help but think that this was a trick question because you never quit this job, you were never allowed to quit this job, you could only step away when you got too old to do it and very few guys at my level ever made it to that point, they always seem to just disappear. When someone would disappear, it was thrown around that the feds got to them and now they were in the witness protection program, but I knew better. "Is there a problem with my work or the way I handle my business chief?" I needed to deflect that question and change where we were going here because this was a fishing conversation and fishing conversations were dangerous. "I mean, I can take on more work if you need me to, Teddy is getting pretty self-sufficient now and doesn't require as much of my time as he used to."

Big Paul turned around again and looked down at his son, "You are a steady hand Xavier, you don't lose your cool in tough situations like Jimmy here." He patted his son on the forehead as he spoke then turned and walked over to the mini kitchen and poured two glasses of Jameson, one of his favorite drinks." He kept his back to me so I couldn't see his face, "I spoke to New Jersey, they are as concerned about this mess as we are." He then turned around and looked at me as he took a sip from his Jameson. "They say they are going to handle Carmine and that other guy themselves." He didn't have any readable expression on his face, and I wasn't sure where he was going with this, "But you don't believe them?" He then smiled, "You see, you are smart, you understand that nobody outside the family should ever be trusted to take out the garbage." As always, I tried to choose my words very carefully with big Paul "and you want me to handle it still?" Big Paul let out a small laugh, "absolutely not". Big Paul had me very confused, something that you could not afford to have happen around him. "No, I don't trust them at all, but I am going to give them time to make it right, personally if the roles were reversed, I wouldn't have made the same deal but that's me." He looked around the room and then looked directly at me, "I opened up a new revenue stream a while back and it was working out really well at first and now it's not." He sipped from his drink, making a slurping sound like he was eating hot soup. "I want my money and you are gonna get it for me." Thoughts were rolling through my mind, I thought I had a good working knowledge of all revenue streams and to my knowledge; Big Paul had no problems anywhere. "Sure thing, just give me the address and a name and I will handle it." Big Paul offered up a slight smile, "excellent, I knew I could count on you, there is a credit card on the table over there, take it, you're gonna need it." I was confused so I looked at the table and sure enough, there was a stack of those credit cards that looked like the cards you get off a rack at a Walmart or Target. I picked one up and looked at it, Big Paul must have sensed my confusion, "The address is in Lucas Arizona."

Now I was really confused and to be honest, a little nervous. "You want me to go to Arizona to collect a debt?" Paul walked over to where I was standing by the table and motioned for me to sit down and after I was seated, he pulled up a chair beside me and sat down. "Yeah, that's right." He methodically took out a piece of paper from his pocket and unfolded it on the table, treating it like it was some ancient treasure map. "A friend of a friend kind of deal, I should have known better." The paper was sort of a hand-sketched map of Arizona with a star to mark the location way down on the border next to Mexico. "This is Lucas, it's a shit town right on the border of Mexico but that is where my guy likes to hide." I surveyed the map, I'd been to Arizona once in my life, I got talked into a hiking trip when I was in college that I wish I hadn't gone on but hey, we all get talked into some stupid stuff sometimes. Hiking the Grand Canyon was too cold for me at the time, but I liked the scenery. It was a three-day hike along a place called the bright angel trail. I haven't been back since and I never wanted to. Yes, it was beautiful but nature, camping, snakes, bugs and not taking a shower for three days just aint my thing.

"You know I will do whatever you ask me to do but damn, I was not expecting to go to Arizona to collect on a debt." He patted me on the arm and took another sip from his drink. "And there is the issue of Teddy." I paused for just a second, but I was trying to think of any way possible to get out of this trip. "I need to check with his tutor and see if maybe they can help but that isn't what they get paid to do." He stopped patting my arm and gripped my forearm tightly, "YOU are the only one that can handle this, and I don't like what I am hearing." I squirmed just enough to get my arm free from his grip and stood up. "I didn't say I wouldn't go I just said I needed to try and make arrangements." I took a step toward the door but turned back around to look at him, I wanted to see what look if any, he had on his face. As expected, he was expressionless. He was always in control. "Give me a few days to get it arranged and I will be on my way." Big Paul stood up and walked over to where I was standing and put his arms around me. "Don't let me down Xavier." It wasn't unusual for big Paul to hug people, but it was really unusual for him to hug me. It was also unusual for him to call me anything but X. He never got near me, and I wanted to keep it that way. He released his grip on me and cupped my face with his hands, all I could think of was the kiss that Michael Corleone gave his brother when he found out his brother had betrayed him in the movie the Godfather except, I hadn't betrayed anyone. He looked me in the eyes with the most serious look I had ever seen, "This is important to me, very important." He paused and released his grip on my face and slowly turned back to where Jimmy was still laying in the hospital bed. "Work it out with her and get going soon." He stood still for just a second then continued until he was standing beside Jimmy again. I wasn't sure if I was excused to leave but I turned to exit, "give Ruby and call, she will set you up."

I've never met her face to face, but I've certainly talked to her many times. She was the lady that set up all travel and handled the credit cards. None of us had our own credit cards but we always had a company card if you could call it that. All the cards were stolen, don't ask me how it works because that was not my area of expertise in the company. I just know that when you had to travel without leaving a trail, you called Ruby. She provided you with cash drops, flights, fake I'D's and whatever else you thought you might need; I was always fascinated by how well it all worked.

I was working out the details of what I would need in my head before I even left the Ice cream parlor; there was a lot to work out, especially with Teddy. I wasn't sure that Madison would let him stay with her so I would have to arrange that before I did anything else, but I did need to call Ruby, so I pulled into a Walmart, put my ball cap on which had a wig attached to it that looked pretty real and a pair of glasses that served no purpose other than to ever so slightly change my looks. You could never be seen purchasing one of those throw away phones now, the camera systems in those stores were so good that the cops starting using them regularly. Even if you couldn't be personally traced to the phone, they could match the activation code of the phone if they found it and trace it back to where it was purchased and then they would use all of Walmart's cameras to place you with the phone when you purchased it. It was pretty flimsy stuff to prove in court, but I never took chances.

After I bought my phone and loaded the minutes on it, I called Ruby. You could never speak to her directly, you could only leave a message in case someone was listening, and my message was always the same, "Hi babe, just letting you know I will be late for dinner. Something has come up at work. Love you." After you left that message, she would call you back from the caller ID your phone left.

Things had been running smooth for quite some time now and that meant that my services weren't needed much. I had a regular route and things were going pretty smooth up until Jimmy got shot. I hadn't spoken to Ruby in a while so I was looking forward to it because she had a sexy voice that could have been one of those 900 number voices, but she was also polite with a tone of the girl next door. True to protocol she returned my call as I was pulling out of the parking lot. "I need to move to Arizona; can you help me?" I could hear her slight chuckle on the other end. Telling her I needed to move to Arizona meant that she would provide me with all the proper ID which included a conceal carry permit and it even had a voter registration card. She would tell you where to pick it up and that would be all the conversation you could have with her. "Of course, I can, that's what friends are for" was her response. She gave me the pick-up information and that would be the end of my conversation with Ruby. The pick-up location was in Ajo Arizona, and she also provided me with the name of my collection, Armando Cruz. I still didn't know what Armando's business was or how much money he owed Big Paul, but I would find out as soon as I met my drop.

First, I would need to go back and talk to Madison and see if she would be willing to let Teddy stay with her for a few days and as I was calculating the best route to get to her apartment building, I realized that big Paul had said "her" at the end of our last conversation. I tried to remember every conversation I may have had with anyone regarding Madison and there were none. The only thing I may have mentioned was that I was happy that Teddy had a great tutor now, but I never mentioned her name or gender or anything else. My mind started to race, did he just get lucky and say, "check with her" and assume that Teddy's tutor was a woman?

My stomach was churning now. Had I been too careless in any of my conversations? I was pretty damn sure I had not been careless which could only mean two things, big Paul was watching me and sending me to Arizona on some made up BS set-up, or I was full of shit and too paranoid for my own good. Either way, I was going to Arizona, and I needed to get Teddy situated before I left.

Chapter 10

Sleepover

Madison happily agreed to become Teddy's full-time caregiver while I was gone, a job that I could tell she truly loved. When I told her that I needed to go to Arizona on business, she didn't ask any questions at all which made the conversation much easier. I started to ask her if she would be willing to let Teddy stay with her for a few days, but she wouldn't even let me get all the words out of my mouth before she started talking about all the things that her and Teddy would do while I was gone. Before she got too far into her planning, I did have to go over the school drop off and pick up rules, and I gave her all the necessary paperwork to be able to make decisions on my behalf should the need arise. Although Teddy was a great kid, he was a little accident-prone and I couldn't afford to have her call me to ask permission to have a cut stitched or to have a broken bone reset. I needed her to make decisions that were best for Teddy and by the time I left her apartment, I had no doubt that she would.

I went over the emergency details about what to do should she not hear from me in the proper allowed time. For this trip, I set the time frame at three weeks. I would need time to find the guy and establish a pattern. People were so routine for the most part that it rarely took more than a week to establish someone's daily habits right down to when they had a bowel movement if you paid close enough attention. The trick was to not be seen while you were watching them. This would be tricky because I didn't know the area at all so I would first need to figure those things out before I figured my collection out. Big Paul just wanted his money for now and there would be no need for rough stuff or anything extreme if I caught the guy by surprise. If he knew I was coming he would definitely change his routine and that would make my job much tougher.

As I was going over everything with her again, I checked to see if she still had the number that I gave her in case something did happen to me, and I didn't return. I know I was being overly parental, but I couldn't help it. The life that I had chosen and the life that I was actually living was getting further and further apart. A guy in my line of work was really not expected to handle all the things that I had to handle as Teddy's guardian, but I wasn't given a choice. Even if I had been given a choice, I would have chosen Teddy. Teddy was changing me; he didn't know what I really did for a living, and I didn't want him to. I needed to keep him far away from that part of my life as much as I could, but he was definitely changing me. I was softer and I was more aware of the finer details of life and how beautiful it could be if you just listened and took it all in. In short, he was making me softer and that was not a good thing for someone like me.

As I stood there going over all the details with Madison, I couldn't help but notice her beauty. I felt something during that conversation that I hadn't felt before. It wasn't that feeling you get when you love someone though, it was that feeling you get when you truly appreciate someone, and you truly care for that person. I knew that Madison would handle anything she needed to handle when it came to Teddy and that gave me the peace of mind that I needed to leave Teddy with her.

When I told Teddy that he would be staying with Madison for a few days you would have thought that I was telling him he was going to Disneyland. I tried to get him to focus on all the other instructions I had for him that included, brushing his teeth, doing his homework, and actually wash himself when he was in the shower instead of just singing. Teddy loved to sing in the shower, so much so that he would forget why he was there in the first place.

Once Teddy calmed down enough to have a rational conversation, if you could call it that, we talked about what he would be doing while I was gone and how I expected him to behave and act like a gentleman. "I won't be a dingle berry, I promise." I shook my head when he said it, I still wasn't sure he had a full grasp on what the term meant but at least he was using it in the right context. His comment about not being a dingle berry reminded that I had one more errand to do before I left for Arizona.

Chapter 11

No man of the cloth

Despite all the backdoor ways I had to track people down, I was having a very difficult time finding an address for this one. Even my contact at the police department couldn't help me pin this guy down. It was a little frustrating but all that meant was that I was going to have to do things the old fashion way and just follow him around for as long as it took and eventually, I would find out where he lived. It was funny, I had done this so many times now, and I was actually very good at it, once I found out where someone lived, I could just about plug in all the details without much more effort.

School let out at 3:15 as it did every day, and I was positioned so that I wouldn't look conspicuous, and I rented a nice minivan for the day so I would look like any old daddy doofus waiting on a kid to come out of school. It worked, I felt like a doofus driving a minivan. I have no idea how people drive around in stuff like this.

I saw Teddy coming out the front gate area along with a bunch of other kids and since I didn't have any idea what this kid looked like I was trying to use deductive reasoning. Teddy said that he had sex with a lot of girls and that he was very popular, so I was trying to find the kid that looked like that description and sure enough, in the herd of kids coming out of school I spotted a tall kid, well built for his age and he had an amazing head of hair. From where I was sitting in my ridiculous goofball vehicle, his hair looked like it had been colored jet black. It flowed nicely over his ears and had some length to the back. He was wearing a jean jacket that looked just a little too big for him and some regular jeans. Thank God he wasn't wearing those hideous skinny jeans that were popular. Teddy had asked me several times to buy him some but being Teddy's legal guardian and big brother meant that I had to make sure that he didn't look like a dork when he got dressed in the morning and with Teddy's frame and size, skinny jeans were simply not made for him. There was no doubt though, this Danny guy was a good-looking kid.

There was the usual pushing and shoving and smacking guys on the arm that apparently would never go out of style for young boys in school. I watched closely for his interaction with Teddy, and I was pleased with what I saw. I feel like I have always been good at reading body language, which has helped me many times in my line of work. If you pay close attention to your subjects, they will generally let you know with their eyes, raised eyebrow, twitching eyelids, shoving their hands in their pockets over and over, shuffling feet, licking lips too much, clearing their throat, looking past you and not at you, or constantly checking around for an escape route to anywhere.

Danny almost always kept his eyes on Teddy, almost like a parent does at the grocery store, he pulled Teddy close to him once and put his arm around him as they were talking to some girls that had walked up and joined the group. This was a clear sign to me that not only was Danny popular, but he was also a good kid. It is not easy for a teenager to befriend a kid with Down syndrome; the peer pressure to be super cool is sometimes just too much. I was glad to see that there were still good kids in school that would look out for Teddy.

Once the kids spotted their rides or began walking away from school, I saw Madison pick up Teddy, which was another thing I was happy to see. Madison actually got out of her car and met Teddy with a hug. Because Madison was still very young and very pretty, Teddy got a lot of catcalls and hollers when she openly hugged him in front of the group. It clearly made Teddy happy that he was the subject of not only Madison's attention, but he was also the center of his friends' attention.

It didn't take long; I was impressed by how quickly so many kids dispersed from what looked like controlled chaos. It also didn't take long for Danny to be by himself, and he didn't seem to be looking for anyone. He looked mature enough but, in the city, he is still an easy mark.

Once everyone that was in Danny's group were gone, he began to walk the sidewalk where I followed him several blocks. He almost lost me because he cut down a few alleys that I would not have used as a short cut, they were the type of alleys you could find yourself in trouble if you weren't careful. I followed him right to where he entered a building that looked like it used to be some sort of church but the sign on the front simply said, "All are Welcome in God's Kingdom". The sign didn't look like it was professionally done but it still looked pretty decent. Needless to say, I was intrigued. This is the kid that Teddy says has sex with a lot of girls and after school he is entering a place like this? Maybe I was being too judgmental and then again, maybe because I had never really had the "talk" with Teddy about boys and girls, he may not know the difference between sex and a kiss.

I made a mental note to clear that up once I got back from this little trip I would be taking to Arizona. When I entered the front door, I was struck with how it smelled. It had an old smell to it, that kind of smell you got when you visited your grandparents house. It didn't stink it just smelled odd for this type of building. People were milling around, some had coffee cups in their hands, some had bottles of water, but they were all doing something. It looked busy but organized. I hadn't had time to spot Danny before some guy dressed in what looked like a priest frock came up and spoke to me.

"May I help you?" He stuck out his hand and said, "I'm Robert, I sort of run the place." I shook his hand and before I could let go of his hand, "Your hands are too soft to be in need of accommodations, so your intentions are either good or bad, which it?" I retracted my hand with a little resistance from Robert. He smiled, "I'm afraid I am overly aggressive sometimes but frankly I don't have the time any more for pleasantries Mr. . . . ?" I smiled, "Richard Tracy, my friends call me Rich." Robert started a slow but methodically perfect smile and then laughed, "So your intentions are bad, I am afraid I can't help you, uh Rich." He turned to walk away, "Unless you need accommodations Rich, please show yourself out, I have work to do."

"Hey, hang on, my intentions are not bad and why are you so quick to size me up and jump to conclusions?" Robert turned back around to look me up and down one more time. "Ok for the sake of argument, you should come up with a better fake name than my childhood comic book hero Dick Tracy. You may think you are quick on your feet my friend but you're not. You are simply a guy looking for someone that either owes him money or you're a cop looking for someone that has perhaps committed a crime." He looked me up and down again, "Cops have no use for fake names unless they are dirty which leads me back to", he paused again, "Your intentions are bad."

I couldn't help but like this guy, he was a straight shooter and he had me sized up in minutes. "Say Robert, you are good at what you do I am sure, but your assessment isn't quite that accurate." He folded his arms over his chest in an impatient way, "Ok, I am listening Dick." I smiled and knew I needed to clear up the fake name. I really didn't want to use my real name for obvious reasons, but this guy had probably seen every trick and con in the book, so it was pointless to try and outwit him now, so I came clean. "Xavier, Xavier Thomas." Robert smiled, "now was that so hard?" Robert pretended to brush something off his frock. He may have been able to read people very well, but I was pretty good at it myself. His brushing of his frock was a signal to me that I had just been defeated in the game of wits we had just had. I was ok with that for now. "How can I help you Mr. Thomas?"

"My little brother called me a dingle berry and I was hoping you can help me with that." Robert flashed a partial smile combined with a confused look on his face, "I'm afraid we don't deal in personality disorders here Mr. Thomas, although a few blocks down, there are the sisters of Saint Rafael adult care center that has done some amazing things with mental disorders and PTSD. Another block down there is a Synagogue that has an amazing social hall that they use for all kinds of community outreach, both are excellent." I smiled, I am sure I could use the polish of Christianity or Judaism but right now I am searching for the young man that taught my little brother the word dingle berry. Robert laughed again, "how old is your sibling Mr. Thomas?" I liked this guy, I tried to put myself in his shoes and thought about what I would do if a grown man came in using the word dingle berry and of course I would think they were an idiot. I really needed to fill in some blanks here for the guy, so I did. "You see Robert," I paused for dramatic effect, "my little brother has down syndrome, he doesn't pick up words like that on his own, nor does he know the meaning. I fully believe that the young man that he has befriended meant no harm in the use of the adjective and I am merely trying to ascertain if Danny, that's the kids name, is being a bully or if he is actually being a friend to my little brother." I flashed a smile, "I am very protective of my brother."

Robert tilted his head to one side and then managed to look me up and down as if he were buying a horse, by the way he was looking at me, I was surprised that he didn't try to inspect my teeth. "Mr. Thomas, fighting your little brothers' battles will not help him in any way. I believe your intentions are good, but I also believe they are wrong." I rubbed my forehead, again for drama, "I can appreciate that from a man of the cloth", he interrupted me quickly, "I am not a man of the cloth, I am a man of faith and I believe in the power of the blood of Jesus Christ, but I am not a priest." I shook my head as if I was agreeing and held up the palms of my hand so that he could see I was not going to argue with him, "I'm just looking out for my kid brother is all man." I put my hands in my pockets, it's hard to be a threat with your hands in your pockets, and "the kids name I am looking for is Daniel, Danny Garcia I just want to visit with him, that's all." Robert gave me a look that I couldn't quite explain; it was a cross between confusion and anger. "Leave him alone, he is a good kid". I was a little confused by this reaction. "Ok, if you say he is a good kid, I believe you, my little brother likes him, and he is very impressionable so I will leave it at that." I looked around the building that was clearly a former church, complete with the stain-glassed windows of Jesus and baby Jesus. "Does he work here after school?" I could see Robert change his expression right in front of me, his entire demeanor changed. "He lives here Mr. Thomas; this is a homeless shelter."

I guess that shook me because Robert took a step towards me and put his hand on my shoulder, and I swear he whispered a prayer or something. "Mr. Thomas, he is one of the best kids you will ever meet. Please leave him alone." I took another look around, "Ok Robert, just tell me why he is here." Robert let go of my arm then took a look around like he didn't want to be heard, "Technically he is a ward of the state, but the state is overwhelmed, as long as he is here, he is safe but if the state gets him in their system, he will end up in a shitty home where the father or mother or both abuse him. He is happy here and I would like to keep it that way." I understood more at that moment than I ever expected to.

Robert told me that Danny's parents were found in their apart-ment, both had suffered gunshots wounds. He also told me that

Danny was the one that found them. The police reports stated that it was a murder suicide, but Robert told me that both victims had multiple gunshots wounds. Robert also told me that Danny's older brother had been missing for quite some time.

"You think the older brother, did it?" Robert shook his head, "I am not sure but what I do know, Danny is a good kid and if I can dodge the state claiming him for another two years, he can make his own decisions." I was still a little shocked by the information I had just heard, "so how do you know I am not a state worker trying to find him?" I put my palms up again, "I mean you gave me a lot of information and you didn't even know me. State workers can have some soft hands too." Someone came up to him and asked him a maintenance question, he answered them and then looked back at me, "State workers don't wear Christian Louboutin loafers Mr. Thomas." He winked and walked away but with his back to me, "We are happy to take donations Mr. Thomas and we are a 501c3."

I shook my head, there were very few guys in the world that could spot more detail on a person than me and I had just met one of them. One of my vice's was expensive shoes. My feet were so wide that it was difficult to find a pair of shoes at regular stores, so I spent a little extra money and purchased very comfortable shoes at a not so comfortable price. At any rate, I would still keep my eye on Danny Garcia, but I wasn't as worried as I used to be. It was time to catch a plane.

Chapter 12

Slim

As I was standing at the check-in kiosk at the airport, something told me to change everything. No one knew where I was going that I knew of, but I liked to stay away from the routines or habits, both could get you in a jam if you were not careful. I had a ticket to Tucson in my hand and I was not checking a bag so changing things up would be easy. I turned to the check in kiosk again and put my carry-on bag down so I could use both hands to tap the check in screen. I found a flight to Flagstaff by way of Phoenix and bought that. It wasn't a direct flight, and it was going in the wrong direction, but I didn't care, I just wanted to change my plans. The ticket was quite a bit more but again, I didn't care. I would just get to Flagstaff, rent a car and drive south to Lucas. It would be nice to take in some Arizona desert scenery, do my job then return home. It shouldn't take me more than a few days to find my mark and then I would more than likely buy a return flight from Tucson. The plane landed with a thud that woke me from my sleep. The Phoenix airport was bigger than I expected, and I had a little trouble figuring out how to get to my connecting flight to Flagstaff but since the connecting flight didn't take off for three hours, I took my time and went through all the gift shops along the way. The place was busy but once you got inside one of the little souvenir stores, things seem to slow down. I found a couple of t-shirts for Teddy that I knew he would like but I would have to explain the one that had the skeleton on the front sitting in a lawn chair with a cigarette smoldering in his hand proclaiming "It's a dry heat." I could see out the windows of the airport, it looked beautiful to me. I had heard that Arizona was an acquired taste. You had to look at it differently and that proved to be true. I could see those big cactuses sticking up, just like the ones you see in John Wayne cowboy movies that I had seen a thousand times because Teddy loved John Wayne movies. Not just John Wayne though, if there was a western on TV, Teddy would watch it regardless of the quality of acting but if John Wayne happened to be in the western, forget about it, it was the only thing that could keep him away from his video games for a few hours and no one loved John Wayne as much as my little brother.

When the small plane landed in Flagstaff, I was taken to a different mental place by the scenery that I could see out of my window. There were pine tree's everywhere, and I swear I thought I saw some snow on the ground. As we stepped off the plane, a blast of cold air hit me which actually felt almost as good as the smell. Holy smokes this place had to be a slice of heaven. I felt like I was in one of those soap commercials that when you took one whiff of the soap, suddenly you were refreshed and dancing around in the shower. I breathed it all in as the attendant lady walked us all from the plane to the terminal. This was definitely a place I could live in once I felt like I had made enough money for me and Teddy. I rented a white suburban. It wasn't my first choice, but this little airport didn't have a lot to choose from. I wanted a car with four-wheel drive, and this was all they had. Even though it felt like I was driving a bus, it actually turned out to be a nice ride and as I was coming down the ridiculously steep highway that scared the hell out of me, I was glad that I had such a big vehicle, maybe if I went over the side of one of these steep cliffs, I might be able to survive in a big ass bus. It wasn't long before the road seemed to flatten out and I felt a little better. I was definitely not going to take a trip back up those roads; I would fly out of Tucson or Phoenix when the time came.

After what seemed like an eternity, I made it to Ajo. The town was beautiful; it looked like something out of a movie. It had the white stucco buildings everywhere, complete with the old Mexican style church with a bell tower and cross that was clearly visible from almost anywhere in the city. There were palm trees that lined every street and even though it seemed like I was in the middle of the desert, the lawns in most neighborhoods were a vibrant green. I fully expected Teddy's hero, John Wayne to ride up on big horse asking me "where you from stranger".

I would make my way to Lucas as soon as I met the drop and got the information, I needed to complete my assignment. Even though I didn't like being this far away from Teddy and was already getting a little antsy to get this trip over with, I wanted to experience a little of this town. I liked the openness and fresh air. I could see for miles, there wasn't much to see but cactus and desert, but I could definitely see as far as my eyes would let me.

I parked the Suburban in a spot close to downtown, I was expecting a meter or something to pay for my parking but there wasn't one. The sun was going down and I was getting hungry. I could hear my stomach growl as I walked along the sidewalk of downtown Ajo. The good part about meeting this drop was that I was supposed to meet them at a small downtown diner. I was told by Ruby that when I found "Pablo's" café, I was supposed to go in, sit at the counter and order huevos rancheros with habanero coffee. Now I've had huevos ranchero's before but never habanero coffee. It didn't even sound appealing since I tend to get heartburn, but no one told me I had to drink it.

"Hola Señor", the older but still beautiful waitress behind the counter said as I slid my bar stool closer to the bar. She looked like something out of a southwest painting. Her jaw was square, her teeth were straight out of a toothpaste commercial, and her hair was silky gray. She wiped the counter in front of me as she smiled and slid a single laminated menu in front of me, "Que`le sirvo señor?" She caught me off guard, I don't know any Spanish but when she greeted me with "Hola" I understood that, and I replied with a confidence that may have signaled to her to believe that I spoke Spanish. She must have seen my eyes go wide and the panicked look on my face so she added, "what can I get you sir?" I smiled and managed a sheepish "Thank you", signaling to her my appreciation for throwing me a translation lifeline. "Uh, I will have the huevos rancheros and some habanero coffee is all thank you." She looked at me up and down as if she were buying a car and needed to check it out more thoroughly, "we stopped brewing the habanero coffee for the day señor" she took the menu from the counter but continued to smile at me, "Is there some other beverage I can offer?" her accent was thick, and she spoke slowly as she enunciated the English words so I could understand her. In this particular situation I felt like I was slowing her down and if I just spoke Spanish I would have probably already eaten and been on my way by now. "Water is fine." She smiled and turned to the little slide through hole in the wall where she handed the orders to the short order cook and they in turn place the completed orders back up on the ledge and rang a bell when they were ready for the customer. She turned back to me and smiled "Aqua que viene su biendo". I had no idea what she said but I understood aqua, so I assumed she was bringing me water. I really needed to work on my Spanish but I wasn't going to be here very long so what was the point. The beautiful silver haired lady smiled at me, "your water is coming right up sir." I looked around the place and could feel the age of it. This little hole in the wall café had to have been here for as long as anyone could remember so I could understand how this would be the place chosen by Ruby as the drop.

The glass of water came just in time. I started nibbling on the Salsa and chips she sat in front of me, and I was not prepared for this salsa. It was delicious but it was definitely hot. Hot to the point that I knew I was going to have some heart burn later, but it was extremely good. To her amusement, I guzzled the glass of water in seconds and set the glass down on the counter, she smiled and refilled the glass so fluidly that I almost didn't notice she had done it. I sat there staring at the bowl of chips, daring myself to grab another one but before I could tempt the heartburn gods, she softly sat the plate of huevos rancheros in front of me. I looked up at her and smiled, the language problems we had between each other wasn't due to body language, she had a smile that could melt an ice sculpture and I tried to be as congenial as my stoic face would allow me to be. "Uh . . . gracias." I was careful not to sound very confident in my knowledge of her language, but I was so careful that I am certain my Mexican "thank you" came out sounding more like "grassy ass". "Señor, I speak English, we are happy to have all of you here in our little heaven." She reached in her apron pocket and pulled out the ticket for my order and placed it on the counter in front of me, "you can pay me when you are ready."

I started working my way through the Huevos Ranchero's and in no time, they were gone. This perhaps could have been the best plate of eggs I have ever had in my life. They were so good, I strongly considered ordering another plate. As I sat there listening to the Angel of moderation on my shoulder argue with the Devil of gluttony, I heard the bell on the front door clang. It wasn't much more than a cowbell, but it made a nice racket, what was odd is that I don't remember hearing it on the way in.

"Hola Louis, la usual?" her greeting was as charming to the tall man in the cowboy hat who seemingly pulled his cowboy hat and leather gloves off in one motion. His face was very dark, so dark that you could see the hat line on his forehead. It was easy to see that he and his cowboy hat rarely parted ways. Even though he was dirty, his clothes were pressed; I was struck by the seriousness of the crease in his jeans. Someone went through a lot of starch to make that happen. I guessed he was close to fifty by the wrinkles around his eyes and forehead. Hell, maybe it was forty; I am terrible at guessing ages. Here I was in a small Mexican café in southern Arizona, sizing up a customer like I did in New York. It could be an annoying habit but a very useful one; I just didn't think I had any use for it here. The tall slender man nodded his head and flashed a smile that defined his dark sundried skin even more. He sat his cowboy hat down on the chair then pulled up another chair at the table towards the back of the café. He caught me staring at him and flashed another smile; I nodded and returned the gesture, only my smile wasn't nearly as nice as his.

I could hear the waitress talking to him in Spanish and by the tone it seemed friendlier than normal, almost like a brother sister conversation but they definitely knew each other well. As she was placing the glass of water on his table the cowbell clanked again and their conversation stopped. I didn't turn around because Louis had already busted me for staring at him, so I tried to look back through the mirror of a very faded Budweiser clock that hung on the wall behind the counter. I couldn't make out things very clearly, but I could see that there were two men, also in cowboy hats, standing near his table. The pretty waitress had quickly made her way back behind the counter and I could now see that her body language had switched from warm, inviting and friendly to one of nervousness. It didn't take a genius to realize that since there was no greeting for the two men from our waitress, she didn't care much for the guys. She pretended to go clean but as I watched her, she kept an eye on the men who were now standing over the cowboy that had just sat down.

The conversation between the men was at first soft and slow but it got louder and more heated. I wouldn't call it a conversation though; the two men that were standing over slim were doing all the talking and then yelling. The waitress made her way behind the counter and ended up right in front of me. She kept her head down as she wiped the counter, but she managed to lift her eyes enough to let me know she was scared, and she whispered, "you should go señor". Now I am not much on butting into business that doesn't concern me, but I hadn't paid for my meal, I hadn't received what I was sent here to get and now a waitress, in a very short span of time had made me feel like her best friend and these two guys were causing me problems in getting what I needed so my logic led me to the conclusion that this had now become my business.

I put my hand on her hand and stopped it from cleaning the counter for a second and winked at her. The look on her face changed from scared to confused and I have to tell you that the confused look made her even prettier. I stood up, gave her a dramatic stretch show, cracked my knuckles, drew in a breath and turned towards the men at the table. I walked over to the table like I knew what I was doing, circled around Slim who was focused on the two men standing over him and clearly trying to intimidate him. I could see he wasn't easily intimidated because as I made my way around him, I touched him on the shoulder, gave him a pat, "Hey Louis, I didn't realize that was you!" I pulled up a chair and saw that the chair that I pulled up had his cowboy hat in it, so I carefully picked up the hat, gently brushed it off in the direction of the two men standing in front of us, sat it on the table and sat down in the chair that used to be occupied by a cowboy hat. "Say man I was wondering where you get your pants pressed, I have been looking for a place that can produce the crease that I want, and I have yet to find it." I smiled and acted like the two men standing above us were not even there, Louis smiled one of the warmest most welcoming smiles I have ever seen, "I am sorry señor, this is the work of Ellalio, he works for Ms. Villalpando and does many chores." I started to reply but one of the men cut me off. He took a step toward me but stopped when I looked up quickly. I have to say I have a look I can flash someone that can catch him or her off guard. It works on Teddy very well when he is pushing me a bit too far. Teddy refers to it as "the look". The man crinkled his forehead and then put his hands on his hips, making certain that in the process, he pulled the jacket he was wearing apart just enough to see the shoulder holster that was home to what looked like a Glock, but I wasn't sure. It was too away too deeply for him to go for it quickly enough before I sent him sprawling but I wasn't ready to do that just yet. "golpealo en la Cabeza!" Now I crinkled my forehead because I didn't understand a word he said. I looked at Louis and shrugged my shoulders; Louis smiled again and let out a little chuckle. I can safely say I really liked this guy. "Señor, my friend here" he used his hand in a sweeping motion says that he would like you to find a conversation elsewhere." Louis smiled and looked up at the man who was now showing clear signs of aggression. "Did he now? My guess is, that he was not so polite in his words and somehow in your gentlemanly translation you cleaned it up for him." Louis nodded ever so slightly then took a sip of his water. Yep, I like this guy, he didn't rattle at all.

The other man was still standing there, the quiet one was just a spectator at the moment, and then I had flash backs of me and Jimmy. I really wasn't sure why other than it reminded me that things can escalate very quickly if you don't keep the upper hand.

I knew I had read them correctly; the loudmouth was in charge. I stopped looking at the loudmouth and turned my attention back to Louis, "He seems angry, and I really need some pants pressed". Louis smiled but then his smile quickly left which told me to turn my stare back to the men. As I turned back towards loudmouth, I saw him reaching under his jacket and in my experience, loud talking idiots should never be allowed to pull a gun because nothing good happens when they do. Luckily in his attempt to intimidate me, he had placed himself within arm's reach of me. The short distance between he and I gave me the opportunity I needed to give him a quick wrap in the groin which immediately caused him to lean forward where I caught him with a very clean uppercut. Before he could recoil back from the punch, I reached in his jacket with my other hand and pulled the gun out of his holster. Before the second man knew it, he had a Glock pointed right as his nose.

His facial expression was comical. He was not sure what to do but I could see he was scared and that was all I needed. I smiled at him and nodded. He understood what I wanted and reached into his jacket and pulled out his gun. He handed it to me and without looking and I placed it on the table close to where Louis was sitting. I then looked down at his shoes and raised my eyebrows. I have to say at this point, I was good at body language and despite our language barrier, the man reached down and pulled another small pistol from his ankle holster. These types of guys always had a backup plan, they thought they were prepared for everything but most of the time, they weren't. Now that I had yanked the fangs out of the snake, I smiled and motioned for the scared man to sit down. He was confused by this gesture at first but when I pulled out a chair and nodded, he quickly sat down.

The loudmouth was still out cold, I was proud of that uppercut I gave him, it was one of my favorites. It is very effective in close quarters if you weren't afraid to step towards your opponent. I have found that most guys are really not keen on getting punched in the face, most were too vain and didn't like the idea of not being pretty, so they try to avoid the blows by stepping backwards as they throw a punch. I wasn't ever pretty enough to ever worry about my looks, so I learned how to throw an uppercut early in life.

I turned to Louis who was smiling at me and shaking his head to indicate that he was amused. "Señor, although I appreciate the intervention, it was not necessary." He looked over that the guy sitting at the table with his hands in his lap, "these caballeros are of no worry, they are like the little Chihuahua that barks and growls but can be easily kicked into the next pasture." Now it was my turn to smile and shake my head. "What is your name Señor?" he stuck out his hand, "I am Louis Arroyo". I took his hand and was struck by the roughness, this man seriously worked with his hands. I was certain because of all the callouses, he could stick his hands on a hot griddle and not feel a thing. "Richard Tracy, nice to meet you". He let go of my hand and smiled. "So, what do these guys want?" His face changed from happy and amused to somewhat angry, "Land, money", then he paused and added "and a woman". I looked at the scared man, "speak English?" I didn't expect a reply, but he gave me one, "see". It caught me off guard, "So what did your friend here say to me?" He didn't answer the question, he just stared at me, "Come on man, I aint gonna hurt you, loosen up, let's be friends." Louis leaned forward, "tell him amigo". The scared man looked at both of us "he says . . . , butt out shithead". I laughed, "well that was a reasonable request, had he told me in English I would have complied, but I don't speak Spanish."

The loudmouth started to roll around a little and moan. He was nursing his nuts a little by rubbing his crotch. I doubt he knew exactly what he was doing because it was embarrassing to watch, much less do. I stood up and walked around Louis to get to the man on the floor. I helped him get on his feet and sat him down in a chair at our table. He protested a little, but he was in no shape to argue much.

"Well, it really isn't any of my business, but I was having trouble enjoying my huevos ranchos and a wonderful conversation with the beautiful waitress". I hit the release pin on the Glock and the clip slid out on to the table, I then pulled the slide back and let the remaining shell fly out on the table. Surprisingly, Louis caught it in the air and gently placed the bullet on the table next to the clip. I repeated the action for the second gun. The gun the man had in his ankle holster was to my surprise a double tap. It is a very skinny gun but should not be mistaken for a toy, this thing was a 9mm and was deadly.

I looked at the scared one that had the ankle holster, "I would like you to take your friend here and go now". The scared man looked back at me then glanced down at the table where the guns, clips and bullets were placed neatly together. I knew he wanted his guns back, even on the black market they were worth a lot of money. "You can take them but leave the clips on the table, I'm not a thief". I smiled as the scared man picked up all three guns, placed his in his holsters and placed the loud mouth's gun in the front of his pants. He then wrestled the loudmouth to his feet and in just a few seconds, the cowbell clanked, and they were gone.

Louis looked over at the pretty waitress and waved for her to come over, "Would you like something else Señor? Let me treat you to some of the best Agave tequila you will find in Arizona." He smiled again and I was struck by the wear and tear on his face but the friendly way he presented himself. "No thank you, I do appreciate the offer, but I am not much of a drinker." I turned to look at the waitress as she was now standing over us, "I would just like the check please". I winked at her to try and signal that I wanted what I came for which was the drop box that had been prearranged. She smiled a sheepish smile, "There is not a charge for your meal sir." I shook my head and pulled out my wallet and as I was doing so Louis spoke up, "your money is no good here compadre". I took out a twenty and laid it on the table, "then let me get the tip." Louis nodded in approval, and I stood up, so I was standing in front of the waitress, "earlier, you said, that you were happy that we are all here, I am traveling by myself." Even though her facial skin was dark I could see her cheeks form a little red, "I am sorry sir, there are other men who speak and act like you that were here earlier. I assumed you were together." She frowned just a bit then offered, "they order the huevos rancheros too." I nodded and then stuck out my hand for Louis to take which he did, "I do like the creases, tell Ellalio he does impressive work."

I turned to the waitress who was staring at me with eyes as brown and beautiful as I had ever seen and put my hand in front of her. She took my hand but as she did, she used my hand like a rope and pulled herself close to me and kissed me on the cheek. It was a soft kiss and she planted it well. I could smell the mix of café food and some sort of rose scented perfume. That was the best cheek kiss I have ever received in my life. As she was close to my face she whispered, "Thank you señor, God be with you." I could feel the flush in my cheeks now, "What is your name?", she replied, I am Elizabeth, but my family call me Lisa." I stepped back away from her, and I started to leave but turned back and asked a question to Louis and I can't even explain why I asked, "what land and what woman?"

Louis looked amused, "The Villalpando land and it is Mrs. Villalpando that interests the two men that just left with no bullets." He could see that I was a little interested in the how's and why's, "I am the foreman for the La Leche Madre ranch, I work for Ms. Villalpando." He smiled, "she has no interest in anything but her ranch." I rubbed my forehead, must be some valuable land for a couple guys to want it bad enough to rough you up over it." He shook his head, "It is not so much the value of the land as it is the quantity." I didn't really understand that but I needed to go and find a phone so I could call Ruby and figure out why I wasn't getting my information. I wouldn't tell her that other guys were here ordering the same thing because I was certain she already knew. Ruby was a set up gal, not a friend. "Gracias Louis, and ma'am, it was a pleasure to meet you both." I started to walk out the door wondering if I had been set up? The thought of men dressed and sounding like me had me a little concerned but more importantly, I was leaving without my package. I pulled on the door and heard the clanking bell, I let the door stay open as I turned back to Louis, "What was the name of that ranch again?" Louis smiled, "La Leche Madre", he took a sip of his water, "It means "Mother's Milk in English but everyone around here just refer to it as the double L".

Chapter 13

Fat Jackie and the Hooligans

I made the short walk back to my Suburban and was struck again by the beauty of this little town. The sun was setting on the horizon and in a few minutes, it would be dark for sure. Based off what I could tell, the city would be just as pretty at night as it was during the day. There was still enough light in the day for me to see the handprint on the driver side window. It seemed odd because it looked like a tiny handprint, maybe a toddler, even a baby. It may have been there when I rented it and I was just now noticing it, but it was cute. It was a perfect little 5-fingered handprint. All one would need to do is draw the turkey feathers connecting the fingers and you'd have that same refrigerator picture that Teddy made for me a few years back for Thanksgiving.

I sat down in my car, bus, or whatever you called these things, and thought about the day's events and especially butting into someone else's business. I broke my own rule of life, which was to stay out other people affairs and even though I had somehow found the rationale for it in that café, I knew I could have easily walked out of there and not said a word. I am pretty sure my conscience wouldn't bother me but there was something about that waitress and the way she made me feel while I was in there. Our encounter was brief, but she somehow got me to like her more than I should in just a few minutes.

The interior light of the Suburban went off which told me that I had been deep in thought for a while and just as they went off, a car passed by, and their headlights flashed inside my car for just a second and I saw it. It looked like someone had licked their finger and wrote the words "not go" on my passenger side window. Seemed odd to see that but again, it could have been there when I picked up the rental, but I thought nothing more of it when I caught a glimpse of a box sitting in the passenger side floor. I reached over and put it on the seat beside me and opened it. It looked to be factory sealed just like a package you'd get from Amazon or Walmart. I opened it and was delighted to see the contents I was looking for. I don't know how they got it inside my rental while the alarm was set but nevertheless, I was staring at a Colt 1911 with three additional clips along with a stack of cash, and a real concealed carry permit for one Richard Tracy from the great state of Arizona, just in case I got stopped by the police. This wasn't a final collection, and I should not need a gun, but I don't know my way around, I don't know these people so I would prefer to have it and not need it. The box also contained an address, which I assumed was the address of my collection. It was time make my way to Lucas.

As I was pulling out of my downtown parking spot, I had to stop to let a vintage looking corvette and one of those rental moving trucks go by before I could back out. Even though the sun was setting quickly, and it was getting dark I could tell that the moving truck had plenty of miles on it. The paint was badly faded, it looked like it might have been yellow at one point in time but now it was just ugly. The corvette was quite the opposite though; I could see that it was a 63 split window stingray with a spectacular silver paint job. I have always had a thing for corvettes; they have their own mystique to them that attracts guys of all ages. Living in New York, I would never own one, but I could sure enjoy the view of the ones I see, and this one was amazing.

Highway 85 south was the loneliest stretch of road I have ever been on. It was unbelievably dark, and I didn't see another car, truck, caravan or bicycle the entire way to Lucas. There were also no radio stations that broadcast in any other language than Spanish available for me to listen to on the way there, so it is a good thing it was a relatively short trip.

Lucas was kind of a busy little town because it was a port of entry into Mexico from the United States. It wasn't as pretty as Ajo, but I guess you could say it had its own persona.

The motel clerk gave me a look up and down like he was going to measure me for a suit. "Where are you from?" Up until this point everyone had finished every question and statement with "Señor but not this guy. He was somewhat greasy with very bad teeth. I couldn't tell if he had just put down a crack pipe or he was cursed with terrible teeth but every time I had to look at him, I got caught up in just how absolutely gnarly they were. I seriously wanted to hand the guy a couple grand and send him to a dentist, but he'd probably not use it for the purposes intended. The clerk at the desk held his stare as he was holding my credit card, "why are you in town?" I held my stare with his, I gave him the look, but it had no effect on him at all. I was certain this guy was stoned, "I'm with Rotary club of America, I am a dentist, and I am here to offer pro bono dental services to underprivileged children of Mexico and fatuous adults of Lucas, you should sign up." He nodded and smiled which was painful to look at. He took my card and ran it through one of those archaic hand machines that you slide back and forth to make and imprint, he never realized the card I gave him was a "newer model" that didn't have raised numbers or letters, so his imprint was blank. I signed his slip, and he handed me a carbon copy of receipt for nothing.

It was an actual key, a real big heavy brass key he gave me to the room. This was something I had never seen. I had heard about the giant room keys of the old days, but I had never seen one until now. I stuck it in my pocket thinking that if I forgot it was there and moved in the wrong direction too quickly, that giant brass key might actually stab me in the thigh. I chuckled at the thought of explaining an injury like that to the emergency room folks and went looking for room 143.

I wrestled the key out of my pocket and laughed again at the size of the thing. When I finally got the door opened, I was surprised by the size of the room, I was expecting it to be smaller, but it wasn't. It had a small little sofa and kitchenette. I am not sure what I was expecting but based off the condition of the company representative at the front desk, I wasn't expecting much.

I sat at the little table in the room and cleaned my gun. I didn't have much to clean it with, but I did a good job considering my lack of supplies. I did not want to use a gun at all on this collection and would do everything I could to avoid it, but I didn't know this guy at all, so I needed to be ready with several contingency plans. I was confident in my ability to keep things calm and rationale in every situation, except when I was working with Jimmy. Things could explode at any moment with him as it had done at the pharmacy and now, he was in the back of an ice cream shop trying to stay alive. I was still wondering if Big Paul blamed me. He didn't seem to, but he was a very hard person to read.

After I hung my shirts in the closet and laid out my things on the bathroom counter I sat down at the little table in the kitchenette, pulled out the cell phone that Ruby provided me in my care package. I had to find Madison's number. I wanted to check on Teddy before I headed out to find Armando.

"Are you ok?" Her voice was reassuring and sweet and I hated it.

I hated that I enjoyed talking to her and just hearing her voice. There was no place in my life for women, especially women as young as Madison. "How is Teddy?" She laughed into my ear, "You didn't tell me how much that kid eats!" I laughed back at her, "I can send you some more money if you need it, he has a healthy appetite", before she

could respond, "I'm sorry I should have left you a credit card for stuff like that." She laughed again, "It's ok X, I got it, really." I looked at my shoes as she was talking and decided I needed a more relaxed pair to wear before I left this evening, "He has asked me if I would marry you at least a dozen times." I was searching for what to say, "I told him I would be happy to, but the decision was a two-way street." I paused, "Madison, I am sorry about his meddling. when he gets an idea in his head, he is like a snapping turtle waiting for lighting to strike." She laughed again, "You are so easy to rattle!" She continued to laugh, "Geez, I wouldn't marry an old fart like you." She let me off the hook, but I know she was partially telling the truth. Madison would make an excellent partner in life for anyone but me. She was simply too young and too good for me. I knew that and she knew that. "I should be back in a couple of days but just in case, you have that number I gave you right?" She gave me a quick "yep" and I told her that if she didn't hear from me in at least 3 days to call it. After a little chatter about food and school and what Teddy likes to wear as opposed to what he shouldn't wear after school. It was fortunate that school had a dress code so everyone wore the same uniform but if it didn't, Teddy would wear some of craziest clothes you've ever seen. The louder and brighter the color, the happier Teddy would be.

I hung up the phone feeling nervous for some reason. I couldn't put my finger on it, but I had that feeling like I should be with Teddy instead of here. I think at that moment from the minute a child is born until the parent is dead, the parent never gets to relax. Since our parents were taken from us way too early, I had become the parent for Teddy and my life began to change. Some changes were noticeably better, and some changes for me at least were worse, like the constant internal worry that I didn't have before I became Teddy's legal guardian was never there. I never worried about much at all, sometimes I would worry about some silly stuff but now that I look back, it was stupid to worry about those things.

I snapped my holster to the right side of my belt, checked to make sure I had my carry permit in my wallet, which I did. I also made sure that there was nothing in my wallet that actually identified the real me. Normally I would at least like to conceal my gun but it was too damn hot to wear a jacket down here and my legs were too thick to hide a gun in an ankle holster so it was better to just let everyone know you had it, besides, it seemed to me that everyone I saw since I landed in Arizona had a gun on their belt, except kids and I am guessing they knew how to use a gun too. Everything was in order; I would walk out that door as Richard Tracy and there was no way of proving it otherwise.

I heard a shuffle outside my door then saw a piece of paper slide under the door. I bent down to pick it up and saw that it was a flyer for a "*Country Music Extravaganza*" to be held in the town square courtyard. The flyer had a picture of George Strait playing the guitar and smiling as he sang into a microphone. It also had a band listed but not pictured as "Fat Jackie and the Hooligans" The flyer made me laugh, there were a few other pictures of people that I didn't recognize but I was sure that George Strait was not going to be performing at the courthouse square in Lucas Arizona. Maybe some of those other folks on the flyer would be, but not King George. Hell, even I knew who George Strait was and I didn't like country music. I also needed to see this Fat Jackie group, with a name like that, they had to be entertaining at the very least. I folded the paper and stuck it in my back pocket. Teddy would want to see this.

Chapter 14

Lupita

The walk from the motel to downtown was nothing but it generated a huge sweat. It was hot outside, and I just don't handle the heat very well. I sweat like no other, complete with sweat rings under the arm pits and sweat pouring off my forehead. By the time I reached the courthouse square I was happy that I wore a white golf shirt, and I was very happy that I was standing in front of what looked like one of those very old drug stores complete with the bar counter, bar stools and booths on the other side that ran the length of the store. I didn't care what it had to offer I just wanted to get out of the night's heat. As I entered the old drug store, I could hear the concert music start up in the distance and damn if it didn't sound like George Strait singing "Amarillo by morning" complete with the crowd cheering as if it really were George Strait. It almost had me thinking that maybe I had misjudged that flyer.

I was expecting a bell to ring when I opened the door, but nothing happened except the guy behind the counter smiled and said, "sit wherever you like", he then pointed at an open booth, "If you want a booth, there is one over there and if you want mindless chatter coming from all directions" he pointed at the two bar stools that were empty, "sit right there." The place was full of men in cowboy hats, a few with baseball caps but everyone had some kind of hat on. I didn't care but I did feel a little out of place since I forgot to bring my cowboy hat with me, but I didn't feel out of place enough to leave because they definitely had the A/C cranked up on high and it felt nice to be out of the heat. Since I have never felt real good about my back being turned towards an opening door, I chose the booth that was open and sat facing the door I had just entered.

A young girl startled me when she touched me on the shoulder, I didn't see where she came from, but she was holding what looked to be like hundreds of beads around her arms and she was lifting her arms straight out like a scarecrow for me to see all the beads as they dangled from her arms. "Cinco dõlares" she smiled and then with all the charm of a 10-year-old girl she said "Please". My Spanish hadn't improved any in the last few hours, but I understood that the necklaces were five bucks. That seemed a little pricy for some fishing line and wooden beads but good lord, what was I supposed to say to a girl that small, smiling at me and holding her arms straight out. If anything, I needed to give her five bucks so she could at least put her arms down. I reached in my pocket and felt for my money clip, I could feel it in my pocket and regretted not taking a few bucks out of it and putting some in my shirt pocket. I couldn't pull a money clip out of my pocket that had at least 5 grand in it comprised of one-hundred-dollar bills. So, without taking the entire clip out of my pocket I wiggled one bill free from the rest and hoped for the best. When my hand broke free from my pocket I could see that it was a hundred-dollar bill.

This situation was now one of life's great dilemmas that was staring me in the face all because a little girl wanted to sell me some beads. I can't pull my clip out and fish around for a smaller bill, I guess I could ask the guy behind the counter to break a hundred but that seemed cheap, I could ask the little girl to break a hundred but that seemed even worse, I could send her away with a no thank you and feel like a complete jerk the rest of the night or I could just give her the hundred dollar bill, take a necklace and tell her to keep the change. Out of all the choices I had, I chose the last one, I pointed at a necklace that seemed to stand out more than the others, she lowered her arms, gently laid the necklaces on the ground in front of the booth and sorted through the necklaces until she found the one, I pointed at. When she found it, she rose up and handed the necklace to me and I handed her the bill. At first, she started to stick the bill in her front pocket without thinking but she stopped to glance at it. When she discovered what it was, her eyes got really big and tried to hand it back to me, "demasiado jefe!" I pushed it back, towards her and as I was doing so, a young boy, not really a boy, maybe a teenager came to the table, put his hand on top of the girl's head, "She says it's too much boss". I sort of waved them off with my hand, "Tell her I won the lottery today, and her salesmanship and timing couldn't have been better." The boy smiled and said something to her in Spanish and she smiled at me and ran toward the back of the store and disappeared. "She has gone to show her mother what you gave her señor, her mother may not allow her to keep it, she doesn't do those things". He looked around the place and then looked back down at me, "Can I bring you a cold beverage while we wait on the verdict?"

The last thing I wanted to do was cause a ruckus but apparently, I had done so. "Look, I didn't have any change, I just wanted to help her out and sit in the A/C for a little while before I go see Fat Jackie and the Hooligans." He laughed out loud and shook his head, "In that case my friend I will bring you two beers, Fat Jackie needs all the help she can get." He disappeared as he weaved his way to the back but then I saw him reappear behind the counter. He poured a beer into a glass with a handle and let a little of the foam run over then disappeared again until he was placing the glass of beer on my table. "It is on the house, your generosity towards my sister is appreciated."

I took a sip of the cold beer and sat back in my booth as the young bar keep walked away. There must not be the same regulations about minors serving alcohol down here on the border as they have up in New York, but I didn't care. I needed to listen to crowd chatter and get a feel for the town. I was also looking forward to hearing fat Jackie and the Hooligans. I don't know why but every time I thought of the band I chuckled. It just seemed like a funny name.

Each of the booth's had a mini juke box on the table that you could put a quarter in and select some songs. As I sat there listening to the chatter in the drug store or bar or whatever this place was, I scrolled through the music. There wasn't much that I cared for, it was full of country, and nothing struck me as being willing to give up a quarter for. The place was lively, and people were laughing and having a good time. I heard some conversations about sex, football, a place called Rocky Point, and someone had a profound hatred for the police.

"You looking for company?" I was so lost in my thoughts and listening to chatter that I didn't notice the girl who just sat down at my booth across from me. "Uh excuse me?" I was not looking for company and I was especially not looking to go to jail, this girl that just invited herself to sit with me couldn't have been more than 16 and that was stretching the age as far as I dared. "Do you want some company baby?" I could feel my skin crawl when she said it, but I could also feel her bare foot press against my crotch under the booth table. I gently pushed her foot away from my privates, "no, I am not looking for company, I am looking for privacy."

She continued to smile at me, her teeth were straight and pearly white against her dark skin. She had some dental work done in order to get teeth that straight. "You need to go do some homework or something kiddo. I aint your guy." I wasn't opposed to anyone making a living, I was in no position to judge but I hated the fact that an underage girl was letting herself be abused for money. "Don't be mad mister, I promise you won't regret it." I blinked my eyes and shook my head, "yes, I would and so will you. Maybe not now but later in life you will." I pointed at the door, reached in my pocket and pulled out another hundred-dollar bill, I folded it under the table so no one could see it then palmed it as I brought my hand up to the table. I stuck out my hand as if I wanted to shake hers and she took my hand. I know she could feel the bill in my hand press against hers and I leaned forward so she would be the only one to hear me. "Please go away. Take the money and leave me alone." I was happy that she took the money discreetly because I didn't want anyone to think that I would sleep with a prostitute child, especially any cop that might be trying to set me up. I just wanted her to go away. She continued to smile at me and didn't move from my booth. She pretended to scratch her chest and I could see her slide the money in her training bra. We sat there and stared at each other for few minutes, "Are you hungry?" She changed her smile and looked around the drug store like she was looking to see who was watching. It seemed very strange to me that she was willing to screw me without knowing me and that didn't make her nervous at all but asking her if she was hungry made her jumpy. "I can't get fat." I shook my head, and a waitress came walking by so the timing was perfect, "hey ma'am, can we get a couple grill cheese sandwiches with one of those pickle spears and some fries?" The waitress looked at me and then looked at the girl, they seemed to know each other and as soon as their eyes met, my forced date for the night lowered her head and stared at the table. I looked up at the waitress and gave her the look, "Do I need to repeat myself?" After the waitress caught my look of seriousness, she was the one looking down at the floor now, "add two sodas to that also."

I don't know why I did what I did but I felt bad for this girl. She was as skinny as a rail, too young to be doing what she was doing, and I was guessing she was hungry. So, technically I paid her 100 dollars for her time, which I am guessing was a lot more than she ever really got from one customer so if I wanted to feed her and let her sit at my booth then I had paid for that right?

We sat there in silence until the waitress brought the food over, I had already eaten in Ajo earlier so I wasn't overly hungry but this was just a grill cheese and fries so I could probably handle that. I picked at my fries for just a little bit as I watched this girl consume that sandwich in record time. When she realized I was watching her eat, she slowed down and put her hands in her lap. "Don't stop, you are obviously hungry, so eat." She looked around the room again but not as long as the last time and began eating her fries. I picked up my grill cheese and put it on her plate, she looked up at me and smiled and without hesitation started eating her second grill cheese sandwich. "What's your name?" In between bites of fries she said, "Lacy". I smiled, "not your stage name, your real name." She glanced up for a second, looked around, swallowed her food and leaned forward and whispered, "Lupita". I was about to say my name, my stage name of course when a hand grabbed her arm and started pulling her from the booth. I looked up and saw a man in a nice suit without a tie. His hair was beautiful. It was the best-looking head of hair I have ever seen on a guy. This man could have been one of the Bee Gee's for sure.

"Time to go honey, you have work to do." He smiled at me as he was pulling on her arm, I reached over and grabbed his wrist and yanked him towards me. He must not have expected it because the look on his face was more shock than fear. "Me and the lady are having a nice dinner and you are being rude." I let go of his arm and he tried to compose himself. He looked at me with his best Billy Bad Ass face, the same face that Jimmy Romano tries to use to no effect on anyone. "You should mind your own business my friend." He adjusted his suit then looked at the girl who was clearly scared now,

"It is time to go Lacy." He reached down and grabbed her arm again and this time she yanked her arm free from his grip and said, "please Armando, I am hungry, and he paid me already!" Armando without hesitation reached inside her bra where she had stuck the money I gave her and slid it into his pocket.

I could not believe my luck! The man I was sent here to look for had revealed himself without me even trying to find him. "Let the girl eat." Armando looked down at me again with a very straight face, "Ok Señor, have it your way, dine with the best tonight. I have everything I need now."

I am lucky I didn't run her off at first like I wanted to. It never occurred to me that Armando was a pimp down here. I had just assumed he was a drug runner but that's what I get for assuming. Armando smiled at me and walked away.

As he walked away, I could see the fear in her eyes, and I hated it. I like to see fear in the eyes of the people that I am trying to collect money from that is owed to us, it always helps with the process, but this was a baby, a young girl that should be doing her homework right now, not slubbing around with old guys making money for a cheap pimp. I was going to enjoy this collection very much.

"Where does Armando hang out? Where will he go with your money?" She looked down at the plate in front of her that was nearly empty now, I knew she was scared but I think I had won her trust and if I stayed with it long enough, she would tell me where to find Armando. "Please, let it go mister." She looked up at me and at that moment I could see the beautiful woman she could become but if she didn't stay stuck in this racket, the softness in her eyes would turn to hardness, then to desperation and then hopelessness. When it got to hopelessness, it would be too late. "Listen, Lupita, I want to help you and I will, but Armando owes some people some money, people that you should be more scared of than Armando and I am here to collect it for them. Once I have what I came for, I will get you out of here. I promise." I patted her on the hand and as I did, she looked down again and I could see a tear rolling down her cheek. "Where are your parents? Where is home for you?" She wiped her eyes then looked up at me, my mother is in Mexico, and I don't know where my father is. She continued to wipe her eyes, I yanked a paper napkin from the holder and handed it to her. Her English was very good but every once in a while, she struggled with finding the right word to fit the conversation. "My mother paid a man to smuggle me across the border and I haven't seen her since then."

I may do some bad stuff, but I am not a bad person. I try to tell myself that as much as possible but one thing I know for sure is I hate child abusers. The girl sitting across from me was being abused and it was pissing me off. The more she talked and unraveled her story for me, the more pissed I got.

"I didn't want to leave but my mother wanted me to have a chance at a better life. She said America would give me a chance to be rich and happy." She looked at her hands and rubbed her wrists, "It hasn't turned out that way." I had already heard enough, I could probably fill in the blanks without any help from her, but she continued without any prompting from me, which to me, was a sign she trusted me. "My mother worked very hard to save the money to pay the man to get me across the border, my uncle, her brother, helped her and said that the man she would hire to take me across the border was a good friend of his and would see to it that I got across the border safely and would get me a good job when I arrived." She fought back a few more tears, "She even gave me pocket money so that I would not be broke when I arrived." I am glad she couldn't see me roll my eyes, but I didn't need to hear more, I was pissed so I tried to speed the conversation up a little, "So they took your money and turned you over to Armando and I am guessing your uncle is a piece of shit, right?" She was nodding her head, "I told my mother that he was always trying to touch me and that I didn't like him, but he was her brother and she said he was just a loving man."

Lupita eventually got around to telling me where I could find Armando, but it took a while. It turns out that Lupita could sing, and she could play the guitar, piano and saxophone. She told me that she wanted to sing and play for audiences, and she wanted to be in a big show in a big city is how she put it. She worked for a rich family in the town she came from, and they had all kinds of instruments in the house. She told me that nobody she knew of in the house played any of them so whenever she could, she would teach herself how to play.

"When I said goodbye to my mother, she hugged me and said that she was going to save more money and come join me when she could. She said I should find a place for us to live." I tried to interrupt her, but I think she needed to "ring out the sponge of her soul" as my mother used to say, "I don't want her to come here now, I don't want her to see me like this." She slid the plate in front of her towards the middle of the table and closer to me, "My uncle took me before he even turned me over to the men that took me across the border" she paused and the tears started flowing without any noise, "He took me! Then he took my money too. I have nothing now, not even my dignity."

I looked around the room to see if anyone was watching and was struck by how no one seemed to care what was going on around them. "Come on, I am going to help you get your dignity back." I stood up, placed a fifty-dollar bill on the table and stuck out my hand for her to take. She needed to feel what it was like to be a lady and not an object and I was going to try and correct that. I hated myself for feeling this way, I am not a Knight in shining armor and for that matter, I don't want to be, but I can't take the thought of this girl getting raped by another man. She needed a break, and I knew I was it. Unless I helped this girl now, she'd be dead in a year.

Chapter 15

The Heart Softens

It felt really odd, well odd might not be the right word, creepy seems to fit the mood better, taking a teenage girl back to my motel room but I didn't have any choice. I needed to get her away from Armando and then go collect Big Paul's money from him.

After I got her situated in the room, I told her to stay put and not to open the door for anyone. I showed her the chain latch at the top of the door and how to close it after I left. I could see in her face that she was scared, and I hoped she wouldn't run away after I left. She had no reason to trust me, hell she had just met me a little over an hour ago. Her own Uncle had abused her and here she was in a motel room with a strange man who was trying to help her but how was she supposed to know that? Her mother was trying to help her too but that didn't turn out well for her either.

As I was getting ready to leave the room, I was giving her instructions one more time, she began to tear up again and in the middle of me telling her what to do if I didn't come back, she practically leaped into my arms. She had her arms wrapped around my neck; she was so light that I barely felt her hanging on me. I didn't know what to do, affection is not my strong suit, so I patted her on the back with one hand but left the other hand dangling by my side. I didn't want her to think I wanted anything more. I let her hold on to me for a few moments but lowered my neck so her feet could touch the ground again. Once her feet touched the floor, she released her grip on me but kept her face pressed into my chest. This girl's sobs were real, her pain was real, and it made me feel angry. I don't care where you come from, children should be protected, not abused. I patted the top of her head with the hand that I had just used to pat her back, I really thought I was getting good at this comforting thing. She pulled away from me, "I don't even know your name." She looked around the motel room and then looked straight through me, how am I supposed to trust you when I don't even know you. You could fuck me like everyone else has!" I understood her position and I really didn't know how to answer her question. "I will be back. Just relax, watch some tv, take a shower if you need to, but I promise, I will be back." I touched the sides of her arms as if I was going to draw her close to me, but I didn't. I didn't want her to feel any threat, "I promise, I won't do that to you."

It was sort of tough to leave her, but I did. She was a vulnerable child and I hated getting caught up in this crap and I just wanted to get her and me out of here. I needed to go find Armando and get moving as far away as I could. I needed to go get my little brother from Madison and figure a way to get out of this business once and for all.

Lupita told me that Armando had a bungalow at the west end of town, she said it was the only green bungalow on the street. She told me that he had people coming to the house all the time. Even though it was a short walk, I took the rental. It was late and I might look out of place, making me easy to spot. I wouldn't need much of an element of surprise, nor did I want one. I always found it was best to just either knock on the door or just open it and go in. There were always so many people coming and going in a place like this that nobody ever stopped to lock a door. It has been my experience that criminals like Armando think they are really smart, but they are actually very dumb.

It was hard to tell what color the bungalow was in the dark but a few minutes of watching the house from my rental I could tell by the activity that I was in the right place. I checked my 1911 one more time, put it back in the hip holster, took a drink of water that I had in the suburban and made my way to the front door. I passed a woman coming out who didn't look very good at all. She looked like she wanted to throw up, so I veered away from her on the sidewalk. I am pretty sure she never even knew I was there.

I opened the front door and stepped inside. There was some soft music playing somewhere, I couldn't tell what kind of music it was but as I got closer to the living room area, I could tell that it was country. The air was filled with smoke and from experience it wasn't cigarette smoke. The crack smell hung heavy in the room. I figured a guy like Armando liked the ladies and there was good chance he was in a bedroom somewhere in the house and I also know that guys like him think they are invincible, so they leave doors unlocked everywhere. They are also really bad at surrounding themselves with idiots.

There was one guy in the living room, but he was out of it, so much that the drool was running down his chin as he had his head cocked back on the couch and his feet up on the coffee table. He still had the rubber strap around his arm, and I am pretty sure the needle was still in. Although I know that most of the money I earn comes from the drug trade in one form or another, but for the life of me I can't see how this guy feels good about himself. I could walk up right now; slit his throat and he'd be talking to saint Peter before I could wipe the blood off my blade. How can anyone allow themselves to become so vulnerable? It is a mystery to me.

I went all the way down to the back of the hall, I knew it was pointless to check the front rooms, Armando would be in the back, the master bedroom, and more than likely I would catch him either asleep or naked doing what guys like him like to do. I was right, Armando was getting "serviced' by a young girl, the room was back lit with some kind of neon lights so I couldn't tell how old she was, but she just looked young from the angle I had. Armando had his eyes closed and didn't see me walk right up to him but when he did, I could see the fear in his eyes.

He jumped up quickly, but the girl didn't jump up with him which was awkward and funny to watch as he stumbled back into the chair he was sitting in. He looked around quickly to see if there was any help in the room but there was not. By now the girl realized something was wrong and she rolled out of the way. She was naked except for the panties and when she saw me standing in the room, she covered her bare breasts with her arms. She and I made eye contact and at that moment she looked older than I first expected but again, I can't tell how old people are. I motioned for her to leave the room which she quickly did. I kept my eyes on Armando because he would be the type to try something stupid. He sat there in the chair completely naked trying to look tough, but it didn't work.

"Didn't realize it was that cold in here chief" I threw him a pair of pants I saw on the floor, "better cover up before it disappears completely." Armando fumbled with the pants but managed to get them on and then he stood up which gave me the opportunity to begin the collection process. I stepped forward and slapped him across the face with my left hand which nearly knocked him over, but he caught his balance just enough for me to slap him again with my right hand and that time he fell back in the chair. I stood over him as he was rubbing his face trying to collect himself and grabbed him by the hair and pulled him to a standing position. Once I had him standing, I used my free hand to grip his neck and once I had the grip, he began to lose air, I could see his eyes widen even more. "You owe my boss some money and he isn't happy about your delinquency." I let go of his neck but slapped him again and this time he dropped straight to his knees with his face staring directly at my crotch. I reached down and grabbed a hand full of hair again and forced him to stand up, "No... No, I don't swing that way shit head, so that won't do you any good." He was standing now, and we were close to the same height, but he was very wobbly. I was amazed by this guy's inability to take a punch. Hell, it wasn't even really a punch, I simply slapped the man and he now looked like he had just gone a few rounds with the heavyweight champ.

"Tell him I'm sorry . . . " He sniveled and groveled, "I ran short this month!" I pulled him towards the bed in the room and sat him down on it. "You have been short a few more than just a month my friend. Where do you keep the money?" He looked around the room which told me that he had the money, but I knew the next words out of his mouth were going to be a lie and that he didn't have it, so I smacked him hard on the ear with a cupped hand. That hurts like hell when done correctly and in this case, I had done it correctly. He howled when he felt the pressure on his ear drum. "Don't even think about telling me you don't have it. Snakes like you always keep your "running" money handy so you can run from your debts." He rocked back and forth holding his hands over his ears hoping I wouldn't bust the ear drum on his other ear and looked up at me with tears in his eyes, "it's in the wall." He nodded straight ahead to a wall that had a full-length mirror hanging on it. I grabbed him by the hair and pulled him to his feet. Armando wasn't as tough with me as he had been with Lupita. With my help, he quickly walked in front of the mirror and removed it with two hands. The sheetrock had been cut away revealing stacks of neatly wrapped bundles of bills. "You want to pull out what you owe Big Paul, or do you want me to just take it all?" I let go of him and he nearly fell down, so I grabbed the back of his neck and held him up. He reached forward and pulled out three bundles of cash and sort of gave me a sheepish look, "You sure that's enough?" I squeezed the back of his neck and watched him wince, "If I have to come back . . ." I left that remark hanging and he reached forward and pulled two more bundles out for me. I smiled when he looked at me and let go of his neck and he immediately fell to his knees. I stepped forward and pulled another couple of bundles out, "This is gonna go towards my recovery fee, it's expensive to travel to Arizona."

I grabbed a pillow off the bed and removed the pillowcase, stuffed all the bundles of cash in it. I took a step toward Armando and put my hand under his chin. "Down here you might be a bad ass, but where I am from, you're a dime a dozen. You take advantage of women and kids because they can't fight back." I looked around the room and was surprised to see the little girl that had been engaged in sex with Armando and it reminded me of Lupita. "And by the way", I slapped him gently to get him to look at me, "I'm getting Lupita out of here, chase her, follow her or threaten her or her family, I will come back and finish you." I slapped him a little harder, "You have my word on it." I turned to walk out and without turning to look at him, "Your slate is clear with Big Paul now, I wouldn't borrow any more money from people you aren't prepared to deal with."

I walked down the hallway back to the front door with the pillowcase full of cash bundles slung over my shoulder. I really had no idea how much money I had but I was pretty confident that I had way more than enough. As I was reaching for the door handle, I heard the gun shot and heard the thud when it hit the bag of bundled cash. Instinctively, I drew my 1911 and spun around, I was about to pull the trigger when I realized the person that had just shot at me was the little girl that Armando was getting "serviced" by when I first arrived. Even in the neon glow of this house I could see she had tears in her eyes, but she was still pointing a weapon at me.

"Put it down kid," I lowered my 1911 and let my arm hang down my side. I was vulnerable and she was unpredictable, but I was not about to shoot a kid. I could see her hand shaking but I couldn't tell what kind of gun she had. From the back of the hallway, I could hear Armando yell, "I said kill him!"

I walked back down the hallway towards the girl holding the gun. The closer I got to her the more she cried. The tears were flowing down her cheeks as I reached for the gun and gently removed it from her hand. I easily pushed her naked body aside and went back into the room where Armando was trying to put his shoes on. I took three quick steps and kicked him in the face as he tried to block the kick. It didn't do any good, my Italian loafer caught him square on the chin and he went sprawling face down on the floor. This wasn't a final collection thank goodness or this guy would have made it easy for me. He sent a baby out to shoot me, all I could think about was "what a prick." I dumped the pillowcase on the bed and inspected the bundles that had just probably saved my life to see which ones had been ruined by the bullet. I found the bundle that had absorbed a bullet intended for me, otherwise I would have been dead or seriously injured. I threw it all back in the pillowcase and then reached into the wall to grab the rest of the bundles. I wasn't going to be nice anymore. He needed to be taught a lesson in manners.

Armando was moaning on the floor, one of his hands were visible to me, it looked like he was trying to do a one arm push up with it. I stood over him and brought my size 11 double E shoe heel down on his fingers with all the energy I had. I could hear the bones crunch which was the desired affect I was looking for. Armando screamed but not long, I decided that Armando needed some broken ribs to go along with that broken hand. Three good kicks to the side of his chest and stomach probably did the job but I didn't want to leave anything to chance so I gave him two more. This guy was a creep and I actually enjoyed leaving him in a really bad way. "I will be back for you later." I wanted him to be scared from now on, either he wouldn't borrow any more money from Big Paul, or he would find a different source. He would have trouble being seen as a tough guy around town with the damage that I left on him.

I stepped back into the hallway where the naked little girl had sat down against the wall and was still sobbing. I stood over her then decided it was best to kneel down. Looking up at someone in the position she was in could be intimidating for a kid, especially this one. She looked up at me and tried to gather herself enough to say, "lo siento". I didn't know what that meant but she looked and sounded genuine. I would later learn that she said, "I'm sorry". Since there was no chance of us communicating, I tried to point at my shirt and pants and then point at her. It took a minute, but she understood, and I helped her stand up. She went into the room where Armando was still moaning and came out holding some clothes in her hands. I motioned for her to put them on, and she did. The two of us made it all the way back to the motel where Lupita was waiting. I had no idea what or why I was doing this but now I had two little girls in my care. I felt stupid for letting myself get caught up in this stupid crap, but I was past the point of no return.

Chapter 16

Poppin Tags

When I entered the room, I saw Lupita lying in the bed watching TV. She had taken a shower and her hair was still wet. She looked more relaxed than I had ever seen her. She had also helped herself to what little clothes I had packed and was wearing one of my knit polo's. I gave her a look that intended to imply that she should asked before she took it, but I don't think it worked and decided to let it go. I could buy some more clothes on the way back.

"She doesn't speak English. Let her know I am trying to help her." The look on Lupita's face when I brought another girl into the room was one of confusion. There is no telling what was going through that girl's head, but it wasn't good, I am sure. She got up off the bed and walked towards us, "her name is Alejandra. She was with me when I crossed." Lupita walked over to where Alejandra was still standing and put her arms around the girl. Lupita was much taller than Alejandra, but I was guessing they were about the same age, an age too young to be mixed up in this mess.

"It is time for me leave now and since I don't know what to do with either of you," I paused, looked all around the room and realized that now I was harboring illegal aliens and no matter what my intentions were, I was in a difficult spot. I raced through my options as best I could. I had never been an impulsive person and took pride in the fact that I always had a plan and here I was with two underage girls without an ID, a bag full of cash, and no plan. "I guess I should ask before I assume, do you want to go with me?" I let that hang in the air while both girls remained in an embrace with only Lupita looking at me. "I guess I can try and straighten this mess out when we get back to New York." I rubbed my forehead, "All I am saying is that you are free to do what you want to, you have choices." Lupita released her embrace of Alejandra but kept her hands-on Alejandra's shoulders and looked up into her eyes. She then let loose a bunch of Spanish words that I didn't understand. She was talking so fast that I felt like she needed to stop and breathe but as she was speaking, Alejandra turned and looked at me, then she looked back at Lupita and nodded her head in the affirmative motion. With that simple up and down motion of Alejandra's head, I now understood that I had just become these girls' guardians, whether I wanted to or not.

Lupita hugged Alejandra again but as she was hugging her, she looked directly at me, "We don't even know your name," she never blinked, her stare towards me was firm and strong, whatever spirit they had taken from her was returning right before my eyes, "but we trust you." Her words hung on me like a brick necklace that I wasn't prepared to wear but what I was prepared for and what had to happen were two different things.

I thought about my options as I stood there looking at two teenage girls in an embrace in my little motel room in Lucas Arizona. I couldn't put them on a plane, bus or train, so that only left the option of driving back to New York and even that option was risky. There were at least two checkpoints along the highway where border patrol stopped you and would often search your car. I didn't know the roads in Arizona well enough to avoid all the check points, but I was fairly certain we could get past the check points with a little rehearsal and practice. Lupita would be easy because her English was exceptional, but Alejandra would be a completely different challenge because she didn't speak a lick of English.

"Do you know where we can get you girls some clothes?" Lupita looked over Alejandra's shoulder then looked back at Alejandra. She spoke to her in Spanish and Alejandra immediately went to the bathroom and closed the door. "I told her to go take a shower and wash the feel of Armando off her. I told her to take as long as she needed." Lupita walked over to the bag that I brought, patted it, "you travel light." She walked over and sat on the bed, "what is your name and what are your real plans for us?" She looked around and her face got hard and her shot daggers at me from somewhere inside her soul. "I've already been fucked by everyone I trusted so when I said I trust you, I also know how that can work against me." I rolled my eyes and shook my head, "don't use that kind of language, real ladies don't curse like that." She laid back on the back on the bed, "I'm not a lady anymore." I sat down on the bed next to her, I put my hands on my knees and drew in a deep breath, "you are a lady, you can never ever believe anything different." She put her hand on my thigh and started to run her hand up my leg and I stopped her, "don't you want the same thing all men want?" I shook my head and drew in another deeper breath, "if I wanted THAT I would have already taken it," I stood up, "stop thinking that short term defeatist crap and help me figure out how to get you two some clothes so we can travel without suspicion." She stood up too and I could see her face was flush with some embarrassment. "Everything is closed but there is a second-hand donation store that I know how to get into." I shot her a look, and it must have made her nervous, "it's right next door, the back-door lock has been broken for several months now." She looked down at her feet in a shameful, guilty way that made me chuckle, this girl had been through hell, unspeakable things had been done to her and she was worried about me judging her for breaking into a second-hand store? This whole day was a fascinating experiment in human nature.

"Ok then, while she is in the shower, I need you to go get some clothes for you both to wear." I reached in my pocket and gave her a 100-dollar bill. "You know they are closed right?" I smiled, "a lady doesn't curse or steal, leave the $100 where someone will find it." For the first time since we met, she smiled at me. I think she understood what I was trying to do. "Nothing revealing," I pointed at her, "jeans, shirts that cover everything and sneakers if you can find them." She turned toward the door then turned back, "what's your name?" I handed her the big key to the room but as she reached for it, I held a tight grip so that she couldn't turn around too quickly, "Richard, Richard Tracy," I held the grip, "make sure you find some underwear for both of you." She wrinkled her forehead, "you want me to put some panties against my kochie that some other skank has worn, would you do that?" I let go of the key and let out a laugh, "you have a point, I just don't want anything sticking out or hanging out." It was her turn to laugh, and I have to say that I enjoyed hearing her laugh. She probably hadn't had much to laugh about in quite a while, and I was glad to I could make it happen. "Ok, Richard. I will make you proud."

I can't understand why anyone would hurt a child, any child, but especially her. Even after all she had been through, she still had a glow in her eyes and a smile on her face, the smile was slight but when she smiled at me as she left that room, I knew I had to get them help.

While I waited on Lupita to return from the thrift store, I packed up everything we had. Alejandra was still in the shower, I suspected she was trying to wash away more than just the exterior dirt. I heard the water stop running and I tensed up. I was hoping she wouldn't come out of the shower until Lupita came back. She didn't speak any English and I didn't speak any Spanish so we would just have to sit in silence for a while, plus I wasn't sure what she would wear out of the shower. I wanted her to get rid of that trashy dress she wore earlier.

The dress was one of those really tight spandex dresses that were designed to show a woman's curves, but Alejandra was so young that she didn't have any real curves yet and she was so tall that she looked like she had an oversized 70's style tube top that went from under her chin to her thighs. Luckily, she stayed in the bathroom long enough for Lupita to return with a laundry basket full of clothes.

Lupita dumped the clothes out on the bed and began sifting through them. She separated the piles, one for her and one for Alejandra. When she had the basket empty, she immediately took off her shirt and was standing naked in front of me, I must have been in deep thought about what steps we needed to take now because I didn't realize she was naked. When I finally saw her freely changing clothes in front of me, I spun around so I could not see her. "You need to not be so cavalier about changing in front of people, especially men." She didn't say anything, "I guess we need to begin a rule book for ladies," I held my index finger up over my shoulder so hopefully she could see me count, "One, ladies don't curse, two, ladies don't steal, and three, ladies don't get naked in front of guys." She responded with "you can turn around now." I turned to see a teenage girl in front of me, not the girl I met in the restaurant. She found a nice pair of jeans and a blouse that was sleeveless and buttoned up the front. Nothing was showing, nothing was poking out, she looked like a girl headed to the mall with her friends. I am not sure if kids even went to malls anymore, but you get the idea. I stuck out my hand for her to shake, she looked a little confused, but she slowly took my hand, "I am Richard Tracy, it is nice to meet you." She got a little embarrassed and her checks became flush enough for me to see the red come through her dark beautiful skin. "I'm Lupita Arroyo."

She looked down at her feet and pulled her hand away from mine, "Well it is nice to meet you Ms. Arroyo." When I addressed her as Ms. Arroyo, even though her head was down I could see a smile develop on her face, "gotta work on that hand shake young lady, too weak." She looked up at me with the smile still on her face, "Can you get Alejandra dressed so we can get out of here?" She nodded and disappeared into the bathroom.

When the girls came out of the bathroom, they both looked incredible. I was first impressed by Lupita's ability to pick out clothes for Alejandra. The clothes were almost identical to what Lupita had chosen for herself but a different color blouse. Both girls now looked like it was Friday night, and they were headed to the mall to hang out with friends and flirt with the boys. I hope they can get back to something like that, but I just think too much damage has been done to them. Neither of the girls were ever going to know normal again but I was going to do everything I could to help them come as close to it as I could.

Chapter 17

Voice of a Killer

I loaded the car with what little stuff the girls had along with my one single small bag. I stuck the pillowcase full of money in the spare tire well located under the back-cargo liner. I gave Lupita the key to the room and asked her to take it back to the front desk. It wasn't long before she returned to inform me that the office was closed and locked. I saw her stick the key in her pocket and thought she should keep it. Keep it as something that represented the beginning of a change in her life, maybe a symbolic key that opened the door to her new beginning. I wasn't sure if big Paul would approve with my meddling in the business down here. Big Paul liked things neat and organized, he wanted to be paid the money Armando and him had previously negotiated and that was it. He didn't like to make noise and I had just made a bunch of noise. I figured once I gave him way more money than he expected, he wouldn't care about how I got it and what I did as I was getting it.

Alejandra sat on the bed with her head down as we loaded the rental. I would catch her staring at me sometimes and she would immediately look away. Lupita helped her get in the back of the

Suburban and Lupita sat in the front seat. I closed the door to the room and as I was getting ready to get in the Suburban, I could hear the music being played nearby. It was a woman's voice and she sounded pretty good. If I wasn't in somewhat of a hurry to get on the road and put some miles behind us and Lucas Arizona, I would stop and see if maybe the woman's voice I was hearing was fat Jackie. Maybe one day I would come back and find fat Jackie and the Hooligans and just enjoy some music.

The road north and out of Lucas was quiet and just as it was coming in, not a soul around. I put my headlights on bright so I could see a little more of the road ahead, but it really didn't help, it was by far the darkest stretch of highway I had ever driven on. Lupita sat straight up looking into the darkness, she was wide awake. Every now and then I would catch her looking back, I couldn't tell if she was checking on Alejandra, who had slumped over in the seat and was asleep from what I could tell but I thought maybe Lupita was looking back to see if anyone was following us. "My mother will never find me now." Her words shattered the silence in the car like someone had thrown a rock through the window. I didn't say anything back to her right away and she continued, "I always hoped that she would cross the border and find me but I was afraid that those men would do the same thing to her that they did to me so I prayed she would come and then quickly pray that she wouldn't." It was almost as if she was talking to the road and not necessarily to me, but she definitely started talking more and more, "My mother is very pretty, she had me when she was too young to have children, but she did anyway." I decided I would interject a little just to let her know I was listening, "where is your father?" Without hesitation, "I do not know where my father is or even who he is. My mother never speaks of him and every time I ask, she always says that I am too young for such conversation." Even in the dark car, only illuminated by the lights of the dashboard I could see her wiping away tears as she spoke, "Here's the deal, if you would have stayed back there, you would eventually be dead, there is no getting around that." I looked at her but then turned my eyes back to the road.

"Why?" I wasn't sure how to answer her question, "Why you'd be dead if you stayed?" She shook her head, "No, why me, why us?" She looked back at Alejandra when she said it, "Why are you doing this? You have your money." It was my turn to shake my head, "I don't know really. I just know I hate what has happened to you girls," I motioned to the back of the suburban with my thumb, "you both are too young to know what you know now." She fiddled with her seat belt a little then put her feet up on the dashboard in front of her, "I guess it really doesn't matter anymore, my life is over." I grunted and cleared my throat, "that's where you are wrong, your life is just beginning, you can't let this hold you back." I could hear her crying and I didn't know what to do. I just kept my eyes on the road in front of me, I don't know why but the darkness of this road made me nervous. "I know some people that can help you get your life back on track, you just need to relax and help me get past those checkpoints." I could see she was about to speak when I saw the blue lights in my rear-view mirror and these lights were right on my bumper. There is no way that this guy pulled out from a hiding space and flipped the lights on, he had to have pulled out and followed me without his headlights on and when he was right on me, he hit the lights. I didn't like this at all. I slowed down, and began to pull over, I was careful not to pull too far over because if you got in the sand, you'd get stuck. "What's wrong?" I could hear the nervousness in her voice as she took her feet down off the dashboard. "I don't know what he wants," Lupita looked behind and told Alejandra to stay down and under the third-row seat if she could. "We didn't do anything wrong so don't worry." I looked out her side of the window and didn't see much, it was simply too dark. I tried to watch as much as I could through the rear-view mirror without moving too much,

I knew from experience that when a cop is behind you, don't move a lot. Act normal and cool if you can and sit still. I felt for my 1911 and it was right where it needed to be, on my right hip. I kept my eyes on the lights behind me and didn't move my head to look at her, "hey Lupita, there is something in the console that I want you to open and get out for me." She started to lean over and look but I stopped her, "You can't look down, just look straight ahead, find the latch, pull it and get it out". She was a good listener and very good at sitting still. "It is the only thing in console so gently reach into it and take it out." She fiddled with the latch, and it finally popped up, I could see the man walking towards the car with a flashlight in his hand, "Move quickly, when you find it, put it where you can get to it quickly." I took a deep breath, "It's called a derringer, it has two bullets and this one has no safety so don't squeeze anything. Just remember all you have to do is point and pull the trigger, just like in the movies. She pulled the derringer out of the console and held it like it was a venomous snake then gently placed it in her lap between her legs, so it was concealed. "Why do I need this if we didn't do anything wrong?" I sort of nodded my head in agreement, "In my line of work, you get a little jumpy and you don't trust anyone," I glanced a look towards my side mirror, and I could see three figures walking towards us, "bad things happen when you do."

I knew something had to be up; you just don't approach a car with three guys. It could have been girls approaching the car; it was so dark I just couldn't tell. I just knew there were three people approaching my car and I had two illegal aliens in the car with me that I was trying to help, but none of that mattered. I went through every single possible action I could go through but decided I needed to be reactionary and just go with the flow. It had worked for me up to this point and I didn't see any point in abandoning that method now.

The knock on the window came as expected and I hit the power button to roll the window down. The night air and dry heat hit me very quickly and reminded me that it was hot down here. "Hey, hello officer." Even though I had just thought about it, I was surprised to see a woman officer staring at me. "Can I see your license and registration please." It wasn't a question it was a demand and she said it forcefully. "What is the problem ma'am?" She bent down and looked through the window, "I won't ask again." She seemed jumpy and intolerant, "yes ma'am, I am going to reach into my back pocket and get my wallet out for you and since this is a rental, I believe the registration will be in the glove box." She was edgy and I wasn't about to get shot reaching for my wallet.

She took my fake driver's license and registration and went back to her car, but I could still see two figures standing at the very back of my car. "What's going on?" The whisper came from Lupita. I pushed the button to roll up my window. I pressed my index finger against my lips to give her the hush sign and she complied. I was trying to think through every possibility, which I knew was impossible. I always expected the bad but generally things for the most part turned out good.

I could see her walking back to the car, but she stopped to say something to the two other figures that were now directly behind the suburban. I quickly rolled the window back down to see if I could hear anything being said but I didn't. "Mr. Tracy" she said as she handed the license and registration back to me. "I am going to need you to step out of the car." I tried to look at her, but she had her flashlight at an angle that made it impossible for me to see her but the thing that had my attention was her voice, it was distinctive, very high tone and very confident. I felt like I had heard that voice before, but I couldn't place it. "What did I do officer?" There was a moment of silence as she allowed me to put the registration in the glove box and I slid the driver's license in my back pocket. "Just step out of the car please." Her voice was like hearing silverware drop onto a stainless-steel counter, it was so clear. "But I would like to know why I am being asked to step out of the car?" I could hear her draw in a deep breath of frustration, "Mr. Tracy, do you see that little red dot on the dashboard right now?" I looked at the dashboard and just above the navigation and radio display I could see a dot that seemed to have a mind of its own as it bounced around a little but then it started to move towards my side of the vehicle and then it disappeared. "It's now pointed at the back of your head, please step out of the car."

I now knew she wasn't a cop, and I knew where I heard that voice before. She was the DHL delivery lady that came to my apartment door as me and Teddy were getting ready to leave the other day. I also knew that the only person that knew I was taking this little collection trip was Big Paul Romano. I now had my answer; he blamed me for his son getting shot. What I didn't know is why this lady posing as a cop didn't just blast her way into my apartment that day and kill me then? She was very convincing as a DHL driver and now she was very convincing as a cop.

"Damn woman, you are really dedicated to your work, I told you I would pick up the package at the local branch." She didn't like that comment, "get out of the car!" I turned to Lupita who was staring at me like she was sad, or felt sorry for me, "Don't sweat it, I will be back in a jiffy." I opened the door and got out of the suburban, "I had a million things going through my head and the number one thing I could think of was Teddy. Teddy made me a better person and he is probably the reason I was trying to get two girls out of the hellhole they were in. The thought of Madison came into my head, I hoped she would call the number I gave her so that she could access the money I had stashed away, and she could take care of Teddy. I hoped that she knew I loved her and wanted the best for her.

"How much is he paying you to do this? Must have cost him a fortune to send me on this little run and have you waiting on me." I could see the gun she was pointing at me and now I could also see the two guys she was with, the Jersey boys. Geez, it had been a long time since I had been snookered and yet here I was, in the desert of Arizona about to be snookered by Big Paul. "I never kiss and tell, you know that." I laughed at her cold attempt at humor; I don't even know you lady. I am quite certain we've never kissed or told." She didn't seem to have a mood for any more humor. "Just get out of the car."

I shook my head in an agreeable fashion and drew in a deep breath so that she could see. I was nervous but not scared, but if I had any chance of making it back to New York to see Teddy again, I needed her to believe that I was scared. "Just gonna say bye, don't shoot me." I leaned across the console and pretended to give Lupita a kiss on the cheek but as I was kissing her cheek, I gently slid the derringer into the cuff of my shirtsleeve. It wasn't much of a chance or a plan, but it was all I had for now. They would take my 1911 that was on my hip, probably frisk me and then they would do whatever they were told to do. There was a good chance that big Paul would want some proof in order to pay up fully. I could see the look on Lupita's face when I actually kissed her on the cheek and fished the derringer from between her legs. I whispered in her ear, "I don't know what is about to happen, be ready for anything."

I stepped out of the suburban and stood in front of the lady pointing the gun at me. "Up against the car." I was surprised that this woman had a highway patrol uniform on that seemed to fit very well. She was obviously very thorough and very good at her job. I thought I knew everyone in the game but apparently, I didn't. I put my arms on top of the car, I was taller than her, but I wasn't taller than Carmine who stepped up quickly to initiate the frisk. I kept my arms tightly glued to the top of the suburban as Carmine did a semi good job of frisking me which included cupping my balls for a few seconds longer than I thought was necessary but he did not make it to my wrist so when he was done groping me and he had removed my 1911, I turned to look at my new lady friend and as I did, I slid my hands in my pockets so I could look relaxed and unafraid but I also wanted to let the derringer slide from my sleeve into my pocket since it wasn't very secure. I still didn't know who Carmine's partner was, but that wasn't important.

"I don't understand why you didn't do your job when you did that package delivery thing. You had me there." I think she answered but I didn't hear it because Carmine hit me in the lower back with a blackjack that sent me to my knees. I thought I might black out, but I didn't. I fought it off and ended up on my hands and knees like a dog. My new lady friend in the cop uniform took the opportunity of having me in a vulnerable position and she kicked me in the face. My chin absorbed most of her shoe but on the upswing, she caught me in the nose. My eyes got blurry and watery for a second. I have been hit harder so I was still ok, but I needed to get to my feet before she put a gun to the back of my head. I was pretty sure they weren't going to do anything on the highway, the risk of being seen, even on the desolate stretch of highway was not worth the risk. I stood up but turned around to Carmine, "Try and hit me with that wuss hammer again and I will shove it up your ass." Carmine must not have liked the threat because he pulled his gun out and pointed it at me, "Stop!" I could hear my lady friend yell from behind, "Not here, you know the plan, stick to it dip shit."

Chapter 18

The Assassination

Carmine's partner took the suburban with the girls in it, and I was forced into the passenger seat of the squad car, but it wasn't a squad car. It was a big white car with a light on the top of it. As I sat there in the passenger seat of that car with my right kidney throbbing from being struck by Carmine's blackjack, I thought to myself that these guys went to a lot of trouble to get to me so they must think I am pretty dangerous. "You guys really played this beautifully, couldn't have been your idea Carmine, you don't have the cerebral acceleration to execute anything as well planned as this." As we turned west off the main highway and down a dirt road, "it sure as hell wasn't your partner, I've seen stalks of bananas with more mental capacity than that guy," so that leaves the DHL delivery lady."

I could feel the rough road under us, and I was counting in my head as I was speaking, trying to get some sort of measurement as to how far we were traveling. I already had a fix on the little dipper so I knew I could find my way back; I just didn't know how far that would be. If you look up in the sky with all those stars, the night didn't seem so dark but if you just look out over the vast landscape of nothingness, it was extremely dark and hard to measure distance. Carmine broke the silence, "You know for someone that is about to take a dirt nap and never be heard from again, you sure are a smart ass." I chuckled at the comment, "makes two of us I guess" I replied. "What the hell does that mean moron?" I chuckled again, I needed to get in Carmine's head, but I didn't know what kind of time I had so I was rushing more than I would have liked, "it means you are too stupid to remember the first rule of assassination Einstein" I let that statement hang for just a second, "you get rid of the assassin." This time Carmine chuckled, I knew the lady in the back that was pointing that gun at my head, probably my own gun, was listening and knew exactly what I was saying, "Come on Carmine, you think Betty Boop back there was brought along just for her looks?" Now I chuckled, "as a matter of fact, when we get to wherever we are going, do a perimeter search for extra holes in the ground. Betty back there can't drag you two Jersey numb nuts very far so the holes for you are probably already there and you are driving yourself to your own funeral.

Since there wasn't an immediate reply from Carmine the brainiac, I knew I was getting to him but so did Betty Boop. "Carmine is right smart ass; you have a little too much spunk for the ride you are taking." I used my right hand to scratch my head, "So, where did you and Carmine meet, e-harmony? How long have you been working together?" I said it in a sarcastic way so that my words would continue to get at Carmine. "Shut up prick." She didn't sound very happy, and Carmine wasn't saying anything. I think I had done enough to get Carmine distracted and thinking about those extra holes in the ground when we get to the extermination site. Even though I had never been the driver or rider on one of these trips, I knew all about them. I knew the planning and I knew they were prepared, more prepared than me and I needed an edge. I had two edges now, I had two shots in my pocket, and I had Carmine thinking about getting a bullet in his own head. The unknowns were how I would handle the girls and how they would handle the girls; I knew there couldn't be any witnesses so they would be eliminated too.

The fake police car started to slow down, "It should be on your right, don't miss it or you go off in the sand." Her voice was so clear and precise, I can't even begin to describe it accurately but as stupid as it sounded, I was thinking that I bet this lady could sing. Carmine strained to see the road in front of him and then he found what he was looking for and we turned and headed north again. I had counted to 1000 in my head before we turned. I looked out my passenger window and got fixed on the little dipper again. My scoutmaster would have been proud at my nighttime navigational abilities. It was scary how much I had retained from my time in the scouts.

I counted again and didn't get past 300 Mississippi before we rolled to a stop. Betty Boop told me to get out of the car and I did. She kept the gun on me the entire time. I looked around and sure enough, there was a hole there already. I glanced at Carmine and not surprisingly; he was looking around for other holes. I don't think they were counting on me having the two girls in the car so I am sure that would distract them a little. I watched Carmine's partner get out of the car, walk around to the passenger side, open the door and force Lupita out of the car. He held her by the arm as they walked to meet us. I could not believe they didn't realize that Alejandra was in the back of the Suburban, my odds of survival just got better. "Did you find your final resting place yet Carmine?" This time Betty Boop smacked me in the back of the head with the butt of a gun; I was hoping that it wasn't my own gun she had just cracked me on the head with.

It was tough seeing Lupita in tears, even though she was so young, she had seen enough of the bad side of life to know what was coming and having to look at a hole dug in the middle of the desert was a tough thing to do. Hell, I was having my own issues with it, but I was more occupied with when to make my move. They were all lazy and we were a good twenty feet from the hole, more than likely they would make me get as close to the hole as possible so all they would have to do is watch me fall in after they pulled the trigger. They would more than likely toss Lupita on top of me and then they would cover us up, drive off in the cars and abandon the rental somewhere. Hopefully not realizing that they had a hidden passenger with them.

"Big Paul said you'd be a smooth-talking smart ass and that I should take delight in shutting you up." I rubbed the back of my head as she kicked me from behind to indicate that she wanted me to move closer to the hole. I needed Carmine or his partner very close, I needed one of them to get mad, lose control and attack me. I hoped that Betty would give me just a little more time. "Hey Carmine, your partner isn't saying much, did he get his jaw wired shut after that upper cut I gave him at Weinstein's?" I laughed; I mean he went down like a schoolboy! I mean one punch for Christ sakes, what a pussy." I laughed and stared directly at the man, and he did exactly what I wanted him to do, he let go of Lupita's arm and stepped toward me. "Hey Betty, I bet you didn't realize that Big Paul paired you up with a couple of grade A whimp's, but then again, maybe you did. You are supposed to dispose of them both too, aren't you?"

That really got under Carmine's skin and he took two steps closer to me, but he didn't attack like I needed him to. I didn't care which one attacked or if they both attacked, I just needed someone to come at me. "Here, look, my hands are in my pockets, take your best shot." I still couldn't tell where Betty was standing but for the sake of the exercise, I had to assume that she was directly behind me and if she was the professional, I thought she might be, she wouldn't stand for this charade very long and would simply pull the trigger. "I bet you wanted me to beg for my life? Well bull shit, I knocked both of you two pussies out with one punch each and neither of you have the balls to take a shot at me now."

I laughed a good hardy laugh and it was more than Carmine's partner could take, he lunged at me, I ducked the punch but stepped into him and grabbed him around the waist. As we both were falling, I was able to spin us in a direction so that I could see Betty with wide eyes, not believing that her partner would be so stupid, and I pulled the trigger on my little gun at the same time she pulled the trigger on hers. My shot made a small popping noise, but it hit the mark, the .22 caliber bullet went right into her throat, and she dropped the gun she was holding. I wasn't sure where her shot went but I heard another shot and felt a burn and sharp pain in my lower hip, but it didn't hurt, so I thought maybe we landed on a cactus or something hard. From the view I had behind his partner I could see Carmine; he was fumbling to get his gun out of his shoulder holster. I now had my left arm locked around his partners' throat, and as we were both lying on the ground, I extended my arm out from under him and I pulled the trigger on the final bullet I had in the chamber. I saw it hit Carmine in the left upper thigh; it had a weird thud sound to it. I am sure it hurt because he dropped to one knee, but he managed to raise his gun and unload the rest of his ammo on us. Luckily, most of the rounds went into his partner instead of me but the ones that found me were good ones. I didn't see Lupita fall to the ground having been struck by Betty Boop's wayward shot.

I didn't see Carmine bleed out in just a few minutes because the bullet that hit him in the thigh, hit his femoral artery too, and it was only a matter of minutes before Carmine went to visit with Saint Peter.

I had a good idea that before things went black that Carmine's partner had done a good job of shielding me from Carmine's bullets, and I also knew that I could hear Betty Boop gagging from the .22 bullet that went into her throat. Unfortunately for Betty, she was going to die a slow and painful death because not only did the bullet cut off her breathing, but it had also paralyzed her from the neck down. No, I really didn't see any of it; in fact, I don't remember any of it.

PART II

Chapter 19

Tio

"**I** took a shot at a coyote and missed. He got a chicken this morning." She looked out the kitchen window as if she were scanning the territory for the murderous coyote with a ravenous appetite. Louis sat at the little breakfast table that was in the middle of an oversized kitchen designed to store and prepare food for all the hands that lived and worked on the ranch. Louis was always in the kitchen before everyone else, even the company cook. He would sit at the table, sip coffee and read. He was an avid reader of all sorts. He especially loved mysteries and "who done its" but he also spent quite a bit of time reading his bible. "I planned to go after him today Miss V but first I have to chase that young bull back into his pasture, he broke free again."

Selina laughed at the comment and turned from the window. She leaned against the stainless-steel kitchen countertop and folded her arms into a comfortable resting position, "He does have an overly aggressive fondness for the ladies," she unfolded her arms and put her hands on her hips, "why do we have to go through this every day Tio?" She shook her head then walked over to the coffee pot and poured her a cup of coffee, two sugars and one cream. Louis had made fun of her coffee mix since the first day he made her a cup of coffee. She had known Louis her whole life. She called him "Tio" which meant "uncle" in Spanish, but he wasn't related to her. Louis was her father's right-hand man, in the old days they called him a range boss but in the modern era, all the "vaquero's" or cowboys called him Capitana. To Selina he was her sounding board, her friend, her advisor and in some regards, her father. "What is it miss V, go through what?" She took her cup of coffee and sat down at the kitchen table with him, "you used to just call me Selina, and somewhere along the way when I wasn't paying attention I guess, you started calling me Miss V and I hate it." Louis never looked up from his book, "hate is a very strong word miss V." She took a loud sip from her coffee then sighed, "ok, I guess hate is too strong of a word, I strongly dislike it."

Louis Arroyo never missed an opportunity to subtly correct Selina when they were together. He would never correct her in front of the cowboys or the staff of which there were many. Louis was constantly trying to maintain some kind of budget or at least something that resembled one at the double LL ranch. Selina was a tough-minded woman, and he was very proud of the way she ran the business, but she was also a softie. He would see someone new working in the kitchen, or the immediate vicinity of the ranch house and he would know that Miss Selina had picked up another "stray" in town. She was a pretty good judge of people but not always. It seemed that when she misjudged people, she misjudged them badly.

"Fine, I don't hate it, but I strongly dislike it." She smiled as she looked at him over her coffee cup, but he never lifted his head from the book he was reading. "You were there the day I was born, you gave me my first beer, you were there when," she paused and looked down at her cup, she started to continue but he finally looked up from his book, "these things are all true but life is a balance" he closed his book and picked up his coffee but he didn't take a drink from it, "should I suddenly become cavalier in the way I show my respect for you? Then so will the others." He then took a sip of coffee but realized that he had let it sit for too long and it was now cold, so he put it back down on the table. Selina had been through this routine with him so many times that when she saw him place the cup back on the table she immediately got up, took his cup to the sink, poured the coffee and then returned it to him with fresh hot coffee. As she sat back down in her chair across from him. Louis smiled, "gracias Miss V." She placed both her elbows on the table in front of her and rested her chin on her now clasped hands, Louis took a sip of his coffee but realized it was now just a little too hot and sat it back down on the table to cool. "Once the avalanche of the flippant familiarity of disrespect begins miss V, I'm afraid it is snow that cannot be put back on top of the mountain." She let out a sigh and shook her head, "you think respect comes from a title or a name?" Louis picked up his cup and tried another sip, "I just want to be me again, not Miss V, or ma'am or anything, I just want to be Selina again," she paused for a second and looked at him, "I just want to be normal again." Louis rubbed the stubble on his chin, he wasn't much on shaving regularly, "no ma'am, respect does not come from a name, it come from the actions of the person wearing the name." She pointed her finger at him in an accusatory way, "see! Even you admit that the name had little to do with it," she sort of laughed when she said it, but he interrupted her slight moment of argumentative victory, "most of our workers do not share the close proximity of your daily actions as I, therefore their respect for you comes from their close proximity to my actions Ms. V," he smiled and nodded his head in an acknowledging way. She knew he was right, she made it a point to let him do his job and to mostly stay out of the way of the help.

Since her father passed away of a heart attack, Louis had become the only man in her life. Tragedy seemed to follow Selina everywhere she went but Louis knew that it wasn't karma or bad medicine, it was simply all a part of some bigger plan for her. Her father was a great man in all regards, but he had his shortcomings too. He built the largest cattle ranch in all of Arizona with nothing but his wit, grit and determination. He worked hard and he played hard. It was nothing for Emanuel Villalpando to work 16-hour days, drink hard for 2 hours with anyone that could keep up with him, sleep for a couple hours and then start the process over again the next day. Louis was the closest person alive that could keep up with the pace of his best friend and boss. Manny as his closest friends called him, always said that without Louis by his side all those years of building a business, he would not have made it. Louis had become the only man in Selina's life, not by choice but by fate and it was a job that he took very seriously.

"Who is to say what normal is? Maybe this is normal for you? Maybe it would be too difficult for others but for you, it is your plan?" She started to say something, but he waved her off, he had been through this morning routine with her many times but today seemed a little different. This morning she was distant, this morning she was troubled, and he could tell. He had known her his whole life and he loved her as if she was his own daughter. "The Navajo's have a saying Cariño," Cariño was the name he called her when no one was around, it was a Spanish word for sweetheart, and it was his way of letting her know that he loved her without actually saying so. He was always careful not to step across the line of being a trusted friend and trying too hard to be her absentee father. He could never replace her father and he didn't ever want her to think that he was trying to. "They say *Walk in Beauty*". Selina tried to smile but it just wouldn't surface, "and what does that mean Tio?" Louis leaned forward and put his elbows on the table, "it means that life is about balance, it means that too much fun and no work is ugly, it means that too much sadness without joy is ugly, it means that too much rain and no sunshine is ugly and too much sunshine and no rain is ugly." She laughed, "you must have forgotten that we live in the southwest where rain is forever lacking." Louis nodded his head in agreement and let out a little chuckle, "I cannot argue that point, but you have always loved the cactus flowers, yes?" She nodded, "Cactus require little to no water, yet they flourish and produce flowers of immense beauty" he put his arms out as if he were Moses parting the sea, "It is God showing us how-to walk-in beauty, it is balance." He put his elbows back on the table, "you are out of balance, you carry the burdens of yesterday into today." She smiled and tilted her head back, "I know." She got up and grabbed a cast iron skillet off the stove, "my stomach tells me that I need a balanced breakfast this morning." She opened the double door refrigerator and pulled a carton of eggs out of it. "You want some eggs Tio?" Louis got up from the table and walked over to the stove where Selina was now cracking eggs into the skillet and put his arms around her. Since the day she was born, he had been intuitive about when Selina needed to be held. Her father, a great man, was not much on affection but he was always quick to tell her he loved her. Louis was quite the opposite; he couldn't get the words out of his mouth, but he was always there to embrace her when he knew she needed it. "What would I do without you Mr. Louis Arroyo." It wasn't a question; it was more of a proclamation. "I am going to skip breakfast this morning and head north and see if I can catch the trail of the coyote." She kept her eyes away from his because she didn't want him to see the uninvited tear that was rolling down her cheek. "Saddle my horse too please, I am going with you."

No matter how much he tried, he could never talk her out of her Vaquero ways. The truth of the matter was that Selina was a better cowboy than all the cowboys that occupied the bunk house. It wasn't because the cow hands were bad wranglers, it was just that Selina Villalpando was better. She could ride and rope as good as anyone had ever seen, including her father and Louis. Louis couldn't ever figure out if the reason that most of the men stayed away from her was because she was a more skilled wrangler than they were or because she was the boss lady. Either way he was happy that none of the current crop of cow hands ever tried anything with her because he would surely set them straight, either with stern words or clinched fists, he would let them know she was off limits. She wasn't ready for a relationship again and he knew it. Selina was exceptionally beautiful and would have made some one very happy if she would show them some attention, but she was still grieving. She didn't enjoy being referred to as a widow but there was no other word for it. Louis always gave her the space she needed to deal with the emotions of losing her husband and he kept others from crowding in on her as well.

Louis may have been getting up in years, but he was intimidating in his own right. He could handle himself very well with anyone that wanted to try. The double L ranch had always had its trouble with illegal's trespassing on their land as they crossed from Mexico to the U.S. Selina would try to help them when she could, and she would leave fresh water for them at certain locations. The double L ranch was vast and in certain locations, water was very scarce. The local border patrol would warn her that she could be cited for a crime, but she didn't care. Selina always took the position that if someone wanted to make a better life for themselves in America and took the risks that these people were taking, then she needed to do everything she could legally to help them. She had windmill driven stock tanks all over her ranch and even though border patrol agents argued that it was illegal, leaving drinkable water in strategic locations was her way of thumbing her nose at law enforcement, the same law enforcement that failed to help her when she needed it the most.

"Ms. V, you don't need to go, I can handle a few simple coyote's, please stay." Selina stood at the stove as she was scrambling her eggs, "no, I need to ride for a few days, it will make me feel better. You know what they say," she lifted her spatula to illustrate the upcoming proclamation, "the outside of a horse is good for the inside of a woman." Louis shook his head, "or man" She laughed, "exactly! Not to mention that Jake still hasn't brought in those broke mouths." Even though he knew it, he hated to be reminded that one of his hands wasn't preforming up to standard and Jake was surely struggling.

Jake was a good kid, but his biggest problem was his daydreaming, and an even worse problem was, his sense of direction. He would get turned around in the kitchen if he stayed too long. To Jake, north was up, and south was down, that was the extent of his sense of direction. Jake came to the ranch, broke, hungry and willing to do anything that helped put a roof over his head and food in his stomach. He had his personal battles with drugs and alcohol as a teenager and ended up on the streets of Phoenix begging for food and money. Selina bumped into him on 6th street coming out of a lawyer's office. At first, she thought he was trying to mug her but quickly realized he was just clumsy. He asked her for some spare change and true to Selina's kind heart, she gave him some money and her famous lecture about self-respect that comes from hard work and how hard work is the first step to independence and that independence leads to freedom. Louis had heard it so many times that he could probably recite it by memory.

Selina may have been a soft heart, but she was tough as any woman or man he'd ever met. She would not tolerate loafers and if you signed on to work for her, she intended to not only make you a top-notch hand at the double L, but she also intended to make you a better person. Jake was in the early stages of his transformation, but Louis had his doubts that he'd ever make a good cow hand. The way Louis saw it, if Jake couldn't find his way out of the bunk house to breakfast, he'd never be able to find a stray or bring in some long-toed cows. Jake could rope, he could handle an unruly horse and he wasn't afraid of hard work, but Louis also knew that it didn't matter what he thought, when Selina made up her mind to help someone, there was no stopping her. He had to admit though, he never thought Jake would make it a week but here he was, one year later from the time he nearly knocked her over coming out of the lawyer's office in Phoenix still trying to be a cowboy.

Chapter 20

Benjamin

Selina stood in front of the mirror, it was something that she rarely ever did and ran her fingers through her hair and just like every day for the past three weeks, when she pulled her hand away from her head, she could see that there were several strands of hair that came with it. She shook the hair on her hand and watched the strands fall into the little trash container beside her dresser. As she stood there in front of the mirror she tried to think of happier times when he was there, times when she might have been standing in this very spot and he would come up behind her and put his arms around her and pull her close to him. He would kiss her neck and whisper in her ear, she remembered the things he would say to her, the way he said them and how good it felt to have him pressed against her. There were some mornings that his caressing would be so intense that she could feel him getting aroused against her. She would blush when she felt him getting larger against her backside as he would put his hands on her hips and pull her tightly against him. At those times she could see them both in the mirror. Looking in the mirror and watching his hands roam every arousal spot on her body was heaven to her. She hadn't ever been touched like he touched her, and five years into the marriage he was still driving her crazy with his hands. As she looked in the mirror, she would see the skin around her neck get red splotches when it was happening because she was generally a shy woman. She would get those red splotches when she got nervous and aroused. She knew what he wanted, and he knew what she wanted, and it was certain that both of them wanted the same thing. Even though she had just gotten dressed, during those moments he would still manage to undress her and carry her back to bed.

It didn't happen every morning, but it happened often enough that everyone knew not to wait on them to eat breakfast. They had been married for five years and even though their morning ritual may have seemed routine, it was anything but routine. Every time he kissed her and touched her; it was like he was touching her for the first time. She could see the look on his face and feel the immense passion in his touch. She loved him with a passion that she couldn't explain, and she was now alone, heartbroken and still grieving because someone had decided to take him from her.

She woke up every morning reliving that awful day, wishing that it was all a nightmare, and that she would reach over to his side of the bed, and he would be there, but it didn't take long to realize that it was indeed real life, and he was not there. Subconsciously before she even began the motion of trying to touch him in the morning, she knew he wouldn't be there. She knew because she wouldn't have to reach for him, he would already have her in his arms as they slept because every night, he tightly cradled her in his arms, pulling her so close to him that their breathing seemed to become as one, as each rise and fall of their chests matched the other. His habit of draping his left arm over her and cupping her right breast as they slept made her smile every time she thought about it. She loved that each night, he held her as if he was afraid someone would try and take her away from him as they slept.

She took one last glance at herself in the mirror then looked for her hat, a wide brimmed Resistol that had plenty of wear and tear and had kept the sun off of her for many years. Ben would try and get her to change hats, but she wouldn't think of it. She had plenty of Cowboy hats that she could wear but this one had settled on her head nicely over the years and it was so comfortable that she would often forget it was on her head. She stuck the Resistol on her head, looked in the mirror and whispered his name and blew him a kiss, "Ben".

Selina met Benjamin Allan Walker when she was in college at Northern Arizona University in Flagstaff. She was getting her mechanical engineering degree and he was getting his degree in business. At the time, all she could think about was getting off the ranch and becoming her own person. She didn't mind ranching; in fact, she was very good at it, but she was the classic kid that wanted badly to see the world and be her own person.

She and Ben met when he entered the women's bathroom at a downtown Mexican restaurant by mistake. She was leaving and he was entering. He wasn't a towering figure but at that moment, standing in front of him in that doorway, he looked like a mountain. "One of us in the wrong place" was the comment he made, and she quickly quipped back, "or both of us are in the right place." She blushed when she said it because it was unexpected for to her, cheesy. He laughed and looked around and realized it was he who was in the wrong place.

When he went to his restroom and her back to her table, she giggled like a little girl. She happened to be on a date, but she didn't care. Much to her surprise, he found her at her table and walked over to introduce himself and apologized for his mistake and shook her hand. When he did, he slid a torn piece of business card in her hand that she discreetly slid into her jeans pocket without her date knowing a thing. For good measure he shook her dates hand and complimented him on his cufflinks and left.

Later that night after she was safely in her own room, she pulled the torn business card from her pocket and looked at it. She laughed out loud when she read what he wrote, "Will you marry me, yes or no?" He had included his cell phone number, but he also made the little boxes kids used in elementary school for her to check yes or no. She tried to sleep that night, but it was nearly impossible, she wanted to call the number, but she didn't want to seem eager or aggressive but something inside her told her that this guy was different. She waited an entire week before she called him, and it was the longest week of her life.

As she finished getting ready, she recalled the first real conversation she had with her future husband, "Hi, I uh . . ." her face flushed and she struggled to get the words out of her mouth, she pulled the phone away from her ear and looked at it like it was broken but she knew what the problem was, her. She was not good at small talk and dating but this was the first time she had actually called a guy back. He interrupted her, "well, did you think about it?" She tried desperately to think about what he was referring to, but her mind had gone blank, she was usually sharp witted but at the moment, she was at a loss for words. She heard his voice on the other end of the conversation again, "I know it is sudden, but I just know." She finally gathered herself, took a deep breath, "you are quite sure of yourself, aren't you?" It was a statement and not a question from her, but he answered it anyway. "God put me in that spot for a reason and the minute I saw you, I knew what that reason was." She started to respond but before the words came out of her mouth he continued, "besides, if I weren't right, you wouldn't have called me back."

"I think you are assuming too much, and you are full of yourself." He started to respond but this time she cut him off, "You better ask me out on a first date before you ask me to marry you." She heard him laugh on the other end but then his voice came to life again,

"Ok, I can probably wait through one date and then ask you, it will be tough though." This time she laughed, "for all I know you may be a murdering sociopath, so I want you to know that I am very proficient in firearms, and I have a conceal carry permit in 4 states!" She really didn't have a permit, but she wanted him to think so, but she laughed at his answer, "then I will feel safe wherever I go with you."

He gave her time to laugh at his comment then he became serious, "would you like to go see a movie and have dinner with me?" The nervous joking and bantering stopped, she knew he was serious, and she wanted to scream into the phone that she badly wanted to go out on a date with him, but she steadied her breathing and replied, "yes, I would like that very much." There was a moment of awkward silence, but it didn't last long. Ben seemed to know how to keep things in balance, "Great! Then we can get married!" She shook her head in amazement even though she thought he was a jokester, somehow, he was conveying the message that he was serious. "Geez, my mind tells me that you are a nut case, but I am going through with this anyway."

She adjusted the Resistol one more time then turned to look back at the bed she had slept in alone. She knew she was depressed and was almost out of energy to keep up the fight with the government, the border patrol, the drug smugglers, the constant tension with the Barstow brothers and now the human traffickers. She had Louis to help her with all of it, but she missed her husband, and she missed her father. It was simply not in her genetic make-up to play the damsel in distress, so she looked back in the mirror, smiled and walked out of the room. Three days on her horse would do her good.

Chapter 21

Big Cat

Louis was saddling her horse as she walked into the barn, "Tio, stop that, you know I can do it myself." He smiled and cinched the front strap snug. "He is a fine animal and enjoys his time with you. I can see it in his eyes when you enter the barn." Louis finished saddling her horse for her before she could do anything but put her arm under BB's neck and stroke him. He threw his head up and down to signal his pleasure and then pawed at the dirt beneath his feet. Selina loved all types of music but when she was trying to sort things out in her head, she either listened to BB King or Van Morrison. Her love for BB King led to her naming this horse after him. She trained this horse herself and her affection for him was renowned. He was beautiful, tall, and dark with three white socks, and he was a top-notch quarter horse that could hold his own with the best cutters on the planet. Selina loved him like he was her child and anybody with a good eye for horses could tell he felt the same way about her. "Don't forget the bed roll and tent." Louis was fiddling with his own horse saddle now and stopped. He lowered his head to the point that his forehead was against the saddle. He was clearly frustrated. "Ms. V you should not be out riding for that long. You know it is not safe." Selina found a curry brush and was treating BB to it, "You know it's my job Tio." He raised his head up off the saddle and turned to look at her, "no Selina it is not, you are the owner, you are the CEO of this ranch now. You don't ride the fences or sleep in tents or line shacks. You lead ma'am, you guide, you make the ranch work with your brains and not your brawn." Selina stopped combing BB and laughed. She put the back of her hand that held the brush against her forehead in a dramatic way, "I believe that is the most words you've ever strung together in your whole life." Louis walked behind his horse and then reappeared with a bed roll and tent, he threw them on the back of his horse and began to strap them down, but Selina stopped him, "nope, you know you have to meet with the vet tomorrow morning and reload supplies." Louis stopped what he was doing and again put his forehead against the horse. He knew she was troubled, and he was worried that she might do something silly, and he was trying to keep an eye on her. If she took off for three days, he would not be able to keep track of her. "The tumultuous river of stubbornness runs deep in your family." She laughed and started brushing BB again, "you got that right Tio." He took the bed roll off his horse and placed it on hers, he tied it down along with the tent. He then went into the little office that was built in the barn just for him and returned holding a rifle and phone. "He slid the Henry repeater in the case and fixed it to her saddle. He looked around and found the saddle bags that had her initials on them (SAW), Selina Analise Walker. They were a gift from her husband the first Christmas they shared as a couple. People around town and on the ranch still called her Ms. Villalpando. At first, she tried to correct them, but she grew tired of it. Even her husband, Benjamin Walker would be referred to as Mr. Villalpando when they were together. He never seemed to mind or let it bother him, but he always politely corrected them.

Louis slid the satellite phone in the bag and closed the clasp, "the sat phone is fully charged. Since I have no influence over you, I hope you will be respectful of my concerns and check in at the appropriate intervals." Selina stopped combing and stroked BB's nose, "Yes Tio, every 4 hours, but since you are with me on the first day can we skip it today?" She laughed and stroked BB some more. "You are troubled young lady, this much I know, and I worry." He finished securing everything on their saddles and mounted his horse. She looked up at him, she could see the love in his eyes, and she knew he was truly worried about her. "I know what you are trying to do Ms. V," he took his hat off and fiddled with the brim as he spoke. "He had nothing to do with those two girls and you know that. You won't find any more clues or answers out there." Selina stopped moving and stood completely still, "then why were they with him?" Louis put his hat on his head, and he pulled the reins to steer his horse out of the barn, he didn't say anything to her he just slowly guided his horse out of the barn.

Selina looked at BB and patted his neck one more time, "I guess that means we gotta go baby." She reached for the saddle horn, stuck her left boot in the stirrup and mounted BB like she had done thousands of times before and began following Louis. As she felt the gate of the horse and adjusted her own motions to the horse, she felt her hip and found what she was looking for, she was thankful that somehow, subconsciously maybe, she had strapped her colt .45 Devil Anse to her belt. She didn't remember doing it, but she was glad she had. It was a single action revolver with a seriously black barrel, beautiful black grips and it was deadly accurate, at least for her. She was an excellent shot with it. She never ventured out on the ranch without it.

"Are we going to talk any as we ride or are we just going to enjoy the moment?" She kept her horse to the right of Louis, a practice that she learned as a child. If you rode with Louis, you stayed to his right, not because he preferred it that way but because he was almost completely deaf in his left ear and if you didn't stay to his right, he wouldn't hear a thing you said. Louis looked to his right and saw her right beside him. BB was slightly taller than Nell, an appaloosa that Louis rescued from a nearby farm. The horse had been mistreated badly and was near death when Louis discovered her. She was tangled up in some barbed wire for what appeared to be several days. It was an accident that he found her. He found her when he was tracking a wayward steer onto a neighboring farm. He gently cut her loose and instead of running away when she was freed, she stood up with her dehydrated wobbly legs and stood next to Louis. He didn't know how long she had been there, but he decided since the owner wasn't looking for her, he claimed her. He managed to get the vet out to the site because she was too weak to make it back to the ranch. Louis stayed with her at that very spot for two weeks straight until she was strong enough to make it back to the ranch. Louis Arroyo was that kind of man.

"I guess that means I get to talk to hear myself talk." Selina adjusted her hat and drew the draw string so that it would not blow off. It was breezy today and strong gusts of winds were very common in this part of Arizona. She didn't have to do much with BB, he seemed to read her mind and know where she wanted to go, all she did was sit comfortably in the saddle and enjoy the scenery.

Since Louis wasn't in a talking mood, she suspected he was mad at her for taking this trip, but she didn't really care. She was in search of some answers, and she knew that if she kept looking, she would find what she was looking for. "Tell me again, please." Louis stopped Nell and turned to look at Selina, he had a look of frustration that she had seen before but again, she didn't care. She allowed BB to trot right by him without looking at him directly and took the lead. "I know you don't want to talk about it." She continued to trot ahead, "my husband was found murdered with two little girls beside him,"

BB flickered his mane as if to support her need for information. "We don't know how the girls got there, who they were and why they were with him," she spoke in a way that indicated she has had this conversation a thousand times and always coming to the same conclusion, "He was not a trafficker, I don't care what the police say."

Louis was the one that found them that day. Selina tried several times to reach him on the satellite phone to no avail. He had gone out to repair a windmill and never returned. The ranch bordered a different country, so everyone knew you had to be careful, for as long as she had been able to remember, there were always illegal crossings but here lately it was like someone had turned the spigot on full blast. Along with the increased illegal crossings came drugs and now human smugglers. The human smugglers were a bad element and left a trail of destruction everywhere they went, and they were leaving a path of destruction right through her ranch.

"I don't know why you want to talk about it, it won't bring him back." She was surprised that Louis answered, she was sure that he was going to be quiet today. Louis leaned forward in his saddle and scanned the ground beneath him as the horse slowly trotted north. "I can't tell if the tracks are old, we haven't had any rain, so I am guessing they are new." He sat straight up in the saddle again. "It is more than one though." He was avoiding the subject Selina most desperately wanted to talk about, "I think we just head north for a while."

For the next four hours the only conversation was the conversation she had with herself. She would talk to herself as she rode, a habit she picked up when she was a little girl, she would follow behind her dad as the two rode all over the ranch. Her dad didn't talk too much but he liked to hear the conversations that Selina would have with her imaginary friends as they rode together. Louis never said so, but he enjoyed hearing her work through her problems with whatever imaginary friends she continued to talk to. Louis realized quickly that when Selina became the head of the ranch through the death of her father and husband that she would have very few close friends, if any, that could understand what she was going through. He also knew that she was a real prize for some wide eyed, get rich quick caballero that wanted her body but wanted her money and land even more.

"I think we stop for a few minutes and let the horses rest," Louis was already getting off his horse when she realized that he had spoken. She pulled the reigns back on her horse just slightly and he immediately stopped. Selina eased out of the saddle and listened to the leather make its noisy leather sounds. She loved the sound that a saddle made when you were climbing on or off a horse. "I think that's a good idea." Selina reached into her saddle bag and pulled out a brown paper bag. "You want a peanut butter sandwich?" Before he could answer, Selina fished around in the bag and came up with two sandwiches and tossed one to Louis. He caught it effortlessly as he was climbing off his horse. Louis was a gifted athlete back in his day, he was an excellent third baseman and an even better pitcher. Everyone said he could have played in the major leagues if he hadn't walked away from baseball to work for her dad. He played in the Arizona-Mexico League in 1952 and was making quite a name for himself as a heavy hitting 3rd baseman who also pitched second in the four-man starting rotation. Selina knew that he loved baseball, but she never understood why he walked away, came to work for her dad and never looked back.

"Do you regret that you didn't keep playing baseball?" Louis smiled instantly, Selina knew that if she couldn't get him to open up, all she had to do was mention baseball. "It is a game, not much more than that." He tried to look away as he said it, but she caught the twinkle in his eyes. She took a bite of her sandwich, chewed for second and decided she couldn't let the moment die or she would never get him to open up to her like she wanted. "You have a point there, but to you, it is much more. Anyone with a good eye can spot the way you light up at the mention of baseball." He looked at her then tossed his eyes back towards the Santa Rita mountains that loomed in the distance. "It is true that I love the game, but it is still a game. I love the strategy and what it means more than the game itself. I love the way each man is an individual but must function as a team." He took a bite of his sandwich but then slid it back into the plastic baggie that Selina had stuck it in, "baseball mimics life and life mimics baseball." He stood up and put the sandwich back in his saddle bag. No one can play baseball by themselves, and no one can play the game of life by themselves, not even the strongest man or woman. Each must have someone to help them, to guide them, to talk to them, to hear them. He paused and petted his horse on its back-left flank causing it to flick its tail in his direction. The horses tail brushed against his face and nearly knocked his hat off. Louis patted the horse again as if to say thank you for flicking him in the face then looked back at Selina, "I will eat the rest later."

Selina took his motions as a signal that it was time to get moving again, this was her trip but as usual, Louis was always playing the role of the ramrod. He didn't like to talk very much, even when he was in a good mood. Selina never stopped trying to get him to talk though, she found that if she could strike the right chord, he would open up ever so slightly, but she had to navigate the conversational waters with him very carefully. If she struck the wrong chord, he wouldn't say another word for hours at a time. Baseball, horses and Elizabeth, were subjects that could get him talking but you had to be careful with Elizabeth, he was in love with her, but he didn't love her enough to give up the cowboy lifestyle. He would go into town as much as he could and eat dinner at the diner where she worked. They would flirt a little but never too much, everyone in town knew that Elizabeth wanted so badly for Louis to ask her to marry him, but he never did. He could talk about Lisa with a smile on his face but if you ever got close to talking about marrying her, he would clam up.

After they got back on their horses from their sandwich break, the horses walked side by side for several miles. It was a quiet ride where you could hear the sound of the horse's hooves clump against the ground. Silence and Selina didn't go very well together but when she was with Louis, she was patient. "Did you see Lisa last night?" Louis didn't answer her, but Selina would not be deterred, "You better marry that woman soon, before someone else does." Selina could hear Louis chuckle a little as he took his hat off and wiped his forehead with his sleeve. Even though it was October, it was still hot in the desert. "Lisa and I have an understanding, Selina." Now it was Selina's turn to chuckle, "that's what you think, but you better stop thinking that way or you will lose her." Louis chuckled again, "you think you know more about love than anyone don't you?" It was Selina's turn to chuckle, "I know more than you and that's the point," she adjusted her position in the saddle then continued, "that is one of the best women in town and you've been stringing her along for how many years now?" It wasn't really a question because she didn't let him respond, "You taste a woman's fruit for 10 years or more, I'd say it's time to harvest the crop." Selina had a way of keeping things simple in the conversation with Louis, not because she didn't think he was smart but because simple was his language. She knew that Louis was extremely smart, but he didn't care much for people that tried to prove how smart they were by using big words. Most of the euphemisms she learned all came from Louis anyway.

Louis started to say something, but Selina kept her part of the conversation going. "You are worried about me, you are worried if you marry her, you won't be able to provide the attention to me that you think I need," she turned to look at him, "that's a bunch of hooey and you know it." Without any warning she drew her revolver and fired a shot. The shot startled Louis's appaloosa just a bit and she stepped sideways away from the noise. Louis quickly turned to look at her and he had every intention of yelling at her for being careless with her use of firearms but as he turned, he saw that she was aiming to their right and she fired another shot. "What the hell is that son of bitch doing all the way down here!" The excitement was in Selina's voice, "He was 20 feet from us and about ready to pounce!" Louis looked beyond Selina in the direction she was still aiming her revolver. At first, he couldn't see anything other than desert sand and cactus but then he saw it spring up with one last burst of energy and lunge at the two of them. Selina fired the third time and this time the mountain lion dropped like a sack of bricks.

Selina started to get off her horse, but Louis told her to sit still, he had never seen a mountain lion this far south and wasn't sure what to think. "Stay on BB, he might be rabid, you never know." Selina, as usual, ignored his advice of caution, "He's dead, that last shot caught him right between the eyes." Louis had no choice now but to dismount and follow her towards the spot where the mountain lion lay dead. Even though Louis knew that the lion was dead, he just didn't like the idea of Selina getting too close to it. "He is a big damn cat Tio." Louis looked down at the mountain lion and had to agree, he had seen plenty of mountain lions in Arizona, especially up around the Mogollon rim but he had never seen one down here. He looked healthy to Louis, "He is a big one, I'd say he is close to 200 pounds for certain." Selina reached down touched its fur, "Mrs. V!" Louis did not like her touching the animal, he was still in disbelief that a cat that size would be down here in the desert. "Louis stop, he can't get any deader. He had three bullets in him which pisses me off that I didn't drop him with one shot, and I had to ruin his beautiful head." She petted him as if he were a house cat, "I may still have Jacknack come out here and see if he can skin him out and mount him for me. I've never shot a mountain lion." Jacknack worked on the Villalpando ranch for as long as Louis had. His real name was

Jack Nackard and he could do anything as far as Selina could tell. He was an expert taxidermist, but he was also an expert cowboy. Like Louis, he was getting up in years, so Selina found things for him to do on the ranch that didn't involve him spending too much time on horseback. Jacknack was thrown from a horse while he was out one day when a rattle snake spooked his horse enough to throw him from the saddle causing him to land in the dry creek bed they were crossing when they spooked the snake, but it also caused him to land on the snake at which time it bit Jacknack on shoulder. Jacknack made it back to the ranch in time to be life flighted to Tucson where he damn near died, not from the snake bite but from the punctured lung and ruptured spleen. Jacknack was a walking miracle as far as Selina was concerned but if you ask Jacknack about it he would just shrug and say that it was all a part of being a cowboy.

Selina walked back over to her horse leaving Louis standing beside the dead mountain lion. Louis was staring down at the mountain lion and cursing himself under his breath. He should have seen the threat before Selina, he was supposed to protect and look after Selina, and he had failed to do so. He found himself getting angry at the mountain lion for having just illustrated to Selina that he was no longer capable of protecting her like he once did. In the past Louis would have smelled the lion, spotted the lion and if not, he would have been riding a horse that would have alerted him to the threat but here he was, a dottering old fool that damn near got them killed by being old and soft. He could hear Selina on the satellite phone talking to Jacknack. She was giving him the coordinates of their location and telling him to bring the Willys. The ranch owned many off-road vehicles but if Jacknack couldn't ride a horse anymore, he would only drive the Willys. The Willys was an old-World War II jeep that he had restored to near perfect condition.

Selina slid the phone back into the saddle bag and walked back over to the dead cat. "Jacknack was excited to have something to do. I gave him the coordinates and he will be here in an hour." She looked around and could see the sun going down over the mountain range to the west. "I am just gonna camp here for tonight, you can head back." Louis let out a deep breath, "I am very sorry Cariño." Selina turned her stare away from the dead mountain lion and looked at Louis with a confused look on her face. "Come again? What are you sorry for?" Louis took his hat off and fiddled with the brim as he spoke. It was his "poker tell" for Selina, she had come to realize he took on this little tick when he was nervous and apprehensive about saying what was on his mind. Make no mistake, Louis wasn't scared of anything that Selina knew except, revealing conversations.

"I should have seen this beast before it got so close, I was unaware that age had dulled my senses and my wits until just now." Selina looked at him with an even more confused look. She started to say something, but Louis started speaking again. "You were right, I have not married Elizabeth because I believe that a man can only truly love and protect one woman at a time and you are my first love, you are my responsibility." Selina put her hand on his shoulder then proceeded to slide her arm completely around him so that he was in her half embrace, "Just because my father told you to look out for me doesn't mean that you can't live your own life. It doesn't mean that you have to give up everything in order to be there to catch me when I fall, fight my battles for me or sleigh mountain lions." She looked down at the lion then back at him. Their faces were so close together that she could see the hair inside his ear. She smiled and for the first time in her life she saw Louis as an old man, one that she now needed to look out for. His job looking out for her was complete and he needed to have a life of his own. She felt a little selfish at that moment for not recognizing it sooner but now that reality had just bit her in the ass, she was determined to do something about it.

"It's time you stop saddling my horse and start saddling hers." Louis lowered his head and mumbled something, but Selina couldn't make it out. "Get on your horse, go to the restaurant tonight and ask her to marry you." She kissed him on the cheek and gave him a strong one arm squeeze then let go of him. Selina turned away from Louis and started to walk back to her horse then stopped and said, "by the way, if I hadn't been trying to flick an inadvertently picked booger off my finger, I would have never seen the damn cat either, age has nothing to do with it, it was luck that kept us both from being cat shit tomorrow." Selina had a way with words too.

Chapter 22

Traditions

Selina watched Louis as he rode south back towards the ranch house. She knew he was hurting on the inside, and she wished she could roll back the hands of time to where she was just a happy little girl getting into all kinds of mischief around the ranch.

Afterwards Selina pitched her small tent, nothing more than three center posts and a flimsy canvas that wouldn't keep the cold night air off her but would certainly keep her somewhat sheltered. She was never worried about snakes sneaking into bed with her on the desert floor, BB was her alarm for any danger. She would tie BB's lead rope through a grommet in her bed roll so that if BB got spooked, he would yank on her covers. BB was very good at detecting snakes but then Selina second guessed his reliability with the thought of that cougar getting so close to all of them without him being able to detect the stalking cat.

The night air was a little chilly so she found a small juniper that would provide enough fire for the evening. Jacknack would be along soon, and he would take this big cat back to the ranch and begin the process of making him a stuffed trophy. She crossed her legs meditation style and did just that. She tried to close out the thoughts of the day and the troubles that kept her from sleeping. She loved the desert; this was her sanctuary. This was where she could find answers through meditation and prayer. She wasn't raised religious but when she married Benjamin, he introduced her to regular church. Technically her family was catholic, and she understood religion but never connected with it until she met Benjamin. When she began combining meditation with prayer, she found that she could cope with life much better. She practiced her breathing and focused on clearing her mind of painful thoughts and simply focused on the desert, the night air, the crackle of the fire and the coyote howling in the distance.

The happy thoughts of her childhood came to the front of her mind as she saw herself running from stable to stable to see how fast she could pet each horse. She loved to climb in the loft and play in the hay that was stored there. When the hay was getting low, she would make her own fort out of the it and could spend hours pretending to be her own boss, making decisions and telling her imaginary ranch hands what to do. She remembered holding her father's hand as they walked the trail that led to the small rock outcroppings that offered up memories of people a long time ago by the petroglyphs, they left for others to interpret. That spot on the ranch was one of her favorites. She remembered her dad telling her stories about the odd drawings on the rocks and how they told the story of fierce and brave warriors from long ago and how those people worked hard to carve out a life on the land that they now occupied and called the La Leche Madre ranch.

Sitting by that fire that night, waiting in Jacknack to arrive she found a peace that she hadn't found in a very long time. She listened to her heartbeat and focused on what was good and right in her life and tried to put behind all that was bad. She came to the realization that she couldn't bring her husband back and trying to make sense of his death was futile. There was no making sense of death only that she must accept it as inevitable and that all things happen for a reason, and it is more in God's hands that it was in hers. She focused on controlling what she could control and learning to cope with what she could not by trusting her creator more than she had in the past.

Selina was abruptly forced out of her thoughts and meditation by the unmistakable sound of Jacknack's Willy jeep as it approached the site. She opened her eyes and starred up at the Stars that were slowly coming to life above her and smiled. She realized that her issues were not that simple and couldn't be solved in a one-hour meditation period here in the desert, but she did feel better. Seeing Louis so distraught over not hearing the Mountain Lion and how she saw herself as his protector now, not the other way around gave her more resolve to be strong than she has had in a very long time. She felt rejuvenated.

The jeep rolled up right next to where she was standing. She waited for Jacknack to turn off the engine before she spoke. Even though it was getting dark, the flicker of the campfire gave her a clear view of Jacknack and he was clearly smiling. "What are you happy about?" Jacknack climbed out of the jeep, "well, it's nice to have something to do for a change, it's nice to be needed." Jacknack had been a part of the Double L ranch for as long as she could remember, it was no secret that he was one of best hands they had, if not the best. His back and neck injury came from a freak accident for sure but from a liability standpoint, the ranch could not afford have him on a horse any longer. The doctor told them that if he was thrown from a horse again, he would more than likely end up dead or paralyzed. It was common knowledge that for a cowboy to be removed from the back of a horse is usually equivalent to a death sentence for a true cowboy, but Selina was committed to keeping him working at the ranch for as long as he wanted to. His wisdom with horses and his instincts for cattle and behavior were unmatched. She could hire a hundred young cowboys and every one of them would work themselves silly all day long trying to accomplish a task that Jacknack could complete in an hour.

"You dramatically underestimate your value to me Mr. Nackard" She watched him swing sideways out of the jeep and gently slide out of it. "Louis and I talked for a minute when we crossed each other's path just now, it's like someone took the starch out of his britches." Selina pushed her hat off her head and let the draw string do its job as it now rested on her back. "Yeah, well we will work on that one later but let me introduce you to the fella that took the starch out of his britches." Selina motioned for Jacknack to follow her to where the cat was still lying stretched out like it was resting on its stomach and stretching its legs. The last bullet that Selina put in him dropped him at the moment he was about to leap. "Well, I will be dipped in sheep shit, would you look at that!" Jacknack bent down and pet the cougar's fir just as Selina had done, "that's one big damn kitty cat." Jacknack picked up on of the cat's paws and placed his hand against it, Selina was surprised to see that Jacknack's hand disappeared. "Geez, he would have eaten you and Louis for dinner tonight for sure." Selina nodded, "yep, I don't fancy being cat shit any time soon, that's for sure." Selina bent down so that she could be next to Jacknack, "in all your time here in the desert, have you ever seen a cat this far down this time of the year?" Jacknack tinkered with the cat's paw trying to get it's claws to extend all the way out, "ma'am, I aint seen a cat this far down ever, never mind what time of the year it is." Selina stood up but Jacknack stayed crouched next to cougar. "He sure aint starving so can't no tree hugger say that he's been run out of his habitat," he paused and ran his hand all the way down the length of the beast, "My guess is, he's got a few double L broke mouths in his belly." Selina knelt back down again, "Jake should have those in by now, shouldn't he?" It was Jacknack's turn to stand up, "aint up to me to be tellin you how to run your spread ma'am but he is dumber than a bag of bent hammers, don't know why you keep trying with that boy. He aint never gonna be a cowboy."

Jacknack acted like he was going to say something else but abruptly stopped. "And …" Selina was never one to let a conversation die so easily. Jacknack didn't say anything, so she tried again, "Go on, you were going to say something else, finish." Jacknack stopped petting the beast and stood up, "I got out over my ski's ma'am, not my nature to speculate or advise." Selina put her hands on her hips, but she forgot that she had her revolver on her hip and decided to fold her arms across her chest instead, "Oh bullshit, you make a living speculating, that's pretty much what cowboyin is, you speculate which way the calf is gonna break, you speculate which bulls are the best for the heard, you speculate which horse is ought to do what, so cut the crap and start speaking your mind around me." Selina was dressing him down and it was for a reason. Selina was always thinking ahead, she knew that she would probably lose Louis to matrimony soon and she would need another ramrod. She figured that even though he couldn't ride a horse anymore he could sure keep the ranch hands in check. "Well ma'am, it's like this, I think for some reason I aint figured out yet, he wants us to think he is stupid. I think he is smarter than the lets on." Selina was somewhat surprised to hear Jacknack say that, but she decided she didn't want to let him know that. Jacknack turned and started walking back towards where he parked the jeep, "where are you going?" Jacknack never stopped walking but answered her over his shoulder, "Gonna back the jeep up and set up the hoist."

Jacknack slowly backed the jeep into the best position to hoist the animal high enough to gut it. It was important to get rid of the animal guts before he hauled it back to the ranch. Selina was still standing by the cougar when he killed the engine. "I thought you'd want to get it back to the ranch." Jacknack didn't say anything as he quickly assembled the A frame hoist that he had custom made for the jeep that was complete with a power winch. Selina stood there and watched him. She was comfortable enough around Jacknack that she wasn't offended with his lack of responses. She had learned over time that a cowboy didn't always respond right away to questions and had their own pace to a conversation.

"You need me to do anything?" Jacknack ran the chain through the hoist then handed Selina the free end of the chain, "secure the hind legs", Selina did as she was asked and felt like she had the giant paws secured. Selina was excellent at field dressing a deer or and elk, but she had never done a large cat. She didn't hesitate in the least little bit, she knew that if Jacknack saw her do anything that was wrong in the process, he would correct her without hesitation. She nodded at Jacknack to signal that she had completed the task and he pushed the button on the automatic hoist handheld control. The motor started winding the slack and soon the cat was hanging by its back legs.

She watched Jacknack go to work on the cat and marveled at his skill with a knife, a very sharp knife. "Aint cold enough to salvage any of this meat longer than another hour so we are having mountain lion for dinner as soon as I'm done", he paused as he inspected an incision he was making as he was trying to slowly peel the hide away from the meat, "we'll both have to explain to the man why we chose not to nourish from that which we have taken." This comment took Selina by surprise as she never figured Jacknack for a religious man. She had been taught that guys like Jacknack, Louis and especially her father, didn't practice a faith very much but they each had their own code, sort of a cowboy code that paralleled the ten commandments for the most part. She knew from experience that Cowboy's weren't saints by any stretch but at the end of the day they always tried to do the right thing, at least the cowboys she grew up with.

"Why Jack Nackard, I never figured you for a religious man." Jacknack continued to remove the hide from cat with the precision of a neurosurgeon, "pull the jeep up about four feet before I slip in this gut pile", he paused then pointe his knife at the pile beneath him but slightly to his right, "hang on", he reached down into the gut pile and pulled something out. It was getting pretty dark so Selina couldn't quite see but she had a good idea, "don't you even think about it", Selina stepped back away from him as she spoke, "it's disrespectful mam." Selina stopped moving away from him, "I'm not eating that heart Jacknack if that's what you are thinking." Jacknack arched his back a little, "mam, this is a magnificent creature, the man sent it to you for a reason, to ignore that is not natural." Selina started to say something witty, but she could hear the seriousness in his voice, "the natives believed that this type of animal was a fierce and respected competitor, and the warrior who bested it can be made fiercer, more spirited and more alive by consuming it's heart." Selina had heard this story from her father, and she had taken a bite of a deer heart when she was old enough to go on her first deer hunt and all she remembered about the sacred event was that she threw up immediately after the sacred bite. Now that she recalled, Jacknack may have been on that hunt with her and her father. "I already ate a deer heart Jack; I am not eating any more raw animal parts." Jacknack turned toward her, took a bite of the cougar heart and stretched his arm out to her. Selina wanted nothing to do with the ritual, but she also knew that deep down she respected the culture, both native and cowboy, she respected the land and didn't want it known that she had blown off spirited tradition. She shook her head no, but it was not emphatic, she let out breath, took the heart from Jacknack, "Fuckin rituals", she then took the smallest bite she could possibly take. Even in the darkness, she could see Jacknack smile. He took the remainder of the heart from her, inspected it and smiled again. "You bring a skillet?" Selina shook her head; she knew what she needed to do and set about doing it.

Chapter 23

Getting to know someone you thought you knew

The fire crackled as Jacknack poked and prodded the contents of the skillet. "Needs more salt." Selina sat back against her saddle as she watched Jacknack shake more salt on the meat that Selina had to admit smelled amazing. "Are you sure eating a cat is not some sort of native taboo?" Jacknack let out a little chuckle, "house cat yes, mountain lion, no." It was Selina's turn to chuckle. It wasn't easy to get any of the old ranch hands to relax around her, but she never stopped trying. She could sense that Jacknack was loosening up a little. "Why are you here Jack?" She was surprised when he immediately answered her. "Your father hired me." She chuckled again, that was not my meaning Jack." He shook head as if he understood then cut a small slice of meat from the skillet. "Don't want it to cook too much, best to be tender." He took a bite from the slice he took from the main cut, then handed what was left of the small cut to Selina. She put it in her mouth, it was still very hot so she had to toss it around inside her mouth just a little before she could fully appreciate the culinary skills of this very quiet cowboy. "Damn, that's good! Backstrap?" Jacknack shook his head indicating that she was incorrect, "Heart". Selina smiled and savored the juicy meat a few seconds more, "way better than the first one." Jacknack laughed.

The two of them sat in silence as they ate the backstrap and the heart. The sounds of the night were as relaxing as the hot meal that Selina had not expected to have that night. She packed enough peanut butter, crackers and Vienna sausages to last her for a few days, but she certainly never expected to eat a meal like this. Although there were no vegetables or side dishes of any kind, she was certain that this was one of the best meals she had had in a very long time. The Backstrap turned out to be even better than the heart and she savored every bite, and the company. She didn't mind that Jacknack was a man of few words.

"Ma'am", Jacknack started to speak but Selina interrupted, "you don't have to MA'AM me, for cryin out loud", Jacknack set his tin plate on the ground and sat forward from the makeshift chair he was using. "Sorry ma'am, there is no taking the manners out of this old puncher." Selina shook her head in disbelief but decided to let it go. She had already fought this battle with Louis, and she had lost every single time. She would never get over how the men treated her around the ranch, especially the older ones like Louis and Jacknack. Jacknack saw an opening to the conversation and took it, "ma'am, it's pretty dangerous for you to be out her by yourself at night, these little rides you like to take aren't even safe for someone as old and crusty as me, much less a woman of your caliber," he paused and looked directly at her, "that's what I mean about being out over my skis, it aint my place to be tellin you this but I'm doing it anyway."

Selina sat there staring at him trying to find the right words to respond correctly. She wanted him to talk to her freely but knowing the men around the ranch the way she did, she knew that if she said the wrong thing he would likely clam up and she would never get anything out of him again. "I know you're right and I've heard the same thing from Louis a thousand times, but I get really upset to think that my parents left me a ranch that I can't enjoy like I am supposed to." She fiddled with her position in the saddle that was being used as back support, "I'm a cowboy as much as anyone on this ranch and if I can't ride and work on what they built, then what's it really worth?" Jacknack took his hat off and placed it on the ground. Selina was surprised by the sight of his head; she couldn't remember ever seeing Jacknack without a hat. It must have shown on her face, "you got something stuck in your mouth?", "well, I've just never seen you without a hat, at least I can't recall." Jacknack picked the hat up off the ground, fiddled around with the brim and ran his index and middle finger all the way around the snakeskin band. "I killed this fella in the stable, horses was kickin up a fuss something terrible so I knew there was something wrong", he had a slight squint in his eyes as he looked up at the stars, "caught me at moment without my sidearm so killed him with my bare hands", he took his eyes off the stars for a second and focused them on Selina, she could clearly see the whites of his eyes in the night air, "I take my hat off at the table, and when I sleep. Sometimes when I am speaking to the man, I show him the proper respect and when I am saying goodbye to somebody as they go meet the man, I do the same." Selina sat forward toward him, "Which is it now?" Selina was extremely shrewd in the way she could use her words and wit to quickly box anyone into a corner without much warning, but it was Jacknack that was doing the boxing tonight. "We aint never sat at the same dinner table till now Ms." Selina now crossed her legs like she was getting ready to smoke a sacred peace pipe.

Jacknack sat forward but he didn't cross his legs, he was long past the stage of crossing his legs, maybe in his younger years but not now. "I don't know what to say Jacknack, I'm sorry." Jacknack looked surprised at the apology, "for what, the fact that we don't take our supper together?" He laughed a belly laugh, "it's the way of the world missus, ranch hands don't eat at the same table as the boss." Selina shook her head, "No, I'm sorry for not ever offering." Selina took her own hat off then reached over and stuck her hand out to Jacknack,

"I'm quite imperfect in so many ways, I guess I can be as narcissistic as the next person but it sure aint intentional, I guess I never really looked around her to see that was valuable and what was important, you are both Mr. Nackard." Jacknack smiled and she could see the perfectly straight white teeth against his dark skin. He took off his glove and shook her hand with his bare hand, an act she knew to be genuine and respectful. His hands were huge compared to hers and she could feel the years of work that had formed every callous.

"I bess be getting on back ma'am, cowhands' libel to talk if I don't get back soon." Selina laughed, "I don't care what anyone thinks, stay a while." Selina held on to his hand for as long as she could then let it go, he immediately put his glove back on, "How long have you worked for the double L?" Jacknack rubbed his chin and looked over at the jeep, "care for drink miss?"

Once they were settled back down across from each other, Jacknack took a small sip from the bottle then handed it to Selina. Selina wasn't much of a drinker, especially whiskey straight from a bottle but there was something about tonight that she needed to participate so she took a drink from the bottle then handed it back to him. She was sure to avoid any expression that might giveaway the fact that the whiskey she had just swallowed seemed to be burning a hole in her esophagus as it slid down her throat. "This here is my favorite, it is an Old Forrester 1897, same year my Great granddaddy made it to Arizona". Selina had just discovered more about Jacknack's history in the last sentence than she had her entire existence, and she was starting to feel guilty. "He was a slave, but he was freed, not really though, he fought for the union and after the war, the army kept him doing the only thing he knew how to do was, be a soldier." Jack took another drink then looked at the bottle as if it was some sort of trophy or prize, "They sent him out here to fight Indians but by then, he had lost his stomach for hurtin folks, so he snuck off one night and never went back." Jacknack laughed, "Hard to wrap a mind around the fact that after spending 30 years in the army and 16 years as a slave, that if they would have caught him, they would have stood him up against a wall and shot him dead for desertion. Imagine that." Selina extended her empty hand to Jack to signal that she needed the bottle back and this time she really did want the drink, she wanted to hear more of this story, and she was determined to do so. "I don't even know what to say, I just learned more about you in the last 5 minutes than I've known about you my whole life." Jacknack handed her the bottle, "no cause to become an alcoholic over it miss." He laughed as he said it and then he watched her take a long drink from the bottle. Selina was surprised to find out that this time, the whiskey didn't burn at all, it tasted quite good. She started to hand the bottle back to Jacknack but she quickly took one more drink from the bottle, "I'm sorry I didn't know all that." Jacknack smiled and crossed his arms, "I will tell you more about how our families met and came together but I have to do some more work on you," Selina was confused about the comment, "what do you mean?" after Selina handed the bottle back to him, Jack sat perfectly still, his only movement was his eyes as he scanned the bottle he was holding. He was still looking at it as if it were sacred.

"You are a good woman, you have a heart the size of all outdoors, you take in strays and treat them like they have been yours forever, you are the only one the barn cat will even go near, and that barn cat is meaner than the rattlesnake I killed." Jacknack smiled as he spoke and Selina felt a calmness she hadn't felt in a very long time as she listened, "You mourn every day because you are now afraid to live. You are afraid to be happy because you have seen so much misery. You think that God wants you to be sad and lonely and that just aint so." Selina didn't expect this conversation from Jacknack and was struggling to respond. "You don't know everything about me Jacknack." Jacknack laughed, took a drink from the Old Forrester then continued, "You was born on Oct 6th, I was there the day you popped out and said hello, screaming with all the lungs you had in your little body. Me and your daddy smoked cigars and drank whiskey while they got you ready to take home." Selina caught herself smiling, she didn't know Jacknack was there for her birth, and she was getting a little embarrassed again. "I held you in my arms and knew at that very moment that they would have to take my last breath from me before I let any harm come to you and you weren't even mine." He took another look around the night sky, "I know that your favorite color is maroon, and your favorite time of the year is spring" he smiled as he stood up and Selina could hear a few bones of his popping, "I know enough miss." Selina was blown away by what he had just said. Jacknack was such a man of few words that she was now speechless. This man that she had known her whole life was telling her things she would never have guessed he would have known. She stood up quickly and approached this kind gentle man standing in front of her and hugged him. Jacknack was not a touchy person, and he was unsure of what the proper response should be, he patted her on the back and tried to return the embrace, but he acted as if he might break her. "I have so many more questions for you", and as she said it, they both heard the rustling brush and the sound of footsteps. Jacknack grabbed her arm and moved her away from the fire and behind the jeep opposite of where they heard the noise.

Chapter 24

Gringo

Selina placed her hand on her hip, it was a habit that she was glad she had developed over time and sure enough, it was where she expected it to be. She hadn't reloaded the three that she used on the cougar so that left her with 3, a rookie mistake and she was silently beating herself up for not reloading when she had plenty of time to do so. She looked at Jacknack who had let go of her arm and was standing closer to the rear of the jeep. She could see that he was fumbling through the back of the jeep. He stopped fumbling when he found the Winchester and retrieved it. Once he had it firmly in his grip, he pulled the lever jacking a shell into the chamber, the action was unmistakably loud and intentional. "Approach carefully!" The rustling and footsteps immediately stopped, and the desert night became deathly silent. Selina could hear a cow bellow somewhere far off in the distance and thought of Jake not doing his job. "Acércate con cuidado!"

Spanish was Selina's first language; her mother would not speak to her in any language but Spanish and her father would not speak to her in any language but English. Her mother and father were adamant that she could speak and understand both languages with ease and they were successful. Jacknack was not as good, but he held his own when it came to conversations of meaning and this was a conversation that he fully intended all to understand. After Jacknack yelled into the night to approach carefully in two languages, they could hear some whispers. From experience, they both knew that voices and whispers could carry through the dessert night and off canyon walls, fooling any recipient into believing that the voice was right over their shoulder. It was a way that people got lost in the dessert, sound carried easily, and it was always deceptive.

Jacknack looked at Selina and put his index finger over his mouth, the universal sign for quiet. He then used the same finger to point down at her .45. She understood but then once again regretted not reloading but then she remembered the belt she was wearing had 6 shells loaded in the back, so she reached behind her and felt for the shells, she found three and pulled them from the belt. Her problem now was ejecting the empty shells in the dark, but she was confident she could do it. She watched Jacknack disappear into the darkness as she got her Devil Anse reloaded to its capacity. She slid the empty shells into her front vest pocket, she didn't want to take a chance of dropping them on the ground and making any noise.

The jeep was just about 20 feet away from the fire that was still burning well, casting a small amount of light off the jeep. She decided that staying by the jeep was too vulnerable, so she moved in the direction opposite of but behind where she thought Jacknack had gone. If he did have to use his Winchester, she didn't want to be caught in the crossfire. She felt somewhat silly for being so jumpy, but she knew that her land had turned into a drug smuggling corridor and now the human smuggling had become even more pronounced. The combination of the two made for some very bad people and some very vulnerable people. She would help the vulnerable with everything she had in her, but she had determined that she would not be bullied or scared off her own property by the bad people. Her husband had been murdered on their own property and to this day not one single person could tell her why. The local Sherriff was corrupt, and the PD was worthless in her opinion and the border patrol was not much better. The FBI wouldn't return her calls, but they did manage to mail her a letter stating that the matter was of "local jurisdiction". Selina was determined to get her own answers.

She crouched down when she felt like she was far enough removed from any flicker of light and as she was bending down, she felt an arm grab hers, she spun quickly while reaching for her revolver but realized just as she was about to unholster it that it was Jacknack. "Sorry but you damn near stepped on me" he whispered. Selina lowered her head in a motion of relief but was still very tense. "There is a lot of people coming this way, maybe 20" Jacknack pointed towards the east, but Selina couldn't see anyone "A gringo and looks like a bunch of kids." Selina shook her head; it was a combination of disgust and sadness. She knew what it was, and she couldn't stop it. "When they heard me yell, they changed directions but now they are headed right back toward the jeep." Selina once again looked toward the East but couldn't see anything and she could feel the anger rising up in her, "I am going to stop them and get them the help they need, I've had enough of this shit." Selina started to stand up, but Jacknack grabbed her arm and pulled her back down, "the Gringo has a A-R ma'am, you have a revolver and I have a Winchester, the odds are not in our favor." Selina once again lowered her head but raised it back up with a steely resolve, "then so be it," she stood up and this time she yanked her arm free of Jacknacks grip and because of this, he stood up with her. Jacknack was well aware of Selina's temper and her resolve when she was mad, she couldn't be talked out anything once she had her mind set on something. The only thing he knew he could do was to try and help her and maybe she wouldn't get killed. "Ok, what's the plan Selina?" Selina was surprised that Jacknack addressed her by her first name, the shock sort of brought her back to the moment, just enough for Jacknack to explain the situation, "the gringo doesn't give a shit about the people he is leading, he has already been paid to get them across the border, his only job now is to hand them off." Selina knew what that meant, it meant that they would be herded into some supposed safe house until they could be milled out to the highest bidder. The thought disgusted her and made her even more angry, but Jacknack continued, "any sign of trouble he will run, shoot us, shoot them or all of the above", he looked East and West, "our best bet is to let him do what I let you do just now". Selina raised an eyebrow but wasn't sure if Jacknack would catch the facial expression of confusion in the darkness so she whispered, "what the hell are you talking about?", she could see Jacknacks rough exterior in the darkness and she thought she caught a very sly and mischievous grin, "he has one direction point in mind which is why he wouldn't change course much when I yelled, he would get lost if he strayed too much so we put ourselves right in his path and let him walk up on us."

Selina and Jacknack slowly and quietly circled back to where they would be directly in the path of the gringo, they were both very careful not to make noise. Once Jacknack was satisfied that they were directly in the path, he moved a few paces away from Selina. The night was quiet as Selina stayed crouched down like a catcher at a baseball game and waited on the despicable human being that was leading these children to their demise. She was mentally tired of everything but tonight, she gathered all her wits and wanted to make a statement to whoever ran this smuggling operation, find a new entry point or suffer the consequences.

She could hear the footsteps getting closer and for the first time since this began, she could see a crowd of people all walking two by two or single file. She felt odd about seeing it, she wasn't sure why, she had seen plenty of new footage showing the flippant way that people crossed into the United States, but it was like she was doing the filming, she felt like she was doing something bigger than herself and frankly struggled with what she was about to do. She wrestled with the idea that she was changing the course of events for some of these people, maybe for the worse but she banished the thought of their fate being something worse than having to turn back instead of going forward. These kids were about to be traded like some sort of commodity, they didn't know it, and that made it worse for her. Every single one of these people had more than likely booked passage via some savory individual that promised them freedom and safe passage to the good ole US of A. It wouldn't be long before the girls and boys for that matter would be forced into prostitution or other unspeakable acts. Those awful images that went off in her head got her blood boiling again and she was ready.

She could see the gringo as he approached, he was wearing a cowboy hat and even though it was dark outside he had on aviator sunglasses, obviously for the purpose of hiding his identity in case someone slipped his clutches and could possibly pick him out of a police line-up.

She eased her revolver out of the holster and flicked the safety button, just as she was doing it, she saw Jacknack stand almost directly in front of the Gringo with his Winchester at the ready, the man stopped instantly and started to swing his A-R into firing position but Jacknack made a show of jacking a round into the chamber of his rifle with the lever, "I will part your head like Moses and the dead sea", the gringo didn't move anymore and all people that were following him froze in their tracks, "drop it now". There was a soft but unmistakable command in Jacknacks voice but even though the gringo didn't move, Selina could see him smile which she found very odd. If a man was pointing a 30/30 Winchester directly at her forehead she would definitely not smile, something was wrong, the gringo had an air of confidence about him that she didn't like, it could only mean that they had missed something. Maybe the gringo had spotters, a fact that annoyed the hell out Selina now that she was just now thinking of it. Jacknack sensed the overconfidence in the man too and drew back the hammer on the Winchester, so that there was no mistaking his intentions. "Easy old timer, we're just passin through." Jacknack made his intentions clear again, "I said drop it", the gringo smiled even bigger, "Old man, I said we are just passin through", "and I said drop it!" Selina decided to stay crouched, something inside her told her that there were more like the gringo, and they would soon show themselves, if she stood now, she would give away the only surprise that she and Jacknack had left. "Say man, maybe your eyes aint to good but I have my gun slung around my neck, if I reach for it to unsling it, you turn that rifle lose on me, so John Wayne, I can't drop it." Jacknack didn't respond right away, Selina was certain he was weighing his options now. Selina's mind was racing and badly wanted to stand up, but she knew that now was not the time, "drop it old timer, these Mexicans aint worth you dying over". There it was, she knew she was right and was now really pissed that she didn't consider a parallel spotter. She knew these guys didn't travel alone. She felt stupid but she put that behind her, if she was stupid then so was Jacknack and they might both be stupid, but they needed to get smart real fast. The second voice came from almost behind her and she could hear footsteps approach her, she held her breath. The man's pants brushed against her shoulder as she was kneeling, and he didn't even feel it. Then, another voice came from her right side, "just shoot the old fucker and let's keep moving".

Selina now heard three voices and could see four men, five counting Jacknack. The first gringo was still smiling, "you want to put down the rifle now old timer. Selina couldn't let Jacknack put the rifle down because he would be unarmed after that. Jacknack always had his buck knife on him but that would be no good if he dropped his Winchester.

She drew in a breath, asked the Virgin Mary for grace and asked the almighty for forgiveness as she stood with her arm extended and devil anse pointed at the last two men to arrive and without any warning pulled the trigger twice, she heard a third shot go off that wasn't hers and she saw the gringo drop directly where he was standing then she spun around to where the fourth man should have been but he was already running through the dessert.

Her arm was still extended and pointed in the direction of the man running through dessert when she felt a hand on her forearm gently pressing her arm down, "easy ma'am" was all Jacknack had to say for her to relax long enough to breathe. "Let him run, the threat is over for now ma'am", Jacknack let go of her arm but stared into Selina's face, "you alright ma'am?", Selina realized she wasn't breathing again and took in a nice size gasp of air, "I think I just took a human life". Jacknack turned in the direction of the men that were now discussing their earthly deeds with Saint Peter, "no ma'am, you took two, before they took yours." Selina walked over to where the first man, the gringo was laying on the ground. His smile was gone and so was most of the top of his head. Selina knelt down beside him, "I couldn't let them make you drop your gun", she touched the gringo's shoulder as if she expected him to wake up. She stood up and walked over to where the two men had been standing together, her precise aim and the devil anse had done exactly what she thought they would do, both men were still leaking blood but not much from what Selina could see in the dark. One man had a hole under his right eye and the other had a hole just above his left eye.

"God forgive me, I've taken two lives." It was Jacknacks turn to kneel down beside the two smugglers, "would you rather be standing over my corpse ma'am?" Selina relaxed a little, but she couldn't shake the feeling that she had just done something terrible, she had violated a commandment. Jacknack began rumbling through each man's pockets, "What are you looking for?" Jacknack found a wallet, but didn't immediately open it, he stuck it in his own pocket and kept searching, "ma'am, there is probably some really scared kids hunkered down out there somewhere, you might want to try and round them up before another cougar gets one of them.

Selina knew he was right; the kids didn't have anything to do with this mess and she needed to help them but all she could focus on was the sound of her revolver as she pulled the trigger and took the life of two men. Here head was like fog all around her and everything was going in slow motion, slow motion that she felt like she was walking in mud, "Selina, my Spanish is not as good as yours, try to let them know they are ok and get them to come to you." Jacknack had finished his search through the pockets of the two men that Selina had taken out and was now going through the one they only knew as the gringo, the one he had dispatched.

"Don't be afraid, you are on my land, and you are safe now. These men that you were with did not have good plans for you! My name is Selina Villalpando, and I will make sure that your trip to America was not for nothing!"

Selina was using her Ranch voice and it was a booming voice that could echo off every canyon wall from Tucson to Winslow without any distortion. Her voice was strong, but it was also clearly the voice of a female. Selina spoke clearly in Spanish and repeated the exact same thing in English. It didn't take long for the first head to pop up out of the brush and cactus and pretty soon she was standing in front of a crowd. The crowd was quiet and even in the darkness she could see the fear in their eyes. She moved forward toward the small crowd and began inspecting each person, she guessed that the oldest might be 16 but all the rest were just children. Her heart was beating fast, and she knew that these children probably saw her kill the men that they were with and even now, she was second guessing herself and Jacknack for not letting them just pass through, if they had let them pass through peacefully, three men would still be alive. She mumbled under her breath in opposition of her own thoughts, "and most of these little babies would be getting fucked tomorrow if they haven't already Selina". She could feel her jaw line become tense as she fought the words from actually escaping her mouth.

She relaxed her jaw and let out a deep breath then looked down at the children standing in front of her. She softened her voice to that of a gentle schoolteacher, "Mi nombre is Selina" she was about to say something when Jacknack came up to her quickly. "They weren't far from the pick-up point ma'am, we have to get out of here, there are trucks coming and I am sure they aren't happy." Jacknack didn't look worried and for all practical purposes he wasn't worried about himself, but he knew what these traffickers would do to Selina before they killed her, and he would be powerless to stop them because he would be dead.

"You ever stuff a Volkswagen Jacknack?" Jacknack shook his but he knew what she meant. Selina looked at the children and instinctively she reached down and grabbed the smallest child close to her, a girl with beautiful silky black hair and placed her on her right hip while she shouted at them "Necesito que todos ustedes se suban al jeep! Rãpido!" The children weren't moving in any direction and Jacknack decided to try English, "Get in the damn jeep!" Selina then reached down and grabbed another child she thought she could carry, another small girl with the same beautiful silky black hair, only hers were braided. Once she had a kid on both hips, she started making her way to the jeep, the other kids had taken the que from Jacknacks booming voice and started to scramble to the jeep. Jacknack grabbed a shovel from the back of the jeep and proceeded to scoop all the cougar guts and what was left of the meat onto the fire along with sand, quickly extinguishing the flames. He started strategically placing each child in the jeep. He was very proud of himself when he turned around to see that there were still two children that were not in the jeep. "Shit".

Selina took BB by the reigns and got him in position, she placed one child on the saddle and then the second, these two girls were not big at all, and BB would have no trouble getting up to full gallop with the three, the problem would be Selina trying to keep the girls from falling off. She turned to look at Jacknack, he had managed to place the two extra children in the jeep by placing one on his lap and the other had to sit on his shoulders. If the situation hadn't been so serious, this would have been comical to see, the jeep looked exactly like pictures she had seen of kids stuffing a beetle. Jack looked at Selina on the horse, "I don't know if we can make it." Selina looked towards the northeast, "We have to try." She gave BB a serious squeeze and he didn't need any more coaxing. He took off with the speed that she knew he had in him. She could hear the power in his breathing as he inhaled air and expelled it like a locomotive. Something inside her made her believe that BB knew the situation required urgency and he was doing his best to get her and these little girls out of trouble.

With her left arm she held the reigns and saddle horn as tight as she could and with her right arm she held tightly to both girls. The wind howled in her ears as she felt BB finding his stride, the four of them were becoming one and the speed in which they were traveling was exhilarating. Jacknack was trailing behind her in the jeep, but he was being more cautious, she had no idea how many kids were in that little jeep, but it was a lot and he was traveling without the use of headlights. He simply followed Selina as fast as he possibly could.

Chapter 25

The Brothers Grim

When there was any kind of bad weather, the cowboys at the double L knew to try and get to a line shack, which was a series of tiny shacks strategically located at some of the furthest points away from the ranch. They contained nothing more than a wood stove and a bunk, just enough shelter and warmth to weather a bad storm. If they couldn't get to a line shack quickly enough, they had a chance to get to one of several canyons that had outcroppings of rock formations that could provide plenty of shelter from rain, snow, or hail but it didn't guarantee warmth.

When Selina was just a little girl, her father would take her on as many overnight trips and long rides as her mother would allow. She would get so excited when her father would say they had to go "northeast" because she knew that meant she would get to visit the cliffs. She loved the cliffs and would stay there all day if her father would let her, but he always told her to respect the cliffs and the shelter they provided as they stood for thousands of years. He called the place Respeto canyon, which in English meant respect. Deep inside Respeto canyon were cliff dwellings left behind by the

Hohokam tribe many years ago, they were hard to find if you didn't know where to look and they provided excellent shelter. She and her father had actually used the cliffs more than a few times to get out of the elements. As far as Selina knew, there were only three people on the ranch that knew about the cliffs and two of the three were headed there now. It was the only place that Selina knew they could disappear and no matter how hard anyone tried, they would not be found.

BB's ears were pinned back, and he was galloping at a speed that gave Selina the confidence she needed. She was proud of her horse, he was no racehorse, he was a cutting horse, and he was not made to win races but today, Selina was certain that BB was taking care of her with his heart, grit and sheer power. She had never been on a horse that was moving this fast in the dark, it was as if BB knew exactly where she wanted to go and was taking her there at breakneck speeds.

Despite the darkness, Selina found the entrance to the canyon and guided BB up a small trail that was not visible from below. Once she had BB behind a large rock formation, she hopped down and then helped both girls down. She knelt down so that she could be at eye level with the two girls, both girls had big eyes and they were very wide. She wasn't sure if they would ever appreciate the thrill of being on a horse that was moving that fast, but she didn't care at the moment, she whispered to both, "Stay right here with BB, he will protect you". Both girls looked confused, so Selina repeated it in Spanish, "quédate aquí con BB, él te protegra". Both girls nodded their heads and Selina made her way back down the trail, she could hear the jeep coming and was at the bottom of the trail when they arrived. She started grabbing kids out of the jeep and quietly telling them follow the trail and she would point at the entrance to the trail.

Jacknack gently dropped the one child that was sitting on his shoulders to the ground. His cowboy hat came off and Selina picked it up for him. She watched all the kids marching up the trail, she envisioned Hohokam children from a thousand years ago marching up the trail towards the cliffs to escape danger just as they were doing now. Jacknack looked at Selina, "what about the jeep?" Selina had already thought of that too, "twenty yards from here is a steep drop off, grab what you can out of it and let it go over the side", Jacknack knew about the drop off, but his stomach churned knowing his one prized possession was about to get destroyed but he also knew that it was the only choice. He pulled the Winchester and a box of shells along with the canteen and some bags of dried food out of the storage box, then handed everything to Selina except the Winchester. "I will be back", he looked over his shoulder and could see the headlights bouncing crazily in the night dessert as their pursuers must have been hitting every ditch on the way to the cliffs. Selina grabbed him quickly and hugged him, "Hurry Jack, no kissing it goodbye." Jacknack smiled at the thought that he might actually stop to kiss his jeep goodbye then looked at Selina, "you have to keep them quiet, the echos.," she stopped him from finishing, "I know Jack, just go!"

Jack jumped back in the jeep and sped off. He stopped when he was close to cliff, "Goodbye girl, I will come get you when I can, don't take it personal." He pushed the shift into neutral and gave her a little push, because of the sand she was harder to push than he expected so he put a little more energy into the shove and then watched her disappear over the edge. He could hear the jeep as it rolled quickly down the ravine then over the cliff. He knew when she was airborne because it got quiet for just a second and then he heard the sickening sound of medal crashing against rocks.

He took his mind off losing his pride and joy and started to make his way back to the trail entrance, but it was too late. The headlights were too close to the canyon entrance, he couldn't risk being seen so he laid flat on his stomach in the brush so he could see the smugglers. He pulled the Winchester up to where he could get into firing position. He wasn't sure if Selina had time to get to cliffs, but he couldn't worry about that at the moment. He focused on staying out of site and on the cars that were quickly approaching.

Two dark color SUVs pulled up to the entrance of the canyon and stropped but no one got out. Jacknack knew from experience that from their point of view right now, the canyon looked like a dead end and technically it was if you didn't understand the cliffs and the brilliant maze that the Hohokam tribe devised thousands of years ago. One person could get into the cliff dwellings and never come out. They might get lost and starve to death, but Selina knew the cliffs better than anyone on the planet and it made him relax a little. The Double L ranch was so vast that most people didn't know about the dwellings and as far as Selina was concerned, no one ever would. She knew that if she let the secret out, it would invite treasure pirates and government officials and they would try to take her land away from her in the name of preservation. Jacknack agreed with Selina and thus the cliffs were a tightly guarded secret between Selina, Jacknack and Louis.

Jacknack stayed in ready position for what seemed like an eternity as the headlights of the SUV's continued to light up the entrance to the canyon. He heard the engines go quiet and then four men appeared at the front of the SUV's. Jacknack was a damn good shot with this Winchester and could take out at least two of them before they knew what hit them, but he had already killed one man tonight and wasn't in the mood to kill anymore. All these guys were trespassing on Double L land but killing someone changed the stakes for where he and Selina could go with this scenario. If they called the local police, with the help of a good attorney they would probably be ok but if they got the feds involved there is no telling what could happen. They could easily claim self-defense but as a defense that wasn't always successful. The third option was to call the border patrol and they would claim jurisdiction, hand the self-defense over to the local and they would take the children back to Mexico of which their parents would have them back across the border in a week.

Four men got out of the SUV's, Jacknack was close enough to hear them talking in front of the SUV lights, "where the hell did they go?" he could see all four of them looking up at the canyon then to each side of the entrance, he appreciates them standing in front of the headlights so he could not only hear them, but he could more clearly see them. He knew two of them well, two men that had been a pain in the family's ass for many years, the Peña's. He always knew the Peña family were behind all the smuggling, but he never really had visual proof until now. The Peña family had a small amount of land but not enough to smuggle as freely as they could across the Double L. They were smart, they may not have had much land, but they owned damn near everything from Lucas to Winslow and they used their legit businesses to wash the money from their trafficking business. They supposedly had backing from the mob on the east coast, but Jacknack never delved that deep. He worked for the Villalpando family and had for many years and that put him in direct opposition to the Peña family. As far as Southern Arizona was concerned it was good against bad and most of the people in Southern Arizona stayed politely out of it. The Peña brothers wanted the Double L land, had the money to buy it but Selina and Selina's father would never sell it to them.

Jacknack listened to them talk about what to do and if they should go into the canyon for just a little but then he heard the coyotes howl. He smiled, the echo's, she was using the echoes. Very few people understood the cliff dwellings the way Selina did, she knew that once you were inside the honeycomb of mazes and cor-ridors, any sound you made, reverberated off every wall and there seemed to be thousands of them up there. One voice could sound like a 100, a hundred voices could sound like a thousand. Selina could sound exactly like a coyote, she was the best at calling them in at night. Once the howling started it began to sound like the place was about to be overrun by hungry coyotes. Everyone knows that one man against a coyote is pretty good odds for the man, but you get 10 coyote's, and the man is gonna lose, every time. "What the fuck!" Jacknack could hear one of the men say, he wasn't sure which one, but he could clearly hear the fright in his voice. The other three men stood there looking all around, fully expecting to be attacked at any moment, "enough of this shit! I aint gonna get eaten!" Jacknack had to fight off the urge to laugh, Selina had done it, she had scared at least one of them and Jacknack knew that fear was contagious, once you got one man spooked, it wouldn't take long for the others to follow.

The brother known as "junior" since he was the first son of the elder Peña spoke, "I need those fucking twins!" The other three men stood still, they all knew not to cross junior, even the little brother "Cito" short for Encito, who was purported to be even more mean than Junior didn't move. Jacknack watched Junior pull a gun from the back of his pants and point it at one of the two other men, "this is the second time you have made me break a promise!" Still illuminated by the headlights of the SUV's, Jacknack could see the fear on the man's face that was now staring at Junior's gun. Junior Peña stood perfectly still pointing the gun at the man, the man staring at the barbell of Juniors gun had his hands up in sort of a begging position but if he was begging, it didn't work, Junior pulled the trigger. Jacknack felt his leg flinch just at the sound of the shot, if it was enough to make him flinch it was surely enough to make a child flinch. The man dropped right where he stood, if it hadn't been real, Jacknack thought it looked cartoonish, almost Wylie Coyote type of stuff. He almost expected the man to stand up and dust himself off.

He raised his Winchester up by propping his elbow on the ground and placed Junior directly in his sites. He could easily put a bullet directly through Junior's head and if he was quick enough on the lever, he could possibly take out one of the other two. He saw Junior turn the gun on the other man, not Cito and the other man immediately dropped to his knees and began to beg for his life. Jacknack felt awkward watching a man grovel like that and in some weird way felt sorry for him, he smiled when he heard the song "Should have been a cowboy" pop into his head.

"You have my merchandise and I want it! Give me what is mine and we will forget this!" Junior continued to point the gun at the man kneeling on the ground, Jacknack swore he could hear the man crying. Jacknack prepared himself to watch another man die this evening when he heard her voice, "You are on Villalpando land! You are trespassing!" her voice was loud and clear; he was surprised that she seemed that close to Junior. Jacknack watched Junior lower the gun he was pointing at the man kneeling and turned towards where he thought Selina's voice was coming from, "Ahhh, now I understand!" Junior turned back to the man kneeling and used his gun to signal to the man to get up. The man not only quickly got up, but he also put their SUV between he and junior just in case Junior changed his mind. "The righteous Villalpando Widow has spoken!" His voice was clear in the dessert night air, "I won't hurt you; I promise. Just give me what is mine and I will leave, no harm no foul Ms. V." Deep down, Jacknack hoped she wouldn't respond but he knew Selina and there was no way she would not, so he made sure that Junior's head was in his sites.

He never expected to see Selina walk out into the open, he whispered to himself, "holy shit Selina, bad idea", he was confused to see that she had her Devil Anse aimed at Cito and not Junior. Junior was no idiot so he took advantage of this by pointing his gun at Selina, "Lower your weapon Junior or I will end your brother's life right now!" Jacknack tensed up as he watched the drama unfold and thought that this couldn't possibly end well, "and I have my weapon pointed directly at you Ms. V" Junior laughed as he pointed his right hand holding the gun at Selina and used his left hand to move in a dramatic flair as he continued, "I would lose a brother yes, the Ranch would lose an owner but I would still be here my friend, and I would have my merchandise." He was laughing as he said it, but Selina interrupted "that is where you are wrong Junior, I have a gun pointed directly at your head" she let that sink in for a second and then he heard her shout his name, "Jack!" Jacknack turned the sites on ground in front of Juniors feet and he squeezed off a round. The dust flew up about a foot from where he was standing. Jacknack shouted "the next one goes right into your fucking head amigo!" Junior stopped laughing, the night became quiet, "Your merchandise aint worth dyin over Junior, you and your friends, including the dead one need to get off my property." Selina said it in such a calm voice, but no one moved, "Now!" Selina cocked the hammer on her revolver for good measure and then stood and watched the three men scramble to retrieve the dead guy off the desert floor and get into the SUV. From Jacknack's point of view, Junior didn't do too much to help his brother and the other guy get the unfortunate one into the SUV.

Jacknack kept the Winchester aimed at the SUV until it was a few hundred yards away from them and then stood up. He shook his head as he made his way to where Selina was standing. As he approached her, "that was an unnecessary risk ma'am, you could have been killed." Selina holstered her revolver, "After the kids were safe, I didn't feel like hiding on my own land." She did have a point, Jacknack shook his head though and as if she was reading his mind, "besides, I knew you were out there Jack."

Jacknack took one more look at the taillights far off in the distance, "You know you just poked the bear, right? They don't just go away mad ma'am; they will come back." Selina looked at the taillights too but didn't say anything, she knew she had poked the bear as Jack called it, but she was tired of tip toeing around her own land, in her mind, she needed to either live in peace on her own land or die trying, there was no in between now.

"Help me get the kids down from the cliffs so we can get them the help they need." Jacknack shook his head again, "I don't see how we can help them very much tonight; we have one horse and no jeep." Selina turned and yelled to the kids that were hiding in the cliffs and yelled for them to come down in Spanish and English. It was dark and things happened so fast that they very well could be some other international visitors that didn't speak Spanish but were more likely to speak English. The smugglers didn't care what nationality their cargo was, they only cared about the money.

Chapter 26

Images

After Selina retrieved the satellite phone from her saddle bag, she called Louis, not the sheriff or border patrol. Whether she was right or wrong in her actions, she had committed a crime that night, and not just any old crime, she had killed two men. The two men she killed would have more than likely killed her and Jacknack, fucked the girls before they turned them over to the creeps and perverts that would surely fuck them again and put them to work satisfying other perverts. The thoughts of what those kids, both boys and girls were headed for sickened Selina to her core. What she was seeing tonight wounded her deeply, instead of providing answers to the reasons for her husband's death and the way he was found, it just sparked more pain and more questions. Questions that opened the spigot of pain even wider and would not allow her to vanquish any thoughts of her husband being found dead with two little girls and it made her angry.

Selina gathered the children at the largest room in the cliffs. Her father told her it was the chief's residence, of course he had no proof to back that up, but she went with it. She chose the room because it was vented with a flue which allowed them to make a fire that would warm them all until Louis arrived with transportation back to the ranch. She had no idea what she intended to do, but her first priority was to get them back to safety.

Not long before Louis arrived with the Ranch pick up, a ford diesel 350 dually that could pull a house if needed, Selina sat with the children and talked, she asked all the questions she thought she could ask. At first, they didn't say much but with a little humor and her natural ability to put people at ease, especially children, they began to share stories of their families. She felt like she was getting close to understanding how some of them got there when the head lights of Louis's truck got everyone's attention. The kids scrambled for the deeper safety of the cliffs and in fact, Selina thought about it too, but she knew it was Louis and not the brothers returning for more fun.   The two girls that held her tightly as BB carried them to safety never left Selina's side, even when everyone else scattered and hid, the two little girls would not turn loose of Selina.

After Selina and Jacknack explained the entire evening to Louis, Louis made his way to the cliffs to collect the children. Louis was quiet as he collected the brood of immigrants and Selina had charged him with returning to the ranch house for the evening.

"Mrs. Villalpando, you cannot stay another night alone here. It is not safe." Louis was nearly pleading as he addressed his boss and his friend.

"I will be fine; the brothers are mad, but they aren't stupid. They will spend the rest of the night doing God knows what drugs and puffing each other's chests up enough to come at me later." Jacknack would never interrupt a conversation between Selina and Louis because he knew the relationship and would never interfere, but he was worried about Selina being so stubborn and spending the night out here alone. "Mam, there are lots more issues to consider than just the brothers." Both Selina and Louis turned to look at Jacknack and both were surprised by his interruption, "there are three other lost souls that wait interment, that problem will not tend to itself ma'am."

There was no way Selina had forgotten about the men that her and Jacknack had set up judgement meetings with God earlier that evening. Selina had never in her life considered how it would feel to take another human life and she was trying desperately right now to avoid the conversation with herself much less a conversation with Louis and Jacknack about it. "I know that Jack, I don't have to be reminded of it so here is the deal", she stopped and pointed at the children that were now loaded up in the truck, "they are my first priority, regardless of what happens to me tonight, tomorrow or whenever, I will not allow those children to endure one more minute of abuse." She then turned her attention to BB, "he is mine, he won't let anyone else ride him and you both know it so there is not one snowballs chance in hell that I am leaving him out here in the desert tonight." She drew in a large batch of fresh Arizona night air and breathed it out slowly to help her steady her voice. "Take them to the ranch, get Lisa to come feed them and look after them until I get there."

Both men knew it would be best to stay quiet and not challenge her, Selina was very strong minded, many called it stubborn, but it was really not stubborn because Selina was smart, she listened very well, and she digested information more rapidly than anyone in the state. She was strong minded at this moment because she had just planted her battle flag. No one threatened Selina Villalpando and got away with it.

Selina climbed on to BB and took a tight grip on his reigns, "I will be back at the ranch in the morning, we will arrange to retrieve Jack's jeep tomorrow and by then I will have figured out what to do with the kids." Selina started to turn away from Jack and Louis, but she turned back to Jack and smiled, "Moses parted the red sea Jack, work on your bible a little more." She turned around again then gave BB a nudge and it wasn't long before the two were out of sight.

Chapter 27

Last Rights

Even in the darkness, Selina found her way back to where she and Jack had hastily left camp. She walked BB around the spot, not sure of what she was looking for or even why she was looking except that she needed answers. Maybe these were the guys that had murdered her husband and those 2 little girls, but she doubted it, they were two young and her husband's murder was almost five years past now. She doubted that the brothers murdered her husband because deep down they were just idiot brothers who followed in their dad's smuggling footsteps, they could be mean but murdering Ben Walker on the Villalpando ranch would not be a wise business decision but maybe she was wrong. After all, no one had been arrested for the murder and there were no serious leads on who might have done it.

Selina slowly walked BB over to where the Gringo still remained. She almost hoped he would have gotten up and walked off with the other dead men after they had heard the word "cut" yelled by a director, but this was no movie. There was no coming back for these guys and she felt sick.

Once BB came to a stop almost right next to the man, she climbed down. As she stood there next to the horse, she argued with herself about not having to do what she was going to do. She reached into her saddle bags and removed the old leather bag left over from a now empty bottle of Pampero rum and removed the silver and Pearl rosary she kept there. She gently pushed BB aside and he complied by stepping back and away which left the man visible on the ground. She could see that his eyes were still open, and he was seemingly looking at the stars. When she was standing over the man, she felt like he was looking at her. The expression on his face was the one of shock or surprise. It unnerved her enough to make her slightly dizzy.

Selina took one last look up at the night sky that was filled with stars, "It is not my place father nor am I qualified to do this since tonight I was the angel of death, I have no choice." She knelt down beside the man and held her rosary tight with both hands and closed her eyes, "This is quite after the fact mister but it's more than anyone gave my husband or those girls," she continued, through this holy anointing may the lord in his love and mercy help you with the grace of the holy spirit. May the lord who frees you from sin save you and raise you up." She touched the dead man on the shoulder and said "amen".

Once Selina searched the man for any information that might help her, she stood up and took a very slow walk over to the men that she had directly killed. She stood over the men for the second time that night but this time she wasn't as shaken. This time she was able to clearly focus on the two men, that lay dead next to each other. She knelt down next to the two men and repeated last rights for them. When she was finished and felt like she had done what she could for now, she looked to the stars again and said, "forgive me Lord".

Selina made her way back to BB who stood waiting for her as patiently as he always did. She could always trust BB to stay focused and not to wonder. She stood next to BB and patted his neck and rubbed his nose. "We have a little work to do tonight boy, it's gonna be a long night." She reached into her saddle bag and pulled out two apples and fed them to BB with her hand. "We will get you good and fed tomorrow but tonight I need your help again." BB looked eagerly at the apples and flicked his head up and down in appreciation and agreement.

Selina took the rope from the saddle and tied it around the legs of the Gringo. "I know for certain you would have killed me, so I don't feel very bad about this." Once she had sufficiently secured the rope around the man's legs she climbed onto BB and wrapped the rope around the saddle horn and gave BB a nudge. Nice and easy boy, no need to rush.

Verde flat wash was about three miles west from where they had camped and that would be her destination. If she had enough rope, BB could have easily drugged all three men together but with her limited supplies, she was forced to shuttle each man one at a time. At first it was unpleasant knowing what she was doing and from time to time her passenger would get stuck behind a cactus and she would have press BB a little harder to force him through. She took no joy in the task, but she carried it out none the less. The sounds that a body makes when it is being drug across the desert floor was not pleasant and she was certain she would remember those sounds the rest of her life.

When she reached the wash, she got off BB and for some reason checked the rope that was wrapped around her saddle. It was tight like a bow string, she shook her head wondering what she was expecting, perhaps her passenger might say "are we there yet?" but since the night remained silent, she stood over the wash. Verde flat wash was dry 300 days a year but when the monsoon run off came from up north, it could quickly look like the Colorado river. It had been raining up north for several weeks, probably snowing on the mountains so a little run off might be expected. Enough to book passage for these guys to Mexico. If the creek never swelled with the coming rains and subsequently swept them south, then the animals would likely stock up while they waited on the rains. Either way, no one would find them here in the wash. There were plenty of overhangs along the banks to stuff them out of site. These men could never be found, not in Selina's mind. She didn't know the law well enough to risk it, but she also knew that the brothers just might phone in an "anonymous tip" to the Sherriff and the Sherriff would be forced to check it out.

She looked for a place easy enough for BB to ease down into the dry wash so he wouldn't possibly turn his foot wrong and found one. She eased BB off into the wash and her passenger followed without resistance. Once she found an overhang that she liked for passenger number one she stopped, unwrapped the rope and got off BB. She coiled the rope back as she approached him. Dragging him through the desert had pulled his shirt over his head making it easy to pull it the rest of the way off. She then removed the rest of his clothes leaving him naked. "Sorry, it's the way it has to be". She began the task of rolling the man under the overhang of the flat wash, which was much harder than she expected, but she managed.

Once she had all three men secured in the Verde flat wash, she removed a plastic trash bag and gathered the pile of clothes she had created by stripping the men of all their possessions and placed then in the bag, looped it around the saddle horn and rode BB out of the creek, it was well past midnight now and she was getting tired. She let BB walk to help ease some of the burden he had carried for her tonight then got down off him and walked in front of him all the way back to the point where she and Jacknack had begun to make camp before they were interrupted.

She unsaddled BB, brushed him thoroughly then gave him a grain bag that she brought with her. Selina was nowhere close to putting the events of the night behind her and at this point she figured she never would. How does one put behind the act of breaking a commandment? She walked around each one of BB's legs and checked his hoofs with a small flashlight, she didn't want him to come up lame. She took the bag of clothing, boots, belts, and all and started a fire. It wouldn't take long for their things to burn to ash, and she needed a little warmth.

Firewood was scarce in the desert, and this would get things going. She sat by the fire with her knees pulled up against her chest and her arms around her knees, a position she took when she needed to think. Even as a little girl, her father would often find her somewhere in the barn, sitting in that exact position.

"Maybe I should just sell the place and walk away BB?" BB didn't respond but he did flicker his ears and she took that as a sign he was giving her to continue, "The cost of raising cattle continues to grow while the price of beef continues to fall." It was if she was running through a checklist in her mind. "We don't have enough good pastureland to keep up with some of the others, we can't go back to raising cotton, hell cotton prices are worse than cattle prices." BB stomped his front right hoof on the ground in agreement, "And there is always the chance that none of it matters because I would be in prison for mur.." She almost got the word out, but she stopped short. "It was self-defense, and it was on my land you know." She unwrapped her arms from her legs and leaned back against her saddle. "The Sherriff is as crooked as a sidewinder though, he'd figure a way to pin it all on me", she looked up at BB who was staring off in the distance, "you know he already tried, well at least suggested that I had something to do with Ben's death." She laughed out loud, "he actually asked me if I was happy with my choices, can you believe that? Me? Happy with my choices? I damn sure was until someone took my husband from me." She pulled her hat down over her eyes then pushed it back up, she leaned over and took the rope from the saddle, stood up and eased it around BB's neck. She was confident that he wouldn't run off in the night, but she just needed a few hours of sleep and one less worry. She looped the other end of the rope around her leg and leaned back. This time she pushed her hat over her eyes. It was peaceful where she was right now, peaceful enough to feel her eyes getting heavy and she dozed off.

Chapter 28

Wide as a House

Selina guessed that she had only closed her eyes for an hour maybe two when she heard what her mind told her were a series of firecrackers and she woke. It didn't take her long to realize that the sounds she was hearing were gun shots and she felt her side for her devil Anse and of course she found it.

BB didn't move a muscle at the sound which made her proud, in fact, she guessed he hadn't moved an inch. He was standing sentry over his trusted friend. Selina decided at that moment she would never have to tether herself to BB ever again. She tried to move quickly but she couldn't, her body ached from the work she had done. She was tired but she didn't want to be caught off guard.

She saddled BB and checked the site for anything she may have left behind. The fire had burned down to ash as expected, even the soles of their shoes were gone. She cinched BB with a grin and thought that if they could just get those floods from up north, her friends would get that free trip into Mexico where even if they were found, they would never be reported. The corrupt local authorities would have nothing but speculation and conjecture, she could handle that. Selina didn't think very highly of the local authorities. Most of them went into their positions with Noble ideas and plans but became corrupt in a very short time. Money for someone who has never really had any is a powerful motivator and can weaken the strongest of men.

The corruption at most of the local levels coupled with the Mexican government's aversion for poor relations with the US made it better for the gringos that might turn up dead on Mexican soil or to just simply remain missing.

She was asleep when she heard the first shots which made it difficult to pinpoint a direction, so she tried to get a fix on where she thought the shots came from and headed in that direction. She didn't rush though, she kept BB at a very slow pace, she didn't want to be seen or heard. The night was getting very ridiculous and the thoughts of selling off her land for a large sum, split the profits with all the long-term hands and walk away filled her still groggy mind but she kept going.

BB's pace was perfect as usual, he kept her steady and going towards where she thought she heard the sounds of the shots. There were a lot of pops and then it stopped as quickly as it started. She was coming up on a slight rise in the landscape. If she had her bearings correct, just over the rise would be a small flat valley that had a couple of dirt roads leading in and out of it from the south and north. She was wide awake now; her pulse rate was climbing the closer she came to the rise. She stopped at the base of the small hill where she and BB would still be out of sight from whatever might be in the valley.

She climbed off BB and removed the Henry rifle from its leather sleeve. She whispered to BB, "stay here boy, I am gonna have a peek." Selina smiled when BB nodded his head in agreement, she believed that she and BB were able to communicate but getting others to believe that was impossible. Selina slowly walked halfway up the rise and then she dropped to her stomach and belly crawled to the top. When she got to the top, she pulled her rifle up to firing position. She could see two cars, an SUV's and some kind of sedan, the sedan had its headlights pointing in a northerly direction and the SUV aiming its headlights in northwest direction making a nice V pattern in desert. She stayed perfectly still and scanned the entire valley with her naked eye but couldn't see much. There were too many dark patches, and she was too far away.

She reached into the saddle bags and pulled a small pair of binoculars out, not the most powerful but better than the naked eye. She climbed back up the hill and resumed the position she had just left. She saw an arm behind the right front wheel of the SUV but that was all could see. "This looks like a drug deal gone bad." She turned to look down the hill at BB, "Best to let this settle itself for tonight." She started to move back down the hill when a slight movement caught her eye. The back-passenger door slowly opened to the SUV. Selina moved the binoculars back into position. "Come on . . . ease on out of there, show yourself you scumbag", she whispered "You are on double L land and haven't been invited." She put the binoculars down for a second then raised the Henry up to a position that allowed her to put the gun sites right down on the SUV door that was opening.

She was trying to balance the rifle and the binoculars but then settled on just using the binoculars with both hands. She gasped when she saw a young girl get out of the car. She couldn't tell how old the girl was from this distance, but she looked pretty young to Selina. "Geez Christ almighty, what are you doing at a drug deal little girl?" She tried to comprehend what she was seeing but she couldn't. There was still no movement other than the little girl and she had dropped out of site behind the sedan.

Selina waited, something bad had happened and somehow this girl was walking around in the middle of all of it. Selina took one more look at the arm that was barely visible behind the tire of the sedan, it hadn't moved. She drew in a deep breath and slid back down the hill towards BB with the rifle in one hand the binoculars in the other. "I'm sorry if I get you in a mess big fella but I have to go see."

She decided the best possible way to get down to where the cars were parked was to circle in a westward direction until she could enter the small little valley from the south. She could see there was a slight entrance to the location carved into the area, probably the same entrance the cars had used to get there. It might take a little bit longer than just riding BB over the ridge and directly into the location but from where she was, she couldn't see if it was safe enough to do so. The last thing she wanted to do was get herself shot, not after the night she had already been through.

She once again dismounted slowly from BB and removed the Henry from its sleeve. She checked the devil Anse's cylinder to find that she was fully loaded. She didn't think she would be scared but she was. She hated the feeling of being scared on her own land and tonight she had decided she had no intention of feeling that way ever again. Even though she was very certain that she didn't want to shoot anyone else, she could not afford to be scared on her own land. This was no way to live and if she could get through tonight, she would begin the change. The actions of earlier were still heavy on her mind so she continued to tell herself that she was not a killer by any stretch, but she was a property owner with rights, and she was bound to protect them.

Her adrenaline was pumping in ways she had never experienced, it was weird to her that it seemed to be heightening all of her senses, but it was also giving her the strength to focus all her energy on the task at hand. She steadied her breathing and slowly made her way through the entrance where she could see fresh car tracks from where her trespassers had entered. She heard something that sounded like a whimper that caused her to stop and crouch down. She held tightly to the Henry rifle and peered around the cactus that was providing her cover from the taillights of the two cars. She could make out the outline of three people lying on the ground but couldn't get the full view unless she moved.

Selina was good at slow walking without making any noise. Her dad had taught her that stealth was the difference between a good hunter and a great hunter. The great ones remained quiet all the time, the great ones didn't rush, and the great ones controlled their nerves. She was focusing on all of them as she slowly peeked around the back bumper of the SUV.

The little girl that climbed out of the SUV was kneeling beside one of the dead men crying. She would hold him by the shoulders for a second and then she would plunge her face into his chest and cry, not loudly but she would repeat this cycle several times. Watching the girl told Selina that she cared about that person. Selina continued to scan the area for any movement, but she didn't see any, it appeared that perhaps she was right, this was a drug deal that went sideways but she couldn't figure out any of the details. There were 4 bodies lying on the ground, when she saw the 5th body, it was a body almost so small she didn't realize it was there. "Good God, what happened here?' she whispered under her breath.

She drew in another breath and decided she needed to walk into the mess. She didn't want to frighten the girl that was leaning over the dead man, for all she knew, the girl could have had a gun too. She slowly stood up with the Henry rifle at the ready position and made a slow and methodical movement toward the bodies that lay almost in a circle. "Fãcil" Selina spoke with slow but very clear tones and then she repeated it but this time in English "easy". Selina walked toward the little girl who was now looking at Selina with tears streaming down her face, but her eyes were wide and fixed on Selina's every move. "Are you hurt?" Selina looked at each person on the ground but unfortunately the headlights did not illuminate some of them well enough. She reached inside her vest pocket and retrieved a small flashlight, "por favor ayudalo!", "please help him" the little girl brushed the hair from the man's forehead as she spoke and looked at him with as much compassion as Selina had ever seen.

Selina knew she needed to secure the area before she tried to render any aide, sometimes in situations like this, the combatants tend to play dead until they know it's safe to skedaddle or attack. Selina looked at the little girl and put her index finger against her lips giving her the quiet sign. Selina first walked to the person directly in front of the little girl and the man she was praying over, Selina was quite surprised to see that it was a woman, and she had her eyes open. She had a small hole in her throat but there was very little blood around the wound. She removed the gun the woman was holding and was thankful that she was wearing her gloves. Selina then waved her hand in front of the woman's eyes to see if there was a response and there was none. She then pinched the woman's nostrils together and counted to 30. The woman never moved. She then tried to feel for a pulse, but she didn't trust her ability to find a pulse and concluded that the woman was dead.

Selina was going through the same steps with the man closest to the little girl when she heard a slight moan, she turned her head far enough to see that the small body furthest away from where all the action seemed to be moving. Selina and the girl that had asked to help her looked at each other, it startled Selina to see the little girl jump up and run over to the other little girl. Selina picked up her pace on checking for pulses and securing the area so she could go check on the little girl.

"Lupita! Lupita!" Selina could see that the girl had blood around her waist and left hip but couldn't see much of anything in the dark. She shined her flashlight on Lupita and could see that she was breathing, but slowly. "Jesus H, I got to get you to a doctor before you bleed to death." Selina looked around, and knew what she had to do, she would have to leave BB here for the rest of the night and get the girl to doctor as fast as she could. "Who are you people, what's your name?" Selina said it in English but then repeated it in Spanish, hoping the little girl would give her some information about what had just happened.

"Alejandra" the little girl wiped a tear from her eyes and told Selina that the other girls name was Lupita. 'Well Alejandra, you need to help me get Lupita in the car. Both Selina and Alejandra picked up Lupita and put her in the back seat of the SUV. Selina looked around the site for anything that she thought she might need to do and decided to do and watched as Alejandra knelt beside the very wide-bodied man, she spoke in Spanish to Selina, "he was trying to help us, they hurt him for helping us." Selina walked over to where she was and knelt beside her, "It's too late for him now, we need to get your friend to a doctor." Just as she was about to stand and force the girl to leave the man moaned. "Alejandra burst out in more tears and wrapped her arms around the man, Selina put her hand in the man's hand "If you understand me, squeeze my hand." The squeeze was faint, but it was there. "Holy shit, you're alive, sure fooled me." Selina looked around knowing that there was no way she had the strength to lift this man into a car and felt a little helpless until she remembered BB. "Mr. you are as wide as a frickin house, this aint gonna be easy."

Selina maneuvered the SUV as closely to the man as she could and then opened the rear hatch door to the SUV. She tied a rope under his arms and then strung it across the top of the SUV then tied it to BB's saddle horn. She may not be able to lift the man into the SUV but if she could get BB to lift him high enough, she could push him into the back and with Alejandra's help that is exactly what she managed to do.

She unsaddled BB and removed his bridle, "you're on your own tonight buddy. I will come back and get you. I promise". She threw the saddle and bridle in the back seat but removed the satellite phone from the saddle bags before she spun the SUV around and headed for the ranch house.

Chapter 29

Doc Spivey

Selina was pushing the SUV through the desert back roads as hard as she dared. She managed to dial the ranch house from the satellite phone and was happy when Ellalio answered. Ellalio was not only good at keeping the clothes pressed and cleaned, but he was also an excellent house manager. He kept the place running smoothly, he was for all practical purposes the operations manager and he did it very well. "I will be at the ranch in an hour, I have two badly injured people with me that need medical attention, one young girl and one man." Ellalio listened intently as Selina explained as much as she could. "Ms. V, you should go directly to the hospital." It made sense to Ellalio that if the people were injured badly then his boss should take them directly to the hospital. "I can't, there is too much to explain so just call Doc Spivey and tell him to get there ASAP."

Doc Spivey was a trusted friend, a friend she had gone to high school with and then to college. He had always had a thing for Selina but despite his good looks, she was never interested. She trusted him though, and knew that he could work on or heal just about anything, he bounced back and forth as the family practitioner and the family veterinarian. Selina could count on Doc Spivey to keep things under wraps, but she also knew he had a code of ethics that would not allow him to do anything illegal. She would have to be very careful with this and choose her words wisely. She would never lie to Doc Spivey, but she needed his help.

When she hung up with Ellalio, she asked Alejandra to tell her everything she knew about the man and the girl. Alejandra told her about how the man had entered into Armando's home, beat him up and took his money, she even told her that she was embarrassed that the man had entered the room and saw what Armando's was making her do to him. She told Selina that she was happy to see the man beat up Armando because Armando was a terrible person and deserved to be beat up but then she told her that Armando had made her shoot at the man and if he hadn't been carrying the sack of money, she would have killed him. She told her that she was surprised that the big gringo did not kill her with his own gun but instead walked straight up to her and took her gun away.

When she was satisfied that she had told Selina everything she could about the big man, she told her about Lupita and how Lupita had helped her get cleaned up and how Lupita had shown compassion for her. She explained that until that man and Lupita showed up, no one had made her feel respected or cared for her since she was separated from her family. She said she was ashamed of what she did and what she had to do. She said that when she was with the group of people that were being "helped" across the border, the men in charge of everyone grabbed her from her sleep one night and did awful things to her. She described how they laughed as they hurt her and how she could smell their stinky breath as she felt the pain of each one. She told Selina that God could never forgive the men for doing that to her and he could never forgive her for allowing them to do it. Alejandra did not see the tears that slowly rolled down Selina's cheeks as she listened to a barely teenage girl talk about how God could not forgive her. Selina discreetly removed the tears from her cheeks as she drove, she drew in a strong breath to steady her voice. "The men that did that to you will burn in hell for all of eternity and you . . . my angel" she paused to steady her voice just a little more, "will eventually sit next to God the father with his arms around you. You've done nothing wrong" She could see the lights of the ranch ahead and figured they had about ten minutes before they arrived, "He sent Lupita and that man to help you, didn't he? There is nothing you have done that requires his forgiveness . . . never ever forget that."

Selina honked her horn so that Ellalio and whoever else might be there would know she had arrived. She eased the SUV into the barn and once she had the vehicle where she wanted it, she jumped out of the SUV and told Alejandra to stay in the car until it was ok to come out. The entire event had played out in darkness for Alejandra so Selina did not want to take the chance that she might see things like dripping blood that could do more damage to her already delicate state.

She was met by Louis, Jacknack, Ellalio and surprisingly Elizabeth. She had forgotten that she had told Louis to go ask her to marry him earlier in the evening or was it yesterday now? She had lost track of time.

Selina was tired but she still had work to do. She looked at Jacknack, "In the tack room behind the shoe wall . . ." she was cut off by "got it". Selina, Ellalio and Louis all managed to pull the big man out of the SUV and place him on a gunny sack gurney they used for sick animals from time to time. Lisa had already pulled the little girl from the back seat and was now being helped by Jacknack who had already opened up the secret door behind the tack wall that Selina thought no one knew about. She was wrong.

The room had two bunks, a wood stove and a sink with an old fashion hand pump. You had to pump a few times to get well water from it, but it still worked. After she and the others had placed Lupita and the man in the bunks, Louis started tending to the wounds of the big man and Lisa began attending to the little girl. Selina looked at Jacknack, "How the hell did you know this room was here?" Jacknack didn't respond quickly enough, Louis spoke for him, "who do you think built the thing Ms. V?" He continued to cut away the clothes of the big man but also continued to speak, "do you think your candy wrappers, beer cans and the ash trays just cleaned themselves up?" Selina rolled her eyes. She couldn't believe that a room that had been her getaway place her entire life was not as secret as she thought. "You know about the marijuana? Never mind- don't answer that."

Jacknack lit the stove as they continued to clean up the two new occupants of Selina's secret room. "Geez Selina- What have you gotten yourself into? You need to call the police, not the doctor." Selina turned to see Doc Spivey standing in the secret doorway. "I went to the house first, but nobody answered, saw the light on in the barn and this is what I find!" Selina started to speak but he cut her off, "I can't be a part of whatever this is for Christ sakes Selina! You know that!" His voice continued to rise, and Selina could see that his ears were getting red which was a sure sign he was angry. "Without taking one step further I can see from here that you have two people that our suffering from gunshot wounds!" He continued "now call the God . . ." but Selina had had enough, and she cut him off and stood as straight as her back would allow her to, "Michael Davis Spivey!" Selina walked over to where he was standing and nearly came nose to nose with him, "I know this much, your first oath is to do no harm!" she stepped back giving her enough room to poke him in the chest, "and by you standing in that doorway passing judgement from your high fucking horse you are doing harm!" She turned and pointed to the man and Lupita, you see two people who might be dying in front of you and choose to go on the fucking moral lecture circuit!", she turned her back to him and grabbed another clean towel from the basket that Lisa had brought to the room, "go call the fucking cops for all I care but these people need a doctor right now, not a judge!"

The room was quiet for a minute because everyone in that room knew that when Selina got pissed it was best to just keep silent, Doc Spivey knew that too. "Get out of the way, let me see", Doc Spivey pushed Selina aside and looked at the little girl, he checked her vitals, shined his light on her pupils as he held her eyelids open, "Well her pupils aren't dilatated, her blood pressure is a low due to the blood loss from this hole in her hip." He looked at Selina and motioned for her to help him turn Lupita on her side so he could see the backside of the wound, if there was one. "Well, there is an exit wound thank goodness so there is no bullet inside her and from the tiny entrance and exit holes, it was not one of those bullets that get wider the minute they hit their target and explode out the back". He gently rolled her back on her back and then stood to look over her once more. "She is lucky, it doesn't appear that the bullet hit any vital organs, but I can't be sure of that without x-ray and MRI which is why you need to take her to the hospital now". He stood up and walked over to the man that was now lying naked on the bunk where Jacknack and Louis were still trying to clean wounds so he could have a better view of the damage. "Best I can tell Doc is that he has 6 and a half holes in him, not sure if there is exits though, to damn big to see the back side of him." Jacknack and Louis stepped aside and let the doc have a look. Doc Spivey pointed at each wound and spoke as he did it, "Left hip, left clavicle, left elbow, left thigh, left calf, left jaw line and what appears to be the marks of a bullet from the left side of his temple to back of his head but it did not penetrate the skull", he motioned for the two men to roll him over so he could check for exit wounds.

Jacknack and Louis rolled the man over and both men grunted as they did it, "Well the bullets in his hip, calf, thigh, elbow all went through him, the jaw line took out two molars and exited just below his ear, and the clavicle has a bullet stuck in the bone somewhere because it didn't exit." He let them men roll him back on his back. Doc Spivey looked around then pointed at the bag on the floor, "give me my bag, He pulled at the middle of the bag and according to Jacknack, it unfolded into a three-tier pharmacy with all kinds of stuff in it.

Doc Spivey took out a vial and loaded a needle full of whatever it was and injected into the man. He then did the same for the little girl, that's a straight antibiotic to help ward off any infections instigated by having hot lead pass through their bodies." He placed the vial back into its chosen spot in his traveling pharmacy. They both need blood, especially the man, he's lost a lot of blood." He looked around as if waiting for someone to concur, "I don't generally carry extra bags of blood with me, would one of you run to the refrigerator and bring me two units of O neg, stat" he waited for second, "Oh wait, I forgot, this isn't a fucking hospital! It's a God damn barn!" He walked back over to his bag and pulled out some more equipment, then grabbed a bottle from the kit. "He handed it to Selina, this is a saline wash, I need you to flush out each wound and wipe it clean as I do the stitch work". Selina did as she was told.

Although most of the bleeding had stopped on both patients, he began suturing up the front and the back side of the girls wound. When he was finished, Selina placed a heavy layer of gauze on the front and the back side of the girl and then with Lisa's help, she wrapped a bandage all the way around her several times. Because of the number of wounds, stitching the man took quite a bit longer than the girl. When the Doc got to the jaw line and head, he looked around the room, "has the plastic surgeon arrived yet?" He gave Selina an angry look and she returned it, "Just do the best you can and quit being a smart ass and if it makes you feel better, I am O negative, and they can have everything I have."

He pulled two saline bags and hooked up a drip system then He handed one bag to Jacknack and one Louis, he then started the IV in the little girl, then in man. He went back to his bag and fumbled around then found what he wanted, "I need to stitch the inside of his mouth where he lost the teeth. Maybe a dentist can help him with some prosthetics later. Selina spoke,

"So, you mean they are going to live?"

"She is for sure, but he needs blood, or he might not."

"I told you they could have all of mine!"

"It aint that simple Selina- I don't have the equipment with me to do that, nor would I if I did."

The Doc filled one more needle from a vial, "this will help with the pain for both of them for now but when and if they wake up, they are gonna hurt like hell, be sure and give them this', he handed Selina a small bottle of pills, "What is it?" he looked at his work on the side of the man's head and decided he had done a good job, "It's 800 milligrams of acetaminophen, a quarter pill for the girl every 4 hours and a full one for that one every two." Selina stood there for a second looking at Louis and Jacknack holding the IV drips, "doesn't that stuff cause addiction?" Doc Spivey turned and looked at Selina, "Why yes Dr. Villalpando it does, you may report me to the governing board of animal husbandry if you do not concur with my treatment regimen."

Selina stuck the bottle of pills in her pocket and shook her head. She knew she was pushing Doc Spivey to his limits. Jacknack spoke up, "How long do we hold these things, Doc?" Doc Spivey turned to look at he and Louis who were both standing beside their patients holding IV drips, "until they are empty or the next nurse's shift change." Doc Spivey closed his bag and walked out of the room. Selina turned to look at everyone, "Lisa, see if you can find something to hang those bags on, a pitchfork and a cinderblock ought to suffice for now." She then caught up with Doc Spivey. "Thank you for the help, Doc" he interrupted her, "I am not helping you Selina, I am aiding and abetting a criminal!" Selina put her hand on his arm, "I know you're pissed Michael, but that man may know who killed my husband", she looked up at the sky, "I know it's a long shot, but I have to try." She then looked directly at the Doc, "No one else will help me find answers and you know it." Doc Spivey put his bag in the back seat of his Escalade and closed the door then he turned and looked at Selina, "I can lose my license for this Selina, there is nobody on this earth worth that, not even you."

Selina knew he was right, he could lose his license but what she also knew was that no one that knew about any of this would ever report him, "You are safe doc, if you don't know that about me by now, then you and I have wasted a lifetime of friendship, but you do what you gotta do." Doc opened the driver's door to his Escalade and started to climb in but turned around, "keep them warm and comfortable and make sure the bandages are changed and the wounds washed without soaking the stitches." He turned, climbed into the cab and before Selina could say anything he slammed the door. She stood there beside the window staring at him, she gave him no facial expression at all then folded her arms like she always did when she was trying to send a message of defiance. She didn't know if he saw her posture, but she wasn't concerned. Even though Doc was married, everyone in town knew that Selina was his first love, some say his only love. She knew that Doc would not alert the authorities, at least not yet.

PART III

Chapter 30

Marty Baxter

After the Doc drove off, Selina walked back into the hidden tack room now used for a triage station. Lisa found the pitch forks, turned them upside down and looped the IV lines around the forks. Lisa was rubbing the girl's forehead with a wet cloth, Louis and Jacknack were standing over the man, inspecting him as if he was a horse for sale at the auction while Alejandra dabbed his chest and forehead with a wet cloth as she had been instructed by Lisa to do. "This baby is burning up; I hope her fever breaks soon, or she may overheat." Selina closed the door behind them so that no one else could accidently walk in and as she was closing the door Louis spoke, "this is the man I met last night, I believe he is an assassin or something in that line of work". Selina walked over to where the two men were standing, "You met him last night?",

"See, Lisa too".

"Where?"

"At the restaurant, he ordered the Huevos Ranchero's for dinner", Selina's sarcasm came out, "and that's how you remembered him? From what he ordered?"

Lisa spoke up, "it was more than that Ms. V." Even though Louis was shaking his head as if to tell her not to talk, she did anyway. "He helped my Louis." Selina folded her arms which was the signal for everyone in the room to start talking, "If he is an assassin, he is an assassin with a heart Ms. V." Lisa continued to wash the little girl with cold water from head to toe but when she spoke, she would stop and look at Selina, "The brothers sent two men to harass Louis and this man stopped them both."

"So, what's with the Huevo'sRanchero's?" Lisa looked at Louis and he gave her a nodding approval, "if a gringo comes into the café and orders the Huevos' Ranchero's with Habanero coffee, we are to call a certain number, wait for an answer and then hang up." Selina rubbed her forehead, "you don't know who you are calling?", "no, we just know that a boy comes by the next day and drops off an envelope full of money, we don't ask any questions." Selina had already heard what Alejandra had told her and had made up her mind that this man was not a bad person, but she needed to know why he was in town. "If he was collecting money from Armando, he can't be that good. Armando's money is sleazy for sure." Louis nodded his head in agreement, "see, but there is something different about him, he is the bully who finds some sort of peace in beating up other bullies." Selina turned to the bunk with the little girl and sat down beside Lisa, "I'm pretty sure he didn't come to Arizona to collect sleaze ball money and take these two girls back as souvenirs. He was probably going to traffic them somewhere else."

Alejandra couldn't understand what they were saying because they were all speaking English, but she was reading the body language and when she decided to speak up, the language shifted from English to Spanish, "I don't know what all of you are saying but I know that this man is good. This man helped me get out of the hell I was in, he helped me clean up, he helped me and Lupita without asking, and we have to help him now," she stopped to wipe the tears from her cheeks as they freely streamed from her eyes, "I don't care if they take me back to Mexico, I want to help him first." Lisa let the motherly side of her show as she stood and put her arms around the little girl.

Selina broke the mood, "where are the other children?" Louis was pulling another blanket over the man lying on the bunk, "They are all at the main house, Ellalio was feeding them all and making sure they didn't have lice, they were all pretty dirty." Louis was still leaning against the wall but spoke, "The sheriff will come snooping around soon Selina, it is almost daybreak." Selina nodded in agreement, "we have to make sure this room stays hidden, no tracks or drag marks or anything leading to a dead end," she looked at Alejandra and returned to Spanish, "Will you stay here and make sure they are comfortable and quiet?" Alejandra nodded and smiled without saying anything. "Louis, you and Jacknack go round-up BB and figure out how to clean up this mess." Jacknack started moving, "and the other bodies"? Selina shook her head as if she didn't know or didn't want to answer. Jacknack could tell from experience that Selina was processing more than she wanted to and she would rather retreat to her "secret" tack room that wasn't a secret anymore. "I will handle it ma'am, the kids have been through a lot.

Selina knew that Jacknack was stepping up and covering for her and she hated it. She didn't like the feeling that someone had to come to her rescue but in this case, she needed time to think, there really was quite a bit to process. The children had not seen her in a few hours and because of the desert chase earlier that night, she felt an attachment to them like nothing she had ever felt before.

Selina entered the back door of the house where she found Ellalio standing next to the stove watching a table full of children eating and eating hardily. Selina looked across the table and it was as if he had prepared a thanksgiving feast for these kids, and they were eating it. Selina enjoyed the site of all those kids, she counted

15 eating a full meal at her table but she was struck by their silence as they ate. Selina grew up with lively conversation around the table with everyone chipping into the conversation as they ate. Not one single child spoke, not even to ask for salt or pepper or anything.

Selina looked at Ellalio and without saying anything, he shrugged his shoulders, he was thinking the same thing, but he was content to watch the children eat his cooking with such gusto. Selina edged her way into a seat at the long table that was designed for ranch hands to use when the bunk house kitchen was closed. She smiled, even though there was no chatter, the clank of silverware and slurping made her smile. These children had not had a chance to sit down at a table and eat for quite some time and Selina was glad to be the one to provide the opportunity.

Selina spoke in Spanish, but she spoke in slow and measured words so as not to seem overpowering. "Is the food good?", there were several nods from the table but still no one spoke, "does everyone have enough to drink?' There were plenty of nods but still no words, she was trying desperately to break the silence, she knew that if she could get the children comfortable enough to speak freely, she would be able to help them more easily. Even the two twins that had clung to her so tightly just a few hours ago, barely looked up from their plates.

Ellalio set a plate in front of Selina, he didn't know if she was hungry, but he didn't care, anytime someone sat at his table, he would feed them. Selina nodded an implied thank you then realized that she was also participating in the silence, "Gracias Ellalio! That is very kind of you, I am hungry as a pig!", she snorted like a pig really loud and almost all the children laughed out loud. There were a few that were reluctant to show any kind of emotion but did manage to look up from their plate and look around to see the others laughing. The two twins each took a big bite out of a tortilla, and both made the same snorting sounds which caused the other kids to play along. The room quickly filled with snorts and laughter; it was a very welcome noise until the gong of the front doorbell sounded. The doorbell was a cross between a large cowbell and a real Zen gong. No one knew where Selina's father found it, but he was so proud of it and had it installed.

Selina had been expecting it, but the children hadn't, and they immediately stopped laughing and snorting. Selina looked up at Ellalio then rose from the table but before she completely stood, she grabbed a tortilla off the plate, pressed it against her face and snorted one more time. The kids erupted with laughter again. Selina left them laughing as she went to go answer the door.

"Why hello Marty, what brings you out this way so early?" Marty Baxter was the Sherriff of Santa Cruz County and although it could never be proven, most of his pay came from the Northern Mexico Trincharis Cartel by way of the Peña brothers or he was being paid by the Barstow Brothers by way of some unknown East Coast mob family, no one knew for sure. He had been investigated by the FBI twice to no avail and he was beginning to feel untouchable. This was a visit that Selina was expecting.

"Good morning Selina, I'm here about a missing person report we received this morning, may I come in?" Selina smiled through the screen, pushed it open so that the Sheriff would have to step back, and she stepped out onto the expansive covered front porch. She could hear the children laughing which meant that the sheriff could also hear them. "Nobody missing around here sheriff."

"Don't be cute Selina."

"Sheriff, I have no reason to be cute with you."

"I'm also here investigating a child smuggling ring." The comment was designed to rattle Selina, but it didn't.

"Why Sheriff, are you finally investigating the murder of my husband and those girls that he was found murdered with...It's only been five years.",

"I said don't get cute Selina." He tried to look beyond her into the house to investigate the sound of children's laughter. "don't recall you having any babies Selina, what's all that noise in there?" Selina smiled, glanced over her shoulder, "Not that it's any business of your business sheriff, but it's bring your kids to work day here at the double L and we are just having a little breakfast before we get going." Sheriff Baxter tried to step past Selina and Selina stepped in front of him, "uh, this is a private party sheriff, invitation only." He stepped back and put his hand on his gun in a show of intimidation, "step aside Selina." The two stared at each other, Selina didn't flinch,

"You're gonna need a warrant Marty, better go get one."

"You know that all I need is probable cause and I can tear this place a part if I want to and I'd say I have probable cause right now."

"What, for laughter? Good luck explaining that one in court Marty." Selina put her hand on her own gun, "You really want to do this Marty?" Selina took her hand off her gun and crossed her arms in the defiant tone that she was famous for.

The silence hung on the porch for a few minutes, "You're fuckin with the wrong people Selina." Sheriff Baxter took his hand off his gun also and started to turn around but turned back to look at Selina, "as far as your husband goes, he fucked with the wrong people too." Deep inside, this infuriated Selina, but she didn't let it show, she was currently in a high stakes game of emotional poker, and she couldn't afford to flinch. "No Marty, YOU fucked with the wrong people."

Chapter 31

Housekeeping

Jacknack and Louis hitched up the flatbed trailer to the big Ford dually and attached the small horse trailer to Louis's Pickup and headed to the coordinates that Selina had provide them which turned out to be about a three-hour drive southeast of the Ranch house. The terrain was very rough in most areas, so the pace was very slow.

Jacknack was first to arrive with Louis slowly easing up behind him. "Damn, she was right, looks like a drug deal gone bad." Both men walked into the heart of where all the action took place and tried to make sense of what had happened. "Most of the shell casings are around this guy and the second-place award goes to this guy" Jacknack stopped and bent down, "girl", he stood back up, "It's a girl, don't make a lick of sense now, especially with one grave." Louis was circling the camp looking for signs of anyone else being there when he hollered at Jacknack, "how many drug deals that go bad pre-dig three graves?"

Jacknack made his way out to where Louis was standing over two other graves dug about two feet deep, just barely deep enough to cover a person but deep enough out here to cover them from ever being found. "Yeah, there is way more to this than drugs." Jacknack looked around with a little more concern in his eyes, "We need to get this shit cleaned up, but we need to figure a few things out first." Louis surveyed the landscape as if he fully expected someone to drive or walk up on them.

"This is a rental, rented to a Lois Kent." Louis was careful not to touch anything with his bare hands, he exited the passenger seat and opened the back of the vehicle, "She was the one with all the grand plans," he held up the shovel for Jacknack to see, "yeah, this one is a rental too, "registered to a Carmine Bev-il-aqua" Jacknack had to sound out the last name in order to get it right and he still didn't know if it was right. "He wasn't smart enough to register a fake name like the girl, no sir, no way that's a fake name." Louis was picking up shell casings "how do you know hers was fake?" Jacknack laughed, "because Lois Lane never married Clark Kent." Louis let out a laugh even though it felt slightly awkward considering where they were. "How do you want to handle this?" Jacknack rubbed his chin, looked around, "I think you go find BB first and when you get back with her, we can load up these cars." Louis looked around at the three bodies, "what about these folks". Jacknack smiled at him then patted Louis on the shoulder, "no point in both of us having that kind of memory." Louis understood, unloaded his appaloosa from the trailer. She was already saddled and ready to go, "I will be back soon, she won't go far." Jacknack never looked up, he just continued to survey the site and formulate a plan.

Jacknack felt a little sinister when he realized that he didn't have to dig any graves, that work had been done for him already. With the exception of the girl, because she had nothing on her, he took all the ID's, wallets, money clips, rings, watches, and even a pair of reading glasses from the former owners and put them all in a plastic bag, then dropped it in the driver's seat of big ford. He managed to drag the men into place then rolled them in the graves face down, these guys needed to be facing where they were going. The woman was easy to get into place and he rolled her in the grave face down also. It didn't take long for him to cover all three.

He searched the back of the truck for the metal detector. A piece of equipment that he had remembered to bring. He turned it on and then began the slow process of sweeping the entire area so that he could detect the shell casings that had been missed by the naked eye. If the FBI, or border patrol or whoever couldn't find a crime scene then that was their problem. He was almost finished when he spotted a Cholla Cactus that would have been in the direct line of fire. He walked over to inspect it and sure enough there were several holes in the cactus with no visible signs of exit holes. He turned the scanner on the Cholla, and it indicated what he already knew. There were slugs inside that cactus. He was digging the last slug out of the cactus when Louis came riding up over the ridge with BB in tow. "Perfect timing, any trouble?" Louis tied BB and his appaloosa to the trailer, "not a bit, what about you?" Louis looked around at a what seemed to be a bunch of nothing now, "nope, you just missed the housekeeper."

The two men winched both cars on to the flatbed trailer and then secured the horses in the trailer. "Do we go directly to town and drop off the cars?" Louis wiped his forehead as he spoke, "I think it's best we take them back to the west barn, wipe them down one more time and then drop them off in the middle of the night at the square. The rental car place will have to figure it out from there, we can't be expected to do all the work."

As they discussed, they moved the cars into the west barn, a barn that was rarely used. It used to be for storing extra hay, but it simply wasn't necessary now, and it needed some repairs, but it was still functional. It had lights and water and that's what they needed. They spent the rest of the day wiping down the cars and searching for anything of value that should not be left behind. The rental papers would be left but anything else would be taken. When they were satisfied that they had sufficiently cleaned the cars they headed back to the ranch where they pulled the flatbed into the main barn.

Selina was looking over the two cars on the flatbed as she spoke "You two look horrible, you need to go clean up and get some rest." Jacknack was helping Louis secure the horses when Selina arrived, "Can't do that just yet Mrs. V. We need to get this shit out of here." Selina looked them over again, "where are you taking them?" Jacknack took his hat off and rubbed his forehead, before he could speak Louis spoke, "Let us worry about that Mrs. V." Once again, Selina did not like the feeling of being protected, "Stop doing that guys! I am big enough to handle things and you both know it." Jacknack started to speak again but Louis interrupted him, "Yes ma'am, we are both well aware of that, but we also know that it is much easier to tell the truth than it is to lie." Selina didn't care for the answer as much as she didn't understand it, "what the hell does that mean?" Jacknack wouldn't let Louis interrupt him again and he powered through the answer, "It means that you Mrs. V, YOU, not us, will bear the brunt of all questions, investigations, inquiries, we are nothing more than the hired help . . . it is simply easier for you to tell the truth, the less you know, the more frustrating you will be for Sheriff Baxter."

Selina knew they were right, she knew it before the conversation even began but she still had the feeling she was being sheltered or protected, and maybe she was but she didn't like it. "He's already been here this morning." Louis nodded his head, "and he will be back again ma'am, that is for certain." Selina wanted to change the subject, so she looked at Louis, "in all this flurry of activity I never got to ask if you asked her?", Louis took his hat off and held it in a nervous way, "I intended to, but the Barstow boys interrupted the occasion, along with the gentleman with 6 bullet holes in him." Selina chuckled ever so slightly, "I guess that would put a damper on an engagement dinner." Jacknack wasn't in the mood for small talk, "Mrs. V, go back in the house please, as soon as the horses are tended to, we are headed out," he looked at Louis, "we will be back in the morning."

It was nearly 3am when Jacknack and Louis arrived at the square. As predicted, the square was empty. The crowd that had gathered to hear Fat Jackie were long gone and all that was left were a few cars of folks that were too drunk to drive home or had gone home with someone else. Jacknack and Louis wasted no time in unloading the cars and carefully parking them in a couple of the spots on opposite sides of the square. They took they keys and set the alarm for each and climbed back into to the big truck. Jacknack steered the big truck in the direction of the ranch as Louis reached in the backseat, grabbed a small igloo cooler and set it on the seat in between the two men. He reached into the cooler and pulled out two oversized cans of Milwaukee's best beer. He opened one and it spewed a little on the window of the cab then handed it to Jacknack, he grabbed the second and opened it with the same result. Louis lifted the can toward Jacknack in a manner of a toast, "to the Double L". The cans clacked together and both men took a hardy gulp from their cans. Jacknack let out a short burp, "that's for damn sure".

Louis sat in silence for as long as he could. The events of the night were weighing on him heavily. Since she sent him away after the cougar attacked them, a lot had happened and for the first time since she was born, he felt like he had lost control, not of her, but of the situation. He felt like he had not lived up to his promises, "Does Mrs. V. have anything to worry about?". Jacknack didn't answer right away, "no, she has nothing to worry about Louis." He knew that was somewhat of a lie, but he was using Louis's own advice, the less you know, the easier it is to tell the truth.

Chapter 32

The Engagement

Selina went back into the house to find that Lisa was sitting at the small breakfast table where she and Louis would often have coffee. Selina took a bottle of 20-year Pappy Van Winkle from the cabinet, grabbed two glasses and sat down across from Lisa. Lisa looked up and smiled and motioned that she didn't want a drink, but Selina wouldn't hear of it. "I've done things and seen things in the last forty-eight hours that I never thought I ever would, I need a drink and I don't like drinking alone." She poured a small amount in each of the glasses and slid one over to Lisa. Lisa looked at it like it was a snake but then relaxed her face a little. "Listen, this stuff is about 5 grand a bottle in the open market, I don't know if it's worth that much, but I enjoy it", she tilted the glass back, then downed all the contents in one gulp. "Ahhh". Lisa picked up her glass as Selina poured another small amount into her now empty glass. Lisa smelled the contents of the glass then took a small sip, "I've never had whiskey before Mrs. V., I don't know what I am supposed to do." Selina laughed as she took a sip, "well I have to warn you that after you have had a sip of Pappy, just about any whiskey you might try from here on out is gonna taste like mule piss." Lisa laughed at the thought then tried another sip but didn't say anything.

"Are the kids asleep now?" Lisa shook her head, pointed to the ceiling, "yes, they want to know when they can go home." Selina looked at her drink then looked up at the ceiling, "find a place to hide 15 children and then sneak them back into Mexico, what a novel concept", Lisa's facial expression changed from soft to a more frustrated look, "It may be close to impossible Mrs. V."

Lisa and Selina sat at the table sipping expensive bourbon and discussing the mess that they seemed to be in. It might take him a while, but Sheriff Baxter would soon come back with a warrant to search the premises. If she couldn't find a way to hide the children, she would be arrested for harboring illegals and then things would get ugly for everyone at the double L. The only way she could ensure that things stayed as normal as it could be for a while, would be to find hiding places for the children, very soon.

"Mrs. V, you have done so much for so many people, you have so many friends, friends you don't even know." Selina shook her head and sipped the bourbon, "I am not following you Lisa and I wish you'd just call me Selina." Lisa looked up at the ceiling and then back to Selina, "You are thinking that the children must all be hidden together, "there are many friends and townspeople that will take them in separately until you can collect them all." Selina smiled at the simplicity and effectiveness of the suggestion. The entire day she had been trying to think of a place big enough to hide them all and it never crossed her mind to hide them separately. "Oh my God Lisa, you are a genius! It is so simple!" Lisa gulped down her Pappy and poured another shot, "do you think you can find say, 8 people that will take care of them, I mean really take care of them?" Lisa nodded that she could and then sipped her pappy, she actually liked the taste of it but only if she controlled the sip. "We can have them all picked up first thing in the morning Selina." Selina smiled, "that is such a relief!".

"Selina", Lisa put her hand on top of Selina's and smiled, "you need some rest, please go lay down and sleep for a while, when you wake, the kids will be fed and on their way to safe families while we figure out what to do." Selina nodded her head; she hadn't slept in almost 48 hours now and she was doing nothing but running on adrenaline. "I still have guests in the tack room that need looking after." Lisa patted her hand, "I will take care of them, please go rest."

Lisa made sure that Selina made it upstairs. Selina sat in the wingback chair in her bedroom and began to take her boots off, but she didn't make it, she fell asleep in the chair. Lisa struggled to remove her boots, so much so that she was certain she would wake Selina with her tugging and shaking but Selina never moved. Luckily for Selina, Louis stepped into the room, he had returned and was looking to update Selina but realized that it would have to wait. Selina was exhausted and there was no waking her up. He helped Lisa pick her up and put her in bed with her clothes on but at least they managed to get her boots off.

Louis stood over Selina for a few minutes like a father stands over a child they have just put to bed. He marveled at her beauty and strength as she slowly breathed in and out. He then turned his attention to Lisa who was standing next to him, "You are so beautiful, so perfect and I don't deserve you but it is now or never", he reached into his vest pocket and pulled out a small box, he knelt down on one knee and looked up at Lisa as he opened the box, "It isn't much, it was my mother's and it is really all I have left from my family," he looked down at the silver band with one small opal stone in it then looked back up at Lisa, "I have been a vaquero all my life, I don't apologize for that but it's time for a change, will you marry me?" Lisa looked down at the man she loved on his knee holding a beautiful ring that she hoped he would offer her some day and that day was here, "of course I will marry you, it's about time you asked me you old fool." He stood up from his kneeling position and put his hands on her hips pulling her close to him, and he kissed her.

Lisa had been his "girl" for almost 15 years, but he never wanted to settle down. When Selina scolded him about not asking her to marry him, he couldn't argue with her. He loved Lisa and that was a fact, but they had never been intimate other than a simple kiss. Lisa had never been married either and was worried that the time had run out on her. She had no children, and she was long passed that stage in life, but she had no regrets. There had never been a short supply of marriage proposals over the years, she had turned them all down. When she met Louis, she knew that he was the one that she wanted to hold her hand as she drew her last breath or vice versa. He was a true gentleman and always treated her with respect and dignity, unlike some of the men that had been in and out of her life over the years. Lisa's life had been anything but easy.

As they stood there and kissed passionately for the first time, with Selina asleep in the bed next to where they stood, Lisa felt like her dreams had come true, the man that she loved was holding her tight, he was pressed against her, and she could feel the emotion of the moment coursing through her veins. She was happy. She hugged him tightly and whispered, "I didn't know you could be so passionate Mr. Arroyo". Louis blushed but she couldn't see it.

They closed the door to Selina's bedroom and walked down the hall. As they passed each door, they checked in on the children that were still sleeping peacefully. "I need to go check on our friends in the barn," Louis couldn't resist as they turned to walk down the stairs that led to the main entrance, he grabbed Lisa's hand and stopped her from descending the stairs, she turned to look at him and he kissed her again. He kissed her passionately again, he could never remember a time in his life that he was this aroused and was afraid that it was showing now, "I thought I might bust inside if I didn't do that one more time". Lisa didn't tell him, but she was glad that he had stopped to kiss her. She wanted to be kissed, she wanted much more but now was not the time and they both knew it. The two were still in their embrace when Lisa slid her hand over his groin where she could easily feel his excitement, Louis was startled by her seductive move but enjoyed the attention, it was attention he had never had before, Lisa looked deep into his eyes and with a very sheepish tone, "I just wanted to make sure that everything works for our honeymoon night." Louis didn't tell her, but he found out that everything worked extremely well the minute she touched him there, far too well. He tried to hold his breath, he tried everything he could think of to keep it from happening, but it did.

Lisa could tell from the expression on his face and the way he wasn't saying anything, what had happened. She removed her hand from his groin and took his hand in hers. She smiled and started slowly leading the way downstairs. Once they were in the main hallway she opened the door to the half bathroom, lead him in and shut the door. Louis was still not saying anything and was becoming more embarrassed by the second. Lisa stood in front of him and unbuckled his belt then unzipped his pants. She slid his pants down around his ankles followed by his boxer shorts leaving him fully exposed and still very erect in front her. She then took a towel, ran some warm water on it and cleaned him thoroughly. Louis fell back against the wall and remained silent with his eyes closed. "That will do for now as she held him in her hands." She caressed him as softly as anything Louis had ever felt, "I'm sorry, but not sorry my beautiful man, don't waste those if you can help it."

No woman had ever seen Louis like that before. He was once bathing in a creek when a woman on horseback stopped and talked to him, but he remained submerged throughout the entire conversation, so he was certain that she hadn't seen his thing. Now, here he was standing in Mrs. V's bathroom letting a woman hold it in her hands. He had to admit that he enjoyed it and as she stood there cleaning and caressing him he could feel the stir and knew that he was about to get even more embarrassed if he didn't get his pants back up so he reached down and pulled his pants and boxers up in the same motion, "I'm sorry Ms. Lisa I am afraid I am not very skilled at this, we need to go check on our friend." Lisa laughed, then washed her hands in the sink and watched him walk out the door, amazed that a man that had seen so much in life had never been with a woman.

Chapter 33

House Guest

When Louis entered the barn, he could see the false wall to the tack room was open and he immediately looked around, Selina and Alejandra were asleep upstairs so there was no reason for the door to be open. He peaked in the door and was relieved to see that Doc Spivey was attending to the little girl. "Hey Doc, I didn't know you were coming back, Selina said you were upset." Doc Spivey stood up from the girl and moved over to the big man. "Upset is an understatement but I am a doctor, and I am not about to let these people die because I didn't do anything,""you think they might die Doc?" Doc Spivey put his stethoscope to the big guy's chest and moved it around as he spoke, "Not now I don't, their progress from last night to this morning is nothing short of amazing. Lupita here, is actually awake." Louis scrambled over to the little girl and knelt beside her, "was awake, she spoke to me for a little but then I gave her another sedative, she needs to rest and let her body heal some more. I would consider moving her out of this barn and into something a little more suitable, actually, move them both." He put his stethoscope in his bag and turned to look at Louis, "the less I know the better off I am." He looked around the room, "where is Selina? I need to talk to her."

Louis stuck his hands in his pockets, "She is asleep Doc, sound asleep, couldn't wake her with a train whistle." The Doc was frustrated with the reply, and he let it show, "I will be back this evening, let her know." Louis wasn't one to suffer bad attitudes very long, in his mind, the Doc could just stay away for all he cared and thought it was rude for the Doc to behave the way he was, "Doc, I don't think she will be awake this evening, I have seen her like this before and she will be asleep for the next 24 hours for sure, maybe longer." Doc grabbed his bag, this bag was different than the one he had last night, this one was much smaller, "then wake her!" Louis saw Lisa walk in the room and wished she hadn't because her presence made him change his temperament, but not much.

"Hold up Doc, Selina didn't ask for any of this, it's been shoved at her. She could have called one of a 100 people that could have helped her, including another doctor but she didn't. She called you, someone she trusts and respects", his voice went from soft and compromising to very hard in a matter of seconds, "why she cares for you I will have no idea because personally her affection for you is the only thing that keeps me from jamming that doctor bag up your pompous sorry ass." Louis took a step towards the Doc. Doc Spivey stepped back to keep the distance between he and Louis. Lisa stepped in between the two men; she didn't say anything but simply stood between the two. "I will be back this evening to make sure these two are on their way to a full recovery, they need to be in the house and not in the barn, if Selina is awake then, I will talk with her but if not, I will be back tomorrow. I suppose there is no rush." The Doc left the room, threw his bag in the car and he was gone.

"The Doc is a good man. He is just scared." Louis looked at Lisa as she spoke, she was calming and beautiful and he felt his mood change. "You are right baby, I let him get under my skin." Lisa put both her hands on the sides of his face and kissed him on the lips. It was the first time there had been any public display of affection between the two and the kiss startled Louis. Lisa laughed at his reaction and decided to change the subject, "how will we get the big man into the house?"

Louis thought about it for a few minutes and decided to wait until Jacknack came back to the barn to address moving the big man. The events of night had caught up with Jacknack also. When he and Louis returned from dropping off the cars in town, Jacknack headed straight for the bunkhouse and hadn't returned. Louis had known Jacknack for many years and throughout that time, Louis had marveled at the energy level Jacknack had. He never seemed to get tired. This sudden display of exhaustion led Louis to believe that something had happened out in the desert that night with he and Selina and it worried him.

He didn't think he and Jacknack could move the man with just the two of them, but he did think that if Selina and Lisa helped, then they might be able to get him into a room downstairs just off the kitchen corridor. He turned to speak to Lisa and saw that Selina was standing in the doorway.

"What are you doing up? You should be sleeping." Selina folded her arms together and leaned against the door jam, "I'm afraid God isn't going to let me sleep much anymore." Not having any idea what she meant and not knowing what had transpired while she and Jacknack were in the desert, Louis managed to place a puzzled look on his face, "what does that mean Ms. V?", she was about to speak but Jacknack cut her off, "it means she has to work some knots out of her rope now." Jacknack pushed his way past Selina, "we need to get these folks in the house and out of the barn before that idiot Sheriff comes back." Louis looked at Lisa, shook his head, "hell I guess nobody needs any rest around here."

"How is he?" Selina walked over and sat down on the makeshift bed that the big man was lying on. "Doc says he will heal just fine, actually said it was remarkable the way that both were healing." Louis walked over and stood next to the bunk, "Doc wants them moved into the house though, he was pretty clear on that part." Selina looked up at Louis then over to Jacknack- "Doc Spivey was here?" Jacknack shrugged his shoulders because he didn't know, he had managed to get a few hours of sleep and that was all he really needed but the sleep had prevented him from seeing the doctor. "He was here, and he was an asshole, I should have kicked his ass but . . ." Selina put her hand on the big man's shoulder and finished the sentence for him, "but Lisa wouldn't let you." She smiled at Lisa who had gracefully and quietly moved towards the back of the room, Lisa had a knack for melding into a room.

"Has he said anything, been awake, moved?"

"He mumbles a lot."

"Like what?"

"I think he is saying Teddy or something similar, maybe ready?"

"Is that it?"

"Madison".

Selina looked around, "well that's a start. Bring the gurney- let's get him in the house."

It wasn't as much trouble getting the man into the house as they had expected. The four of them managed to get him comfortably in a room just off the entrance to the kitchen as planned. He mumbled throughout the entire move. Selina tried to make some kind of sense of it, but she couldn't. "Well, I heard him say Madison but that's about it." She dabbed his forehead and neck with a washcloth that Lisa had brought into the room. "I thought I heard sporting goods, but it wasn't clear enough to make out."

Louis put his hand on Selina's shoulder as she sat next to the new occupant of her home, "You need to rest Mrs. V", she looked up at him and he could see the bags under her eyes, "He is where he needs to be right now, all we can do is wait." Selina continued to wipe his face and neck, "I want to talk to him when he wakes up, I want to be here when he does."

Louis could feel her pain, since her husband had been murdered, she was not the same. She was now missing a piece of her soul that he didn't think she could ever get back. She was expecting, at least hoping that this man would wake up and solve the mystery of her husband's demise and why those girls were killed alongside him. Louis heard the talk around town and even on the ranch, people thought her husband had become a human trafficker as a side hustle. Louis knew it wasn't true, but people were going to talk and when they did, they would say some awful things.

"I am sending Jacknack back to the cliff's ma'am, he will be back in a few days, where there is one Mountain Lion, there is certainly two. We need to chase them back up to the north country." Louis was holding his Stetson and was fidgeting with it, Selina caught the "tell", "what else Louis?" Louis looked down at his boots like a shy child, "Lisa's father is still alive, it was something that I was unaware of," he paused giving Selina the opportunity to urge the words out of him, "go on, and . . . " Louis looked up at her, "He lives up in Winslow," Selina stood up from where she was sitting beside her new unconscious house guest, "geez Louis, just say what is on your mind", Louis looked around the room, "it is a private matter ma'am, may I speak to you in the kitchen?"

Selina and Louis walked across the hall to the kitchen and Louis shut the door behind them. "I know this is bad timing ma'am, but it is proper to ask the father for the hand in marriage. I would not be a gentleman if I did not." Selina poured a cup of coffee, "Why the rush and what if he says no, what will you do then?" Louis fiddled with his hat again, "come on Louis, just tell me, I am a big girl", Louis looked around the kitchen to make sure no one was listening, "Lisa and I had an encounter in the guest bathroom that should only happen between a husband and a wife", he cleared his throat, "I do not wish to tarnish her reputation in any way and if her father says no, I will still marry her, I am merely extending the courtesy and respect a gentlemen should." Selina looked at Louis with amazement, "out here in the desert, with nothing but cows and cactus, you are worried about being a gentleman and protecting a woman's honor." It wasn't a question as much as it was a statement, she walked over to Louis and put her arms around him, she squeezed him tightly and he returned the embrace. "Do what you have to Louis," Louis could hear the snivels come from her and couldn't quite figure out why she was crying. "The world needs more men like you Louis, go protect your woman's honor my friend."

Chapter 34

The Awakening

Once the house became quiet, Selina made herself a drink, an Old Fashion, one of her favorites as long as it was made with Sazerac, any other form of spirit in an old fashion just didn't taste the same. She sat down at her desk and leaned back in the leather high back chair swivel rocker and looked up at the vaulted ceiling of what used to be her father's office. When he passed away, she avoided using the office out of respect and it just felt odd to her. Her father had the massive I beam, and trusses brought down from a lumber mill in Happy Jack, a small town just south of Flagstaff. The wood used specifically for this office was amazing and she had always enjoyed the way this office felt and the way it smelled. It reminded her of her father and at the moment, she wished he was here to help advise her on what to do next.

She had committed a crime; a serious crime and two men would never breathe again because of her actions. She had two badly injured people in her house at the moment that were probably wanted for crimes of their own, well, maybe not the little girl but certainly the man with 6 bullet holes in him was more than likely a criminal and if that were true, she is now aiding and abetting. Her head was spinning as she thought about how everything would eventually play out when Alejandra walked into the room.

Since her arrival here at the ranch house, Selina could tell that she was loosening up some. She was definitely quiet, but she was moving about the house freely now. At first, she sat in her room until someone came to check on her and retrieve her for meals. She was understandably scared, and Selina had the feeling that she was only acting out the existence that she had been subjected to. She was more than likely told to stay in her room and out of site until she would be summoned to service a customer if that is what you call it. Selina knew she had been raped repeatedly and she knew that she was very fragile.

Selina spoke to her in Spanish, "you look more beautiful toady than you did yesterday, and I thought that was simply not possible!" Selina was serious but she was also trying to give this little girl back some of her dignity and hopefully improve her self-esteem. Alejandra smiled a sheepish smile that made her look like a little girl again. "How are you today?" Alejandra did something that Selina was not expecting, she slowly walked around the huge desk that Selina was parked behind and when she reached Selina she bent down and wrapped her arms around Selina's neck. Selina embraced her as best she could from a sitting position which was awkward but before Selina could stand and hug her, Alejandra crawled into Selina's lap and embraced her even tighter, like she was a frightened child, which she was.

Selina held her tightly as she began to cry. Alejandra wept with everything she had. She cried as she spoke, "I am so terrible, I am tainted now, I can never go home, and I have no place to stay here, please don't send me away." Selina rubbed the child's back as if she was a toddler and began to whisper to her and slowly use the rocking motion of the chair to help calm the young girl. "You are safe with me child, no one will ever hurt you again. I will not send you away and I will not let anyone take you from me." Selina stroked the back of her head, feeling her soft hair slide against her fingers, "You will have to help me though and it will not be easy."

Selina let her cry some more until she felt like the pain of her experience was slowly seeping out of her. "Look at me baby, Alejandra released her grip from Selina enough to lean back and look at her. The tears continued to stream down her beautiful face, "from now on, you are my niece from El Paso." Selina wiped the tears from Alejandra's as she spoke, "no one needs to know anything more than that." Alejandra placed her head back on Selina's shoulder, she wanted nothing more than to be a little girl again, the little girl that crawled into her mother or fathers lap when she was hurt or scared or just needed to be held, unfortunately, that innocence had already been cruelly taken from her and Selina was determined to help restore some of it.

Selina sat there with Alejandra on her lap for over an hour. She could feel Alejandra relax in her arms and eventually she fell asleep. She heard the knock at the door, it was more of a pounding, whoever was at the door was not happy. Selina reached for her phone on the desk with Alejandra still asleep and used the app that showed the video of the front door and porch area, and she could see the Barstow brothers along with Sheriff Baxter. She shook her head in frustration and tried to get up, but Alejandra was a little bigger and heavier than she expected. She managed to get out of the chair and carry Alejandra to the leather couch that she used to take naps on while her father worked at his desk.

Before she could make it out of the office, the sheriff and the Barstow brothers were standing in the office with her. "Wow Marty, I hope you have a warrant in your pocket and when did you appoint these two knuckle draggers as deputies?" Marty Baxter walked further into the office like he owned the place and started fiddling with a civil war musket that her father had refurbished and was now hanging on the wall. "Careful Marty, it still works." Barry Barstow took a step further into the office and Joe Barstow stayed in the doorway. "You are such a smart mouthed girl Selina, always have been." The sheriff pretended to aim the Musket at nothing then hung it back on the rack, "I see this girl sleeping on your couch and I need to see her papers." Selina took a few steps towards Alejandra who was still sleeping soundly. "Two things Marty, one, you haven't shown me the warrant that allows you to invade my home and two," she held up 2 fingers, this aint Russia, we don't show papers here." Marty walked over and stood in front of Selina, "Who is she?" Selina smiled and looked at the Barstow boys as she said, "none of your fucking business." Marty did something that she didn't expect, he punched her in the face and knocked her to the floor in front of where Alejandra was still sleeping. It hurt but she had been hit harder, she was a little woozy and knew she wasn't ready to stand but Marty reached down and grabbed her by the throat and started to lift her off the ground. Selina was wishing that Jacknack and Louis were still here but they weren't so she would have to figure this one out by herself. Because she was in the house, she didn't have her pistol with her. There was a gun in the desk drawer, but she was going to have trouble getting to it.

"Shut that smart mouth of yours, didn't I?" Marty squeezed harder around her throat and laughed, "I have been waiting to do that for a long time. Selina smiled which showed some blood on her teeth, "that's all you do Marty, wait. You never do a thing, you're too stupid to actually accomplish anything." Marty punched her again and then let her crumple to the floor. "Well today is different, today I shut you up long enough for me and the boys here to have a turn." Selina was even more dizzy now, but she never lost her spunk, "yeah well it's the only way any of you ugly fucks would ever get laid."

"We just want the land Selina, there is no need to let it go any further." She knew it was Barry speaking but she was trying to collect her thoughts. The second punch that Marty landed had cause her left eye to swell quickly and it was now closing rapidly. "Old Marty has been itchin to fuck you forever, and I think he intends on doing it." Barry laughed as he spoke but then slowly strolled over to where Selina was still on the floor. He knelt down next to her, "I wouldn't mind a turn myself, but I am not that kind of a guy. I like to court a woman a little bit", he smiled showing his perfect white teeth that she was sure that he paid a handsome price for, "before I fuck her". Barry continued to kneel next to Selina and he looked in the direction that Alejandra was laying on the couch, now pretending to be asleep, "I bet that little Mexican Philly has been rode a few times already. I would imagine she is still pretty tight though," Barry stood up and touched himself in the groin, "come to think of it, I'm pretty horny right now for some young cooz.

Marty reached down, grabbed Selina by the hair and forced Selina up off the floor. Selina winced but she was not about to show any pain or scream, she would never give these pricks the satisfaction. Marty pulled her close to him by keeping one arm around her neck and he used his other arms to cup Selina's ass and pull her tightly next to him and he began to rub his crotch against her, Selina could feel the vomit rising in her throat, the thought of Marty Baxter sticking his thing in her or anywhere on her was just about more than she could stomach.

"I'd let the lady go if I were you." The voice was strong but somewhat raspy, "I don't think that's gonna happen today." Marty released his grip and Selina stumbled back on to the couch, right smack on top of Alejandra. Alejandra could no longer fake sleeping anymore and she tried to embrace Selina as they both somehow ended up in a sitting position on the couch.

Every head in the room turned to see that Joe Barstow was lying on the ground and a man standing in the doorway wearing nothing but boxer shorts pointing a gun in Marty and Barry's direction. It was the man that had been shot in the desert and left for dead. Barry tried to reach his brother but the man in the boxer shorts pulled the hammer back on the gun he was holding which caused Barry to stop in his tracks. "Don't worry, he will wake up shortly, I just put him to sleep. I'm borrowing his gun right now, but I have no intentions of giving it back"

Marty stepped away from Selina but not any closer to the man pointing a gun at him, "I am the Sherriff in these parts mister and you better put that gun down before you get into some serious trouble!" The boxer shorts man continued to point the gun at Marty, Selina saw a sinister smile come across his face, "from where I am standing, you look like a weasel piece of crusty shit." The man smiled even bigger, "come here Sheriff weasel", he waved the gun in a gesturing motion to come closer, but Marty didn't move, the man fired a shot that struck one inch away from Marty's right foot and Marty jumped away in fear. "I will put the next one right in your fucking foot if you don't get your ass over here." The man didn't raise his voice, he stayed calm, Selina had the sense that this man was a killer of some sort.

Marty practically sprinted over to the man in the boxer shorts until he was standing in front of him. Selina's eyes got really big, and she may have even gasped when the boxer short man struck Marty in the eye with the barrel of the gun, but he quickly pointed the gun back at Barry as everyone in the room watched Marty fall to the floor, grasping his eye in pain. "When you see that shiner in the mirror when you get home tonight, remember it, remember who gave it to you, burn my face into your memory because if you every hit a woman again, my face is the last thing you will ever see."

He looked over at Barry, "You gentleman need to leave, now." The room was deathly quiet, Selina was in somewhat of a confused state as she looked at Alejandra and they both couldn't believe what just happened. Barry bent down to help the Sheriff up and between the two of them, they managed to get Joe up off the floor. "You aint heard the last of this mister. You shouldn't butt into other people's business", Barry said as he tried to move passed the boxer short man in the door, "You think? I know idiots like you never know when to quit and you all end up dead, eventually." Boxer short man discreetly touched his wound that was on his hip and Selina could see that it had begun to bleed again. Marty had Joe's arm slung over his neck as he tried to help drag him out the door. Selina could see that his eye was swollen shut like hers and oddly, it made her feel better.

Selina looked at the man standing in the doorway in boxer shorts that used to be her husbands. Lisa must have put them on him sometime during his stay. She watched him step aside and let the men go through the door. As they passed each other Barry spoke again, "You have no idea what you've done." There was no response from anyone as they walked out of the house. Selina heard the front door close, and she let out a breath of air. Alejandra wrapped her arms around Selina again and began to sob. Selina rubbed her back but had to let go of her as she realized that the man that had just snapped out a coma long enough to keep the corrupt sheriff from doing what Selina always knew he wanted to do, was no longer in the doorway.

Selina took Alejandra's hand as she rose from the couch, the two walked over to the desk, opened the drawer and took the Sig p320 out of that drawer that her dad kept there. She cleaned it every week despite the fact that it hadn't been shot in over 6 years. The two moved toward the door to find the hallway empty. She checked the front door and could still see the dust cloud created by the intruders that were forced to leave before they got to do what they wanted.

Alejandra begged her not to shoot him, she continued to repeat that he was a good man and that he rescued her. Selina reassured her that she was not going to shoot him, but she was trying to help him.

"Didn't you see that he was bleeding again?" Alejandra admitted that she didn't see much because she was scared. The two ladies walked briskly through the kitchen, back to the room he had been resting in.

He was there, partially on the bed and partially off. He managed to get everything from the hips up back on to the bed, but his legs were still on the floor. Selina could see the blood pool on the white sheets, "Help me get him on his back before he bleeds to death!" Alejandra and Selina wrestled the somewhat oversized man into the bed and on his back. She ran into the kitchen and started to boil some water; she didn't know what else to do other than to make sure that she got the bleeding to stop. "Ellalio!" she screamed for Ellalio, she knew he would be in the laundry room playing the guitar in between washes and drying or starching everything in sight, but he would be close. Then it occurred to her that if he heard that gunshot, he might be hiding. Ellalio was a good man, but he was not a fighter. His flight or fight response was always flight. "Ellalio!" she screamed again as she was grabbing towels. She dipped some of the towels in the pot of hot water and took a handful of clean dry towels into the room across the hall. She began applying pressure to the wound on his side because it was the one bleeding the most but nearly every wound that Doc Spivey had patched was now open and bleeding.

Ellalio finally came to the bedroom, "Sorry miss V, I was a little scared when I heard the shooting," Selina didn't care, she knew what to expect from Ellalio, he did what he was supposed to, and he did a great job of it. He wasn't hired for his masculinity. "It's ok Ellalio! Call Doc Spivey and then help me get this bleeding stopped on this man before he dies!" Ellalio stood in the doorway for a second, "Now Ellalio!" Ellalio bolted out of the room and returned quickly after he called Doc Spivey.

Chapter 35

The Black Eye

Doc Spivey showed up at the ranch in record time. He was carrying his big black bag again as he entered the house without knocking or ringing the doorbell. Ellalio caught him in the foyer and ushered him into the room that contained the once bleeding man. Selina had managed to get all the bleeding stopped, the wounds redressed and dried before the Doc arrived.

"What the hell happened Selina?" Doc put his bag down on the dresser adjacent from the bed. He checked the man's vitals then looked at each wound like a jeweler would inspect a diamond, he was thorough. "We got a visit from the Barstow's with the help of Marty of course." She was keeping her swollen eye out of sight from the Doc, she wanted him to focus on the man and she knew the minute that he saw her he would stop what he was doing and attend to her. Love was a strange thing. "Things got a little rough and somehow he managed to wake up and intervene, I'm glad he did."

Although Selina had already stopped the bleeding, Doc re-stitched the wound on his hip that had opened up during the scuffle. Doc finished and reapplied the bandage, he placed his instruments in his bag neatly, Selina watched his movements, he was methodical about everything. "I can't keep coming out here Selina, you have to get him to a hospital and let them provide 24-hour care until . . ." Doc finally saw Selina's face, he reacted just as Selina had expected, "Good God Selina!" He quickly reached into his bag and found the small little light used to look deep into someone's eye, Selina could see his hand was shaking now. He was steady as a rock when he was working on the man but when it came to Selina, he became very nervous, "The Barstow's did this in front of the Sheriff?" Selina chuckled a little as Doc lifted her chin up then gently eased the slit that used to be her eye socket apart, but he failed. "Damn it!" He shook his head and started to make a move for his bag again, but Selina caught his arm, "it's ok Michael, I am fine.", Doc grabbed her wrist so he could get a feel for her pulse rate, "Like hell you are! I can't believe Marty stood by and let this happen!" Selina took the hand that Doc was holding and slowly raised it up to his face then gently touched his cheek, "Michael, stop. I am fine."

Selina and Doc stepped across the hall into the kitchen and sat down that the table that she and Louis worked out the problems of the world every morning. "Is he ok?" Doc continued to stare at the swollen eye. Selina snapped her fingers in front of his face to get him to focus on the question and not the eye, "You say he got up, choked a man out and ran everyone off?" Selina nodded her head in approval of the cliff note recap of the story she had given him in the other room. "Yes, that's about it. He just showed up in the doorway, took out a man as quietly as a mouse eats cheese on a pillow, we never saw him or heard him until he was pointing a gun at Marty and Barry.

Doc stood in front of Selina and looked her over again. "You probably have a fractured orbital socket, Selina. You need to press charges against those goons!" Doc looked around the kitchen, "you have a drink somewhere?' Selina smiled her incredible smile and went to the cupboard that held the spirits. "Wellers work?" Doc nodded and she poured two glasses. "As soon as I leave here, I am going right to Marty's office and remind him what his job is!" Doc was still upset at seeing Selina's condition. Selina reached across the table and touched his arm, "Michael, it was Marty that hit me, not the Barstow brothers. This is something you need to stay out of." Doc Spivey took a sip of his drink and laughed, "that's pretty hard to do when you keep calling me back out here Selina." She returned the laugh, "good point."

Selina placed her drink in front of her, "I promise not to call you back, maybe." Selina smiled as she said, "is he going to be ok?" Doc explained that his blood pressure was normal and complimented her on getting the new bleeding stopped. He commented on the guy's strength and resolve and then listened to Selina as he coaxed the day's events out of her. "Marty is out of control; I can't believe he is doing this! He used to be such a good decent man." Doc Spivey downed what little Weller's he had left in the glass, "Selina, why don't you just sell the ranch to them." Selina looked down at the table, "They are offering you 75 million dollars for the ranch!" Doc stood up in frustration, "You know damn well that this ranch is not worth that amount of money!" Doc shuffled his feet a little then put both hands on the table and bent over using his arms like a preacher grasping a pulpit. "You know that, Selina!" Selina looked up at her lifelong friend, "then what Michael?" She too stood up "my father is buried here, my mother is buried here, there mothers and fathers are buried here.", she paused, "not to mention that I would be selling out my country", she walked over to the bottle of Weller's and poured another small amount for herself. "You know they only want the land to traffic drugs and people without impunity."

Doc Spivey, took his empty glass and placed it in the sink, "the problems at the border are government problems, not yours Selina," he turned to face her, "You can't fix what you don't control." Selina knew the advice was decent, but she was not in the habit of quitting or backing down from a fight, "Tell that to the two little girls sleeping upstairs that have had their innocence taken from them by unscrupulous people" she took a sip again, "like the Barstow brothers and now Marty." Doc walked over to where she was standing and put his arms around her, "you know they won't stop. You got lucky this time, maybe the next time they finish what they started?" Selina let the Doc hug her and frankly, it felt good. She needed the hug at the moment, and she knew he meant well. She pulled away from him, "you're a good man Michael Spivey, I am lucky to call you my friend." Doc shook his head, "you at least need to put some ice on that swelling. You're gonna need that eye when they return." Selina gave him a sheepish smile, "thanks Doc. I will keep that in mind." Doc turned to leave, "You never answered my question Mike, is he going to be ok?" Doc Spivey laughed out loud, "Selina, that man is a beast. With six bullet holes in him, he should be dead but somehow, he manages to wake up and keep three guys from raping you and he goes back to bed. He will be just fine. Keep his wounds clean." He turned and left the kitchen, only stopping long enough to grab his big black back and leave.

Selina walked next door to the bedroom where he was sleeping. She pulled up a chair and started talking to him as he slept. "Thank you for what you did today. Alejandra and I owe you a debt of gratitude." She adjusted the quilt that covered the man. "I really wish you would wake up so we could talk. I have so many questions to ask you." Selina sat there, staring at the man that had earlier woken up from a coma and somehow neutralized three men that were invading her home. "You know something about my husband's death, I just know it." She reached over and gently stroked his cheek and forehead, "I promise to take care of you," she looked him over from head to toe, "they aren't going to be happy with you now. They will try to get even but I won't let them." She stood up, looked down at him, "they won't catch me off guard anymore, I will be ready next time."

Chapter 36

Breakfast and the naked man

Ellalio and Selina sat at the table having coffee, oatmeal and bacon that Selina had made for the both of them. She normally would have had breakfast with Louis, but he had not made it back from visiting Lisa's father. Lisa was at the café this morning, so it was just her and Ellalio. "Got another plate?" Selina looked up and saw Jake take his hat off and hang it on the Elk Horn rack beside the entrance. "Well, I thought you'd gotten lost Jake!" Selina stood up to grab another plate, "I did." Jake replied. Both Ellalio and Selina laughed out loud. "North, South, East and West Jake, it aint that hard." Jake sat down at the small table normally reserved for Louis and Selina, "sun rises in the east and sets in the west." Jake said thank you as Selina sat the oatmeal and bacon in front of him, "thank you Mrs. V." Jake didn't say much but he tore into the bowl of oatmeal like it was his last meal. "Moss grows on the north side of the tree Jake; we've been over this." Jake nodded his head but continued to eat and in a matter of minutes, the bowl was the empty and the bacon had been devoured. He slurped the glass of milk that Selina gave him, leaving a nice milk mustache that he seemed proud of. "I'm sorry ma'am, I was starving."

Jake sat there at the table for an hour telling Selina and Ellalio about his adventure that lasted far longer than it should have. There really wasn't much to tell but Jake could weave a good story out of nothing, and he was doing a good job at the moment. "Did you at least find the stock?" Jake sipped the coffee that Selina poured for him and nodded, "yes ma'am, I did but we all damn near starved before I got them back." Selina laughed. "I just don't understand how anyone can struggle with directions as bad as you Jake." Ellalio stood up, took his dishes to the sink and began washing them, "ma'am, when the sun is setting, I know that is west and when the sun is rising, I know that is east but it seems to me I would have to follow the course of the sun all day in order to know east and west and if I happen to get turned around in my saddle, I just don't know which way is which.", he sipped his coffee again, "and I ain't seen much moss growing down here in the desert.". Selina shook her head then froze as she him in the doorway.

"I hate to trouble you, but do you know where my clothes are, and can I borrow a toothbrush?" The man was standing in the kitchen doorway, naked as the day he was born. He didn't seem to mind that he was naked and tried to hide nothing. Selina had seen him naked already but that was when he was nearly dead. Now, here he was standing in her kitchen with everything exposed. Jake looked up, "Damn man! Put some clothes on for Christ's sake!" Selina smacked Jake on the back of the head in protest of his comment, "I would brother, but I am at a loss for where they are." Ellalio stopped washing his dishes, "I have some clothes ready for him as you requested Mrs. V, I will go get them." Ellalio dashed off to the laundry room.

Selina walked over to him and stood there looking in his eyes. He looked dazed; his pupils still seemed abnormally wide to her. "Why don't we go back to your room, and we can at least wrap a sheet around you until Ellalio gets back with some clothes." He complied and turned around with Selina following.

"Who the hell is that?" Jake was right behind Selina as she followed him into the bedroom. "He is a house guest, haven't you ever seen a house guest before Jake?" Selina used her sarcasm to break the tension in the air, "of course I've seen a house guest before, but I don't recall seeing one come to breakfast with their tally whacker hanging out."

She followed him into the bedroom at the same time Ellalio returned with an arm full of clothes. "Here are some clothes for you senior." Ellalio handed the arm load of freshly starched clothes to Selina. Selina looked at the man standing in front of her then picked out clothes for him. "You haven't had a bath for quite a while, would you like to sit in a tub for a while or just stand in a shower? I am sure it would be good for you." He stood there for a minute, clearly still dazed but then looked at Selina, "I'm sorry I am a little confused. Where is the bathroom?"

Selina took him down the hall to the bathroom. "There is a toothbrush and toothpaste in the top drawer. You can find pretty much anything you need, if not just let me know." She turned to leave but then turned back around, "I think I need to stay with you through this, you are in pretty rough shape." He didn't say anything but just stood there, naked, looking at the shower and then broke the silence with, "how long has it been?"

Selina leaned against the wall, "well, since we found you on my ranch, full of holes and leaking from every one of them, almost two months." The man looked at her then back at the shower then stepped into the oversized shower and turned the water on. "Try not to get those stitches on your hip wet, I wouldn't worry about the rest too much, but that hip just opened back up the day before yesterday."

Selina kept her eyes on the man in her downstairs guest bathroom shower. She wished she could leave him to fend for himself because she wasn't crazy about watching a strange man take a shower, but she was determined to find out if he knew anything about her husband's murder. "What's your name?", since she didn't get a reply, she thought maybe that she had not spoken loud enough for the stranger to hear her, so she spoke up, "What is your name?" She looked at the man in the shower now with his arm extended out against the wall of the shower with his head looking down at his feet. All she could see was his backside at the moment. "I was hoping you would help me with that", was his reply.

Selina watched the man lean his head into water as if he was trying to get away from the conversation, but she could tell there was more to it than that. He pulled his head out of the water and reached for the soap. As he was washing himself, "I don't know mam, I really don't know." Selina let gravity slide her down the wall of the bathroom until she was sitting on the floor in front of the shower with her knees drawn up to her chest. "Don't bull shit me mister, I'm not in the mood for games." The stranger continued to wash himself but didn't speak. "How the hell do you not know your own name!" Selina buried her head in her knees, "I just want to know what happened to my husband mister. I don't care what trouble you are in, or who you are running from or why you were shot, I just need answers." She looked up as she heard the water stop. The man kept his back to her as he spoke, "can I trouble you for a towel?" Selina used the strength in her legs to push herself back up to a standing position and retrieved a towel for him. "Here is your towel", he didn't turn around, "don't you want it?" He stuck his arm out but kept his back to her, "geez, you are being modest now?". She partly stepped into the shower with him to hand him the towel since he wouldn't turn around, "you just showed up for breakfast with your thing hanging out and now you are shy?' He took the towel and slowly dried as much of himself as he could then wrapped the towel around his waist so that he could turn around. "I didn't have much of a choice this morning, I am sorry ma'am." He stepped out of the shower and looked around the bathroom for clothes or a robe.

"I put your clothes on the linen basket over there", Selina pointed to an oversized wicker basket. He spotted the clothes and walked over to them, "I know I am intruding, or at least I think I am, and I know you've helped me a lot, but if you don't mind, can I please have the room to dress privately?" Selina felt a little embarrassed that she hadn't really thought of letting the man dress by himself. He was moving very slow and by his motions so far, she could tell that there was pain for him with each move he made. "I promise not to run off, I really can't at the moment."

Selina waited in the hallway outside the bathroom. In just a few short minutes she heard him ask for her, "ma'am". She opened the door, and he was still naked, but he had his back to her. "I can't do it, I can't get my clothes on, I can't bend over. I am sorry". With his back to her, Selina managed to help him step into the underwear that Ellalio had brought him. She then helped him step into the jeans Ellalio also provided. She was impressed that Ellalio managed to pick out the correct size for him. "Maybe we shouldn't button that top button until that hip heals up a little more." He nodded his head in agreement then finally turned around so he could see Selina more clearly. Up until now, his head was in such a fog that everyone looked blurry to him. The shower had done him some good and he was seeing things much more clearly. Selina reached for the T shirt that came with the clothes then put it back down on the linen basket. "Why don't we get a button up shirt instead of a pullover. Ellalio had not factored in the inability for this man to raise his arms enough to get a shirt pulled over his head.

She took the man by the arm and slowly led him out of the bathroom, "do you want to lay down?", he shook his head no as they walked along the hall, leading back to the kitchen, "I am very hungry ma'am, I could sure use something to eat."

Chapter 37

Meet Dick Tracy

Selina sat across from the stranger and watched him eat his eggs and bacon with gusto. Ellalio and Jake kept their distance, both were reluctant to leave the boss alone with a stranger. "You don't know your name? You don't know why you are here?" Selina took a sip of her coffee, "and you don't know why you were shot." Selina sat her coffee on the table then leaned forward on her elbows, "don't eat so fast, you haven't had any solid food in quite a while." The stranger looked up at her, took one more scoop of eggs from his plate and shoved them in his mouth. He then slid his plate toward Selina even though he had not finished everything. "I didn't tell you to stop eating, just don't eat so fast."

"Ma'am, you've obviously been very kind to me, you made sure I didn't die, and I don't even know your name." Selina smiled as she saw something on the stranger's face that she hadn't seen in a long time, complete sincerity and vulnerability. "Selina, Selina Villalpando" she stuck her hand across the table to offer a handshake greeting, "it's nice to meet you Mr . . ." he slowly reached across the table to take her hand, "I really don't know ma'am." Selina had hoped that the continuity of the conversation and the normal greeting would coax the stranger's identity out of him, but it didn't work. He seemed very lost, very vulnerable and to a certain degree scared. "It's nice to meet you Mrs. Villalpando but I think I need to leave you folks." Selina laughed, "you don't know your name and you plan on leaving? To where?" He once again looked around the kitchen, nodded at Ellalio then turned his head back to Selina, "I know this much, I have been shot, left for dead and that's it." He took a sip of his coffee then made a face that showed his lack of appreciation for coffee then sat the cup back down, "I can't risk whoever shot me, coming back and maybe shooting you folks." Selina laughed again, "let me fill you in on some stuff, maybe that will help jar your memory."

Selina sat at the table with the man, filling him in on everything she knew about him. She told him about the girls and even had Lupita and Alejandra come to the table for a while to recite their portion of the story, but nothing worked. He was a blank slate of memory. The more information they gave him the more confused and frustrated he became. "That almost brings us up to point where you woke up out of your coma-like condition, disarmed a man, shot a hole through the floor of my office and kept a crooked sheriff from . . ." she paused and looked at Alejandra and Lupita, two young girls that had already been abused in such a way and thought better of finishing her sentence. "Well, nevertheless, you helped me when I needed it." The stranger looked at the two little girls that had just told him that he rescued them from a horrible condition then looked at Selina and her still slightly black eye, "looks like I was a little late to the party", he motioned towards the black mark under her eye, "Oh this, I've been kicked harder by horses, no big deal."

"So, in all of the stuff you found at the place where you found me, there was no ID, money . . . " he paused to rub his forehead, "nothing". Selina lowered her head then looked back up at the stranger, "there was an ID, but I am pretty sure it is fake. It looks real enough but I'd bet the ranch that it is fake." She got up and opened a kitchen drawer, then placed the wallet in front of him. He picked it up slowly and saw the dried blood stains on it, "mine?", Selina nodded her head in agreement. He opened the wallet and took out the driver's license, "looks real to me", he turned the card over to the donor side and then went back to the picture side. "So, I am Richard Tracy?" Selina laughed, "what's so funny? It says right here that I am Richard Tracy from Winslow Arizona." Selina stood back up, went over to the same kitchen drawer she pulled the wallet from and retrieved a comic book in a plastic sleeve. She set the Vintage Dick Tracy comic book in front of him, "first edition, first run, first everything, last estimate says that it is worth close to a half a million." She sat back down, "my dad loved your work as a gum shoe private I, he couldn't get enough. I remember the day he finally tracked down the owner of this and how excited he was to finally obtain it." She crossed her arms and then leaned back in the chair a little, "I thought he overpaid for it back then, but I was wrong. My dad was one hell of a businessman."

The two went back and forth for almost 2 hours at the table with no luck in changing his mind that the ID was fake. He claimed it was a mere coincidence because Richard was a common name. "That may be so, Dick" she emphasized the Dick part, "but I have lived in Arizona my whole life, and I can promise you that you are not from Winslow Arizona." He rolled his eyes and shook his head, "you got it all figured out huh? Why can't I be from Winslow Arizona?", she leaned forward on the table again, "because your accent is too thick. East coast if I ever heard one."

Selina got up again, pulled a bottle of Wellers out of the cabinet and poured two glasses and set one of them in front of Dick Tracy. He looked down at the glass then back up at Selina, "it is 9am in the morning", Selina took a sip, "at least you have some understanding of social norms and proper etiquette." He took a sip of the Wellers then winced. "Wow that's harsh". He set the glass back down on the desk and was about to speak when Louis & Lisa walked into the kitchen. Selina immediately jumped from her seat and ran to Louis, "You're back!! I was afraid you weren't coming back!" she let go of Louis and then hugged Lisa with equal enthusiasm. "Well?" Selina smiled and reached down to grab Lisa's left hand, and she found what she was looking for. "You did it!" Lisa had a wedding ring on her finger. Lisa blushed but clearly enjoyed the attention, "I guess Daddy gave his blessing?"

Louis grabbed the bottle of Wellers and went to the cabinet to grab more glasses, "I know it's early, but we need a toast Ms. V." Louis poured Ellalio, Jake, himself and Lisa a small amount of Weller's then raised his glass, "to Mrs. Elizabeth Arroyo, the woman that God has sent to me, may she forever tolerate my idiocy." He emphasized the E at the end of Idiocy so that it would rhyme with Me. Selina thought it was clever and everyone, but Richard Tracy laughed.

"I see Mr. Tracy is among the living now." Louis polished off what was left of his drink and set it down on the table. "My friend, it is good to see you are up and moving." He gently patted Richard on the back, "I am surprised that the brother's henchman hasn't come to settle the score with you yet." Richard shook his head as if he didn't understand and Selina added, "I forgot that you and Louis had met already." In all the excitement of arriving back home and making a toast, Louis had not noticed the faint black eye that Selina still had and when he did, his mood changed swiftly, "What happened Ms. V?" Selina tried to ease his easily recognizable mood change, "the brothers did come by, but they brought Marty with them. Marty wanted more than land and Mr. Tracy here", she nodded at the stranger sitting at the table still looking confused, "stopped them dead in their tracks." Louis was not happy with the news, no matter how much Selina tried to soften it. "Thank you again Mr. Tracy, you seem to have a knack for handling bad situations." He patted Richard on the back again then continued, "They will not stop Ms. V, not until they are dead, and I say it is time for me to arrange their meeting with Diablo."

"Hang on there Mr. Eastwood, we aren't killers." She knew that Louis did not know about her time in the desert with Jacknack and the actions that she took in order to save those traffic children and she would never tell him about it. She knew that Jacknack would not tell either. "Besides, how do we know that Mr. Tracy here isn't a cop?" That caused Richard to speak, "Alejandra said that I went to collect money from some guy named Armando" he looked around the room and directly at Alejandra, "cops don't collect money" then he caught himself, "unless I am a bad cop." He lowered his head as if he had discovered some awful truth about himself. "That's true Mr. Tracy but something tells me that you aren't a cop, I don't know what it is, maybe it's the fake ID but I am almost certain you are not in law enforcement", Selina put a mischievous smile on her face and finished with, "maybe enforcement, but certainly not law enforcement."

Richard sat there staring at his drink, Selina could see the agony on his face as he desperately tried to remember any detail about himself or anything that would help him. In a way, she felt sorry for him and in a small way, she envied him. If she lost her memory, she would not be able to remember the death of her husband and all the bad things that were happening now. Louis broke the awkward pause, "where is Jacknack?" Selina was quick to answer, "he managed to winch his jeep out of that ravine, and he has been in the barn fixing it since the day you left." Louis shook his head; he was still angry at the sight of Selina with a black eye. "Marty will come back Ms. V, I am surprised he hasn't already. Selina stood up from the table, "maybe he will but he certainly isn't in a hurry", she looked at the stranger at her table with his head down, "Mr. Tracy embarrassed him and the brothers very easily. They knew Jacknack and you were away and figured they had no opposition, or they wouldn't have tried that little stunt." She patted Louis on the shoulder, "now they know we have a full complement of capable people at the ranch, they won't be in a hurry to come back" she paused, "but you are right, they will try again for sure."

Chapter 38

Romeo

Selina rose very early; she was having a hard time sleeping. Mr. Tracy had been with them for almost four months now. He still had no idea who he was. At first, Selina and pretty much everyone on the ranch believed he was not telling the truth. Louis suggested that maybe he was running from someone or something and he wasn't ready to face it yet. Doc Spivey told them that sometimes, our brains had a way of shutting out what it deemed might harm us, especially during traumatic situations. It was hard to tell but he told them about battlefield blindness. The mind gets so traumatized by the horrors of war that it closes off the vision. She had convinced herself that if she could get his memory working again, he would know what happened to her husband and those little girls.

As she walked to the barn, she felt the morning air and although it felt much better than the heat, she hadn't realized the weather would be this chilly, especially in the desert. She saw the light come on in the barn as she was about to enter it. "You're up early Ms. V, something wrong?" Louis was pouring water into the coffee pot that they kept in the small barn office where Louis kept track of all ranch business which mostly consisted of vaccination and health records for the animals on the ranch. He was meticulous in his record keeping. "Just can't sleep señor." Louis continued his morning task but also continued to speak, "he may never get his memory back Ms. V, you should try and reach that conclusion more quickly." Selina was petting B.B. through the stall opening and he was enjoying the early morning attention. "You may be his keeper for the rest of your life if you don't report him and his condition to the authorities." Louis got the coffee brewing. The mixture of fresh brewing coffee and the clear morning air made Selina nostalgic. She would hang out with her father in the barn when she was little. She especially enjoyed the cold winter mornings of the desert along with the coffee smell her dad would brew. Louis continued, "although I hate to lose a good hand Ms. V."

Selina stopped petting B.B. and turned to look at Louis, "do you think he is a cowboy and just forgot he was? He sure is good with horses, hell he is good with everything." Louis walked back over to the coffee pot that was now finished giving life to the morning elixir and poured himself and Selina a cup of coffee. He walked over and handed the cup to her then leaned against the empty stall next to BB's. "No Ma'am, he is a city gringo for sure. He just listens, watches and learns." Louis took a sip from the cup, "he is very smart Ms. V but . . ." Selina cocked her head to one side, "but what?" Louis frowned, "he is dangerous Ms. V. I saw how easily he disarmed and disabled two men at the café and . . ." Selina set her cup on the stall ledge next to BB's, "stop dragging it out Louis, tell me what you are thinking." Louis nodded his head as if he agreed but stuck his hand up as if he was asking her to stop, "I am still working through it but . . . he enjoyed it, almost as if violence makes him happy." Selina looked around the barn, "you mean the same violent man that rescued two little girls from the hell they were in?" Selina sipped from her coffee cup making a loud sip noise she was famous for, "if it weren't for that man, those girls would either be dead or near fucked to death by now."

Louis walked into the tack room without his coffee and came out with a blanket, saddle and bridle. "That's what I can't work out." He opened BB's stall, "I am not going anywhere today, Louis, no need to saddle him." Louis continued to saddle BB, "yes ma'am, you are going riding, you are taking the gringo." Selina laughed, "I most certainly am not, I am not riding out into the desert with a strange man!" Louis never stopped what he was doing, "I am going to Ms. V". Selina entered the stall and watched Louis saddle her horse, "better tell me what's on your mind Mr. Arroyo."

Louis emptied his thoughts he had been having. He always operated under the notion that "the outside of a horse was good for the inside of a man" and he was determined to keep Mr. Tracy in the saddle long enough to maybe help the man work through some of his memory issues. "You think us putting him on a horse for a couple days is going to magically flip a switch in his head? You already said he was a city boy Tio". Louis nodded his head, "if you have a better idea, I am listening." Selina picked up a comb and brushed BB's mane, "I guess I need to go pack my travel bag, but I am not sure this is the right approach."

"Ellalio will have breakfast ready for us and then we can head out." Louis finished buckling BB's billet strap then lead BB out of the stall. "Does Mr. Tracy know he is going with us?" Louis nodded, "yes ma'am, I told him he needed to learn more about cowboyin in the open." He laughed when he said it, "he actually seemed excited at the idea of rising a horse for several days."

Louis and Selina walked into the kitchen from the cook's entrance and saw that Ellalio indeed had breakfast ready for them and Mr. Tracy was already eating. When Richard Tracy saw the two come in from the outside, he seemed embarrassed. "I'm sorry ma'am, I didn't know you guys were already up. I thought I was early. I should have checked." Selina stopped, crossed her arms, "why would that bother you Mr. Tracy?" Dick Tracy looked around as if he was seeking help, "uh ma'am, it is my understanding that the hands don't eat before the boss and the ramrod, unless they are in the bunkhouse." Louis looked at Selina and flashed a smile and decided to speak, "it's ok Mr. Tracy, however, I did not saddle your horse so maybe you can do that while Ms. V and I grab some breakfast." Mr. Tracy shoveled some more hash browns in his mouth and nodded in agreement. He stood up from the table and headed out the door.

Ellalio set two plates loaded with everything under the sun on them onto the table and asked what they wanted to drink. "Who taught him what a ramrod was?" Louis smiled and shook his head, "that's what I am trying to tell you Ms. V, he has read everything available in the house about ranches, cow hands and the work. When he can't find a book, he reads the internet." Louis took a bite of his bacon and then shoved some eggs in the mix. Selina sat there and watched him chew because she could tell there was something else that he wanted to say, "the other day he asked me if he could look at our breeding calendar." Selina showed her interest by cocking her head to one side, "I am not kidding, the man is a sponge, he remembers everything, and he seems to be enjoying it. Never in my life have I had a tender foot get up to speed so fast."

They both sat there and ate as much as they could but didn't say much. Ellalio left the kitchen and came back with Selina's travel pack. A pack that didn't have much but toothpaste, toothbrush, a first aid kit, and one change of clothes but in all the years Selina had been on the ranch, she had never ever used the change of clothes while she was out.

Lisa came in the kitchen; she was as pleasant as ever. Selina thought she had become even more beautiful since her and Louis had been married. "Good morning, Lisa." Lisa poured a cup of coffee and sat down at the table next to Louis, "good morning, Ms. V."

Selina patted her travel pack and thanked Ellalio for getting it ready, "wasn't me, I just brought it down, Mrs. Arroyo got it ready." Selina smiled and looked at Lisa, "then you know your husband is going for a long ride with me and Dick Tracy." Lisa leaned over and kissed Louis on cheek, "yes ma'am, I need a little break, but I will be here when he gets back." Selina let her face show her confusion, "break from what?" Lisa ran her hands through Louis's hair and looked at him like there was no one else in the room, "Mr. Arroyo has quite an appetite for love Ms. V." Instantly, Louis's face became flush with the embarrassment for having his desire for sex with her so openly talked about at the breakfast table. Selina blushed a little too, but she enjoyed it very much. "Well come on Romeo, try and remember that this was your idea." Selina grabbed her hat from the rack and out the door she went.

Chapter 39

Rattlesnake Anyone?

"Holy mother! What is that!" Selina smiled as she saw the excitement in Dick Tracy's eyes. They had been riding for two days, slow and methodical, taking in everything that the ranch had to offer. Both Selina and Louis explained everything from all the different cactus plants to the long nose bat migration that had always creeped everyone out, but they were harmless. "We just call it the cliffs". Dick got off his horse, a horse that he had been working with for the last two months. Selina was very impressed with the command and the bond he had developed with an animal that had never been ridden before Dick Tracy started working with him. "They are the ancient dwellings of the Hohokam tribe and its home for the night." Dick had a shocked look on his face, "we can actually go in them?" Selina smiled as she continued to sit on her horse, "well, they are on double LL land which means they belong to the Villalpando family." Louis got down off his horse and Selina did the same. "Do we just leave the horses here?" Selina led BB around Dick Tracy, "nope, follow me."

Selina led the men and their horses up the trail to the cliffs. When they arrived at the bottom entrance Selina gave some instructions to Dick, "this place is sacred to me, and it probably was to the Hohokam too. That's why they built it here, you can't see it from the valley. You have to know it is here to find it." Dick stood at the entrance and looked straight up at the different layers of dwellings that seemed to stretch to the sky. It seemed to him that it was impossible to build something like this in modern times, how the hell could they have done it back then? "Don't take anything, don't scratch your girlfriends name in the walls, use the fire pit you see through there and tonight when you lay down, you have to give thanks to the earth gods." Dick looked at her like he didn't believe her, "I'm serious, it's our way of giving thanks for letting us stay and protecting us from the elements."

Louis tried to stable the horses and properly hobble them for the night, but Dick wouldn't hear of it. He tended to all the horses which included oats and brush. When he was done, he joined Selina and Louis in the center dwelling with the fire already burning in the pit. "I've never seen anything like this. I am speechless. I may not have a memory, but I damn sure know that I am spending the night in a place that people have spent the night in thousands of years ago. I can't get my head around it."

Louis left the dwelling for a time then returned with a dead rattlesnake in his hand. "Supper time Dick." Dick jumped up from the ground because he wasn't sure the snake was dead, "is it dead?' Louis laughed, "I wouldn't eat a live one." Selina laughed, "just wait, you'll like it. At least you won't go to bed hungry.

Louis showed Dick how to skin the snake and then spent some time explaining how to tan and cure the skin in case he ever wanted a hat band or a pair of boots. "There, a little corn meal, salt and a skillet and you are going to taste heaven." Louis was laughing as he said it. Dick shook his head; he knew he was being picked on.

Selina spent the evening explaining how she used the cliffs as a child and how she believed that they had protective and healing powers. "My dad first brought me here when I was a toddler. In fact, these cliffs are some of my earliest memories as a child. I can never let anyone know they are here, or they will attract a bad element. It is very rare that I bring anyone up here, especially since I have only known you a few months." Dick crossed his legs into the meditation position and watched the fire, he had to admit that the place had a mystique about it, and he knew he was experiencing something that very few people in life would ever experience. "I don't know what to do with you Mr. Tracy. You can't stay here forever, you may have a wife, a family, you may have people that are worried about you and want you back." Selina paused and then stirred the rattlesnake meat that was now sizzling in the pan. "It aint fair to them."

Louis took over the stirring for Selina when Dick responded, "and I could be a bachelor and a very bad person, I could be a drug smuggler, hell I could have been a human trafficker for all I know. Either way, the people that obviously wanted me dead will certainly find me again if you report me to the authorities." Selina nodded vigorously to each of his points as he spoke. When he was finished, he looked dejected, he looked defeated. "Mr. Tracy, it has been my contention that I would rather face life than hide from it, consequences be damned." Dick sat there contemplating what Selina had just said and realized that she was correct. It didn't help the feeling that if she reported him to the authorities, he might as well write his obituary.

Louis stirred the snake meat some more and proclaimed that it was ready. As he was skewering a slice for each of them, he spoke, "Ms. V, there is one thing that must be cleared up before you report Mr. Tracy," Selina bit into her slice of snake and found it to be too hot to eat just yet, "what's that?" Louis watched Dick stare at the meat on his skewer as if he was expecting it to come alive and bit him. "The circumstances by which you found him. There are many details that should not be made public." Selina understood what he was saying and thought about it as she chewed her rattlesnake dinner. The night air felt wonderful to Dick Tracy, even though he didn't know who he was, he somehow knew that he wasn't a camper, and he definitely wasn't a cowboy, but he also knew that he liked what he was doing and what he was experiencing now. It was the thought of possibly having family looking for him, wondering what happened to him. The worst thought of all was that he could be a bad person, he could be a killer. After all, he had handled that gun proficiently when he disarmed that man in Selina's office. He was lost in thought when Selina snapped her fingers in front of his face.

"I said, how's the rattlesnake? Where did you go just now, you were a million miles away." He took bite of the snake meat, "It wouldn't be something I'd order or take someone out on a date for but it's not bad. Needs some salt." Louis laughed, "I forgot the salt, so you'll just have to endure."

The conversation was lively for a while then Louis laid back on his blanket and in no time was asleep. Selina continued to stoke the fire as they talked but Selina did most of the talking. It felt awkward for Dick because he was unable to offer much up in the conversation. Usually when you have a conversation with someone, you draw on your knowledge and life experiences, Dick didn't know what kind of knowledge he had, and he had no life experiences that he could remember, and he sensed that Selina understood this very well and did most of the talking.

Dick had come to appreciate and enjoy this environment. He admired Louis and how he handled his day, his manners and politeness while keeping his intimidation factor at a pretty high level. Dick knew that Louis was Selina's best friend and confidant, there was no mistaking that relationship. He had reached the conclusion that you'd have to kill Louis before you could ever get to Selina. Louis had shared in conversation with Dick that he would get to Marty and the brothers and when he did, they would wish they had never been born. When Louis told him that, he found it odd that he wanted to be a part of whatever revenge Louis intended to extract on those men and he didn't even know them.

He loved looking at Selina although he tried to be discreet about it. Since he had cleared the cobwebs out of his head and regained his strength, he had become very aware at how naturally beautiful she was. She carried herself in a way that had so much smoothness to it. She never seemed to rush; her movements were seemingly choreographed. She struck him as the type that never spilled a drink or dripped ketchup on her shirt. She woke up with a purpose every day and she set out to fulfill that purpose. He wished he could help her solve the mystery of her husband's death, but he couldn't.

"Well Mr. Tracy, I am all talked out and tired." He snapped back into the moment again and nodded in agreement. "Ma'am I uh . . . " he was struggling to get the words out, "I am uh . . . grateful for everything you have done for me." He smiled at her, but he wasn't sure she could see it through the darkness and the flickering light cast off by the fire. "You could have left me for dead." Selina leaned back against the saddle she had propped up, "Mr. Tracy, somehow, I know that you are a good person. I don't know how but deep down my gut tells me that when push comes to shove, you will always do the right thing." She pulled a blanket up over her torso, "Good night Mr. Tracy, don't forget to give thanks to the gods for the accommodations." Dick looked around, "you were serious about that?" Selina closed her eyes, "very" was her reply.

Dick sat there next to fire for a few minutes as he watched Selina fall into a deep sleep. He enjoyed the moment as much as anything he had done since he began his journey of regaining his memory and healing from the wounds. Watching this beautiful woman close her eyes and fall asleep as fast as anyone could was a blessing that he should be giving thanks for.

He quietly stood up and went to the outer walls of the cliffs, far off in the distance he could see the soft glow of what he believed were the Tucson city lights but he wasn't sure. He stood and looked out over the desert then looked up at the sky and simply said "thank you" then returned to his makeshift bunk by the fire. He closed his eyes as he listened to the crackle of the fire and the quietness of the southern Arizona desert. This must be like heaven he thought as he drifted off to sleep.

Chapter 40

I'itoi

"*Xavier we have much to discuss.*" The voice was clear, but it had a very pure but broken style of dialect. It was as if someone who's natural language did not fit the words they are using. He tried to open his eyes, but he couldn't. He felt his arm being tugged but he was tired and didn't want to wake. "*Xavier, we have much to discuss*". He tried to respond but his mouth would not open as it trapped the words that he had sent from his brain to respond. He knew he was mumbling and tried even harder to open his mouth to let the words out, but he couldn't.

He rolled over on his back, his eyes were closed but he felt as though they were wide open. He could see the man, at least he thought it was a man bent down next to him. "*Who are you?*" again he was merely mumbling but he knew what he wanted to say, he simply couldn't get the words out of his mouth. It all became very frustrating. "*The more pressing question is who are YOU?* The man stood up as he spoke. He was not very big, but he was adorned with the most amazing silver jewelry Dick had evert seen. Silver that had been inlayed with jade and turquoise that hung from his ears, nose and freely dangled around his neck. He was bare chested, a point that showed such amazing definition. It was as if he was sculpted by some master hand.

Dick tried many times to speak as the image of the man became clearer with each passing second. "*Stand up Xavier, walk with me.*" Dick shook his head to indicate that he did not want to walk with this man, Dick was actually frightened by the site of this man. How come Selina and Louis were not waking so that they could help him deal with this unwelcome intruder. It was as if the man was reading his thoughts when he said, "*it is YOU Xavier, that is an intruder. This is my home; this is where my creations dwell for eternity.*"

Dick finally stood up from his sleeping position and stood in front of the man. From the ground, Dick expected to be taller than this man but as it turned out, no matter where he stood, this man was always taller than him. "*Why do you keep calling me Xavier? My name is Richard.*" Dick shook his head and rubbed his eyes, he had to be asleep. Maybe this was one of those lucid dreams. It had to be. Maybe the rattlesnake meat was tainted with some hallucinogen? The man began to walk through each dwelling in the cliffs and surprisingly, without any reluctance, he followed the man wherever he went.

When they entered each room, Dick was surprised to see people in each of them. There were children playing with a basket and a small round rock. Women were working a loom in one room, and in another, several men looked to be playing some kind of game, but Dick couldn't figure it out. At that point he firmly believed that he should not have eaten the rattlesnake. The two men seemed to be walking through the entire cliffs, unnoticed. "*You must find your place Xavier; you are out of balance with nature*".

"*Ok stop! Is that my name? Xavier? Who am I? Am I a bad person!*" The questions that had been nagging at him came bursting out of his mouth and he was certain that Selina and Louis would wake and come find him. "*Who are you?*" He was frustrated and it was beginning to show. Just as he was about to reach out and touch the man, the man turned, *"I am I'itoi"*. He put his arm back down and stood staring at the man in the amazing jewelry, wearing nothing but what looked like a leather kilt. A beautiful leather bag adorned with beads sewn in the shape of a mountain lion that seemed to move when I'itoi moved. *"Well hunky damn dory, it is nice to meet you I . . . whatever, but I want some answers!"*

I'itoi stood there at the edge of the cliffs looking out over the vast desert. *"I am not familiar with your demands, nor do I have any concern for them! You must learn the difference between want and need before you can begin your journey of balance Xavier."* After being firmly put in his place, Xavier stood there next to the man in silence staring out at the desert waiting for more when he noticed that there were no glowing lights in the far-off distance. *"I'm sorry sir, I know I am dreaming but that is still no excuse for rude behavior."* Xavier stood there in silence for what seemed to be an eternity before the man spoke again, *"I am the man in the maze, I am the creator of my people, I am the air waiting to breathe life and I am the sun that cracks open the seed and I am the rain that nourishes the seed until it is ready to nourish those who work to harvest it"* he paused then turned his entire body without moving a muscle so that he was facing Xavier, *"that is who I am"*. Xavier was struck by the beauty in this man's face. He was perfect in all regards. *"You are in my home, you are with my people, you are trapped in my maze."*

Xavier closed his eyes, *"can you help me get back in balance?"* Xavier felt a peace come over him he hadn't felt since before his parents died. *"There are many that seek your protection, but they alone are not an exit to the maze, you must right the wrongs of past and the present, you must walk a life of beauty, one of peace before you can exit the maze."* I'itoi swept his hand over the vast desert landscape, *"this I tell you will not be easy; it will not bring immediate peace to your life, but it will lead you out of the maze and back to the one called Teddy."*

Xavier gasped for air and bolted upright. He sat there on the floor of the cliff dwelling trying to gather himself. He looked around and saw that Selina and Louis were still asleep. He stood up, rolled his blanket up and went to the fire. He was more excited than he had ever been in his life. He couldn't wait any longer, it was time to go home.

"Selina, wake up. He tried to whisper but his excitement prohibited him from doing so. Selina raises up and runs her hands through her hair, the firelight flickered against her skin and Xavier could see that there wasn't a single time throughout the day that Selina wasn't beautiful. "What is it? What's the matter Mr. Tracy?" By this time Louis was sitting up watching the exchange, "I aint Dick Tracy, my real name I'm Xavier, Xavier Thomas and I need to get back to my little brother now."

Selina stood up, "that's one helluva change from last night". I could see the apprehension in her eyes, I could see the distrust as easily as anything I had ever seen before but somehow, I needed to tell her and Louis what had happened during the night, but I didn't know how without them thinking I was a total looney tune. "Look, I know it will seem weird, but you have to hear me out.

Selina found the rock bench that was carved out many years ago. She sat on it as she had done many times since she first discovered the cliffs, she always had the same thought, how many people before her had used this bench. "Ok, Mr. uh . . . what is your name today, I didn't quite catch it?" I could hear the sarcasm in her voice now, Louis had taken a seat next to her. It appeared it was now time for me to hold class with everyone on their seats.

"I had a dream last night that was as real as anything I have ever had." I looked around the cliff walls and marveled at its beauty, something I had been unable to grasp until I was given a private tour. "I saw people here, lots of people and a man sort of ushered me around . . ." I couldn't finish because Selina interrupted me, "you met I'itoi." It caught me off guard and I guess the expression on my face revealed my confusion, "how the hell did you know that?" Selina put her hands on her knee as she crossed her legs and shook her head, "well I'll be damned."

"Yeah, I did. He's the one that told me and by the end of the dream I knew who I was". Selina looked at Louis who was as confused by the conversation as he could be. "He said he was the keeper of the Maze and a bunch of other stuff that maybe I will remember later but right now, all I can think about is that I have a little brother with down syndrome that I need to get back to."

The three of us spent the next hour in that dwelling going over every detail of my life, I held nothing back. I felt uneasy sharing that I worked for the mob in a specialized capacity which is what brought me to southern Arizona. The details of my own life came flooding back into my head with so much veracity that I had trouble keeping up with it. I remembered the night of the shooting and could even recount the details of how I got to that spot in the desert, but I could not recount the entire shooting. "Where are the girls? Are they ok?"

Selina stood up and walked to the edge of the cliff and looked out over the beautiful desert sunrise, "I'itoi came to me when I was a little girl", she chuckled a little, "I could never get anyone to believe me, even my father", she laughed again, although he played along like he believed me, but I knew he didn't." She turned to look at me, "Are you a bad person Mr. Thomas?" I was knocked a little off balance by the question, but this lady had every right to ask me whatever she wanted, she had saved my life and I owed her more than I could ever repay. "Ms. V, I believe that I have tried to walk a fine line between good and bad ever since the day I made my first collection for Big Paul." She now walked over and stood right in front of me, "that's now an answer Mr. Thomas." I slowly drew out a breath, "to my little brother, I am not.", at the moment, that's all that matters to me." Louis now stood up and began his line of questioning, which was more pragmatic than Selina's.

"If this mob man sent you here to be murdered because he believes you got his son killed, yet he has had no confirmation," Louis paused then looked at me, "what will stop him from finishing the job." I started to answer but he interrupted, "I don't care either way, but it appears that your presence here has put Ms. V in a very bad position, it could have possibly put her in danger now", Louis became very stern in his look, "and THAT, Mr. Thomas is my concern". I understood where he was coming from, he had been her protector for most of her life and he wasn't about to let no mob guy jeopardize her safety.

"I understand, that's why I need to get away from all of you and I have to go find Teddy." Selina looked out over the desert again then turned back to me, "I don't believe you are a bad person Mr. Thomas, not for one minute. I think you are a good person that has made some bad choices." I was relieved that she said that, but I tried not to let it show. "I appreciate that ma'am." Selina started picking up her bed roll and anything else that had been brought into the cliffs, "I guess we need to head back so you can get to your little brother, we are a day's ride from the house so that should give us time to formulate a plan." I started gathering my things as did Louis, but I couldn't help but ask the question, "what plan?". Selina stopped what she was doing, "you think for one minute that this fella you work for will just stop his attempts to get even with you?", she laughed again, "Mr. Thomas you are in some pretty deep shit. You don't just pop into New York, pick up your little brother, and then what? Where do you go?" She had a point, and, in my excitement, I hadn't had a chance to work out the details.

I hadn't wanted to work out the details. My first thought when I got my own brain back was to get to Teddy. To be completely honest, the moment of clarity that comes with a rebirth or an awakening is amazing and overwhelming. I couldn't believe how much I loved that guy and how bad I felt for leaving him not knowing what happened to me. All I could think of after that old Indian got through with me was Teddy. My brain was working in ways that I had never experienced before. "Mr. Thomas, I want to help you, please let me." Selina walked over to me and put her hand on my shoulder. Her touch sent chills throughout my entire body. I looked at her for the first time since I became alive again, she was amazing. I don't think I had ever seen someone so beautiful and so true. I was searching for words, and I couldn't find them. She changed my entire focus for just a second. She was like a bolt of lightning, so much so that I slightly recoiled from her touch. "I'm sorry Mr. Thomas, I didn't mean to be too forward or startle you. It is difficult for me to realize that I am meeting you for the first time." Selina touched me again. I had to give it to her, she was fearless, "the man I have known for the past four months is gone.

Chapter 41

First Name Basis

"Ms. V, I am not a good man, you are gonna want to distance yourself from me." I was surprised that I knew how to remove the saddle from a horse and put all the tack away. I easily removed the bridle from this beautiful animal that had just carried me across the desert and back into his safe place in the barn. I was in a hurry, but I had to curry him and give him his feed. He had become my horse since I woke up, but what amazed me at the moment was that I felt like I had a connection to him.

Selina stood there and watched me remove the saddle and curry the quarter horse named Baxter. Baxter was a big horse but gentle as anything I had ever experienced. "You keep telling me that Mr. Thomas but from what I have seen, you are a very good man." Selina leaned her back against the stall that held me and Baxter and continued to speak, "I want to go with you to New York. I want to help you get your brother back and then I'd like you to come live here." Selina folded her arms and put her head down in a manner that suggested she had just divulged a secret she shouldn't have.

"First off Ms. V, I would appreciate it if you would just call me

Xavier or just X if you want to. I am very uncomfortable with the Mr. Thomas stuff." Selina smiled at me and let off a little laugh, "Ok,

Xavier, but only if you call me Selina.". I was slightly confused by her proposal, even though I found I enjoyed it, I was not a ranch hand. I had come to love horses and the work that they required. Hell, she didn't even know I was a day trader. I felt like she was way out over her skis on this one, especially since she had no idea who she was dealing with.

"Ma'am, you barely know me, you only know what I have told you, you don't know all the things that I have left out and will never tell you about." Selina walked over to me and put her hand on my forearm, and I had to admit, it caused the hair on both of my arms to stand up. She may have noticed my reaction, but I wasn't sure and honestly, didn't care. My mission in life now was to find and secure Teddy and Madison and once that was done, I would deal with Big Paul.

"Xavier, look at me" she kept her hand on my forearm and I reluctantly made eye contact with her. "I am not suggesting that I would interfere with your business, what I am suggesting is that I can help you get your brother and friend back here, out of the way and safe from the ominous reach of whoever you work for." This comment made me laugh as I spoke, "Selina, the people I work for are the reason I am here." I looked around the stall then back at Selina, "you also have your own set of problems here in Arizona." Selina nodded in agreement but continued anyway, "you're right, very right and that's why I would like you to come back and help me." She took a step away from me and removed her hand from my forearm, "just consider it please." As she was leaving the stall she spoke over her shoulder, "The money that you were sent here to recover is in the safe in my office, Louis can get it for you." What I couldn't see was the sadness on Selina's face as she left the stall.

I looked at Louis and he gave me a confused nod accompanied by the shrug of his shoulders. "She carries the weight of the world on her shoulders, she is a fixer, she wants to fix this for you and for her." I understood what Louis said to me better than he knew. I am a fixer too and I don't sleep well when I can't fix my problems or Teddy's. "She is family to me Amigo, I have known her all her life, I know when she is happy, when she is sad and when no one else does. She thinks she is clever in the way she hides her emotions, but I see it clearly and most of all, I see the change in her demeanor when you are around, she is much happier."

I tried to ingest and digest what he was telling me, and I think he was trying to tell me that Ms. Selina Villalpando had a crush on me, but I didn't say it out-loud. I nodded as if I was confused and technically, I was. Selina Villalpando was amazing and had no business being with a well-dressed knuckle dragger like me. "Can you get me the money out if the safe Louis? I need to get to New York before it's too late, hell it may already be too late." Louis nodded his head and started to exit the stall then turned to look at me, "walk with me my friend, Selina has spoken her peace, now let me speak mine."

As we walked back to the ranch house Louis spoke of Selina as if she were a saint and after listening to him, I believed that he believed that she was. He told me about the day they found her husband and the day her father died. I knew she carried pain like a pocket full of change, but I had no idea the scope of what she was going through. "You are the first man in a very long time that has not made one single effort to win her love", he swept his right arm across the open desert to illustrate the vastness, "many from all over these parts have tried but all have failed, she sees through the bull shit very easily." He stopped walking and so did I, "Most only want the money that comes with having one of the largest ranches in the Southwest." He kicked the ground, and then there are those like the sheriff that want other things. I will kill him for what he tried to do." I shook my head, "I like it here Louis, I had no idea I would enjoy this cowboy stuff the way I do but I need to get to my brother before some very bad people get to him, if they haven't already." I drew out a long slow breath "and as far as the sheriff is concerned, he didn't do what he wanted to and he aint worth going to prison over" Louis flashed a smile at me that I remembered from the first time I met him in the little diner, "Before I leave, I will apologize to her for not being able to stay and thank her for all she has done for me." Louis laughed, "you must have missed the part about Ms. V going to New York with you, she is inside ordering the plane to be ready." Now I really was confused, "what plane? What are you talking about?" Louis continued to walk towards the house, with me trailing behind him. "You are a good man Amigo, you just haven't been convinced of it yet," he paused and looked directly at me, Selina intends to convince you."

There was no way that Selina can go to New York with me. I had too much to do and there was no way that I could look out for her, I wasn't even sure I could look out for myself just yet. I had been in this peaceful spot currying animals like I didn't have a care in the world, and I had probably gotten dim witted and soft.

I walked into the office with Louis and with a few quick turns of the dial, Louis had the mammoth sized walk-in safe opened and was handing me the duffle bag. I had no idea the safe was even there. It was hidden behind a huge hand drawn painting of Poncho Villa riding across the desert with his men. I learned that the painting was specifically commissioned for the purposes of hiding a giant safe. I was staring at the safe when Selina came into the office. "It doubles as a safe room. My father basically had the house built around it." She sat down at her desk, "it's all been arranged, we for New York leave in one hour."

"Ms. V . . ." she held up her finger and I got the message, "Selina, you can't go to New York with me. This is a mission better accomplished alone."

This woman was different than any other woman I had ever been around. She had a body language and a confidence level that suggested that she could will her way to bend spoons with her mind if she wanted to. I knew she couldn't do that, but she was nearly impossible to say no to. "I don't need a plane Selina- I can fly commercial out of Tucson." She shook her head and her actions almost reminded of Big Paul except she was definitely not ugly, and she was definitely not a criminal. "Will you be checking the bag with the money, or will you just carry it on and have them check it at security?" I raised my eyebrows because I honestly hadn't thought things that far through. I tried to pretend like I still had a clear idea of what I was going to do, "I make one phone call to a lady named Ruby and she will have me back in New York in no time." Selina shook her head again and scrunched her forehead so I could visibly see the lines, "then why did you say you'd fly commercial first? Why didn't you say you'd call Ruth?" I really didn't have a good reply to that except that, "it's Ruby, not Ruth." Selina paced around the room now with her arms folded across her chest like she was a lawyer addressing the jury, "I stand corrected", hell, she even sounded like a lawyer at that moment, "So this Ruby person arranges your travel, pickups and provides you with all the details," she stopped pacing and looked at the painting of Poncho Villa, "the same Ruby that works for the guy that tried to have you killed?"

I could see now where she was going and I had already reached the conclusion that I couldn't trust anyone, I couldn't check a bag with a shitload of cash in it without getting noticed and busted. The money itself probably was sprinkled with some kind of drugs so the dogs would be all over me. "I can't accept the charity, Selina. This is my problem not yours." My words had barely left my mouth when she went into Lawyer mode again, "oh I beg to differ, you became my problem when we found you leaking blood all over my ranch." She then turned and looked at me, "my plane leaves for New York in one hour with or without you."

Chapter 42

Piper Malibu

Jacknack was assigned the task of driving us to the airport. He had now restored his World War II jeep after having pushed it down a ravine but thankfully, it wasn't street legal, so he didn't take us to the airplane hangar in his jeep. Until now, I had no idea an airstrip even existed until we drove up to it. We walked into the hangar, and I froze in my tracks. "Struck by its beauty or just afraid to fly?" Selina gently punched me in the shoulder as she said it, but I didn't move. "It's a Piper Malibu." Selina looked surprised when I identified the plane, "You know your Planes very well Xavier, I am impressed." She kept walking but I still didn't move. Was this fate, it was almost as if I was intentionally being tested now. I had been shot to pieces, nearly died and now I am supposed to get on the same type of plane that killed my parents?

Selina realized something was off, so she stopped, turned around and came back to me. "What is wrong with you?" I shook my head and set my duffle bag on the ground beside me, "I only know what kind of plane it is because that is the same plane that crashed with my parents in it", I realized the slip and corrected myself, "same TYPE of plane that crashed with my parents inside it." Selina looked at me with the most beautiful compassionate look I have ever seen on anyone, "I didn't know that, and I am so sorry." She looked at the plane and then looked back at me. "I am a great pilot, I have filed a flight plan, I know what I am doing, and we will be fine. Trust me." I bent down and picked up the bag that contained the collection money, I still had the shoulder bag hanging around my neck that had a double stack 1911 made available to me by one of the New Jersey boys. I couldn't be sure of that; it very well could have been Betty Boop's, but it just didn't seem to fit her personality. I knew through experience that this gun would have been wiped clean, untraceable by any measure and if anything had happened to Teddy or Madison, I fully intended to use it to extract revenge, but it would never ever be traced back to me.

"I just need a minute to get my mind around this." I started a slow walk towards the plane and when I reached the wing, I touched it with my hand. I stood next to the plane and felt emotions that I wasn't expecting. My parents had been gone for quite a while and I had come to grips with the loss but somehow, seeing this plane made it all real. I saw my dad sitting in the pilot's seat with his headphones on and mom sitting right next to him, both smiling and waving at me as they took off on their last flight. "Do you want to delay take-off Xavier?" I shook my head and made my way to the entrance door. "Put your bag back here" Selina motioned towards the small compartment at the back of the plane. "Keeps the weight balanced. I am probably over precautious, but I understand planes as well as I understand horses."

We sat there in the front seats, she offered to let me sit in the back, but I was not interested in being chauffeured, I wanted to get to New York ASAP, and I wanted to see it in through the front window. Selina motioned at the head set in front of me as she was adjusting her hers. "It's easier to talk to each other during the flight."

I put the headset on as I watched her go through her preflight check list. She was definitely thorough, and having lost my parents in a plane crash, I appreciated that. As we taxied out of the hangar and onto the runway she stopped, completed one more preflight check-list. I could hear her voice over the headset, I thought the headsets weren't necessary because this was a very nice plane, and it was quiet enough to manage without them. I know what my old man paid for his and Selina's was quite a bit swankier than his. "We have about a 1000-mile range, but I don't like to push it that far, we stop and refuel in Lubbock first then we have maybe . . . three more refuel stops." She tapped the fuel gage for effect, "your job on this flight is to make sure that this doesn't read zero." She laughed when she said it and she could see I wasn't amused, "I told you, I filed a flight plan which includes all the necessary stops for refueling." She shook her head, "lighten up Xavier, we will be at Blue Dart Aviation by this evening." I shrugged my shoulders and started to speak but she hit the throttle and did some of her pilot stuff which threw me back in the seat a little. I could see the landscape around me moving faster than I ever experienced from this seat and then it all slowed down once we were airborne. I had to admit that the feeling of being in the co-pilot seat of a plane that flew this fast was incredible.

"Where is the Blue Dart place?" She reached beneath her seat and pulled out a map and handed it to me, "it's an FBO attached to Teterboro, you can see I circled it." I looked at it, "why Jersey and not New York?" she smiled, "I figured your friends in New York might have connections with all the FBO's around that city so as a precaution I moved us to Jersey." I thought she was being overly precautious, but I liked her style of thinking. "They might have some sort of gangster BOLO out on you." It was my turn to smile, "These guys haven't heard from me in several months, they think I am dead which is what they wanted." I looked out over the terrain as we con-tinued to climb, "if they think they were successful, then they will leave Teddy alone but if they get any hint that I am still kicking, they will use him as leverage." I explained the phone number that I had given Madison and had also made her sign a contract that she would use the number if I didn't return and to do exactly what they said. I never in a million years thought I would ever have to use this service, but I had paid handsomely for it for this very reason, to protect Teddy.

"What if she didn't use the number?" I had thought of that too, but I just felt like Madison received the seriousness of the message when I covered it with her. "I am ninety nine percent certain she used it." Selina cocked her head to one side, "you good with those odds?" I really didn't want to think about it, but it was good that she was forcing it out of me. "Yeah, I trust her." Selina nodded but then added, "are the people behind the phone number associated with uhh . . ." she tried not to use the word directly but then stopped, "by the way, this plane is equipped with a flight recorder so just be careful", I gave her a thumbs up sign "no they aren't, it is totally separate." Selina nodded again.

I filled in all my life details for Selina which included having my traders license and even included some very specific trades that I have instigated over the last few years that had made me and several other people a considerable amount of money. The more I spoke about my love for the stock market the more I realized how much I missed it. I didn't tell Selina, but I made up my mind in that plane that I was done with collecting and would only pursue an honest living going forward. "Do you ever entertain leaving Arizona, maybe getting out of the cattle business?" Selina gave a slight smile, "I never think about leaving Arizona, Arizona is my home and I love it, but I do think about getting out of the cattle business every day."

Me- "Seems like it pays the bills"

Selina- "It really doesn't, every year it gets harder and harder"

Me- "could have fooled me".

I looked around the cabin of this 3-million-dollar plane as I said it. "I will have to change directions soon or there will be no double L ranch in five years." That threw me off a little, from what I had seen, the ranch was huge but maybe I had mistaken size for profit.

Selina quickly changed the subject, "Where will Teddy and Madison be?" I knew they would be in Greenwich Connecticut in a nice little cabin in the woods. Greenwich was a wealthy place, and it was hard to move in that town without being noticed. You'd think rich people would be more apt to mind their own business, but they were the nosiest of all classes of people. That's the reason I chose that location as the fallback position for Teddy and Madison. "They will be in Connecticut ma'am." Selina adjusted her headset a little, "Great then we will land in Greenwich instead of Jersey." I was going to argue simply because I didn't like to be told what to do but since I didn't formulate a plan for this situation that actually included being flown in on a private plane, the thought just hadn't occurred to me, and she was right. This way we could land in a small airport in Greenwich, get a car, grab Teddy and Madison and put them on the plane with us. "Can we get a rental car in Greenwich?" Selina smiled; we will find out as we get closer to the FBO. I can talk to them directly.

"Once we have your little brother and the caregiver, what do you plan to do?" I rubbed my chin, "I just need to get them to a safe place away from the mess I created," she interrupted me, "that's a given, and you know what I mean with that question". I started to see Selina differently than I did when I didn't know who I was. At that time, she was a nice lady, somewhat standoffish but nevertheless, very nice. She was also the boss. Now I was looking at her in a way that made me apprehensive about telling her anything because I didn't want to make her an accessory after the fact. "Once they find out that they failed in their attempt, they will never stop. I have to think that one through." Selina took her eyes off the incredibly complicated looking dashboard and turned completely in her seat so she could look at me directly, "Please consider relocating to Arizona." I shook my head as if I would consider it, "and be what, your ranch hand?" I smiled, "I just don't see that as a viable solution." I looked at her, my god she was beautiful, this may have been the first time that I actually saw her in a way that caused me to momentarily lose my train of thought, but I recovered quickly, "I have to figure a way to end this, or it will never stop."

I could hear someone talking in the head set but it was nothing but a bunch of gibberish to me, but Selina seemed to understand it all, "copy that". Selina let me know that Eberhardt aviation in Greenwich was giving her permission to land and confirmed a rental car upon our arrival. I had never flown via private plane and realized very quickly that I liked it. I also liked seeing the small airport and runway line up in our front window. Watching a plane land from the front seat was incredible to me and I decided that I needed to learn to fly my own plane.

Chapter 43

Cabin in the woods

The entire drive to the cabin was tense for me. My legs were cramping up which was a sure sign that I was nervous. I had to control it, or it would get the best of me. I wondered if Teddy would be mad at me or would Madison maybe have not followed directions and went her own way with Teddy. I was kicking myself because if they weren't at the cabin, I had no idea where they would be.

I turned the small SUV down the long winding dirt road that led to the cabin my dad owned and took us too almost every holiday and every weekend he could possibly squeeze in for us. He loved it out in the woods and for the most part, so did I but not as much as him. Teddy loved it out there too. He would always sulk when it was time to leave. He loved the sounds, the wildlife and especially the fishing.

The cabin sat on ten acres, modest for some of the other "cabin get-away's" that were scattered throughout Connecticut. There was a stream about 100 yards behind the cabin that was as beautiful as anything you could see in a picture. After Mom and Dad were killed in the plane crash, Teddy and I would spend quite a bit of time fishing that stream. It always seemed to calm him, and me. I wasn't a big outdoor type, but I knew that my dad and Teddy spent a lot of time at this place, and I knew I needed to let Teddy deal with the tragedy in his own way.

I saw the cabin in the distance, and the thought occurred to me that maybe Teddy and Madison made it out here and Big Paul found out. I was getting antsy again and decided to pull off into a secluded spot in the woods and make my way to the cabin on foot. "Why are we stopping?" I drew in a huge breath, "I am being very cautious. These people are crafty and could be waiting on me. I should have thought this through and came at night but there is no turning back now." It was getting later in the evening and the sun would be down soon, but I couldn't wait. Selina started to reach for the door handle, and I stopped her. "If you go with me and it is a trap, two things can happen and neither of them are good for you." Selina pulled the door handle anyway and we got out at the same time. "If they are waiting for me, I will be forced to handle it which would make you an accessory to a crime or," I rubbed my forehead, "or worse." Selina put her hand on the top of the SUV and shook her head. "You know Xavier, you aren't the only one with skeletons in your closet." I put up my hand to illustrate that she didn't need to tell me anything, "Yes we all do but I don't want to see you get hurt or get into something that would jeopardize your family and business back in Arizona."

I opened the back hatch to the SUV and took out the bag that held the Colt 1911 that I had with me when all hell broke loose. I removed it from the bag and slid it into the back of my jeans. "Just stay here for a few minutes. I know you are used to being in charge but not here, not right now." Selina lowered her head, it had been a while since she had been told no by anyone and could tell she didn't like it, I didn't care.

I closed the hatch and began to walk around the car so I could make my way through the woods along the creek. That approach was the safest way to not be seen. Selina surprised me when she stepped in front of me and put her hand on my chest to keep me from taking any more steps. She surprised me again when she hugged me, one of those tight hugs that your mom, wife, or girlfriend gives you when they are worried. "You've been away from them for nearly 6 months now. Half a year has passed. Do you really think they would park someone at that cabin for 6 months waiting to see if you come back?". I couldn't explain to anyone today why I did it, but I returned her hug. I gave that woman a hug like I had never given a hug before and that is simply not me, "No I don't but I am not willing to risk your life on it, so stay here." I let go of her and began cutting across the backwoods to the stream.

Once I reached the stream, I followed it all the way to where I thought the back of the cabin had been. The woods were denser than I remembered, and it was difficult to tell exactly where the cabin was. I remembered being able to see the cabin from the stream but not today. As I made my way through the woods, I focused on steadying my breathing and reducing my heart rate. I needed to be prepared for anything that could happen and it was impossible to think clearly when you were approaching the state of hyperventilation. I can't say I was close to that, but I can say that the thought of seeing Teddy again had me so excited that my hands were shaking.

I stopped when I could clearly see the cabin. I was careful to stay out of site. I stood silent and still for what seemed like an hour but in reality, it was probably only 10 minutes. I saw movement in the windows but couldn't identify who it was. I moved closer and chose the kitchen window to peek into. It was the one that was least used because it really had a view to nowhere but trees. I took a breath, held it, and slowly peered into the window. My heart sank when I saw two guys I didn't know. They definitely didn't belong in my family cabin. I didn't see Madison or Teddy, so I moved to the two bedrooms on the east side of the house. I tried to look into the first window in the back of the cabin, but the drapes were closed so I moved to the next one. It was all I could do to keep from jumping through the window when I saw Teddy. He was laying on the bed asleep. I didn't see Madison and I began to worry. Maybe she put up a fight and they silenced her. I had no idea, but I knew I needed to make a move quickly. Before I could decide what, I needed to do, I wanted a better look in the front window. If it was just the two guys then I could easily get the drop on them but if it was more than two guys, my odds went down dramatically. I also didn't know if maybe Madison was in the front room with them or maybe she was in the bathroom, and I couldn't afford to have her get hit by a stray bullet. The walls of the cabin were serious size logs so there was no way a bullet would travel back and hit Teddy.

I slowly edged towards the front porch which I knew would be to my disadvantage, the porch was huge, and the planks creaked. What I used to consider an endearing quality of cabin life was now an impediment to getting my brother back. I sat on the ground and slid my boots off so that I could soften the sound. I eased one foot on the porch and slowly put my weight on it. I was about to fully stand on the porch with both feet when the front door began to open. I quickly moved back out of view and hoped that whoever just came out wouldn't look to the east side of the house. "Hey Jeff- you know what's nice about being out in this backwoods Grizzly Adams shit…?" There was no reply but from the sound I could tell what was happening. "You can piss off the front porch and nobody gives a shit!" the voice was laughing, and I could hear the sound of his piss stream making mud out of the dirt.

I took that as a good sign for me, he called out to just one guy inside the house named Jeff. Jeff finally replied when I heard him walk out on the front porch also. Jeff also decided he needed to whiz so they were both on the front porch and I decided that now was the time. One man with his fly open and the other bragging about being able to. I steadied my nerves again and eased the 1911 out of the back of my jeans. I eased the safety off and drew in a breath. I slowly eased around the side of the house so that I could fully see both guys, "make a move boy's and this is the last piss you'll ever take." Both men froze and to my surprise, both men managed to shut off their streams. Something I had found over my lifetime that was nearly impossible to do. I couldn't remember if I had racked a shell into the chamber but since it was a double stack, I decided that for affect I would rack one anyway. If I lost a shell, no big deal. I was certain there were not 15 guys in cabin.

"Who are you boys?" One man started to turn, "you turn around and I swear on everything that I believe to be righteous and good in this world, I will splatter your tiny brain all over the woods and bears will eat you for dinner tonight. "Now, who are you?" The older of the two spoke, "we are guys you don't want to fuck with." I chuckled, "yeah, everyone says that right before I introduce them to God." I stepped on the porch and just as I was fully on the porch, I heard a gunshot. I didn't feel anything, so I was certain I wasn't hit. I was not about to take my eyes off these guys, and I truly did not want to kill them, so I quickly moved in behind them with my back to the front cabin wall. This way I could see in all directions and didn't have to worry about my back. It was at that moment that I was preparing to drop these two guys and move on to whoever was shooting at me when I heard her voice, "Xavier, you are clear, there was a third that came out the back of the cabin, heavy emphasis on was." I let out a breath, damn, that is the second time she has saved my life. "Now, I am going to ask you for the last time, who are you?" Selina joined me on the front deck, her devil anse still at the ready. Neither of the men spoke, "Hold these guys right here, if either of them twitches, farts or burps, put a bullet in their fucking head." Selina did as she was asked and I entered the cabin, I checked all the rooms and behind every door on the way to get Teddy. Teddy was always a sound sleeper and when I got to him, he was still asleep.

I stood over him for a moment and had to fight back the tears. I missed this guy, and I couldn't help but feel that I let him down. He was probably scared and didn't understand what was happening. I sat on the bed next to him and rubbed his back, "hey . . . Teddy man, it's time to go home buddy." It took a few shakes and whispers and he finally roused. When he saw me, he leapt from the bed and into my arms. It was at that time that I let the tears freely run down my cheeks. "I'm sorry buddy, I promise I will never let you down again." Teddy squeezed me as tight as he could, "X-man! Where have you been! I needed you! They were mean to me and Maddie!" I pulled him away so I could look at him, "where is Madison buddy, do you know?" Teddy buried his head in my chest and began cry even louder and through his sobs I heard him say "they took her into the woods, and she hasn't come back!"

I could feel my blood beginning to boil, and my anger welled up inside me, but I hid it from Teddy. "Ok Buddy, I will go find her, I want you to come with me and meet a friend of mine." I helped Teddy find his shoes and when he finally had them on with the sneakers tied, we walked out on the front deck. "Teddy, this is Selina, she is our friend. She is gonna take you to our car while I clean up the cabin." Teddy flashed his smile at Selina and despite the fact that she was pointing a gun at these two goons, I could see in her eyes that she was immediately in love with my little brother and for the first time in my life, I was in love with a woman. This woman. Selina Villalpando.

I was not surprised to see Teddy cling to Selina as the two walked away from the cabin towards the car. Once they were out of site, leaving just me, Mutt and Jeff on the porch I began to find out what was going on. "Which one of you is Jeff." Neither spoke so I walked up behind the older one and reached into his back pocket and pulled his wallet out of his pants. "Nice to meet you Jeff," I lowered my 1911 at angle and shot him in ass. He screamed and fell to the ground; I thought

I actually heard him crying. "Now, sir, what's your name because if I have to reach into your pants to find your wallet, your shot will go into your spleen because I am tired of playing fucking games with you numb-nuts. "It's Tommy and go fuck yourself." I laughed and then hit him in the back of the head with the butt of my 1911strong enough to send him sprawling on the deck. I was careful not to knock him out because I wanted to know where Madison was and who ordered them to snatch my little brother. "You mother fucker! I am going to kill you!" I bent down and grabbed him by the back of the head by his hair and yanked as hard as I could "You, my friend are about to go through more pain that you have ever experienced in your short miserable life." I picked him up through his screaming protest. Jeff was still clasping his ass. I knew I had angled the gun just enough that the bullet probably left four holes. I've done it before, you can't sit on anything soft or hard for many months and its painful as hell, but I didn't kill him. I didn't want to.

I drug Tom inside the cabin and hit him again with the barrel of my gun right across the bridge of his nose. It would break his nose, cause some seriously blurred vision and he would bleed profusely. His pain would give me enough time to go retrieve Jeff and his new five holed ass from the front yard.

Once I had both on the living room floor of the cabin, I started asking them who sent them and where Madison was. They weren't cooperative so I took the living room lamp and yanked the cord free from the lamp leaving the cord plugged in and me holding two bare exposed lamp wires. I touched the wires to Jeff's ear, and he screamed and jerked his head away. I did the same to Tom and he reacted the same way. I laid the wire down then went to the kitchen and found the zip ties I had used to string meat from the trees to keep the bears out of it. I zip tied their hands together and tied their feet. They weren't going anywhere. Both would scream and cuss but then I would touch them with the exposed wire, and they would stop.

"Please man! Stop it! Stop this and we won't say a word to any-one!" I could tell that Jeff was getting weary and he was close to the breaking point, so I turned my focus to Tom. I had to admit that Tom was pretty tough and took quite a while to get him to the point I wanted him. "Where is Madison? This can all be over if you tell me where Madison is." I touched the open wires to Tom's crotch, and he screamed but his time I applied the pressure to the wires so that he couldn't wiggle away. The pain delivered directly to his nuts had to be intense because he pissed himself. "She is in the woods man!" Tom was crying as he spoke, "Jeff didn't want to fuck her in front of the retard, so we took her in the woods." Hearing that pissed me off and I shoved the wires in his mouth and began to beat him with everything I had. "Did you fucking kill her!" I yelled as I smashed every bone in his face. When he was no longer resisting and had become unresponsive, I moved my attention to Jeff. "You, mother fucker are gonna take me to Madison now!" I cut the ties off his legs and yanked him to his feet. He screamed but when I cuffed him with a back hand, and he shut up. I ushered him out the door and stopped, "which way fuck stick!" He nodded his head towards the east, and we began to walk. It was more me walking and dragging him.

After we walked about 75 yards into the woods, I saw her, and my heart sank. Fury blew over me like a hurricane and I smashed the back of Jeff's head with my gun. He fell unconscious to the ground, and I ran to Madison. She was naked from the waist down and was handcuffed to a small pine tree. These fuckers had raped and killed her because of me, and it was more than I could handle. Just as I got to her, I saw her leg move. I panicked because I didn't have a handcuff key, so I shot the handcuffs off her. It was reflexive. I bent down to my knees and puller her up close to me and held her in my arms. All I could do was cry and tell her I was sorry. She was somewhat out of it, but she managed to whisper, "took you long enough, you big lug."

I picked her up off the ground and cradled her in my arms. I started walking back towards the cabin and as we passed Jeff, still laying on the ground, I raised my 1911 and shot him in the face. I couldn't help it. He had hurt Madison and THAT I could not forgive. The shot made Madison grasp me tighter around the neck. I said out loud so she could hear, "Jeff is settling up with God now Madison, he will never hurt you again." As we made it to the cabin, I walked through the front door looking for a blanket. I wanted a blanket to wrap around her because I didn't want Teddy to see her like this. I sat Madison down on the couch and laid her head back. I needed to deal with Tom now.

I kneeled down next to Tom and whispered in his ear, "Your hands are tied but they are in front of you, your ankles are strapped tightly. I have disabled your car, so it won't run, and you are 30 miles from civilization", I looked around the cabin then back down at the man with fear in his eyes. I reached for the knife on my hip and pulled it out, I rolled him over on his back and he screamed in pain again. I raised his shirt and then plunged to knife deep enough into his stomach to accomplish what I wanted. He screamed like a child, and I was happy about it. I took my fingers and stuck them into the slice I had made in his stomach and found his intestine, all while he was screaming. I began pulling out his intestine and he continued to scream. I walked out the front door still pulling his guts out as he continued to scream. It was sadistic I know, but I was mad as hell. Men like this needed to end life badly. When I reached the front porch post I wrapped his intestine around the post and walked back in. I went to the sink and washed my hands while I listened to tough guy scream and cry. I walked back in and bent down again, "here's the deal tough guy Tom, you aint gonna die real soon but make no mistake, you are going to die." I pointed out the front door, "I am going to leave your gun out there at the end of your guts, if you can drag your ass out there before the bears start snacking on your insides while you watch, you can shoot yourself in the head or you can shoot the bear." I laughed and stood up, "just know that bears usually take more than one bullet to drop and that's all I am gonna leave you, one fucking bullet." I went over to the couch and picked up Madison. "Before I go, tell me who sent you Tommy?" Tom was about to pass out from the pain, "It was Paul man, please help me! Don't let the bears eat me!" I laughed as Madison and I walked out the door, "don't worry Tommy, the raccoons, coyotes and wolves will probably get to you before the bears do, they are much quicker."

Chapter 44

If that Mockingbird don't sing

When Teddy saw me carrying Madison towards the car he jumped from Selina's arms, opened the door, and ran to me. I put Madison in the back seat of the SUV and told Teddy that she had been hurt and he needed to make sure she was warm and didn't move. Being gentle was never one of Teddy's specialties but watching him try to be gentle was something special. He put his arm around Madison and pulled her close. He stroked her hair and began to softly sing the nursery rhyme, *hush little baby don't say a word, momma's gonna buy you a mockingbird.* It was his favorite song when he was a toddler, and it was something that we had all sang to him to help him go to sleep at night.

I looked at Selina and for a second, I was sure that she saw the evil in me. I was sure that she knew that I had just killed one man and left another at the threshold of it. I could feel the blood rushing to my face, and I felt ashamed. "You got them back without dying Xavier, nothing more than that." She flashed the soft smile of compassion at me and again, I saw how beautiful she was, but I also saw that after what I had just done, there was no way that a woman of her caliber should ever be with a man of mine.

I looked down at my shirt and saw some blood splatter on me then looked up at Selina, "they uhhh, they, they treated her poorly. We need to get her out of here and to a doctor." I looked back at Teddy then backed the SUV out of the woods and onto the gravel road leading back to the highway. "If it's not too much trouble, I would like you to fly them back to Arizona and I will meet you there when I have finished my business here," Selina remained quiet, "I'm sorry you had to do what you did back there but thank you for saving my life, again."

It was dark as we drove the narrow road out of the woods, Selina had not said a word until we made it back to the main road. "You don't have to do what you are going to do you know," I felt her hand gently land on my right thigh and I felt the hair on my arms and the hair on the back of my neck tingle like they had just felt a small jolt of electricity. "All of you can come to Arizona with me and perhaps have a fresh start in life, I know a great school in Tucson that would be perfect for Teddy," she paused and gently squeezed my leg, "please don't do this."

I didn't immediately say anything back because in all honesty, I was trying to sort things out in my head and come up with a scenario that allowed me to get on the plane with Selina, Teddy and Madison and never return to this place. "He won't stop Selina, unless I stop him first."

The other benefit of flying your own plane was that you could drive your rental car right up to the plane. It would be awkward carrying Madison through an airport, battered, and bruised with blood splatter on most of my clothes. I eased the car as close to the plane as I could. I loaded Madison on the plane and despite her petite structure, was not an easy task. Once I had Teddy and Madison situated comfortably in the back of the plane, I returned to the tarmac to find

Selina standing there looking at me. "I guess there is nothing that I can say or do to talk you out of this?" I shook my head no, "alright then, I will take care of them," she motioned her head toward the plane then folded her arms across her chest. The attendant at the FBO handed her some paperwork and she signed it and handed it back to him. He started to walk away and that's when it hit me. The FBO had to have been the tip off source of information for big Paul. I grabbed the clip board from the attendant looked at it and saw the flight plan with the destination Tucson. I yanked the sheets off the clipboard and stuffed them in my pocket, "hey Mister you can't do that!" Selina seemed a little shocked by my action and I could tell she wanted an explanation, "the FBO tipped off big Paul that we were coming, that's how they found the cabin." I grabbed the FBO attendant by the throat and pulled him close to me. I reached into his back pocket and found his wallet. I let him go and he gagged a little, "you're in big trouble man! You just assaulted me!" I looked at his driver license, I grabbed his shirt and pulled him close to me as I spoke, "no, Charlie Beckett, you're in big trouble," I took his license out of his wallet and shoved it in my front pocket, "I know where you live, I know where your family lives, if anyone ever finds out we were even here tonight, I will hunt you down and slice the throats of everyone you love and make you watch me when I do it! You got that?" I could see the fear in his eyes, and he nodded that he understood. I let him go, "now, get the fuck out of here."

Selina's facial expression had changed from shock to blank, she didn't know what to think or say at that moment. "This is my world Selina; you're playing my game now and it aint pretty. This is the man I have been trying to tell you about, he is not a good person." I looked at the plane then back at Selina, "I will come for them very soon."

From the outside gate of the FBO I watched the plane taxi to its assigned runway and take off. I felt relief that they would soon be safe. I also felt the horror of my parent's plane crash and worried that maybe by letting that thought creep into my head at that moment that I had put some bad karma towards their flight home. I tried to put it out of my mind, but it wouldn't go away. If they made the same stops for fuel on the way back, they should be home and back on the ranch by morning.

Chapter 45

Delbert to the rescue

After I watched the place take off, I made my way back to the city. I found the number I needed in my bag, used the phone that Selina left in the car and called the lobby of Madison's apartment, and I got the voice that I wanted. "Hey Delbert, how you doing man?" Just as I expected, this guy was extremely good at his job, "I've so hoped that you would contact me." His voice tailed off into a whisper, "this is Mr. Thomas correct?" I was nodding my head because I was amazed at this guy's recall for voices and names, "yeah buddy it's me." I waited for a response, but the phone stayed quiet. I got the feeling he couldn't speak freely. "Hey if you are being watched just listen, smile and pretend that you are happy and carefree," there was no response, "I need to get into Madison's apartment," there was more silence and then he started rambling, "oh my goodness that is so exciting! Mom is going to be so surprised!" He paused like he was listening, "of course your secret is safe with me! Thanksgiving is going to be wonderful with you home this year!" I couldn't believe that her building was being watched but it also made me feel I had the upper hand now. The fact that men had been at the cabin and now someone was watching Madison's apartment meant that Big Paul was scared and being scared meant weakness. "Ok, my friend, any chance I can get in the building the way you let me out?" Delbert remained silent and I could only imagine that he was pretending to be happy to be talking to me, "Absolutely Myron! I can certainly arrange that, but I can't do it now because I am the only one watching the desk tonight. I get a break in one hour and I can send you all the information then, will that work?" I let out a breath, "I owe you my friend, I will see you in one hour."

I pulled into the parking garage of Madison's building close to the secret door that Delbert had shown me nearly 6 months ago. I sat in the car and waited. I figured the garage was being watched also so I had to be careful. Right on time, I saw the small narrow door open slightly and I grabbed my bag and slid out of the car and crotched down behind the other cars in the row as I made my way to the door.

The hallway seemed to be even smaller and tighter than I remembered but as I entered the door, there was Delbert, smiling. He hugged me as if I was a long-lost friend and, in some way, I was. "I must tell you Mr. Thomas, he showed up yesterday and won't leave. I haven't seen Ms. Madison in so long but I have taken care of everything so that her mail doesn't pile up and her apartment stays active if you know what I mean." I gave Delbert a good squeeze, "She is pretty beat up right now, but she is safe. I need to get into her apartment to clean up and grab some of her things," I started moving down the hallway as I was speaking, "of course I can Mr. Thomas."

We walked down the hallway and had some small talk as we walked and then we entered the super's office. When we got to the office I stopped. "Listen Delbert, you have been good to me, and you have sure been damn good to Maddie and I will repay you, but I need one more favor." I stood in front of him and looked directly at him, "what can I help with Mr. Thomas?" I put my hand on his shoulder, "give me 30 minutes in Madison's apartment and then send the goon watching you in the lobby up. Make him think you are doing him a favor by being sleazy and underhanded, the sleazier the better. They love that shit," he was nodding and smiling at the same time. "I won't make a scene, but I swear you won't see or hear from him again." He laughed and hugged me again; he also gave me an ass squeeze which I could tolerate based off his cooperation. "I will have that asshole delivered to you on a silver platter my beautiful friend."

He led me to the back elevator and gave me Madison's key card. 30 seconds later I was entering her apartment. I quickly changed clothes and checked my 1911. It was loaded and ready to go but for this one, I couldn't make any noise. He wouldn't expect me to be there, so I had the element of surprise on my side.

After my quick shower and change of clothes, I ate a can of tuna mixed with some mustard, checked my watch and it had almost been 30 minutes. I killed all the lights in the apartment and positioned myself to the left of the front door. It gave me the best room for mobility and adaptability.

Just like clockwork, I could hear Delbert's voice loud and clear coming down the hallway. I loved that guy; he was talking loud enough to alert me that he was coming. I could hear him right outside the doorway, "she has been gone all day but since you said you were a friend of hers, I don't see any problem with a quick welfare check, but I have to tell you that per company policy, I am not allowed to go in the apartment, but you can." I heard the buzzing sound of an electronic deadbolt moving and I steadied my breathing. Once the door opened a man stepped inside and I heard Delbert tell the guy that he would wait for him in the hallway, "no need, I can let myself out, run along now" was the man's reply. Before he had time to locate the light switch I had him in a reverse choke hold. Wrestlers called it the "sleeper hold" because if you did it right, you would cut off the flow of blood supply to the brain and the target would pass out only to regain conscience not long after the pressure is removed from the carotid artery. The man fought back relatively well but not well enough. We knocked over a lamp and broke something else, but I didn't know what it was. About 3 minutes of heavy battling between the two of us I could feel this dude's body go limp and I eased myself and him to the ground. By now, Delbert had flipped on the light and was standing beside me smiling from ear to ear. "I'm so impressed Mr. Thomas you are so strong!" Delbert was flirting again, I had to admire his tenacity.

"Say Delbert, look in that bag and see if you can find a couple of zip ties." I motioned with my head because I was still applying pressure to this dude's neck. Delbert did as he was told and handed me a handful of zip ties. "I let the man slowly fall over to his side as I released my grip from his neck. I quickly put his hands behind his back and secured them with a zip. I then secured his ankles with two zips, and I was done. Now, I just had to get him out of Madison's apartment.

"Is he dead?" I looked up to see Delbert in what I would consider a panicked look, "no, he is just taking a nap right now." I stood up and grabbed him by his shoulders, "you should get back down to the desk and forget what you have seen here but before you go- I need access to a maintenance closet or someplace that won't see activity for a few hours." Delbert snapped out of it then hugged me again and of course he gave me the butt squeeze, "down at the end of the hallway is a maintenance closet, I will open it before I go back down." I smiled and sort of pushed him off me, "you're a good dude Delbert. I will make sure you are taken care of." Delbert left happy and for some weird, strange reason, that was important to me.

After I had Madison's uninvited house guest tied and harmless, I sat down and wrote a note; *I could have easily ended your life, but I didn't, the next time I will not hesitate, I have your wallet along with ID.*

I went to her kitchen and found a stapler on the counter and smiled, perfect I thought. I opened the stapler, walked over to the hired thug from Big Paul's crew and stapled the note to his chest. He was still passed out so he wouldn't feel the pain until he woke up.

He wasn't a very big guy, so it was easy to lift him off the floor and make my way down the hallway to the maintenance closet. I put him in there but removed his ankle zip ties. He would need to get up somehow and figure a way out. Unless he was an imbecile, he would figure a way out. I wasn't a killer, at least that's what I told myself.

Chapter 46

End of Big Paul

I sat a block away from the ice cream shop watching everything. I didn't know what their systems of "check ins" were but I knew eventually they would know that the goons from the cabin didn't check in and then they would realize that the goon from Madison's apartment didn't check in, and they would know that I was real. No more speculation, no more hesitation either. Paul would add more security around him very soon, so I had to go now. There was no more waiting.

I had a great view of the back of the ice cream shop. I knew there would be no chance I could enter from the back of the ice cream shop and my chances of entering from the front would be difficult too. I watched the customers going into the ice cream store, they seemed to be having a great day for sales because the foot traffic was heavy.

It didn't take me long to realize that the customer activity was more muscle that Big Paul had put on site to deal with me. I decided I would have to leave and go to his home and stay a while. He would not expect me to be there, he would not expect me to know where he lived but I did. I wasn't sure if his wife would be home but at this point I didn't care. She would be collateral damage. You can't fuck with my little brother or his caregiver and not expect the wrath of God to descend on you. Paul had never seen me mad. For most of my time with him, I was the peacemaker. I collected without having to bash very many "customers," I hated that part of it. I really didn't want to hurt anyone, but I would if I felt like you were a weasel and lie to me, I didn't mind so much. Big Paul had been and done both. He lied to me and then he was a weasel and tried to use Teddy to keep me in check. I intended to inflict pain on him and anyone that got in my way from doing so.

The alarm was easy to disarm, I knew the system and it was simple. None of these guys with fancy alarm systems could actually remember all the codes so most of them were still set to factory code of 1-2-3-4. Big Paul was no different. After I deactivated the alarm, I waited to see if anyone stirred but nothing happened.

It was a big house, and I would need to do a semi-thorough job of checking for collateral damage. I went through every room downstairs and was somewhat relieved to see that the master bedroom was not occupied and didn't find anything of any significance in any of the other rooms.

I made my way upstairs, checking every room and I found nothing. When I was satisfied that I had the house to myself, I went back downstairs, grabbed a beer out of the fridge, went to the garage and found the circuit breaker for the downstairs kitchen and garage door entrance. I figured he would get some muscle to bring him home and he would enter through the garage. If he didn't, I was flexible. I would sit at the bar in the kitchen and wait on him.

My cell phone began to vibrate, I saw that it was a 520-area code, so it was coming from Arizona. "Yeah" I said in my lowest voice, the voice on the other end was easily recognizable. "You don't have to do this you know, just come back here and we will figure it out." I shook my head in disbelief and didn't say anything, but I didn't need to,

"We are all here, we are all safe, I am getting Madison the medical attention she needs, and Teddy loves the place." I didn't reply, I simply hit the power button on the phone, let it shut down and put it in my pocket. I was in no mood to change my mind.

I went through two beers before I heard the entrance door from the garage open. I had re-armed the alarm so he would not suspect anything. I heard the beeps of pressing 1-2-3-4 and I pulled my 1911 out of the back of my pants. The shell had already been racked so I simply moved it out of its safety position. I heard the constant sound of a light switch being flipped on and off. "Well shoot!" I heard loud and clear, and my stomach churned as I could easily tell that the voice was female, his wife was home.

I heard her footsteps come towards the kitchen where I was sitting, and I heard her flip the light switch there with the same results. "Son of a bitch!" I could hear her very clear because she was now no more than 10 feet from me. My eyes were adjusted to the dark but hers were not so I could see her, but she couldn't see me. When she dropped her purse and keys on the bar, I slowly stood up off the bar stool I had been sitting on for the last two hours. She didn't hear a thing until I had her by the throat and whispered into her ear, "I won't hurt you if you cooperate," I strengthened my grip on her neck and pushed her against her giant refrigerator. I eased my grip on her neck but did not let go, "walk with me and if you scream or cause me any problems, I will kill you in the worst and most painful way you could ever imagine."

Even in the darkness of the kitchen, I could see her eyes were wide and she was scared so I was comfortable that she wouldn't cause me any problems. I guided her to the living room where I tied her hands with a lamp cord that I yanked out of the wall. "When does your husband get home?," she didn't answer so I decided to talk instead, "your husband tried to have me killed and he damn near succeeded," I sat down on the ottoman in front of her. "I work for your husband, you see, he blamed me for your son getting shot but the fact is, your son was a hot head and he got himself shot, if he would have listened to me, that wouldn't have happened." She was shaking her head as if she disagreed, "don't shake your head, I don't lie," I started to continue but she interrupted me, "he's dead."

She proceeded to tell me that Jimmy never came out of the coma, he died in the back of the ice cream shop almost 6 months ago. She told me that he did blame me, but she didn't know who I was, until now. She also told me that Paul would be home soon. She informed me that he kept a very regimented daily schedule which was ill advised for a mob boss. Guys like Paul were so insulated from the real world that they all fell into a trap of consistency and consistency could get you killed, and I intended to prove it.

"I can talk to him; I can tell him to stop this non-sense!" Her voice was shaking and squeaky, I thought she was going to cry but I really didn't care. "There has been enough of this!", she was crying, killing my husband won't bring my son back." Her voice tailed off to a whisper, but I would kill this lady if I had to, and her tears wouldn't help her. Big Paul managed to bring out the worst in me, and I hated him for it, knowing I was capable of anything. Teddy and Madison were in good hands, they didn't need me anymore. Selina would take care of all of them.

"Shut up," I stood up and looked out the back-patio window at the pool, "I have a job to do." She frantically shook her head, "you don't! I swear! I can make him stop! You can . . . ," her voice stopped, I heard it too, the door to the garage opened, I turned the light off to the living room and put my hand over her mouth, I whispered, "make a sound and you die with your husband tonight."

I heard the sound of the alarm code being entered into the system for the second time tonight, third if you count my entry. The refrigerator door opened and the distinctive sound of a beer bottle opening. I could feel this woman's body shaking and I knew she was crying, she tried to stand but my grip was far too tight, I forced her back down without ever having to move my hand that covered her mouth. I tapped the barrel of my 1911 on her thigh so she would focus on that instead of saving her husband. She tensed up when she felt the barrel of the gun on her leg, that's when I heard him walk into the living room and I turned the lamp light on.

Big Paul looked as calm as a cucumber in the crisper. He never flinched at the site of his wife with her hands tied and a man holding his hand over her mouth. He was so calm that it caught me off guard and I had to refocus. Guys like Paul didn't get where they are by panicking and it was my mistake thinking that he would get rattled by my presence. Sitting there on the couch with his wife I realized I had overestimated my ability to understand the situation.

"I hoped you would be here; I was disappointed you didn't stop by the ice-cream shop, but I knew you were too smart for that." He walked over to where we were and sat down. "How do you want to do this, quick bullet to the head or do you plan to extract some pain from me?", he took a drink from his beer like he didn't have a care in the world, "does my wife get a bullet too?" he smiled and took another sip of his beer, "she has nothing to do with my business."

I took my hand off her mouth but hung on to her, "neither did my brother or his caregiver." Paul didn't say anything, so I spoke, "yeah that's what I figured." Paul sat there smiling at me like he knew what was about to happen and he was happy about it. "Is there any room to negotiate or are you set on making yourself a target for the rest of your life?", he took another drink, "I've already let family know you want blood and since you are a part of the family, there is a process for grievances like this one and any deviation from the process ends badly for everyone." I laughed then pushed his wife out of the chair and pointed the gun at her, "Since she aint in the family or the business, there isn't any process, right?", I put a bullet in the top of her foot, and she screamed in pain. She would never walk on that foot the same again and I didn't care. "God Dammit! That was not necessary!" Big Paul jumped out of his chair and went to his wife. He held her close to him as she cried, "nor was it necessary to rape Teddy's caregiver and leave her for dead in the fucking woods you piece of shit!" I hit him in the face with the barrel of my 1911. He went sprawling on the floor which caused his wife to scream even louder. I put the gun against her temple, "shut the fuck up or you will never scream again!". I was amazed at how quickly she went silent.

Paul rolled back towards me, I could see him reaching for his ankle, I leaned over and took the small 380 out of his ankle holster before he could get to it. I was somewhat impressed that he had the discipline to not reach for it until now. I was growing tired of his routine, but I needed one question answered, "look at me!" Big Paul did as he was told, "Many years ago there was a guy that owned a sporting goods store, what happened to him?." Paul shook his head like he didn't know so I hit him again, "you do know! I heard you talking about it. Now aint the time to lie Paul" I leaned closer to him, "where is he?" Paul rubbed his head again, "he's buried up in Orchard." I knew where he was talking about, I had never been a part of burying anyone, but I knew how it was done. There were a few spots across the state that were used as disposals. Orchard was actually Buffalo.

I had what I needed now. I put the 380 that I pulled from his ankle holster and pressed it against his ear, "I didn't know they did that to her, I didn't give the order to do that, and you know it!" "Then that makes me the only guy you ever had on your payroll that actually followed your orders," I pulled the trigger and big Paul slumped over in the floor. He would never give another order to anyone. His wife screamed again, and the thought crossed my mind to put a stop to her screaming as I had promised her earlier, but I showed restraint.

I looked at the back-patio door and slid it open, there was nothing but woods behind big Paul's house. I took the 380 and placed it in his hand, raised his arm and fired a bullet directly out the patio door. Big Paul would now have the gun shot residue on his hand. I wiped the gun with my shirt then placed it Paul's hand just to get some prints on it. Once I was comfortable with my work, I dropped the gun on the floor next to his body.

I stood up and walked over to where his wife was still crying. I grabbed her by the back of her neck and forced her to her feet then helped her get to the chair that she and I had been sitting in when Big Paul got home. "Your name is Annamarie, right?," through her whimpering she managed to shake her head yes to confirm. "Ok, listen to me, your husband tried to have me killed, he took my little brother who has down syndrome and tried to use him as leverage against me" I put my hand on her back, "I have six bullet holes in me because your husband gave the order to do it." I gently rubbed her back to try and get her to calm down so she would listen to me more carefully, "the men your husband ordered to kidnap my brother decided to rape his caregiver and leave her for dead." I stood up for no other reason than to stretch my legs, "you married a mob guy, and you knew the risks so don't try and pretend you had no idea what was going on."

I went to the kitchen, found a bottled water in the fridge, and returned to give it to her. "Here . . . take a drink." She took the water and took a long drink. "You have a choice, you can make up whatever story you want about the hole in your foot and the hole in your husbands head, but whatever story you make up, will not involve me." I pulled her hair so she would look up at me, "I will hunt you down, if you think the pain in your foot is bad, the next time you'll beg me to put a bullet in your head." She looked at me and stopped crying when she saw my face, she could see what Teddy call's "the look." Most of the times I have given Teddy the look, it was for show, not serious like this. When she saw the look on my face, she shook her head in the affirmative direction. "Good, now I am going to leave so practice your story for the cops when they arrive but . . . you can't call them for a least one hour," I patted her head, "got it?" She nodded in the affirmative. "Every time you limp on that foot, think of me, and then look over your shoulder."

Chapter 47

Can I talk to him?

I had to stop by my place and pick up some things that I would need, mainly, papers for Teddy, shot records etc... No one in the family would believe that big Paul shot himself and eventually they might figure out how that piece of human debris died. His wife would not tell, I was certain of that. I had scared her enough to last the rest of her life. The mob wouldn't lean on her or try to force any information out of her, oddly, for as barbaric as they could be, they were very coded and guarded of the wives, especially the widows.

My apartment smelled unlived in. It's that smell you get when no one takes a shower, flushes a toilet or cooks. It smells stale and it made me sad. I can't explain it, but I wasn't coming back. This had been my home and Teddy's home for so many years now. If it weren't for that idiot that I had just sent for his meeting with God, I would be tucking Teddy in bed and I would be reviewing trading in the after-hours market to spot a trend. I loved looking for trends, blips on the screen that no one else caught or noticed. I was good at it and if I wanted to get away from this city and this life, I would need to get better at it, lots better. I would need to make up the loss of income in order to take care of Teddy.

I was tired now; I needed some rest before I made my way back to Arizona. Sleeping in my own bed would be a change of pace but it was something that I badly wanted to do. I made one more pass-through Teddy's room, packed a bag with all his favorite clothes and made my way to my own bed. It was the first time in nearly half a year that I slept in a familiar place.

The alarm on my watch went off at 6am but I silenced it as quickly as it awoke me. Normally I would spring out of bed but not today. I was still tired and the adrenaline that I was using to finish my business in New York had evaporated. Now, all I could feel was the aches and pains brought about by being shot. Spending two months in bed didn't do anything for my strength although the work I was doing around the ranch helped build my strength back to a decent but not former level. I closed my eyes and rolled over on my back which was how I now preferred sleeping.

The knock on the door woke me, I looked at my watch and it was now 7am. Even when I lived here before all hell broke loose, nobody knocked on my door at 7am. I sat up, grabbed the 1911 off the nightstand and made my way to the door. I stood beside the door, took another look at my 1911, removed the safety and racked a round into the chamber so it could be heard on the other side of the door.

"Who is it?" I said but when I said it, my morning voice of not being fully awake slipped out and it didn't come out as strong as I would have liked so I said it again, this time with much more force. "It's Robert, Robert Mason from the shelter Mr. Thomas." I am glad he couldn't see my face because I was really struggling with knowing a Robert Mason from the shelter and then it came back to me. He was the guy in the frock that I spoke to when I was trying to find the kid that Teddy was so high on. I flipped the dead bolt and then opened the door. In my haze, I forgot to put on pants, and I was standing there in my boxer briefs.

When the door swung open enough for me to see, there was Robert from the shelter and a teenage boy with a small bruise under his eye, standing there. "Mr. Thomas, I apologize for the early intrusion, but may we come in?" I shook my head in a way that signaled I was confused but I stepped aside and motioned for the two to enter my apartment. "I'm sorry fellas, I wasn't expecting anyone, let me put some pants on."

They followed me inside the door, and I closed it behind them. After I put some pants on, we sat down in the living room. "I'm sorry father, I didn't expect company this morning and I wasn't expecting to stay long enough to receive guests anyway, what can I do for you? "Robert put his hands together and placed them on his lap, "first, I will restate that I am not a priest so please just call me Robert," he looked at the teenage boy, "this is Daniel Garcia, the boy in which you made an inquiry," I shook my head but didn't say anything. The silence hung in the air, making me feel uncomfortable so I said, "nice to meet you, Daniel."

Once I broke the silence which indicated to me that Robert expected me to acknowledge the boy properly. "Daniel has been through quite a lot the last few days and he has some concerns about your younger brother." I was certainly more interested now than I was just 5 minutes ago, "Concerns in what way?" I looked at Daniel and he looked at Robert which in turn caused Robert to take over the conversation, "it seems the day before yesterday, Daniel and Teddy were exiting the school when some men tried to take Teddy right there in front of the school," he put his hands on his knees and rubbed them, "a woman who was also there to pick up Teddy tried to fight with them but Daniel says it was to no avail so he tried to help and the men roughed him up as well." Robert looked around the room and I now understood where this was going, and I needed to clear it up quickly so I could get them out of my house, and I could get going in Teddy's direction.

"Daniel, I assume that is where you got the bruise?" He nodded, "Teddy said you were a good guy and I now realize that. I am indebted to you for looking after my brother the way you have." I looked directly at Robert, "without saying much more than necessary," it was my turn to clasp my hands together and lean forward on my knees, "in my past line of work there were some people that would like to have terminated my services and used Teddy to enhance the negotiations." I looked back at Daniel, "I got Teddy back from them yesterday and he is now safely visiting friends far away from here." I stood up, "as a matter of fact, I need to get going if I intend to have dinner with Teddy tomorrow night, it's a long drive." Neither Robert nor Daniel took the hint, but Daniel spoke and honestly, it got to me, "can I talk to him?"

This kid, who was orphaned and probably felt like he had the weight of the world on his shoulders was concerned about my little brother. I can't explain how that made me feel other than it felt good to know that Teddy had friends that cared so much about him. I felt good for knowing that and bad for thinking that Teddy didn't have any friends of this magnitude. "Young man, you are everything that Teddy said you were, and I feel bad for having doubted him," I walked over and sat next to Daniel, "again, without saying much, it's not a good idea for me to contact Teddy, just know that he and the woman that tried to stop the goons from taking Teddy are safe now."

Robert stood up; I could see that he was now in a hurry to leave. I am sure that he finally managed to piece the puzzle together a little more clearly now and was ready to get the two of them out of the way. "Daniel, do you have a cell phone?" He shook his head indicating that he did not, "ok, hang on." I went back to the bedroom where my bag was and found one of the cell phones I had purchased from a convivence store that I knew didn't have a working camera. I opened the package, quickly activated it, wrote the number down and went back into the living room. I handed the phone to Daniel, "when you get a call on this phone, it will be from me and Teddy" he looked at the phone then back up at me, "yeah it's a flip phone, not much you can do on it other than talk but when the time is right, we will call you and maybe we can arrange for you to come out and visit Teddy."

Daniel looked at Robert then back at me with a smile, "Teddy is really the only friend I have, at least the only one I trust. I was just worried about him is all, I'm sorry for waking you up." I smiled back at Daniel then looked over at Robert, "I know where to find you father so expect a call from me because I'd like to be a part of this young man's future if at all possible." It was Robert's turn to smile, "Once again, I am not a priest." He stuck out his hand and I shook it, "I look forward to hearing from you Mr. Thomas."

Chapter 48

Return to the Double L

When I walked into the ranch house, they were having dinner, it seemed very odd to see Teddy and Madison sitting at the table smiling and laughing. No one saw me enter the house, I was very careful to approach the house with caution. I wasn't sure about the hornets' nest I had just kicked out of the tree so caution would have to be my motto for the rest of my life.

I stood back away from the entrance to the big bench style dining room table and listened to the chatter for a moment. I knew standing there watching this scene that I was at a fork in the road with my life. I knew that going back to New York was not an option, but I also knew that I wasn't a ranch hand either. I might have been good at it, but I didn't enjoy it as much as trading stocks.

As I stood there looking at all the people around that table, I realized that in some small way, I had changed the trajectory of everyone in that room for good, and bad reasons.

Alejandra sat at the table along with Lupita. Lupita was sitting next to Teddy, and I could tell that Teddy was happy. I thought about where Lupita and Alejandra would be had I not intervened in such a way, and I knew there was no doubt that they were better off now. As I was soaking in the farm life "Norman Rockwell" scene in front of me, I felt an arm reach around my waist and pull me close. I looked down at the hands that were around me and could tell they were Selina's. I didn't say anything and what surprised me the most was that I didn't try to push her away like I did with every woman that ever tried to get close to me. Her embrace actually felt wonderful.

She whispered in my ear, "follow me stranger." She released her embrace, and I turned around to follow her. We walked out the side door towards the barn without saying a word until we got to the barn and that is when she began to speak with more conviction and clarity than I had ever heard someone speak with before, " Teddy is a great kid, he loves it here, he loves the horses and I think it will do him good if you would just stay here, "she closed the distance between the two of us until she was standing right in front of me. It was safe to say that she was the most beautiful woman I had ever seen and for the first time since I consciously met her, I was noticing every perfect feature on her face. "I know who you are Mr. Thomas, I know what you did for a living, and I know the reasons you did it." I started to speak but she would not let me, "you are capable of bad things but only when you are pushed, that much I know," I also know that only a person with a good heart can care for someone like Teddy the way you do."

We stood there staring at each other as I waited for her to finish, "Madison is a good girl, she loves Teddy, that's easy to see and to some degree I think she loves you too," I raised my hand in an effort to stop her but she plowed ahead, "I am not saying that you love her or that there is a relationship waiting to brew between the two of you because of the way young Jake has fawned over her since we landed, it is safe to say that he is smitten."

Selina folded her arms, "what those men did to her is reprehensible, but she will recover, "she looked towards the house, "Doc Spivey said she is of strong mind and has the make-up to put that stuff behind her." It was my turn to speak now, "I put her in a bad spot, and it is my fault, for that, I am ashamed and will never be able to forgive myself for putting her and Teddy in such an awful position." Selina stepped closer and put her hand on my forearm and honestly, it felt like I was being touched by some kind of magic wand that sent tingles up my arm and then into my spine. "How they found her I will never know but the FBI called here yesterday to inform her that they had found her father's remains," she cracked a small smile that made her look even more beautiful than she was before, "apparently they got an anonymous tip that led to the discovery of several missing persons." I smiled back at her because she was smart enough to figure out without having to say anything that I was the anonymous tip she was referring to. Because they had never found Madison's father, the two-million-dollar life insurance policy held by the insurance company would not pay off. Now that his remains had been unearthed, Madison could have what was rightfully owed to her. Madison was still young, and two million bucks probably wouldn't last her a lifetime, but it would sure make things a lot easier on her.

I couldn't help but stare at Selina, standing there in her jeans and cowboy hat, she looked amazing. Her ponytail swung from side to side with each turn of her head. It was almost like a worm on a hook just waiting to catch a fish. At that moment, I was almost happy being the fish.

Selina now stepped forward and put her arms around me, her head was on my chest. The impact of her head hitting my chest knocked her hat off, but she didn't bother to pick it up. "I know you think you are a bad person, but I know better Xavier Thomas," I could feel her squeeze me tighter and once again, I didn't resist, "I've done some things that I am not proud of too, in time I will tell you, but just trust me when I say that there are ten things the bible says you can't do and I have violated my share of them." I didn't say anything because something told me that she wasn't finished.

She released her grip on me and pulled away just enough for me to see her face, "Jacknack is getting old, Louis has found love and that leaves me with Jake." I put my hands on her arms just below the shoulder, "what are you trying to say Ms. V?" Selina stepped back away from me, and I let go of her arms, "I want you to stay here, you, Teddy and Madison can all stay here and stop calling me Ms. V."

I didn't know how much she wanted to hear but I needed to clear some things up, "ok Selina, you don't really know me, you don't know what kind of trouble I will bring to you and I may be out of line by saying this but it needs to be said," I looked around to see if anyone had snuck up on our conversation and when I was comfortable that they hadn't I continued, "You are so far out of my league that it aint even funny and even if you were," I put my hands up like I was being arrested, "I have no desire to be Mr. Villalpando."

When we started the conversation, we were very close but when I got to that point in the conversation, we were a few steps away from each other. I could see her looking at me and smiling, she glanced toward the house, took two steps then practically jumped into my arms. Selina Villalpando kissed me like I had never been kissed and for the first time in my life I didn't try and fight it off. She felt like she was a part of me, a simple yet complicated infusion between two people. My mind was screaming for me to leave the barn, go grab Teddy and leave this place but my heart was telling me to stay with this woman.

"Xavier, all I have thought about for the last five years was finding out what happened to my husband, and I may never find out but what I do know, is that when you came out of your coma and you started working around here, I stopped thinking about solving the mystery and started thinking about moving on." I kept my arms around her because it felt incredible to hold her this way. "As you already know, I have my own brand of trouble with the local Sherriff, the brothers, the trafficking through my land and the list grows every day. I am certain I can fight it all without you, but I would much rather do it with you."

I placed my chin on the top of her head and held her as tightly as I could. I needed to talk to Teddy and for that matter, Madison. She was in this mess because of me, and I would not under any circumstances hurt her, even if it meant walking away from Selina. "I'm at a loss here Selina, I never expected to be in this position," I rubbed her back as softly as I could but honestly, I wasn't good at this stuff, I knew my limits. "I need to go inside and see Teddy, enjoy the moment with him and Madison. They have been through as much, if not, more than me the last six months. "He is going to be so excited to see you, I just love that kid." I was releasing my grip on her but suddenly stopped and pulled her close to me again, I looked into her beautiful eyes, leaned forward and kissed her. Selina was the first woman that I had ever instigated affection. It felt good to cross that threshold and I knew at that moment that she was destined to be Mrs. Xavier Thomas.

Chapter 49

Things are sure going to be different

Selina held my hand as she led me out of the barn and back to the house but just before we were about to enter, she let go of my hand and looked at me, "just one more time for good measure Xavier, I want you to stay here with us." It was dark but I tried to put a confused look on my face which I don't think she could see very well, "us?". Before we entered the house, Selina hugged me and said, "Ok, you win, stay with me."

I opened the door for her and let her enter before me. When we reached the dining area where everyone was still chattering like it was a Thanksgiving meal, she entered and said, "look what the cat just drug in." All the chatter stopped, and I felt a little uncomfortable, but my uncomfortableness quickly went away when Teddy sprang from his seat at the table and jumped into my arms. Teddy was a pretty big kid, and he nearly knocked me over, but I managed to stay on my feet. Madison quickly followed Teddy. The three of us stood in that doorway, with everyone watching as we hugged. Madison managed to look up at me through some watery eyes. I held her gaze while Teddy still squeezed as tightly as he could. "I'm sorry Madison,

I won't ever let anyone hurt you again." Madison gave me a smile and then put her head somewhere between my arm and Teddy's head. It was a three-way hug and without question, it was the best feeling I have had in a long time.

"I am so glad to see you, Teddy!", I squeezed the back of his neck as I said it, "I won't ever leave you again, I'm sorry buddy." Teddy looked up at me with the biggest smile, which was typical for Teddy, he could light up a room with his smile alone. "Do you forgive me?" Teddy continued to smile but said, "can we stay here now?' I wasn't expecting Teddy to hit me with the question so quickly, but I should have known better, Teddy has no filter when it comes to understanding things and saying what he is thinking. "I'm kinda hungry Teddy man, can I eat first?" He laughed and hugged me again. Teddy would not let go of me the rest of the night. He chattered in my ear at the table and everywhere else we went after dinner. He took me to the barn and showed me all the stalls that he had cleaned and how the horses all took to him and his sincerely genuine touch. As we were going through the tack room and he was explaining what every piece of equipment was for, I remembered Danny. "Say champ, hang on, someone wants to talk to you", I took out my phone and hit the speed dial for the phone I gave to Danny. After a few rings the voice on the other end was certainly Danny's, "Hey my friend, say hello to Teddy" I said, then handed the phone to Teddy.

I could see Teddy's incredible smile explode from his face and I couldn't help but laugh when I heard Teddy say, "Danny! You dingleberry!" I let them talk until I could tell that Teddy was running out of things to say, "hey buddy, I would like to speak to him when you are done."

Madison walked up to us as Teddy was handing me the phone. She started petting Selina's horse which appreciated the extra attention she was getting, "Hey Danny, I wanted to thank you for what you did for Teddy and Madison . . . no way man . . . you did everything you could . . . I know you tried like hell . . ." This kid was apologizing for not being able to stop two mob goons from taking Madison and Teddy! I could not believe I was talking to a 15-year-old boy. "Hey, let's get past that, ok?" I smiled at Madison when she looked at me, "I spoke to Mr. Mason from the shelter, and he thinks I have a good shot at gaining custodial rights to you if you wanted to live with me and Teddy?" There was silence on the other end of the phone for quite a while, "are you serious?", I wanted to laugh but I thought he might take laughter at this moment the wrong way, "very serious man, all you have to do is approve it and I will start the wheels in motion. Mr. Mason already has the papers ready to submit to the state." I closed the phone shut and stuck it in my pocket.

"So, you are going to stay here?" Madison had the sweetest voice of anyone I knew, "and you are going into the adoption business?" I couldn't help but laugh, "sure looks like doesn't it." Madison came directly to me and put her arms around me. I was getting used to having beautiful women hugging me by now, "Maddie . . . I am sorry about what happened to you, if I could change it I would." Madison let go of her grip on me and pulled away just enough to see her smile, "Xavier, you are some piece of work," she playfully patted me on the chest, "I know it was you that found out where my dad was buried, I know it was you that drug me out of those woods and I know it was you that sent those despicable men to hell, where they belong." She patted my chest again, "do you intend to adopt me too?." It was my turn to chuckle, "I will if you will let me." Madison returned the laugh and this time she stood as tall as she could and kissed me on the cheek then stood in front of me, "I know you would Xavier Thomas, but I am not up for adoption, besides, I am a city girl, I belong in the city, not here in the barn with smelly horses."

Madison and I walked through the barn and then out into the yard. The night air felt good. "Selina wants me to stay too but I told her no already. She is quite the woman you know,," there was no arguing that point so I just nodded my head, "She offered to fly me back to the city and that part I said yes," I chuckled "I would have said yes to that too, beats the hell out of commercial," Madison laughed, "I was a little beat up on the last flight so I didn't get to enjoy it too much so I am looking forward to the return flight." I put my arm around her as we walked, "you know that I will always be there for you if you need me. I owe you more than I can ever repay." As we reached the back door to house she stopped and looked at me, "I love you Xavier Thomas," she kissed me on the cheek again and then she entered the house.